THE MISSING MAID

THE BAKER STREET MYSTERIES

HOLLY HEPBURN

B
Boldwood

First published in Great Britain in 2024 by Boldwood Books Ltd.

Cover Photography: Shutterstock

A CIP catalogue record for this book is available from the British Library.

Paperback ISBN 978-1-83533-745-5

Large Print ISBN 978-1-83533-741-7

Hardback ISBN 978-1-83533-740-0

Ebook ISBN 978-1-83533-738-7

Kindle ISBN 978-1-83533-739-4

Audio CD ISBN 978-1-83533-746-2

MP3 CD ISBN 978-1-83533-743-1

Digital audio download ISBN 978-1-83533-737-0

Boldwood Books Ltd
23 Bowerdean Street
London SW6 3TN
www.boldwoodbooks.com

To Barrow in Furness Library, who first introduced me to the adventures of Sherlock Holmes

'I confess that I have been as blind as a mole, but it is better to learn wisdom late than never to learn it at all.'

— SIR ARTHUR CONAN DOYLE, *THE MAN WITH THE TWISTED LIP*

1

When Harry White looked back, many years later, she supposed she owed almost all of her incredible adventures to the unlikeliest of people – a Mr Simeon Pemberton, Assistant Manager (London and Middlesex) of the Abbey Road Building Society on Baker Street in London. Had he not formed a most inappropriate, not to say entirely unprofessional, attachment to her while she worked as his personal secretary, Harry might never have read the letter that set her on the exhilarating yet perilous path that would shape the rest of her life. Not that Mr Pemberton had any idea how profoundly his petty revenge would affect her, of course. He had only meant to seduce her, with scant regard for her feelings in the matter, or those of his poor wife, and his incredulous outrage when she had rebuffed his advances had hardened into malice and led him to exact the only punishment possible.

'I'm afraid there's been a departmental reshuffle, Miss White,' he said, thin lips unsmiling beneath the bottle-brush moustache that Harry knew he took excessive care to groom each morning. His pouchy eyes glittered with unspoken resentment as he regarded her across the vast mahogany desk. 'As a result, your services are no longer required.'

She stared at him, indignation and shock momentarily threatening her impeccable self-control. He couldn't sack her – she had always been a model employee and surely a sudden termination would raise eyebrows in other departments of the bank, leading to awkwardness she was sure he would prefer to avoid. And while she was certain Mr Pemberton had no idea of her true status in life, or her family connections, he must have observed that she was not quite like the other young ladies who worked for the Abbey Road Building Society; along with an air of quiet competence, she exuded a genteel self-assurance that hinted at steel beneath her porcelain-doll features. It was probably what had caught his eye in the first place and it gave her a small measure of comfort now. No, she decided as her heart rate returned to normal, he couldn't mean to sack her.

Smoothing the herringbone pattern of her soft wool skirt, Harry folded her hands in her lap and took refuge in glacial politeness. 'I see.'

'Fortunately, I've been able to locate a vacant position in another department,' Mr Pemberton went on. 'A back-room role that requires no understanding of the banking business. I believe it will suit your abilities perfectly. You are to start this morning – immediately, in fact.'

It was barely nine o'clock. He hadn't even allowed her to remove her hat before summoning her to his office, much less pick up any of the work she'd left unfinished the previous day. 'I see,' she said again. 'There are a number of tasks I should complete—'

'Immediately, Miss White,' he cut in brusquely. 'That means right away, since you seem unsure. The work you have left outstanding can be picked up by your replacement. She will also send any sundry personal items or detritus to your new department.'

A glimmer of triumph played across his pudgy features and Harry knew he was daring her to take the bait, to give him a reason to do what he so clearly longed to. She was almost tempted – it wasn't as though she needed to work after all – but she was blowed if she'd give him the satisfaction. Her family prided themselves on graciousness in the face of incivility; their family motto was *SUIS STAT VIRBUS – He stands by his own strength* – and she had no intention of letting this odious creep of a man see that he had rattled her. There wasn't much at her desk anyway, perhaps a peace lily and some rather fine Fortnum and Mason biscuits, an old pair of leather gloves that she could live without.

Summoning up a bland smile, Harry rose. 'Of course, Mr Pemberton. If you'll tell me which department, I'll report there now.'

The crispness of his reply did nothing to disguise his evident self-satisfaction. 'It's the post room,' he said, pushing a white envelope across the polished wooden surface of the desk until it rested within her reach. 'You'll find it in the basement. Ask for Babbage; he'll show you where you are to work.'

It was another insult, calculated to elicit a reaction. The post room played a vital role in the everyday running of any banking institution but it was no place for a woman of education and refined manners. Harry had no doubt that Mr Pemberton expected her to throw her hands up in anger and alarm. 'Of course,' she said, taking the letter with steady fingers. 'Thank you.'

Turning, she crossed the wood-panelled office, heels clicking on the parquet floor. Simeon Pemberton let her reach the door before he spoke again. 'One final matter, Miss White. It may be that your new colleagues indulge in gossip and tittle-tattle about other departments of the bank, but I would remind you that everything occurring within these walls remains highly confidential.'

It was possible he meant inside information about who might be defaulting on a loan or increasing a mortgage but Harry would never share details like that and besides, she couldn't imagine many of the post room staff caring. No, Pemberton meant his lascivious eye and bumbling efforts to seduce her, she thought. He didn't want any whispers about that to work their way around the gleaming new building, much less her emphatic rejection of his advances. She paused in the door frame and met his forbidding frown with a coolly raised eyebrow. 'Understood, Mr Pemberton. You may be sure I will remain as professional as ever.'

Head held high, she closed the door and set off in search of her new office.

* * *

Neither the magnificent marble staircase in the entrance hall nor the gilt-edged elevator beside it serviced the post room. To reach the basement, Harry was obliged to make her way beyond the bustling, chandelier-lit showiness of the public areas and into the rear of the building, where the considerably less grand service lift conveyed her underground.

When the metal doors slid open, they revealed a brick-lined corridor illuminated by a row of light bulbs in the ceiling. The distant clang of machinery and cheerful raised voices floated towards her, and a curious aroma hung in the air, the oily tang of industry mingled with the scent of cigarettes and manual labour. Harry fought the urge to wrinkle her nose as she stepped out of the lift; it was a stark contrast to the hushed, flower and furniture polish order of the offices upstairs and something of her determination to show Mr Pemberton that she would not be cowed wavered. But she hadn't been raised to shy away from difficulty, even though she was well aware her life had not involved much struggle so far. Once again, she straightened her shoulders and went to find Mr Babbage.

The corridor opened into a wide rectangular room that was a maelstrom of noise and confusion. She stood for a moment, taking in the enormous, noisy contraption that dominated the centre of the room but whose exact purpose she couldn't immediately define, the men in checked shirts with no jackets who scurried around it, the hustle and hullabaloo and fug of cigarette smoke that made the whole scene hazy. Most of all, she observed the total absence of female workers. And then one of the men noticed her.

He stood still and stared, mouth agape as though he had never seen a woman before. His sudden stillness caught the eye of the worker beside him, who also stopped moving to gawk. The raucous shouts began to die away and, before Harry could gather her wits enough to speak, every man was staring in a way that made the hairs on the back of her neck prickle.

'Can we help you, miss?' called one, stepping forward and removing his cap. 'You ought not to be down here.'

Harry cleared her throat. 'I'm looking for Mr Babbage. Is he available?'

Her accent, well-spoken and proper at the best of times, sounded shrill and horrendously misplaced above the thrum of the machinery. The spokesman frowned but turned to shout over one shoulder. 'Mr Babbage, sir? There's a – a lady what's asking for you.'

The door of a side office opened and a stout, red-cheeked man came hurrying out. Harry was instantly reminded of a jolly garden gnome, the kind her aunt had gone crazy for the previous summer and dotted around the gardens of Abinger Hall until it felt as though they were being overrun by cheery little men. He stopped short, goggling at the sight of Harry, then seemed to pull himself together. Eyebrows bristling, he hurried forward. 'I'm Albert Babbage. What can I do for you?'

His tone wasn't blunt but nor was it especially cordial. Nevertheless, Harry met the enquiry without flinching. 'I'm to report to you for work.'

Mr Babbage gawped at her, astonishment written all over his florid features. 'For work? *Here*?'

Uncomfortably aware of their audience, she nodded and took the envelope from her handbag. 'Perhaps this will explain things.'

For a moment, Mr Babbage merely stared at the white oblong, then he seemed to recall where he was. He glanced furiously at the men around him. 'Dunno what you're all looking at,' he snapped with sudden but palpable irritation. 'Haven't you got work to do?'

As one, they busied themselves and Mr Babbage turned his attention back to Harry with a bemused expression. 'You'd better step into my office,' he said, indicating the door through which he'd just passed. It wasn't until they were both seated, on opposite sides of a heavy oak desk, and he had given Harry another perplexed look, that Mr Babbage pulled out the letter and began to read. Harry took the opportunity to take in her surroundings – post room-themed pamphlets dotted the walls, some yellowed and torn with age, along with procedural posters and instructions. An open cabinet hung in one corner, revealing row after row of shining brass keys, each neatly tagged. A hefty set of weighing scales sat on a sideboard. Here, as in the main room and the corridor, Harry detected the oily bite of metal and machinery. Beneath it lay the ingrained odour of sweat and hard work, and perhaps a hint of tobacco.

With a surreptitious glance through the windows at the engine room beyond, Harry reminded herself that this was Simeon Pemberton's attempt at revenge. She had to rise above it.

Mr Babbage looked up. 'This won't do, I'm afraid. It won't do at all.'

Harry dragged her gaze from a fire safety poster and fixed her attention upon him, wondering what the letter suggested. 'Are you not in need of secretarial support?'

'Well, no,' he huffed. 'That is to say yes, there is a vacancy but it's not... I didn't expect—' He broke off to eye her helplessly and took a deep breath. 'We can't have a lady of your... your credentials working down here, Miss White. Only an idiot would have suggested we could.'

She allowed herself a brief flicker of amusement. 'I think we agree on that.'

'There must be some mistake – a miscommunication,' Mr Babbage went on, frowning to himself. 'Because there is a job to be done but...' He trailed off, fixing his gaze on the letter once more, then glanced up at Harry and sniffed. 'Wait here. No, on second thoughts you'd better come with me.'

Harry didn't quite heave a sigh of relief when they took the service lift to the first floor and returned to the quiet elegance of the corridors she knew well, but she felt the tension in her muscles ease. Mr Babbage led her past a number of closed doors before he found the one he wanted. Instructing her to wait, he disappeared inside, leaving her to study the unadorned wood panels with no inkling of who worked within. When he reappeared a few minutes later, a weight seemed to have lifted from his shoulders. 'I've found you an office,' he explained, heading back the way they had come. 'I daresay it's not what you're used to up on the fifth floor, but it'll be a darn sight better than anything we've got in the post room.' He glanced sideways as though sizing her up. 'Yes, a darn sight better.'

He must be wondering what her crime had been, Harry thought, feeling the faint fire of indignation warm her cheeks. Whatever Mr Pemberton's letter said, she knew it wouldn't be anything resembling the truth. 'What is the position I shall be filling?' she asked.

Mr Babbage huffed. 'Didn't Pemberton tell you? It's a secretarial role, mostly filing and correspondence. Replying to letters, that kind of thing.'

She frowned, remembering the noise and chaos of the basement. 'Then why send me to the post room?'

'Why indeed?' Mr Babbage grumbled. 'Although strictly speaking, the correspondence doesn't relate to the business of the bank so maybe that's it. Stuff and nonsense if you ask me but it falls under my remit, right enough. I've just never known what to do about it and it's getting out of hand.'

Harry felt her brow crease even further. Letters that weren't Abbey Road Building Society business? Stuff and nonsense? What could that mean?

'Ah, here we are,' her companion said as they arrived at a shabby door set just before the bend of the corridor. It bore the number 221 but looked very much like a broom cupboard to Harry. Even so, Mr Babbage slotted a key into the lock and pushed the door aside to peer past. 'Not what you'd call plush but you'll be comfortable enough.' He shook his head. 'More comfortable than downstairs, at least.'

Moving back, he gestured to Harry to take a look. Beyond the light from the corridor, the room was shrouded in darkness. She felt for the switch just inside and flicked it upwards, filling the small space with weak yellow light from an overhead bulb, and she realised her first assessment had almost been right – it practically was a broom cupboard. There was a chair and a desk, with a typewriter taking up most of its surface. A narrow filing cabinet stood in one corner with a forlorn black telephone resting on top. There were no windows, no skylights, no view to the outside world. The walls were blank, with the occasional oblong smudge that suggested a picture might have once hung there. At least there was a carpet, Harry thought as she stepped inside and her heels sank into the crimson wool. She wouldn't have been entirely surprised at bare floorboards.

'Well,' Mr Babbage said from the doorway, 'I'll leave you to settle in. One of the lads will be along shortly with the first batch of letters – all you need to do is type a short reply and then file the original with a copy of the response.'

Harry stared at him. 'What kind of letter? How will I know what to say in my reply?'

Mr Babbage coughed. 'All will become clear, Miss White. Ring down once you've opened a few and we can discuss a standard response.' His eyes met hers then and she saw pity in his gaze. 'I'm afraid it's going to be very dull work. Dull but necessary, for all that it's stuff and nonsense.'

Almost subconsciously, she stiffened her spine. 'I'm sure I shall do my best.'

He gave a little shake of his head as he walked away. 'Call down to my office when you're ready. Goodbye for now.'

Harry gazed after him for several long seconds, then surveyed the room again. After a moment or two, she drifted towards the desk and ran her fingers across the keys of the typewriter. They were dust-free and the ribbon seemed to be new. She sat in the chair, listening to the silence. Nowhere in the bank could be considered noisy – apart from the recently discovered basement, Harry allowed – but on the fifth floor there had always been a discreet background buzz. The genteel murmur of conversation in offices and corridors, the clack-clack-clack of typewriter keys, the clip of well-heeled shoes on the polished wooden floor and the ring of the telephone. But in this apparently forgotten corner of the building, there was no sound. She might be the only person there.

The drawers of the filing cabinet were empty. Harry lifted the telephone, listened briefly to the dialling tone, then sighed and drummed her fingers on the metal of the cabinet. Her previous work at the bank could not be described as interesting – her brothers frequently asked her how she bore it – but she had always taken a quiet satisfaction in an immaculately typed, neatly filed document, enjoying the knowledge that while she was not stretching herself, she was good at the work. She liked earning her own money too; the granddaughter of a baron had no title to inherit and needed to make her own way in the world. Usually this was by marriage to a suitably wealthy husband but Harry had no intention of being forced to settle for such a match. So her job, though frowned upon by her family, was more than just employment – it was a declaration of independence. And that was why she was determined not to let this sudden change in role disturb her.

Things would work out, she decided, and carefully removed her hat. Seeing nowhere to hang it, and making a mental note to requisition a coat stand, she laid the hat in the empty filing cabinet and reached into her handbag to retrieve the Agatha Christie novel she had been enjoying on the train that morning. It wasn't her habit to read on the bank's time, but what else was there to do?

Almost an hour passed before Harry heard the squeak of a wheel in the corridor. It was followed by a knock at the door. She lowered the paperback. 'Come in.'

Slowly, the door was pushed back and a youth peered in at her, dressed in the same familiar red and gold livery that the bank's doormen wore. Harry didn't recognise his amiable, freckled face but that was hardly surprising; as Mr Pemberton's personal assistant, she hadn't been responsible for handling the post. 'Got a sack of mail here,' the youth said, gesturing vaguely at the shiny brass trolley behind him. 'Where do you want it?'

Harry almost laughed. The office was barely big enough for the furniture it contained – there weren't many places for him to leave a sack. But she swallowed her amusement and pointed to the corner on his left. 'Over there, please.'

She watched with undisguised curiosity as he hefted the hessian sack from the trolley and deposited it on the carpet. It was full, just as his grunt of effort suggested, and once again Harry found herself wondering at the nature of the letters contained inside. Stuff and nonsense, Mr Babbage had said, but the sheer volume confused her. Who were all these letters to, if not the bank? And who could they be from?

'That's the lot,' the post boy said, scratching beneath his brocade-trimmed hat with the cheerful air of one who has completed his task. 'For now, at any rate. But I reckon you'll be a regular stop on my delivery route now, given how much people write to him.'

The words only increased Harry's mystification but she managed a polite smile. 'Then I suppose I'd better introduce myself. I'm Miss White.'

'How d'you do? Most people call me Bobby,' the youth replied. His eyes travelled around the room, taking in the single light bulb and lack of decoration in thoughtful silence before his gaze came to rest upon the novel splayed cover upwards on the desk. 'Like them kind of books, do you? Detective stories and that?'

Harry nodded. 'Yes, I do.'

Bobby looked pleased with himself, as though he'd solved a puzzle. 'That must be why they give you this here job.' He gave himself a little shake and stepped backwards into the corridor. 'Cheerio, then. Prob'ly see you tomorrow.'

The squeak of the trolley receded, leaving Harry alone to stare at the bulging sack. None of this made sense – what could her taste in literature have to do with anything? But now at least she had something to do. Getting to her feet, she took the few steps needed to cross the room and tugged the rough brown material apart.

The sack was filled with a jumble of envelopes, all shapes and sizes, in assorted shades and decidedly mixed in quality. The handwriting was neat on some, an untidy scrawl on others, but the name and address on every letter was a variation on the same theme:

Mr Sherlock Holmes
221b Baker Street
London

Harry could only stare in open-mouthed astonishment. Whatever she'd been expecting, it wasn't a bag full of letters to – well, to someone who didn't exist. And yet they weren't incorrectly addressed, nor had they been misdelivered: the Abbey Road Building Society headquarters did occupy numbers 219–229 Baker Street, undeniably encompassing the fictional address of Sherlock Holmes. But surely people didn't write to him there. Surely they understood their letters would go unread... Still blinking, Harry gathered up a handful of letters from the top of the slithering pile and took them back to her desk. She slit the first envelope open and began to read.

Mr Sherlock Holmes
221b Baker Street
London
NW1 6XE

43 Myddelton Road
Sandy
Bedfordshire

13th April 1932

Dear Mr Holmes,

I am writing to you for help with a most terrible crime. The police have been worse than useless and I am at my wits' end. I believe my neighbour cruelly murdered his wife in the dead of night last month but no one will listen. I am certain that a man of your brilliance will see the truth of things immediately. Please grant me an appointment so that a killer may be apprehended and justice served.

I await your reply by return.

Yours faithfully,

Mr Benjamin Grantly

Harry blew out her cheeks, wondering whether Mr Grantly had abandoned hope of receiving a response, given it was six months since he'd written, or whether his neighbour was still under suspicion. Putting the letter to one side, she opened the next. This was from a Miss P Bellows, the distressed owner of a missing cat, who claimed she had been the victim of international pet thieves. Another writer accused a local vicar of embezzling church funds. Several claimed sightings of Holmes' nemesis, Professor James Moriarty, in locations from Dover to Aberdeen. As Harry's incredulous gaze skimmed each entreaty, she was sure of one thing: few of these purported crimes would have snared the interest of the great Sherlock Holmes.

Puffing out another breath, Harry stacked the sheets of paper neatly on top of each other. Now she understood why Mr Babbage had said the correspondence wasn't really anything to do with the bank. The letters had evidently been allowed to pile up, a minor problem it was easier to ignore until the sheer volume meant the problem was no longer minor. Something had to be done to address it. *Someone* had to address it and, however improbably, it appeared that someone was Harry. It was certainly a long way from what she had expected to do when she'd arrived at work that morning.

Lifting the heavy black telephone onto the desk, she consulted the internal telephone directory she found in a drawer and located the post room extension. Mr Babbage answered on the fifth ring and grunted when Harry introduced herself. 'I suppose you've got a better idea of the job now.'

'I have,' Harry said. 'Although I must say, the correspondence is a little... unusual.'

There was a hollow laugh. 'Downright foolish, if you ask me. It started arriving as soon as we opened the doors. We had a look at a few, thinking they were meant for Sir Arthur Conan Doyle, but we soon realised – well, to be blunt, that it was our problem, not his. A duty that comes with the Baker Street territory, so to speak.'

Harry eyed the spidery handwriting on the paper before her, and then gazed at the sack leaning against the office wall. These letters hadn't been written in admiration of the author of the Sherlock Holmes stories but in appreciation of Mr Holmes himself. Every correspondent ardently believed not only that the great detective was a real, flesh-and-blood person, but also that he could and would solve their mysteries. They had each set pen to paper, some in frustration, others in desperation, all in hope and anticipation that Sherlock Holmes would heed their cry for help. Mr Babbage was right, a response was most definitely needed – one that was sympathetic but firm – and that was something Harry could hardly imagine would be forthcoming from Sir Arthur Conan Doyle himself, given that the great man had sadly been dead for several years.

'Yes, I see what you mean,' she said, as her future suddenly stretched away in front of her. 'There are so many letters.'

Mr Babbage seemed to hesitate, then rallied. 'You'll soon get on top of things. Like I said earlier, all you need to do is whip up a short reply and pop it in the post, then file the copies and move on to the next one.'

'What am I supposed to say?' she asked, lifting the first letter from the pile and scanning the hopeful words. 'And who should the reply be from – the bank?'

Again, Mr Babbage paused. 'No, not the bank. From Sherlock Holmes – the *secretary* of Sherlock Holmes.' He gave an uncertain chuckle. 'That's you.'

Not for the first time that morning, Harry wondered if she was still asleep and dreaming. 'And what should the reply say? Given we're going along with the pretence that he actually exists.'

There was a huff from the other end of the phone. 'I don't know. Tell them he's dead – no, don't tell them that, we could get into a lot of hot water, legally speaking.' He stopped, as though thinking. 'Say he's not taking any new cases at the moment. Yes, that works.'

Harry considered what she knew of Sherlock Holmes' character, having read and enjoyed the stories written about him, and then recalled the distressed tone in some of the letters. 'I'm not sure that's going to work,' she objected. 'Holmes is always declaring he isn't taking new cases and then something juicy comes along and he's off on the trail. They'll just write again, more desperately.'

'Then be firm,' Mr Babbage said, starting to sound exasperated. 'Tell them he's retired and living in the countryside and doesn't care about crime any more. Say he's got a new hobby now like – like bell ringing or gardening or something.'

Once again, Harry pictured the familiar image of Sherlock Holmes, deerstalker hat on his head, and tried to imagine him cheerfully indulging in bucolic bell ringing. 'I don't think—'

'You'll come up with something, Miss White,' Mr Babbage cut in jovially. 'The sooner you get started, the better we'll all feel, eh? Goodbye for now.'

Harry stared at the silent receiver, then replaced it on the cradle and moved the telephone back to its home on top of the filing cabinet. She sat still for a moment, wondering for what felt like the hundredth time how she had come to this, and then gave herself a brisk mental shake. Simeon Pemberton had sent her here, doubtless hoping she would refuse to lower herself to such ridiculousness, and she wasn't about to give him the satisfaction of being proved right. Besides, there was a job to be done – not glamorous or flashy, but a job, nonetheless. These letters needed a response, a kind and soothing reply that let the writer down gently, and that was something Harry could provide with her customary calm efficiency.

Reaching a decision, she took the topmost letter to Sherlock Holmes from the pile she had opened and smoothed it out on the desk, skimming over the words to refresh her memory. A slight frown creased her forehead as she decided how to word the perfect response, then from the desk drawer she extracted a sheet of inky blue carbon paper and laid it between two sheets of plain letter paper. Rolling all three pages carefully into the typewriter, she lined up the carriage and, with a final decisive glance at the return address on the letter, she began to type.

2

Over the weeks that followed, it quickly became clear to Harry that she had vastly underestimated the mind-numbing monotony of her new role. At the end of the first day, she had risen from her desk at four o'clock sharp to don her hat and coat, pausing in the doorway to survey the neat stack of answered letters on the desk and choosing to block out the still-bulging mail sack in the corner. The number on the door as she closed it brought her up sharp – someone had a sense of humour, it seemed – but she had turned the key in the lock with fastidious care and made her way to the ground floor, where she'd smiled at Patrick the doorman, and taken the Underground from Baker Street to Piccadilly.

She'd had no doubt that the excellent London Library in St James's Square would house the complete works of Sir Arthur Conan Doyle among their labyrinth of shelves and stacks and she was not disappointed; the librarian offered her original copies of *The Strand* magazine in which many of the Sherlock Holmes stories had first appeared, as well as leather-bound copies of the five short story collections that had followed to feed the growing public appetite for the detective's adventures. Arms aching a little with the weight of the compilations, Harry had returned to her small apartment in Mayfair, eaten a hurried supper of steak and kidney pudding, and spent the rest of the evening immersed in fiendish crime.

In the morning, she had returned to the office and retyped the letters she had produced the day before, because Sir Arthur Conan Doyle himself had given her the perfect cover story – in *His Last Bow*, he had referred to Holmes having retired to the South Downs to keep bees. Clearly, Mr Babbage hadn't been as far off the mark as Harry had supposed.

But once she settled into the task, the monotony began to tug at her spirits. The letters themselves were often diverting, if wild and sometimes laughable. Having renewed her acquaintance with Holmes through the books she'd borrowed from the library, she couldn't help imagining his reaction to these demands for his services. Every now and then, she came across one that caught her eye and caused her to wonder whether it might have made a good Sherlock Holmes adventure or contemplate how the detective might have solved it. She never varied her response, however:

> *Thank you for your enquiry. Unfortunately, Mr Holmes is no longer available for consultation. He is retired from detective work and has for some years been living in Sussex, where he is a much-respected beekeeper.*
>
> *I am sorry not to be able to help further but wish you every success with this distressing matter.*
>
> *Yours faithfully,*
>
> *R. K. Moss*
>
> *Secretary to Sherlock Holmes*

Initially, she had considered using her own name to sign the letters but she suspected the bank – or at least Mr Pemberton, if he ever came looking – might view that as a grave impertinence. Her next idea was to use one of Conan Doyle's minor female characters as a *nom de plume* but that felt somehow both disrespectful and foolhardy – those who wrote to Sherlock Holmes were very likely ardent fans of the world the famous detective inhabited. They would register a name stolen from a story and probably write again to demand an explanation.

After some deliberation, Harry had settled upon the tried and trusted stalwart of many mystery novels – the anagram. The letters of Sherlock Holmes' name had given her a number of possibilities that would not look out of place in one of his own stories: Heckler Shloom sounded like a wealthy American businessman being blackmailed by his mistress, Horses Hemlock put her in mind of a shady bookmaker with links to a nefarious gambling ring. The only name she could make with an ounce of believability was Rochelle K. Moss, which she abbreviated to R. K. Moss in order to muddy the waters further. But once that initial burst of creativity was over, the reality of typing the same words over and over, day in, day out came to weigh heavily on her spirits. It wasn't as though she had colleagues to relieve the boredom – her daily visits from Bobby and his post trolley provided some brief respite from the solitude but for the most part, it was just Harry and the never-ending stream of letters.

As the weeks rolled by, she began to wonder whether her determination to stick things out was misplaced. And then, one Tuesday morning, she opened the envelope that changed everything.

It was the sender's address that first caught Harry's eye. The village of Foxley was around five miles from her family's estate in Surrey and while its houses and shops didn't lie within the Abinger lands, she knew several members of the household staff and groundskeepers came from there. It also boasted a very fine public house that Harry's brothers spoke well of, and an excellent cricket team, all of which flashed through Harry's mind when she saw the address. Who on earth in Foxley would be writing to Sherlock Holmes? And, more importantly, why?

Frowning, she scanned the neat handwriting and observed the letter was from a Miss E. Longstaff, of No. 5, The Cottages. Miss Longstaff was writing on behalf of her family on the delicate matter of her eighteen-year-old sister, Mildred, who had moved to London to work as a maid but had vanished in mysterious circumstances.

The police have been no help. A newspaper advertisement offering a modest reward only attracted the worst kind of swindlers and liars, none of whom could prove they had seen Mildred. I beg you in the strongest terms, Mr Holmes, to use your formidable skills to find her. She is a gentle country girl, hard-working and diligent and most proper in her conduct. With each passing day my fears grow that something dreadful has happened. Please help us, sir. I do not know where else to turn.

Harry's frown deepened as she studied the letter. It was well written in a looping cursive script, with flawless spelling and an excellent grasp of language and grammar: whoever Miss E. Longstaff was, she appeared to have enjoyed an education that went above and beyond that offered by the average village school. What was more, if everything she claimed was true, she was in pressing need of help. Why, then, had she chosen to consult a man who did not exist? It made no sense to Harry, who enjoyed a crime novel as much as the next person but had never been fooled into thinking the detectives she admired were real. And yet Miss Longstaff was not alone. The letters Harry spent her days answering were testament to that.

The paper and envelope offered few additional clues about the sender, being inexpensive but perfectly adequate. The date beneath the address was over a month old and when Harry examined the envelope, she saw the postmark was the same day, which suggested urgency on Miss Longstaff's part. No big surprise after her revelation that the family was afraid for the missing girl. And yet quite some time had passed – perhaps this Mildred had turned up safe and well in the meantime. Almost certainly she had, Harry told herself as she rolled fresh paper into her typewriter – wasn't her aunt constantly bemoaning the flightiness of housemaids?

Her fingers flexed as she prepared to type the standard reply. She laid them on the keys, poised to let them fly, and stopped to gaze pensively down at the looping handwriting. There was really no way of knowing whether Miss Longstaff's sister had been found, short of asking and that was impossible. But it was a possibility that Miss Longstaff had written again, in greater desperation, and that subsequent letter might be waiting in the pile of envelopes Harry had long since sorted into date order, ready to work methodically through. Pushing her chair back, Harry got to her feet and selected the two oldest, elastic-bound bundles and carried them to the desk. She flicked slowly through, comparing the handwriting and postmark on each envelope with that of Miss Longstaff's letter, but none matched either in penmanship or the postal district neatly stamped above the Baker Street address.

Undeterred, Harry moved on to the next bundle, and the next. By the time she reached the final cluster, all of which bore a postmark dated in the last week, she grew more and more assured that her original supposition must be correct – Miss Longstaff and her sister had been reunited. Until she recognised a familiar hand on a fresh, unopened envelope. It didn't have to be a further entreaty, Harry told herself as she reached for the letter opener. It could be that Mildred had been found and the conscientious Miss Longstaff was simply informing Mr Holmes that his services were no longer needed.

But deep down, Harry thought it unlikely; if the girl had turned up Miss Longstaff would most likely have forgotten she had ever written to Sherlock Holmes. And her suspicions were instantly borne out. The letter begged for help – the family's concern ate away at them all. They were not wealthy but they would endeavour to pay anything Mr Holmes asked to have word of Mildred. Desperation poured from the page, tugging at Harry's heartstrings even as she understood there was nothing she could do to help. Sherlock Holmes could not and would not be moved to investigate, because he did not exist. With an uncharacteristic groan of frustration, Harry settled once more with her hands on the typewriter keys and began to type.

She got little rest that night. Her dreams were punctuated by glimpses of a phantom girl, who led her on a chase through London's landmarks, always tantalisingly close but somehow also just out of reach. When Harry jerked awake sometime around dawn, she gave up trying to sleep again and lay staring at the ceiling as pale tendrils of yellow crawled across the alabaster. In her dreams, it had not been Sherlock Holmes who had been searching for Mildred Longstaff, it had been Harry herself, an idea so preposterous that Harry might have laughed if she hadn't been so unsettled. Yet that was what her fevered brain seemed to be demanding, regardless of the ridiculousness of the undertaking, and the after-effects of the dreams were hard to shake off.

Eventually, Harry got up and made her way across the still-slumbering city to Baker Street, arriving early to immerse herself in the dullness of her work. But that only seemed to make things worse – she could not stop thinking of Miss Longstaff and her parents, silently watching the door each day for news from their last great hope. At length, Harry found the standard letter she had typed to Miss Longstaff the day before and sat looking at it for a long time. Perhaps she might call – but no, it was madness to even think of it. The family wanted the brilliance of the world's greatest detective, not meaningless platitudes from a member of the local aristocracy. What good could she do? Unless...

The idea was so audacious, so utterly against the trust placed in her by the bank, that Harry felt light-headed even thinking it. Yet it persisted in her head, growing in noise until she had to give it proper space. It was an incontrovertible truth that Sherlock Holmes could not uncover the whereabouts of Mildred Longstaff but that did not mean there was nothing to be done. What if Harry sought information about the missing girl and reported back to the Longstaffs under the guise of Holmes?

She gave herself a mental shake. That would never work – she was not even a man, let alone anyone's idea of a master detective. But Mr Babbage had dubbed her secretary to Sherlock Holmes. What was to stop her taking a little liberty with the title and replying to Miss Longstaff in that capacity? She could request more information, do some digging in her spare time and see what she could find out. No one at the bank needed to know. It wasn't as though anyone was checking up on her, after all – apart from Bobby and Mr Babbage, no one seemed to remember she was there.

Rolling another sheaf of papers into the typewriter, Harry sat without moving for several minutes. The difficulty was that time was now pressing. Mildred had been missing for almost two months already, and correspondence between the Longstaff family and Holmes to gather further details might take weeks. Harry was due to return home to Abinger Hall that weekend – what if she took a trip to Foxley village and presented herself to Miss Longstaff as Sherlock Holmes' assistant? She could ask questions of the family, perhaps even request a photograph of Mildred... it would be a much more efficient approach than writing and awaiting a reply. And she could do it all under the guise of R. K. Moss – no one need know her true identity. Making up her mind, Harry began to type.

Wednesday 5th October, 1932

Dear Miss Longstaff,

Thank you for your recent letters to Mr Holmes regarding your sister, Mildred. Unfortunately, Mr Holmes is no longer available for consultation. He is retired from detective work and has for some years been living in Sussex, where he is a much-respected beekeeper.

He has, however, asked me to investigate on his behalf and share any findings with him, in order to try to locate your sister. Accordingly, I shall visit you at 2 p.m. on Saturday 8th October, at your home.

Mr Holmes is keen to render his assistance and has asked me to assure you there will be no fee. I look forward to meeting you.

Yours faithfully,

R. K. Moss

Secretary to Sherlock Holmes

Harry reread the letter several times once it was complete, anxiously considering its tone. She had tried to use the trademark arrogance of Holmes to overcome the lack of social grace in demanding an interview at such short notice – there wasn't time to allow Miss Longstaff to write back. Would Holmes' reputation for brusqueness, combined with the family's undoubted gratitude at receiving his attention, be enough to get Harry past the front door? Time would tell, she supposed. The lack of a fee would help – in the first instance, she had no idea how much assistance she could truly offer and in the second, she had a sneaking suspicion that taking any kind of payment on behalf of a fictional character might amount to fraud. Better to avoid that altogether, she felt. But it still took her until lunchtime to pluck up the courage to add the envelope to the pile of others that would soon be collected by Bobby to be processed in the post room. And it took all her strength not to run after him once he had taken it, whistling cheerfully as he trundled along the corridor.

She stared at the closed door of the office for a long time, wondering whether she'd made a terrible mistake. Eventually, she filed her copy of the standard letter with all the other standard replies she'd sent so far, hid the letter from R. K. Moss inside a folder at the bottom of the filing cabinet, and opened the next envelope.

3

It was a perfectly crisp autumn day when Harry navigated the lanes from her family home to the village of Foxley. The roads were strewn with coppery leaves that had flung themselves from the branches and the sky was a deep cornflower blue. Another time, Harry might have savoured the luxury of her brother's cherry red MG, which he'd grudgingly allowed her to borrow without too much interrogation; driving was one of her great pleasures, inspired by the motoring adventures of Baroness Campbell von Laurentz, who had written a book on the subject and had been a frequent visitor to Abinger Hall during Harry's formative years. But right now she found the enormity of what she was about to do dampened her spirits. What if the Longstaffs saw through her ridiculous assertion that she was working for Sherlock Holmes and called the police? Or worse, what if they laughed in her face?

Nevertheless, she found a parking spot on the edge of the village, tucked her golden curls under her hat and straightened the no-nonsense skirt suit she'd chosen for its dullness. With a bit of luck, she looked the part. All she needed now was to convince Miss Longstaff and her parents that she was R. K. Moss, secretary to the greatest ever detective. The thought made her feel exhilarated and ill at the same time.

The door was opened almost before Harry's knock had died away. A young woman of around seventeen stood there, pale but composed in a neat, emerald-green dress that matched the colour of her eyes yet contrasted beautifully with her striking auburn hair. 'Yes?'

Harry considered her. From the style and tone of the correspondence, she had assumed Esme Longstaff was older than Mildred, perhaps in her twenties. 'Miss Longstaff? Miss Esme Longstaff?'

The girl frowned. 'Yes, I'm Esme Longstaff.'

Harry cleared her throat. 'I'm R. K. Moss. I assume you got my letter?'

'Oh,' Miss Longstaff said, her cheeks reddening a little. 'But I thought...'

She trailed off and Harry understood the cause of her uncertainty. It seemed they were both guilty of making assumptions about the other. 'You were expecting a man, perhaps?'

Miss Longstaff's blush deepened. 'No! That's to say, we wondered but—' She seemed to pull herself together and stood back to allow Harry to enter. 'It doesn't matter. Thank you for taking the time to see us. Won't you come in?'

Harry did as she asked. The hallway was narrow, with a low ceiling and whitewashed walls. She wiped her feet and declined an offer to leave her hat and jacket, then followed Miss Longstaff into a small parlour crowded with a pair of faded chintz sofas, several occasional tables and a dark wood dresser against one wall. A fire smouldered in the small fireplace.

'My parents,' Esme said as Harry edged her way into the room. 'Mama and Papa, this is Mr Holmes' assistant.'

The couple exchanged looks. Anticipating further frowns, Harry strode towards them. 'R. K. Moss,' she said again, interjecting as much authority as she could muster into her voice. 'A pleasure to meet you. Mr Holmes sends his regrets – he's not as young as he was and doesn't travel these days. His arthritis, you understand.'

The detail seemed to mollify them. 'Of course,' Mr Longstaff said from his position beside the fireplace, and shook Harry's outstretched hand. 'We're grateful you could come.'

Esme shook her head. 'You must have had a long journey. Can I offer you some tea?'

Somewhat guiltily, Harry recollected her uneventful fifteen-minute drive. But there was no way she could refuse the offer without appearing rude so she smiled. 'That would be most welcome.'

Once Esme had left the room, Harry turned to her parents, who were older, less vibrant versions of their daughter. Mr Longstaff's hair was grey, his face lined, but his eyes were the same vivid green as Esme's. Harry could easily imagine Mrs Longstaff turning heads in her younger years but she now gave the impression of a once-bright painting that had faded with the passing years. 'Mr Holmes was most distressed to hear of your situation,' Harry said, surreptitiously crossing her fingers. 'Perhaps you could give me some background information while we await tea. How long is it exactly since you heard from Mildred?'

Mr Longstaff pressed his lips together. 'About three months now. She went to London for work, took a job as a maid at a fancy house in a well-to-do area. At first, everything was fine – she wrote twice a week, sent money when she could.' He fixed Harry with an almost fiery look. 'We didn't ask her to – told her not to but she sent it anyway. Said she wanted to help with Esme's studies.'

It had been clear from the letters that Esme Longstaff was well educated. Perhaps there was a private tutor involved, Harry thought. 'I understand,' she said, perching on the edge of a sofa and reaching into her handbag for a notepad and pen. 'What happened next?'

'We don't know.' Mrs Longstaff regarded her from her seat on the opposite sofa, her eyes already damp with tears. 'Mildred suddenly stopped writing and our letters to her were returned. When Mr Longstaff went to the address, we were told she'd been let go. For stealing!'

Her voice rose sharply on the final word and she pressed her hand to her mouth as though to prevent a sob from escaping. At the fireplace, Mr Longstaff made a restless gesture. 'It wasn't true – it couldn't be. I told the housekeeper, Mildred has her head screwed on – she'd never take anything that wasn't hers. But she wouldn't listen.'

'What did they say had been stolen?' Harry asked.

'Some jewellery – a necklace or something,' he said dismissively. 'But it couldn't have been Mildred. She's not a thief. The job was worth more to her than a bit of jewellery.'

Harry nodded. He sounded stout in his belief, although it wouldn't be the first time a parent had defended their offspring against the evidence. 'Of course not,' she said soothingly. 'Did they involve the police at all?'

Mrs Longstaff closed her eyes. 'It would have been better if they had – at least we'd have someone else who would have seen her before she disappeared. But they just sent her packing, didn't want any trouble. I don't know why she didn't come home.'

It was a shame she hadn't, Harry thought, but there might be any number of explanations for that – pride, embarrassment, a determination to make her own way in the city. Stranger still that the police had not been summoned, which suggested to Harry that the stolen item hadn't been especially valuable, or that it had been recovered and Mildred's employer had preferred to avoid any fuss. Either explanation was possible.

Her musings were interrupted by Esme, returning with a tray of tea. She laid it on one of the tables and turned an enquiring look

Harry's way. 'Milk, no sugar, thank you,' Harry said, then returned her attention to Mr and Mrs Longstaff. 'And you've heard nothing more from Mildred?'

'Nothing,' Mrs Longstaff murmured. 'We tried to find her – Mr Longstaff scoured half the city and we even put an advert in the newspaper, appealing for information, but nothing useful came to light. It's as though she vanished.'

Harry thought of the London she knew, vast and sprawling and growing month by month. Behind the gloss of the bright lights lay a warren of dark alleyways. It would be easy for a scared country girl to take a wrong turn and find herself somewhere undesirable. The question then would be how lost she might become.

Esme handed Harry a cup and saucer. 'I wrote to her employer, begging for more information, but it was hopeless.' Her lip curled. 'The domestic staff are beneath their notice, unless their tea arrives cold or the fire isn't lit.'

Realising she could not hold her cup and make notes, Harry slid the saucer discreetly onto a nearby table and held her pen over the notepad. 'Her employer, yes. Who was that?'

'Lord and Lady Finchem,' Esme said. 'They live in Mayfair. I can give you the address if you'd like it.'

'Yes, please,' Harry replied, keeping her face composed even though her mind was racing. She was sure her mother had mentioned a Lady Finchem in the past – it had to be the same one. 'Do you have a photograph of Mildred? It might help me to find her.'

Esme finished pouring the tea for her parents and rose. 'Of course. Although you'll probably recognise her by her hair – it's red, like mine.'

She handed over a grainy black and white photograph that showed two girls, perhaps in their early teens, both of whom bore a striking resemblance to Mrs Longstaff. One was taller – Harry guessed that must be Mildred – but there wasn't much difference otherwise. They were in a garden, their heads tilted towards each other, and smiling as though sharing a secret joke. It was a lovely picture, and reinforced the sisters' bond, but it was too old and indistinct to give Harry much more than a general idea of Mildred's appearance. 'Thank you,' she said, handing the photograph back. 'Are her eyes green too?'

'A family trait,' Mr Longstaff put in. 'My grandfather used to say we had a chip of the Emerald Isle in our hearts that lit up our eyes.'

Irish ancestry, Harry noted to herself in case it had any future relevance. 'Did Mildred ever mention any friends in London?' she asked. 'Anyone she might have gone to?'

Esme shook her head. 'She hadn't been there long. There wasn't anyone she spoke about in her letters, just the girls she worked with and we couldn't speak to any of them. The housekeeper wouldn't let us.'

Harry frowned. 'But you went to the police – afterwards, I mean. Didn't they make enquiries?'

At this, Esme's eyes flashed. 'Fat lot of use they were – took our names and nodded and said they'd look into it, but they never had any news when Papa rang them. Just said enquires were ongoing. That's why we put the advert in the newspaper.'

'Yes, I was going to ask about that,' Harry said, glancing at her notepad. 'Did you have many responses?'

'None that brought us nearer to finding Mildred,' Mr Longstaff growled in disgust. 'Plenty of swindlers, taking advantage of our terrible situation and more than half of them were women. I suppose we should have expected it, but we hoped someone might have seen her.'

'And none of them had?' Harry asked.

Mr Longstaff uttered a derisive snort. 'All of them claimed they had but if everyone who came forward had seen Mildred in Mayfair that day, there wouldn't have been room to swing a cat.'

Harry frowned. 'How did you establish they weren't telling the truth?'

Esme Longstaff leaned forward. 'The advert referred to a young woman in distress and gave the date Mildred left Lady Finchem's employment,' she said. 'It asked for information about her movements in the Mayfair area, but I kept something back. I deliberately did not include the colour of Mildred's hair in the description. If the respondents could not tell us that detail, we knew they were lying.'

Harry eyed the girl with renewed respect. Her shrewdness and self-assurance belied her tender years. 'Well done,' she said. 'And none of them happened upon Mildred's hair colour by chance?'

'None,' Mr Longstaff said flatly but Harry felt a subtle shift in the room, an intangible sense that something was being left unsaid.

'Papa—' Esme began but her father cut her off.

'None, I tell you,' he said, his expression darkening. 'As Miss Moss here suggests, there were bound to be one or two who guessed correctly. It doesn't mean they had seen Mildred.'

Mrs Longstaff pressed a hand to her mouth. 'I refuse to believe it was her.'

Harry looked between the three of them, taking in Mr Longstaff's forbidding glower, Mrs Longstaff's distress and their daughter's obvious discomfort. What was it they did not want to reveal? 'Mr Holmes often finds the least consequential detail to be the most vital clue,' she said quietly. 'Perhaps you should allow him to be the judge.'

It wasn't actually a lie – Sherlock Holmes did solve his cases by observing something that seemed trivial to everyone else – and it got the desired result. Mr Longstaff scowled for a few seconds longer, then waved a despairing hand at Esme. 'Tell her, then. Not that it will help, since it was not our girl.'

'We received a letter from one of the park keepers in Hyde Park,' Esme said. 'A Mr Blunt, of Serpentine Lodge. He claimed to have seen a young woman in the park, around the time Mildred would have been leaving Lady Finchem's. He described her well and said she was clearly upset.' She paused, her eyes grave. 'And she was not alone.'

That changed things, Harry thought. A park keeper was a more credible witness than a member of the public. 'I see. May I ask who she was with?'

'An older man, supposedly,' Esme replied. 'They were arguing, which was what caught Mr Blunt's attention in the first place. The man had taken hold of the young woman's arm, and she was trying to pull away.'

Alarm bells began to ring in Harry's head. 'Go on.'

'Of course, Mr Blunt continued to investigate,' Esme said, her gaze downcast. 'But as he got nearer, the girl pulled herself clear. She took off through the park and disappeared.'

'Did Mr Blunt discover what the argument had been about?' Harry enquired, making notes.

'Yes—'

'Mildred is not a thief,' Mr Longstaff broke in. 'The park keeper was mistaken. It couldn't have been her.'

Harry turned her eyes to Esme once more, who sighed. 'Mr Blunt said the man accused her of picking his pocket. He caught her red-handed and was about to march her to the Royal Parks police when she got away.'

Mr Longstaff shook his head. 'That's how we know it wasn't Mildred. She wouldn't have the first idea how to pick a pocket.'

It was on the tip of Harry's tongue to say that the girl in Hyde Park had not known how to pick a pocket either, given that she had been caught, but she judged it best to keep the observation to herself. Esme cleared her throat. 'I agree that it cannot have been my sister, but I can give you Mr Blunt's letter, if you think it will help.'

'Thank you,' Harry said, and the girl got up to rummage in a dresser. She handed an envelope to Harry, who tucked it into her notebook to read later. It was important she kept an open mind, she reminded herself. Mildred's family evidently could not bring themselves to think the worst of her, but as Sherlock Holmes was fond of saying, when the impossible had been eliminated, whatever remained, however improbable, must be the truth. And it was certainly possible that the Longstaffs' love for Mildred had blinded them to her descent into crime...

'I must say again how grateful we are that you came,' Esme said as she took her seat on the settee once more. 'It seems nobody cares about finding Mildred. Nobody except you and Mr Holmes.'

Shaking away her dark thoughts, Harry glanced at Esme Longstaff, so capable beyond her years, and then at her parents, paralysed by sorrow and despair, and shook off the last vestiges of guilt at deceiving them. She would find out what she could, and present her findings no matter what they revealed. 'Please give me the address in Mayfair,' she said, pen poised purposefully over her notes. 'I'll start there.'

4

The grandeur of Abinger Hall always took Harry's breath away. Viewed from the ornate, wrought-iron entrance gates, attended on either side by rearing stone stags, the house was initially dwarfed by the twin rows of silver beech trees that stood sentry along the long avenue. It drew the eye, even in the distance, but Harry supposed that was the whole point of the avenue – to encourage visitors to contemplate the magnificence of the building as it loomed to full size before them. With three storeys of sandstone splendour, punctuated by rows of windows and dotted with decorative carved crests and swags, it announced that this was the home of a family with wealth and status. To Harry, it was where all her worries usually fell away.

After parking the MG beside the winged stone steps that swept upwards to the double doors, she gave the bonnet an affectionate pat and then removed her driving gloves. Driving was a pleasure she missed, living in London, but she had little need of a car in the city. Between the Underground, regular buses and the ubiquitous London cabs, Harry found she could easily get wherever she needed to go. But outside of London, a car meant freedom, which was why she had nagged her parents into letting her learn to drive in the first place. Perhaps one day she would follow in the tyre marks of Baroness Campbell von Laurentz and drive across Europe with nothing but a map and the spirit of adventure to guide her. She'd need her own car for that.

'Good Lord, you actually brought her back in one piece.' Her brother, Sebastian, was making his way down the left-hand staircase, an expression of mock surprise on his face.

'You knew I would,' Harry replied, holding out the key. 'I'm a better driver than you, Seb. That's why you let me borrow her.'

He cast an eye over the gleaming red bodywork and silver trim. 'Can't argue with that. Don't tell Rufus, though. He's asked to take her out for a spin a few times and I've fobbed him off with tales of an unreliable fuel line.'

Harry smiled. At twenty-two, their youngest brother had yet to develop a sense of responsibility, relying instead on impish charm and a smile that was hard to resist. His siblings had long ago learned not to lend him anything they wanted to see again. 'Sensible,' she told Sebastian. 'I'm doubly honoured you didn't try that on me.'

'I wouldn't dream of it,' he replied mildly. 'You'd demand a mechanic's report and then I'd be caught out in a terrible fib. Much less trouble to let you have your way. Did you have a successful jaunt?'

Harry thought back to the pale, anxious faces of the Longstaffs as she had taken her leave. 'I think so, yes. Listen, you wouldn't happen to know where Mama is, would you?'

'In the drawing room, I think. But ask Chesterton when you get inside – he always knows where everyone is.'

Chesterton had been the family butler for as long as Harry could remember and he did have an uncanny awareness of everything that occurred within his domain.

'Excellent,' Harry said, and started towards the stone staircase. 'Thanks again, Seb. You're a good sport.'

On the drive back from the village, Harry had decided an indirect approach would work best with Lady Finchem. If she arrived on her Mayfair doorstep as R. K. Moss, demanding information about a disgraced maid, she would not get very far and ran the risk of drawing attention to both herself and her investigation. But if she called on behalf of her grandmother, Baroness Abinger, the door was certain to be opened and an audience granted with Lady Finchem herself. Before that, however, Harry needed more background and there was no one better to consult than her own mother. Evelyn White's knowledge of London society was encyclopaedic; even a whisper of scandal would not have escaped her gimlet gaze.

The entrance hall was empty when Harry pushed back the door, its spotless tiled floor gleaming in the sunlight. The air was rich with the scent of furniture polish and roses, a particular mix that always told Harry she was home. A grand staircase embraced the wood-panelled walls, curving upwards to split left and right, its red carpet adding a vibrant splash of colour, and a magnificent chandelier hung from the beamed ceiling. Once upon a time Harry supposed it must have been lit with candles – she could only imagine what a pain it had been to tend. Craning her head back, she allowed herself to be distracted by the sunbeams dancing on the crystals. And then a door opened and the butler materialised.

'Hello, Chesterton, I was just about to call for you,' Harry said.

'Indeed, Miss White,' he replied with his usual impeccable politeness. 'How may I help?'

'I'm looking for my mother. Have you seen her?'

Chesterton nodded. 'I believe she is in the library. Shall I have some tea sent up?'

'Maybe later,' Harry said, reaching up to unpin her hat. 'Thanks, though.'

She found her mother exactly where Chesterton had suggested she would, curled up on a sofa with one of the family's two Labradors at her side. Tiggy's tail thumped lazily when Harry approached but she didn't get up and Harry could hardly blame her; a spot by the fire was not to be relinquished lightly. Winston did get up and bounded over to greet her, ever hopeful that there might be a treat in his immediate future. Harry ruffled his golden ears and surreptitiously fed him one of the biscuits she always kept handy when she was at home. Both Tiggy and Winston were supposed to be working dogs but neither had displayed the least inclination to retrieve anything other than a ball, and they were now beloved pets.

'You'll make him fat,' Evelyn said, as Tiggy raised her glossy black head to fix Harry with a reproachful look.

'He walks too much for that,' Harry replied, crossing to offer the second biscuit to Tiggy. 'They both do.'

The library was one of Harry's favourite rooms. Lined with floor-to-ceiling bookshelves that carried an answer to almost any question, and a thousand stories besides, it usually had a roaring fire in the grate and somehow seemed to retain its warmth even on the coldest winter day. It was no hardship to sink onto the settee opposite her mother and absorb the peace of the room. No hardship, that was, until Evelyn raised her blue-eyed gaze from the book she had been reading and fixed Harry with a penetrative stare. 'The Honeywells said they invited you to dinner last week but you declined on the grounds of ill health. Is anything the matter?'

Harry picked at a loose thread on the arm of the settee. 'There's nothing the matter with me but Julian Honeywell is an insufferable bore and his wife drinks too much.'

Her mother tutted. 'Most of the people I know fall into one of those categories.' She paused. 'Many of them fall into both. But I'm sure I don't need to remind you that the Honeywells have a sizeable estate in Hampshire, as well as a son just a few years older than you.'

Subtlety had never been her mother's strong point but this was flagrant even for her. 'Good for them,' Harry said evenly. 'I'm still not going to dinner with them, much less marrying poor Philip, so you can stop scheming. Apart from anything else, you know very well that I'd have to give up work if I ever got married.'

'Would that be so terrible, darling?' Evelyn's eyes were wide. 'I know you modern girls value your independence and I really do applaud you for sticking it out so long, but surely the novelty is wearing off now. Aren't you just a tiny bit bored?'

Harry's thoughts flew instantly to the multitude of unanswered letters, to the standard reply she typed out over and over each day. The correspondents themselves weren't boring – she was often amused, shocked and horrified by their scandalous accusations and desperate entreaties – but she had to concede the work itself was not diverting. If it hadn't been for her steely determination not to allow Mr Pemberton to get the better of her, she might have resigned weeks ago. And yet if she had, she wouldn't have discovered the letter from Esme Longstaff, which was proving to be anything but boring. She shook her head. 'No.'

Evelyn studied her steadfast expression for a moment, then sighed. 'I can see there's still no reasoning with you. But there's no need to cut your nose off – why not accept the odd evening invitation? I'm sure Lawrence or Sebastian would be happy to accompany you when they're in town.'

Harry almost laughed. She could imagine how thrilled her elder brothers would be at the thought of being dragged to dinner with the insufferable Honeywells. Their evening plans were more likely to involve one of the new nightclubs that seemed to be springing up everywhere, and Harry would rather not know what went on there. It was time to change the subject, she decided. 'Speaking of invitations, do you know much about the Finchems?'

The conversational leap was clumsy enough to make Harry wince but her mother didn't seem to notice. 'Henry Finchem drinks too much and his wife is an insufferable bore. But they're very well connected – Henry is in the House of Lords and has a house on Farm Street, as well as an estate in Wiltshire and something in Scotland.' She tapped her book thoughtfully. 'Old money. Two grown-up sons, as I recall.'

Was that why the housekeeper hadn't called the police? Harry pondered as she filed the new information away. Perhaps Lord Finchem's role in Westminster made him wary of the inevitable publicity that would arise from a police investigation. 'Are Lord and Lady Finchem in London currently?'

'I imagine so. Parliament has been awash with debate about the hunger marches, if the newspapers are to be believed, and Lady Finchem revels in feeling important. She'll be in London all right.' Evelyn raised a curious brow. 'Why do you ask?'

Harry smoothed her skirt. 'They came up in conversation,' she said carelessly. 'I forget where but I thought I might see if Lady Finchem wanted to contribute to Grandmother's charity efforts.'

'Probably,' Evelyn said, shrugging. 'Although I can't see why you'd start with the Finchems. There are plenty of society ladies who would fall over themselves for an excuse to drop the Abinger name into polite conversation. Eugenia Honeywell, for example.'

Her mother's determination to pair her off with the first man she deemed eligible made Harry want to grind her teeth. But perhaps it was something she could use. 'Two sons, did you say?'

She watched her mother through her lashes, waiting to see if the bait would be taken, and was gratified to see the line twitch. 'Then again, why not set your sights high?' Evelyn said. 'I'm sure

Lady Finchem would be happy to help. Let me see now, tea at the Ritz is always a good idea.'

It undoubtedly was, Harry thought, but it wouldn't allow her to visit the scene of the crime. 'I'd be happy to call on her in Mayfair,' she said. 'You can tell so much about a family from their home, don't you think? The family as a whole.'

Once again, the inference was not missed. Evelyn's eyes gleamed with a faraway look, causing Harry to wonder whether she was imagining a romantic first encounter with the Finchem heir in the hallway. 'I'll write to Phyllida immediately,' she said, and paused. 'Shall I join you? Good first impressions are so important, after all.'

'No!' Harry hoped she didn't sound as alarmed as she felt – she could hardly draw the conversation round to Mildred with her mother breathing down her neck. 'I mean, of course they are but I think I can manage to take tea without embarrassing myself or the Abinger name.'

For a moment, Evelyn looked doubtful, then she smiled. 'Of course you can, darling. Do wear something smart, however – perhaps the blue hat with the peacock feather? It brings out your eyes so beautifully.'

Giving herself an inner pat on the back for clearing a tricky obstacle, Harry nodded. 'Yes, Mama,' she said meekly and turned her attention to Winston, who was snuffling insistently at her hand in search of further treats. Now all she had to do was winkle the details of Mildred's disappearance from Phyllida Finchem without arousing suspicion, while dodging her two sons. How hard could that be?

* * *

The Finchem residence on Farm Street was a white-fronted, four-storey Georgian town house with a grey slate roof and black iron railings separating it from the street. Harry made her way there straight from work on Friday afternoon, and if anyone at the bank had noticed her slightly fancier outfit, they had not mentioned it. Then again, she'd encountered no one but the doormen – Bobby and his brass trolley had been conspicuous by their absence – and they had simply tipped their hats in the same way they always did. Checking the address once more, Harry rang the bell just before four-thirty.

Her mother had been as good as her word and had written asking when Harry might call. Lady Finchem had responded with pleasing alacrity, and so Harry found herself enjoying the dubious thrill of undertaking her first foray into detective work. When the glossy front door opened, it revealed a sombre butler in an immaculate black tailcoat. Harry was not surprised by his formal attire and imperious manner; from what her mother had said, Phyllida Finchem set great store by appearances.

'Lady Finchem is expecting you,' the butler said when Harry gave her name. He took her hat and coat with a slight bow. 'This way, please.'

The marbled hallway was larger than Harry had expected and dominated by an Axminster-carpeted staircase that rose majestically to the upper floors. The butler led her beneath a showy gilt chandelier towards a door on the left and ushered her into a drawing room. 'Miss Harriet White,' he intoned.

A tall, grey-haired lady rose from the Queen Anne armchair she occupied. 'Miss White, such a pleasure to meet you,' she said, advancing towards Harry. 'We'll take tea in here, Dobbins. Thank you.'

Bowing, the man backed out of the room. Lady Finchem waved at the sister of the chair she'd been occupying. 'Won't you take a seat?'

Harry did as she suggested, taking the opportunity to study the room. If she hadn't already known from her mother and the sought-after address that the Finchems were wealthy, the contents of this room alone would have confirmed it. From the elegant furnishings to the gold-flocked wallpaper and antique vases that adorned the broad mantelpiece over the large fireplace, everything about it screamed money. The pearls Lady Finchem wore around her neck were worth a small fortune and Harry felt a flicker of disquiet; if the jewellery Mildred was alleged to have stolen was of similar quality then it was no surprise she had been dismissed.

Pieces of the puzzle were starting to drop into place and Harry didn't like the picture they were creating. With no good character references from her previous employer, it was highly unlikely Mildred would be able to obtain another maid's position and certainly nothing with a family like this. But the details of that were what Harry was here to uncover. 'Thank you for the invitation, Lady Finchem,' she said, perching on the chair opposite the older woman with a bright smile. 'I do so appreciate you taking the time.'

'Not at all. We must all do what we can to help those less fortunate than ourselves. I am always happy to assist Baroness Abinger with her charitable efforts. Such a formidable woman.'

'Quite,' Harry said. She adopted an earnest expression. 'But as you say, we must do what we can, especially when there is so much unemployment. My grandmother is most especially anxious to aid women and children, those who find themselves in poverty through no fault of their own.'

Lady Finchem inclined her head. 'A worthy cause. The men may help themselves but we women must band together.'

Her voice rang with compassion but the words themselves sounded hollow. Harry couldn't imagine Lady Finchem visiting a poverty-stricken village with food and clothing the way her grandmother did. 'We must,' she said. 'Why, only last week there was a sad case of a young woman who—'

She was interrupted by the sound of a throat being discreetly cleared at the door. Dobbins appeared, followed by a young maid carrying a tea tray. The butler gestured her forward and the girl, who Harry guessed to be no more than sixteen, approached the table nearest to Lady Finchem. Her face was pinched and anxious beneath the frilly white cap. The cups rattled in their saucers and Harry saw her hands were shaking as she slid the tray onto the table. The noise made Dobbins frown but the tray was delivered safely and the maid stepped back with a relief that was almost tangible. Lady Finchem inclined her head. 'Thank you, Polly. That will be all, Dobbins. I shall pour out today.'

As Harry watched the maid and the butler leave, she decided to abandon her attempt to drag the conversation around to fallen women and seized on a more immediate opportunity. 'Reliable domestics are so hard to find,' she said, sighing. 'But you seem to have matters well in hand.'

'Dobbins is an absolute godsend,' Lady Finchem replied. 'But good maids are difficult to come by. Polly can be a nervous creature but she appreciates how fortunate she is, at least. It seems many young girls are afraid of hard work these days – I've lost count of how many I've had to let go for abject laziness.'

So much for banding together, Harry thought wryly. 'I sympathise,' she said, and tried to recall some of her Aunt Valeria's complaints about household staff. 'So few know how to lay a fire, for one thing. And the sulkiness when one pulls them up – no humility or gratitude that you've taken them in. I blame the cinema – it puts ideas in their heads.'

A faint frown creased Lady Finchem's forehead and, for a moment, Harry wondered if she had adopted the role of put-upon employer rather too enthusiastically. But the other woman nodded. 'Exactly so. But as you observed, I am happy to say we have no such troubles currently.' She waved a genteel hand at the tray. 'Tea? Would you prefer milk or lemon?'

'Milk, please, if you'd be so kind,' Harry said, as her hostess began to pour, sending bergamot-scented steam rising into the air. 'We had to let one girl go when the silver teaspoons started to go missing – it transpired she had half a canteen of cutlery in her room. Can you imagine?'

A thin-lipped smile crossed Lady Finchem's face. 'Most certainly. We had a similar situation here, although the girl brazenly refused to admit she'd done anything wrong.'

Harry raised her eyebrows. 'Teaspoons?'

'Not teaspoons,' Lady Finchem allowed. 'A sapphire bracelet.'

'Good heavens!' Harry declared, doing her best to look scandalised. 'Did you have her arrested?'

The other woman sighed. 'We thought it best to avoid police involvement.' She handed Harry a cup and saucer with a prim tilt of her head. 'My husband's position, you understand.'

'Of course,' Harry said, gratified that her initial hunch had been on the money. 'But even so...'

'The bracelet was recovered,' Lady Finchem said. 'No loss was incurred. The girl was simply let go.'

Harry took a sip of tea. 'And there was no doubt of her guilt, I presume.'

'None,' Lady Finchem replied decisively. 'The bracelet was found under her pillow, in one of the attic rooms.'

Rooms she probably shared, Harry thought, if the servants' quarters at Abinger Hall were anything to go by. 'What happened to her?'

'I really have no idea. She packed her things and left, wailing and protesting her innocence the entire time. Dobbins had to escort her to the end of the street.' The older woman gave a delicate shudder. 'It really was a most distasteful scene.'

Harry could picture Mildred's distress all too clearly, and it brought to mind the quiet despair that hung over the girl's family. She forced herself to smile sympathetically at her current hostess. 'How tiresome it sounds. And you never heard of her again?'

Lady Finchem hesitated. 'Not directly. I understand concerns were raised by the girl's family, some weeks later. Dobbins and my housekeeper suffered a visit from the police, enquiring as to her whereabouts.' She sniffed. 'Obviously they were unable to help.'

The information tallied with what Harry had learned from the Longstaffs but she doubted Lady Finchem's staff had tried very hard to help the police with their enquiries. Regardless of that, nothing she had heard so far brought her any closer to establishing what had happened to Mildred once she had left Farm Street. The idea of such a young woman alone and distraught on the streets of London made Harry queasy. She frowned. 'Did she have any friends that you knew of?'

The temperature in the room seemed to drop several degrees and instantly, Harry knew she had asked the wrong question. Lady Finchem drew herself up. 'My dear Miss White, I don't concern myself with the affairs of housemaids,' she said. 'Especially not those who steal.'

'Of course not,' Harry said quickly, feeling a blush creep up her cheeks. 'Forgive me, but you described it so vividly that I found myself quite caught up in the scene. Was she a seasoned criminal, do you think?'

'I haven't the faintest idea,' Lady Finchem said firmly. 'I have more important matters with which to concern myself. Now, about Baroness Abinger's charitable work – what is it you require from me?'

Judging there was nothing more to be gleaned, Harry outlined a charity dinner her grandmother was arranging, but behind her cool façade, her mind was whirring. If Mildred was innocent, who had hidden the sapphire bracelet in the attic room? But Lady Finchem's determined lack of interest in Mildred's plight inflamed another, more pressing question in Harry's mind: it sounded as though the girl had been in a vulnerable condition when Dobbins had banished her. Where might she have run? Directly north lay Marylebone, and beyond it Middlesex. To the east was Oxford Circus, littered with traps for an unwary young woman. South was Green Park, which was a pleasant enough space during the day but who knew how different it might be after dark? And to the west was Hyde Park – bigger and perhaps even more dangerous at night than its sister space. The only credible sighting of a woman matching Mildred's description had come from Hyde Park. Could that be where her feet had led her in the dazed first minutes after being ejected from the house?

Recalling her assurance that she would not embarrass herself in Lady Finchem's company, Harry forced herself to focus on what the older woman was saying. The conversation gravitated to society small talk, during which Harry listened much and contributed little. She breathed an inward sigh of relief as the teapot ran dry and her audience with Lady Finchem came to a close. Her hostess's sense of entitlement and conceit grated on Harry's nerves and suddenly she couldn't wait to escape the drawing room. Promising her grandmother would be in touch in due course, Harry allowed Dobbins to escort her back to the marbled hallway, where he presented her with her blue hat and coat. 'Thank you,' she said, and glanced airily around. 'Tell me, how many maids do you employ here?'

His neatly groomed eyebrows twitched at the unexpected question but he was far too professional to show his surprise. 'Three, Miss White. One in the scullery and two for general duties.'

Harry summoned up what she hoped was a vacuous smile. 'Wherever do you find them? I'm in need of a maid at home but all the applicants have been wretched so far.'

Dobbins did not smile back. 'I believe the housekeeper consults Mrs Haverford when she has need of domestic staff.'

'Mrs Haverford,' Harry repeated as she ran the name through a mental list of her mother's acquaintances and came up with nothing. 'Who is that?'

'A person of excellent taste and reputation,' Dobbins said. 'She runs an extremely select employment agency catering to the finest families.'

'Oh, I see,' Harry said, widening her eyes as though she had never heard of such a thing. 'Where can I find her?'

'Her offices are on Portland Square.'

The crispness of his tone suggested further details would not be forthcoming. But it didn't matter – Harry had got what she wanted. Peering into an extravagant gilt mirror that gave the chandelier a run for its money in the ostentation stakes, she adjusted her hat and fastened it with a pin. 'Thank you, Dobbins. I'll visit first thing on Monday morning.'

Expressionless, he opened the front door and waited for Harry to take her cue. 'Good evening, Miss White.'

Dusk had fallen but the electric street lamps glowed as Harry stepped past the iron railings to the pavement. At the kerb, she paused to glance up at the Finchem house, past the broad bay windows that graced the upper floors to the small attic casements. Had Mildred Longstaff stood tearfully in this exact spot before being marched away? The thought made Harry fizz with indignation. But just as she was about to turn on her heel and cross the road, a curtain twitched in one of the windows above the glossy front door and she got a jumbled impression of movement. Unless she was very much mistaken, someone was watching her leave.

5

It had been Harry's plan to go straight home but Dobbins' mention of Mrs Haverford had roused her interest and, instead, she found herself heading once more for the London Library in St James's Square, where she scoured several recent copies of *The Times* until she found what she was looking for.

> Mrs Haverford's Bureau of Excellence
> Purveyors of Discreet and Dedicated Domestic Staff
> Satisfaction Assured
> Enquire at 66 Great Portland Street, Lon W
> Telephone – Marylebone 1854

The advertisement was a bold, eye-catching square in the middle of the densely printed columns of *Situations Vacant* and *Positions Wanted*. Harry could see its appeal – why give oneself eye strain by poring over the minuscule newsprint, go to the trouble of contacting one or several candidates and taking a chance on their honesty or suitability when a single call to Mrs Haverford would resolve the matter? Undoubtedly, her services came at a premium but that wouldn't be a problem among the wealthy. Hadn't Dobbins confirmed as much? Perhaps Mrs Haverford had been involved in placing Mildred with the Finchem household, Harry mused as she made a note of the address and telephone number. It was a place to start, at least.

She began her weekend by taking a Saturday morning stroll around Hyde Park. An instructive five minutes with a map had shown her the most likely entrances Mildred might have used had she wandered there upon leaving Farm Street. Mr Blunt's letter did not give much detail but did reveal he had encountered the arguing man and woman just north of the lake. As Harry tried to retrace Mildred's steps, she found herself passing a small house set back from the path. It was a single-storey sandstone building with a well-tended garden surrounded by black iron railings. Two chimneys smoked from the tiled roof and the sign beside the front door read *Serpentine Lodge*, the address Mr Blunt had given in his letter.

Biting her lip, Harry weighed her options. She could write to the park keeper, asking for a meeting. But where would he send his reply? It didn't seem wise to declare herself secretary to an imaginary detective among the wider public, or offer up the bank as a correspondence address; she could not imagine Mr Blunt would take her seriously if she did. But Harry didn't want to give her own address, either, which would reveal her identity should anyone come looking and endanger both her job and her reputation. And yet here she was, practically on the doorstep of a potential witness. She couldn't just walk away – could she?

The door of the lodge was opened by a round, pleasant-faced woman of about thirty. 'Hello,' she said, looking Harry up and down with undisguised curiosity. 'Can I help?'

'I hope so,' Harry said. 'I'm looking for Mr Blunt, the park keeper. Is this the right address?'

'It is,' the woman said, and she frowned a little as she considered

Harry more closely. 'I'm his wife. Is there something wrong – a problem in the park?'

'No, it's nothing like that,' Harry reassured her. She held up the letter. 'I just wanted to ask him a few questions about an incident he witnessed some time ago, that's all.'

Mrs Blunt's wariness increased. 'Are you a solicitor?'

The suggestion caught Harry by surprise. During the war, plenty of women had filled jobs previously undertaken by men and now they often worked side by side. But she wasn't sure she knew any female solicitors. That seemed to be a profession that was still overwhelmingly dominated by men. 'No,' she told Mrs Blunt. 'I'm not a solicitor. I'm looking for a friend who went missing in Mayfair. I understand Mr Blunt might have seen her.'

'Oh,' the woman said, and Harry saw the light dawn in her eyes. 'Well, he's about to go to work, as it happens. Maybe he'll have time to talk to you first. Wait here.'

She closed the door. Harry waited, listening to the faint murmur of voices drifting through the open window. At length, the door reopened and a tall, slender man in a smart black uniform that reminded her in no small measure of a police constable, peered out at her. 'What is it you want?'

Harry held up the envelope Esme had given her. 'Mr Blunt? I'm here about your letter to Mr and Mrs Longstaff, of Foxley village.'

'Oh yes?' he said, displaying mild irritation. 'What about it? I spoke to Longstaff already, told him what I saw.'

'I know,' Harry said apologetically. 'I'm afraid he doesn't want to believe his daughter could be a thief.'

'And you do, I suppose?' the man asked.

'I have no idea,' Harry said, with total honesty. 'But I'm a friend of the family and I'd like to hear your story. Have you got a few minutes to tell me what happened?'

Mr Blunt huffed and Harry expected him to refuse. 'I'm going to work now. You'll have to walk with me.'

Harry found herself grateful the weather forecast on the wireless that morning appeared to be wrong; there were clouds overhead but it was not yet raining. 'Of course,' she said. 'Lead on.'

'Like I told Longstaff, it was late in the evening,' Mr Blunt said, as Harry fell into step beside him. 'Dusk was falling so I had my eyes peeled for trouble. I heard shouting, went to investigate and saw a young woman struggling with a man. At first I thought she—' He stopped and glanced at Harry. 'Never mind what I thought at first. As I got nearer, I realised he was accusing her of robbing him. She was screaming that she'd done no such thing. Then she saw me and that was that – she was off like a hare.'

All of which matched what the Longstaffs had told her, Harry thought. 'What made you think it was Mildred Longstaff you saw?'

The park keeper shrugged. 'The advert in the newspaper said she was eighteen and had gone missing in the vicinity of Farm Street. The young woman I saw was the right age, and she was in the right place at the right time. Seemed like it might be her.'

Harry nodded, almost to herself. Was it possible Mildred was not as innocent as her family wanted to believe? 'So you contacted the Longstaff family – what then?'

'I told them what I saw, gave them a description and all that. At first, they were excited – their girl had red hair too, although that wasn't in the advert.' Mr Blunt paused to shoo some children out of a flower bed and then resumed his story. 'And then I told them she was a thief and they got all shirty. Said it couldn't have been their girl.'

'What about the man she was arguing with?' Harry asked. 'Did he want to make a complaint?'

'No point,' Mr Blunt said pragmatically. 'The girl had vanished –

no sign of her. I wrote it up in a report, in case any of my colleagues ran into her around the park but she hasn't been back.'

Or no one had seen her if she had, Harry thought but did not say. 'Did you get the victim's name?'

A faint smile flickered over the park keeper's face. 'Oh yes. It was Mr Lake, would you believe? You meet a fair few Mr Lakes in the darker corners of an evening. One or two Mr Flowers to break up the monotony. I met a Mr Bench, once.'

He was so determined to avoid revealing the reason these men might be in the park at night, unwilling to give their real names, that Harry wasn't sure whether to feel patronised or protected. She forced herself to remember why she was there. 'And you never saw the girl again? She never came back?'

'Not that I've seen,' Mr Blunt said. 'I think she was scared off.'

Which was perfectly possible too, Harry decided with growing unease. 'Perhaps you could let Mr Longstaff know if she does,' she said.

'I already told him I would,' the park keeper responded. 'But he said not to worry. It wasn't his daughter, you see.'

Recalling his steadfast refusal to accept Mildred had done anything wrong, Harry could easily imagine Mr Longstaff's vehemence. 'Thank you for talking to me,' she said to Mr Blunt. 'You've been very helpful.'

It didn't mean anything, she reminded herself as she walked back to her apartment. She could not match the brilliant reasoning of Sherlock Holmes but she could attempt to follow in Mildred's footsteps. With this in mind, she spent the rest of her Saturday morning considering the best way to approach Mrs Haverford's Bureau of Excellence. The obvious thing would be to continue the story she'd cooked up for Dobbins – that she was desperate to find a reliable and trustworthy lady's maid – but that would not give her a plausible reason to ask specifically about Mildred. If the agency had been responsible for placing her with the Finchems then it was very likely a sore subject and not one that Mrs Haverford would enjoy being raised. Harry was also reminded of the need to conceal her identity. She was taking a terrible risk by investigating at all – if she was discovered it would be at the cost of her job and who knew what else. Her alter-ego of R. K. Moss might also lead back to the bank, via the Longstaffs. What she needed was a disguise, one that would allow her to glean the information she sought without raising suspicion.

After standing for several thoughtful minutes in front of her wardrobe, Harry packed an overnight bag and took the Saturday afternoon train to Surrey, where her grandmother was only too delighted to accept her help in sorting through bags of old clothing to go to the needy. And, after some wrestling with her conscience, Harry telephoned Mr Babbage on Monday morning to regretfully let him know that she was afflicted by a terrible headache and would not be at work that day. Then she dressed herself in the serviceable but worn skirt and jacket she had borrowed from her grandmother's charity bags, darkened her golden curls with brown boot polish and scraped them into a bun covered by a dowdy hat, and tried not to grimace as she pulled on a pair of worn-down shoes.

Her aunt had once told her much could be inferred from a person's footwear and Harry didn't want to ruin her disguise by wearing shoes that were too well made and unscuffed. Lastly, she used make-up to create subtle dark circles beneath her eyes and hollows in her cheeks. When she surveyed the overall effect in the long mirror, she found herself pleasantly surprised by how different she looked. It wouldn't fool anyone who knew her well – there was nothing she could do to change the colour of her eyes, unfortunately – but she was confident of fooling a casual observer. In short, she looked like hundreds of other young women who came to

London in search of employment and while she couldn't claim it was the kind of masterful disguise worthy of Sherlock Holmes, it wasn't bad for a first attempt. It would do for Mrs Haverford; she didn't actually want to acquire a job, after all.

Harry's first call of the morning had been to the employment bureau, seeking an appointment. She had been brusquely advised that no appointment system was in place – would-be domestics should attend the offices and wait to be seen. Realising she might very well wait all day, Harry had reluctantly accepted a sacrifice would have to be made at the bank. Her only consolation was that hardly anyone would notice her absence.

Mrs Haverford's Bureau of Excellence occupied the first floor of a smart terraced town house midway along Great Portland Street. A cluster of brass plaques beside the black front door revealed the property was shared with several other businesses: the ground floor belonged to a Dr Birch, General Physician; the third was split between Randall and Sons, Accountants; and the enigmatically titled Obelisk Inc. Harry pressed the buzzer for the employment agency and, after a short wait, the door was opened by a sour-faced woman of around forty. Her demeanour did not improve as she surveyed Harry. 'Here for work, are you? Follow me.'

She wheeled around without waiting for a response. Blinking at her rudeness, Harry almost snapped an outraged, 'I beg your pardon?' at her retreating back. But then she remembered who she was that morning – not Harriet White, granddaughter of Baron Abinger, but Sarah Smith, lately of Lambeth and now in search of a maid's position. Perhaps this was how all young women seeking domestic work in London were treated. It was a thought that caused Harry to grind her teeth with indignation, even as she experienced a tiny flicker of guilt that by some happy accident of birth, she had never been treated that way herself. Swallowing her unexpectedly complicated feelings, she followed the woman into the wood-panelled hallway and up the stairs.

On the first floor, she was led into a room lined with benches. These were filled by an assortment of men and women of varying ages, whey-faced but presentable, some flicking through newspapers or magazines but most exuding an air of hushed resignation. Those who looked up eyed Harry without interest, which eased some of her sudden jitters. So far, at least, her disguise seemed to fit.

'Name?' the dour woman demanded.

Harry cleared her throat. It was time to put the amateur dramatics skills of her youth to good use. 'Sarah Smith, if you please,' she said and almost winced. The Cockney accent that had sounded so convincing before leaving Mayfair sounded ludicrously false now but the woman didn't seem to notice. She looked Harry up and down, as though assessing her worth. Her gaze lingered on her face for a moment, which caused Harry's heart to stutter; surely she couldn't have been rumbled already? But the woman merely nodded once. 'Wait here.'

Without a glance at the others, she crossed the room to pass through a door in the opposite wall. Nerves settling, Harry watched her go. The woman hadn't offered her name so Harry decided to dub her Lemon Drop, because it looked as though that was what she was sucking. She turned her attention to the already full benches, where no one met her gaze except for an older man at the far end, who grinned lasciviously. 'Plenty of room here for a pretty thing like you,' he said, rubbing his hands along his thighs in awful invitation. 'Come on, don't be shy.'

There was an outburst of vicious tutting and muttering from the assembled women. One of them – a black-haired girl Harry guessed to be in her early twenties – scowled and rolled her eyes. 'That's enough of that, George Newlyn,' she called loudly, and shuffled along the bench to make room for Harry. 'You can sit here, if you like.'

'Thanks,' Harry said, subsiding gratefully into the space.

The girl stuck out a hand. 'Beth Chamberlain – pleased to meet you.'

Her accent was perfectly Cockney, exactly the kind Harry had been aiming for. She took a moment to observe the differences in vowels and consonants, then did her best to mimic them as she shook Beth's hand. 'Sarah Smith. Charmed, I'm sure.'

She held her breath for a moment but Beth's expression didn't alter. 'Don't mind old George,' she said, glancing dismissively along the bench to where the old man was now whistling tunelessly. 'He tries that with all the new girls.'

'Does he?' Harry asked, then frowned. 'Here often, is he?'

Beth shrugged. 'Most days, same as the rest of us. Unless Mrs H finds him a bit of work and then he disappears for a few weeks. But he always comes back eventually.'

The thought of spending more than one day in the cramped waiting room made Harry feel slightly faint. 'How long have you been here?'

'Just today, this time round,' Beth replied. 'Things didn't work out at my last place – slight difference of opinion with the butcher's boy, you might say – so I'm back on the merry-go-round again.' She studied Harry with sudden interest. 'How about you?'

'First time,' Harry confessed. 'My old man up and died, leaving me without a penny.'

It was a story she'd rehearsed, planning to roll it out in her interview, but it didn't hurt to test it a little now. Except just like her accent, it had sounded better in the privacy of her apartment. Beth raised both eyebrows. 'Your old man – you mean your husband?'

Harry hesitated. She hadn't realised the slang might have more than one meaning. Which was more plausible, husband or father?

'Cor blimey, no,' she said, covering her indecision with what she hoped was amused dismay. 'I mean my old dad, God rest his soul.' Crossing her fingers, she begged silent forgiveness from her own father, who was very much alive and well and probably enjoying his pipe in the library even as she spoke. 'He went so sudden, I didn't have time to put by any savings.'

Beth eyed her doubtfully. 'You won't get far without experience,' she said. 'But you've got a pretty face – that goes a long way sometimes. How did you find this place?'

Harry opened her mouth to say the newspaper, then changed her mind. 'A friend recommended it. She came here when she first arrived in London. Mildred Longstaff, do you know her?'

She watched Beth carefully for a flicker of recognition. 'No. But that's no surprise, if she's working. It's only them as needs a job in here.'

Harry lowered her voice. 'That's the thing – she had a job and lost it. Through no fault of her own, of course.'

'Of course,' Beth repeated, her gaze suddenly knowing. 'Master with wandering hands, was it?'

'An accusation of theft,' Harry confided. She cast her mind back to Lady Finchem's flinty expression. 'She didn't do it, of course, but that didn't stop them from throwing her out on her ear. I thought she might have come back here to find another job.'

'I haven't seen her if she did,' Beth said, shifting on the bench to gaze thoughtfully up at the ceiling. 'This place she worked – it wasn't in Mayfair, was it?'

The question was innocent enough – many of the properties in Mayfair employed domestic staff – but there was something in her tone that made Harry wary. 'Could have been,' she said vaguely. 'I don't know where exactly.'

Beth gave her a brooding look. 'Only you got to be careful round them parts,' she said quietly. 'Things ain't always what they seem, 'specially not in the really fancy gaffs. I heard about a girl who—'

But what Beth had heard was interrupted by the reappearance of Lemon Drop in the doorway. She glanced around the room until her eyes came to rest upon Harry. 'Sarah Smith. Mrs Haverford will see you now.'

Loud grumbling broke out, with an accompaniment of scowls and dirty looks that caused Harry's cheeks to flood with embarrassment. She glanced apologetically at Beth. 'Sorry.'

The girl shrugged. 'Don't be. Like I said, a pretty face goes a long way sometimes. Good luck.'

Aware that Lemon Drop was waiting, nevertheless Harry wavered. She wanted to know what Beth had been about to reveal but there was no way to ask now, not without drawing considerable attention to them both. She settled for a more innocent-sounding question. 'Will you be here when I come out?'

'Probably,' Beth said, and winked. 'Unless Mrs H lands me a plum job at the palace.'

Harry couldn't help smiling. 'Maybe I'll see you then.'

There was a loud huff of impatience from the door. 'When you're quite ready.'

She did not dare dally any further. With another apologetic look at Beth, Harry crossed the room and followed the woman along the wood-panelled corridor to another office. This one had three additional doors in the walls opposite, all of which were closed. A long mahogany desk cut the room in two, behind which sat a grey-haired, bespectacled woman tapping briskly at a typewriter. She did not look up as Harry entered.

'Take a seat,' Lemon Drop instructed Harry, pointing to a row of four empty chairs opposite the desk. 'I assume you can read and write?'

'Yes,' Harry said, perching on one of the chairs. The wooden seat was hard – she hoped she didn't have to spend much time sitting on it.

The woman handed her a clipboard and a stubby pencil. 'Fill this in. We need all the relevant particulars, including the name and address of your last employer. Give it to Margot here when you're done.'

'Thanks,' Harry said, taking the clipboard. She glanced at the sheet of paper it held – apart from spaces for her own name and address, it required her hair and eye colour, and her height. 'Why do you need to know all this?'

'So we can check you are who you say you are.' Lemon Drop smiled but there was no humour in her expression. 'You wouldn't believe the things some criminals will try to get through the door of a wealthy house.'

Harry almost asked how many young women were robbing houses but stopped herself just in time. Weren't the papers full of reports about the daring, all-female gangs who were terrorising London's streets? Perhaps that was who Lemon Drop was referring to but Harry didn't get the chance to ask. With an impatient gesture at the clipboard, the woman left by the door she and Harry had just used, leaving Harry alone with Margot and the staccato clack-clack of her typewriter.

After a moment's consideration, Harry began to write, taking care to disguise her elegant cursive handwriting as much as she could. She listed her home as 12 Sophie Street, Poplar – a slum she had recently read about in the papers as being targeted for redevelopment by the local council – and added two inches to her height. Recalling Beth's doubts about her lack of domestic experience, she made up three maid's positions and put Mr and Mrs Honeywell as her last employer. The latter was a slight risk – perhaps Mrs Haverford knew of the Honeywells and even provided staff for them – but by the time the deception was confirmed, Sarah Smith would have vanished. Casting her eye over the form one last time, Harry decided she was satisfied. She rose and placed the clipboard on the desk. 'Finished.'

Margot stopped typing. She collected the board, glanced at it and stood up. 'Wait here.'

She disappeared through one of the doors in the far wall, closing it behind her. Harry took advantage of her absence to study the room. The floor was bare but free of dust; the walls were freshly painted. Several filing cabinets stood against one wall, tall, with three deep drawers each. There were no windows. The desk was heavy; the typewriter looked expensive. A big plant sat on the desk, its leaves glossy and wide. There was a stack of letters beside the typewriter that Harry longed to take a look at, but she didn't want to risk being caught. Instead, she let her gaze travel around the office again. It was entirely unremarkable – no posters or paintings adorned the walls, no name plaques were attached to the doors. In fact, Harry's overall impression was one of anonymity, perhaps even of impermanence – from what she could tell, the contents might be emptied in just a few hours. It was not the kind of place she would have associated with the likes of Lady Finchem but then she supposed none of Mrs Haverford's illustrious clients ever came here. That was what housekeepers were for.

The door opened and Margot reappeared. 'This way.'

Steeling herself against a sudden barrage of butterflies in her stomach, Harry crossed the room and stepped past Margot. The first thing she noticed was the plush red carpet – her shoes sank into it as she walked. A fire crackled in the chimney breast along the right-hand wall, removing the dank chill that had been noticeable in the rest of the building. Bookshelves flanked the left wall. Two tall windows in the wall opposite the door faced out onto the street, dressed in heavy red curtains, and Harry couldn't help contrasting the warmth and comfort with the peeling paintwork and hard wooden seats of the waiting room. But for all that, the focus of this room was another desk, topped with green, gilt-edged leather, and the straight-backed woman who sat behind it. She stood up as Harry entered and smiled. 'Miss Smith. Won't you take a seat?'

Her voice was pleasant, with no obvious accent, but Harry thought she detected the stubborn hint of London even so. She sat in the seat facing the woman, noting the soft click as the door closed behind her, and took refuge in the poor social graces of her character. 'Are you Mrs Haverford?'

The other woman inclined her head. Harry guessed she was nearer fifty than forty; there were crow's feet around her eyes and her platinum curls owed much to the bleach bottle. But her make-up was immaculate, even if the scarlet lips were perhaps a little much for a Monday morning, and the overall effect was of a woman who was used to receiving attention. Harry decided to soften her manners. 'Pleased to meet you,' she said.

'Likewise,' Mrs Haverford said, glancing down at the desk where Harry saw the sheet she had just completed. 'So you're looking for a maid's position – is that right? And you've previously worked as a general maid.'

Harry nodded, even as she wondered how she could turn the conversation around to Lady Finchem. Now that she was here, facing Mrs Haverford, she was beginning to wonder whether she was wasting her time. As far as she could tell, there was nothing specific here to suggest Mildred had ever visited the offices. But it was too late to back out now – she had to continue with her plan. 'That's right.'

Mrs Haverford tapped a crimson fingernail on the desk. 'You were most recently employed by a Mr and Mrs Honeywell, not a family I am familiar with, unfortunately. Why did you leave?'

The admission gave Harry some small relief. At least she wouldn't be immediately caught out in a lie. 'They took on a new housekeeper, who brought her own maid,' she said, and adopted what she hoped was an injured expression. 'I wasn't needed no more.'

'I understand,' Mrs Haverford replied. 'But you're honest and biddable? Prepared to work hard? Loyal?'

The last word was accompanied by a fierce stare that almost made Harry flinch. She nodded again. 'Yes, Mrs Haverford.'

The other woman pursed her lips. 'On your feet, then. Let's take a look at you.'

The demand surprised Harry but she obeyed all the same, taking care to round her shoulders as though she carried the worries of the world there. Mrs Haverford rose too and came around the desk to study her. Harry's pulse quickened – her disguise was not designed to withstand close scrutiny. Would Mrs Haverford detect the gleam of blonde beneath the boot polish on her hair? Might she notice the white smoothness of Harry's hands that belied her claim of being a maid? Hands that had never scrubbed pots or hefted a coal scuttle. Why hadn't she thought to wear gloves, for goodness' sake?

'Good bone structure,' Mrs Haverford said, placing a finger beneath Harry's chin to tilt her face from one side to another. 'But how blue your eyes are. Quite remarkable.'

Harry took her chance. 'My friend Mildred says they're bluer than the sky.'

Was it her imagination or did the name cause a shadow to cross the older woman's features. 'They're certainly very noticeable,' Mrs Haverford said, frowning. She sat at the desk once more and shook her head. 'I'm afraid we don't have any positions that would suit you at the moment. But next week may be different. You're welcome to call again next Monday morning.'

Harry's hopes sank. She was being dismissed without discovering anything useful. It was time to throw the dice and gamble everything. 'Oh, but my friend Mildred heard of a job going with Lady Finchem. It's always been my dream to work somewhere real fancy like that – Mildred said you were the woman to ask.'

This time there was no mistaking the flash of recognition, or the ice in Mrs Haverford's tone when she replied. 'Your friend is mistaken. There are no vacancies in that household.' She paused to eye Harry with disfavour. 'But it seems you have ideas above your station, Miss Smith. It's not for my workers to decide where they will work. They go where I tell them and they never, ever question it.'

The genteel veneer slipped with her irritation, revealing traces of a rougher accent that wouldn't have been out of place in the docks. Filing the information away, Harry lowered her gaze and took care to look chastened. 'Yes, Mrs Haverford. I didn't mean to —'

'A good housemaid knows her place,' Mrs Haverford cut in. 'I suggest you learn yours before coming here again.' She rang a small golden bell and no sooner had the tinkle died away than the door behind Harry was opening. 'Show her out, please, Margot.'

A hot tide of frustration washed over Harry as she left the room. She had no intention of risking another visit to the agency but now that she had met her, she felt certain Mrs Haverford knew something of what had happened to Mildred at the Finchem house. Exactly what that was remained a mystery and Harry suspected she could not unlock it. To do that, she would need help – help from someone who was already inside...

The crowd in the waiting room had grown in her absence – several newcomers were clustered in the middle of the room and the air was moist. Harry cast a hurried gaze across the benches – George Newlyn was still leering in the corner but there was no sign of Beth. She tried to make eye contact with one or two of the other women but they avoided meeting her gaze. 'I was hoping to see

Beth,' she said, trying to sound casual. 'Does anyone know where to find her?'

No one answered. Margot folded her arms. 'You could try the door,' she said pointedly.

Once again, Harry looked around the room in mute appeal. She was met only by George's gap-toothed grin. 'I'll tell you where she lives. Just you come and sit here so I can whisper it.'

Deciding not to dignify the offer with a response, Harry marched across the room to the door and closed it hard behind her, blocking out his wheezing laughter. Out on the street, she took several long breaths to calm her jangling nerves and cool her heated cheeks. More in hope than expectation, she glanced both ways in case Beth was there but the girl was nowhere to be seen. Harry cursed under her breath, more and more convinced she had missed an opportunity and that Beth Chamberlain might have been a useful ally.

As she crossed the road, she toyed with the idea of hanging around to watch the entrance, but the hairs on the back of her neck were prickling in warning. There had been nothing terribly unpleasant about her visit to Mrs Haverford's offices, George Newlyn aside, and yet she couldn't shake the feeling that not everything was quite as it seemed.

Weariness washed over her as she glanced up at the first-floor windows of 66 Great Portland Street and she reluctantly decided there was nothing more to be achieved there. Now that the adrenaline of pretending to be Sarah Smith was wearing off, she felt a sudden desire to scrub the make-up and boot polish away and be herself again. Resisting the temptation to hail a cab, she made for the nearest Underground station and the safety of home.

6

As the week progressed, Harry had to concede she was at something of a loss. Her enquiries had revealed little in the way of new information and she had no idea where to go next. She approached several charitable organisations running hostels for women and girls who found themselves with nowhere to stay – while the volunteers were always sympathetic and keen to help, Harry's enquiries ended in the same way each time: none of them recognised Mildred Longstaff.

Discouraged, Harry began to lose heart. It seemed detective work was considerably more difficult than the pen of Sir Arthur Conan Doyle suggested and, for the first time, Harry felt the magnitude of what she had undertaken. This was not a story and there was no game afoot – Sherlock Holmes could not sweep in to find Mildred in a flash of deductive brilliance. There was only Harry, and a devastated family who waited in dreadful anticipation of news. How could she have been arrogant enough to assume she would solve the mystery with ease? But she would not compound her mistake with cruelty. If she did not make a breakthrough in the following days, she would write to Esme Longstaff and report her regrettable lack of success.

On Saturday morning, she decided to lift her spirits with a visit to Selfridges Department Store. Shopping never failed to make her feel better and there was a fine suit in the window she thought would do very well for work. Oxford Street was as bustling as ever but once past the elegant clock and stone pillars that guarded the grand entrance, Selfridges itself was an oasis of blissfully fragranced calm. There were crowds here too but voices were hushed, as though her fellow shoppers were keen to preserve the illusion of gentility, and somehow it did not seem busy.

Harry lingered at the ground-floor perfume counter, tempted by a beguiling new scent from Paris that her mother would doubtless denounce as scandalous, before taking a slow stroll through the endless displays of clothing. Other shoppers passed her by, in ones or twos, couples and friends and families, pointing at dresses or pausing to stroke the fabric. The suit Harry wanted was displayed in the corner nearest Haberdashery, artfully nipped and tucked around a mannequin to show it to best effect, and she studied it critically for several minutes, imagining herself wearing it.

'Lovely, isn't it?' The question came from an assistant only a few years older than Harry. 'Does madam know what size she requires?'

Nodding, Harry opened her mouth to reply but she was interrupted by a hoarse shout from the direction of Haberdashery, and the pounding of running feet. She looked up to see a group of young women running towards them, coats flapping, their expressions determined as they pushed aside anyone who got in their way. Behind them, a man was following, waving his arms and shouting. 'Stop them!' he bellowed furiously. 'Stop, thieves!'

Instantly, Harry understood what was happening. These shoppers were not in Selfridges to buy the items on display. They were members of the infamous shoplifting gangs that plagued London –

fashionably dressed women and girls of various ages who wore coats and dresses with concealed pockets in order to steal whatever caught their eye. If apprehended, they had been known to fight and scratch their way out with more fury than caged tigers, leaving injured shop assistants and chaos in their wake. It was the first time Harry had encountered them in the flesh, although she knew much about them from the front pages of the newspapers, and she found herself rooted to the floor in shocked fascination.

'Not again!' the assistant at her side moaned as the thieves drew near. 'They was in here yesterday an' all.'

They were making for the door, Harry realised, hoping to reach the street where they would undoubtedly scatter like rats. Faces flashed past and she had a confused impression of breathless fear and laughter, as though they were half enjoying this desperate chase. The thought caused a bubble of indignation to rise in Harry. Without thinking, she stepped neatly sideways and stuck out her foot.

It made contact with an ankle. There was a squawk of panic, which turned into a tumult of cries as several bodies crashed to the floor. The lead runners looked back but did not stop. Those on the ground scrambled back to their feet as the mob of pursuing security guards and shop assistants bore down on them. The girl nearest to Harry clutched at her leg, glaring balefully up at her from beneath an oversized, floppy hat that was not at all fashionable. 'You'll pay for that,' she snarled.

Harry raised her eyebrows. 'I rather think you will, actually,' she said, and reached out to snatch the hat from the girl's head.

Several things happened at once. The hat came away in Harry's hand, setting a cascade of bright coppery hair free. The nearest security guard roared in triumph as he spotted his fallen quarry. The assistant at Harry's side squeaked like a startled mouse. And the girl glanced briefly upwards into Harry's startled eyes before jabbing out a fist to land a vicious rabbit punch beneath her ribs. Harry doubled over, gasping in shock and pain, the air temporarily dragged from her lungs. A second later, the hat was ripped from her grasp and the thief was on her feet again, wrapping her voluminous brown coat around her and tearing along the aisle towards the exit.

Harry straightened, blinking back tears and staring after her in stunned disbelief. Unless she was very much mistaken, the girl she had just been face to face with was Mildred Longstaff.

Wheezing and clutching her midriff, Harry lurched after her, almost colliding with the guard as she did so. Mildred was fast – shoppers were scattering before her and she had a clear path to the door. Harry gritted her teeth and ran faster. If the girl reached the street there were any number of places she might hide. Harry had to keep her in sight at all costs. 'Mildred!' she shouted, hoping that hearing her own name might cause the girl to slow. It made no difference. If Mildred had heard, she showed no inclination to stop. Which made sense, given she might very well be arrested for shoplifting if she did. Harry kept up her pace, eyes fixed on Mildred's copper hair. If she could just catch her...

She had gained some ground by the time Mildred burst through the grand entrance and vanished from view. Another infuriated roar split the air – Harry assumed the gang had targeted items of high value. Ignoring the guards, she hurried after her.

The scene that greeted her outside the store was one of jarring normality. Pedestrians strolled along the pavements, and taxis mingled with motor cars on the road, chugging noisily past. Harry peered first one way, then the other, and growled in frustration. How could Mildred have vanished already? Then a flash of incongruity caught her eye the other side of Oxford Street, a figure in a large hat scattering the tide of walkers. Determined not to let the girl get away, Harry was about to step out in pursuit when the blare of a horn sent her leaping back. She gasped as a red double-decker bus thundered past, followed by a gust of fume-laden wind that had her rocking on her heels.

By the time Harry had recovered her composure, Mildred was gone.

'You ought to take more care, miss,' a passer-by admonished, his expression disapproving, but Harry barely heard. She was scanning the other side of the street, trying to second-guess her prey. The girl might have taken refuge in one of the other shops but Harry thought it unlikely – her instincts would have been screaming at her to get away. It was much more likely she would making for the Bohemian kaleidoscope of Soho, hoping to become anonymous among the drinking dens and pubs.

Harry was about to make a second attempt to cross the road when another sudden movement caught her eye. An immaculately dressed girl of around nineteen had rounded the corner of Duke Street, where Harry seemed to recall Selfridges had a side door. She was panting slightly and glancing over her shoulder, as though she feared pursuit. Whatever she saw seemed to set her at ease; as Harry drifted towards the window display, she watched the girl straighten her shoulders, run her hands lightly over her dress in the manner of someone checking they had all their belongings, and turn briskly to cross Duke Street, leaving the department store behind.

Keeping her gaze fixed on the goods in the shop window, Harry counted to thirty, then followed. She couldn't be certain this girl had been part of the gang Mildred had been running with – couldn't even be sure she was a thief – but her suspicions were aroused. Following her might be a waste of time or the trail might lead to Mildred. Only time would tell.

It did not appear to have occurred to the girl that she might be being followed, although she kept up her lively pace. Harry maintained a discreet distance, pausing every now and then to gaze at a shop window while keeping one eye on her quarry. When the girl crossed the road, Harry did too and suddenly realised her destination: Bond Street Underground station. Perhaps Mildred had made her way here too and was now somewhere in the labyrinth of tunnels that lay beneath London's streets, lost to Harry all over again.

She sped up, determined to keep the other shoplifter in sight. Bond Street only serviced one line, which meant the girl could only go east towards Oxford Circus or west towards Marble Arch, but it was imperative Harry knew which way she intended to go. Jostling her way past several other travellers, who tutted at her poor manners, she joined the queue for the booking office two people behind the girl. When she reached the clerk, Harry peered past the bodies in front of her and strained to hear the girl's destination. 'Elephant and Castle, please. Third class.'

She passed over some coins and took her ticket. Harry waited impatiently for the customers in front of her to be served and moved to the front of the queue. 'Elephant and Castle, third class.'

Hurrying to the circular staircase that led to the platforms, Harry peered ahead for a glimpse of the brown felt hat. Now she knew which station the girl was going to she could relax a little, perhaps even board the train in a different carriage to prevent her from realising she was being followed, but first Harry needed to ensure they caught the same train and that meant she could not back off too far. She used her fellow travellers as cover, pretending to study the posters on the arched walls even as she watched the girl.

The journey to Oxford Circus was uneventful. Harry waited until her quarry had stepped from the train and moved along the platform to slip after her. She stayed as close as she dared on the Bakerloo Line, sensing this was the time she was at the greatest risk of discovery. When she had dressed that morning, she'd had no idea she might need to blend in with the crowd; her cloche hat was a lamentably bright green, with perky white feathers attached to a gold brooch on one side. It was not, Harry had to admit, ideal for undercover work but going hatless would be even more noticeable. As the train juddered along the darkened tunnels, she reached up and unobtrusively removed the brooch. It wasn't much but perhaps it might help.

Elephant and Castle was not an area of London Harry was familiar with but the hustle and bustle that assaulted her senses on leaving the Underground station reminded her very much of Piccadilly Circus. Lorries and buses trundled across the junction, directed by a policeman who seemed indifferent to the noise and danger from the passing vehicles. A tram rolled by, following silver tracks that bit into the road.

Harry blinked several times as she took in the scene, then remembered why she was there. The girl was heading east, waiting to cross the busy thoroughfare. Settling in behind her, Harry did her best to remain unobtrusive, even as they left the smarter streets behind and ventured into a maze of narrow roads. These were home to ugly, smoke-blackened brick houses, sandwiched together so tightly that they seemed to hunch over the thin street to block out the sky. Paintwork peeled from window frames and tattered fabric hung behind the glass, where there was any covering at all. One house seemed to be abandoned altogether, with no glass in the windows and no front door. Rubbish jumbled with decaying autumn leaves across the doorstep. Overhead, clothes lines criss-crossed the street between upper floors, carrying grey, sagging items that had no hope of drying in the damp chill of November.

Harry hung back as she passed beneath them, aware she was horribly out of place and certain she would be observed at any moment, but the girl she was following did not look back, not even when she reached her apparent destination – a house towards the end of the street. Harry watched her vanish inside, counted to one hundred, and began to walk along the road.

Number 25 Tea Cutter Row was in no better state than its neighbours; the windows were grimy and the door had an ill-fitting look, as though it had warped in its frame. No lights shone inside in spite of the gloomy day but that was hardly a surprise; it was only a little after midday. She didn't pause outside the house and, when she reached the end, she turned the corner into Britannia Avenue and paused beside a slender alleyway that cut between the back of Tea Cutter Row and the next street along, uncertain of what to do next. The grimness of the area sapped some of her confidence. Even the best parts of London were grey compared to Abinger Hall but she had never been somewhere as impoverished as this.

She forced herself to think. There seemed little to be gained from passing along Tea Cutter Row again, unless she could invent an excuse to knock upon the door of number 25, but she had nothing on her person that might give her a reason to do so – no charity tin or basket of foods she could offer. In fact, she imagined anyone knocking on the door of any house in this area would be met with extreme suspicion or even outright hostility. And yet she had come all this way, had tracked the girl to this lair. What had been the point if she simply turned tail and went home?

Painfully aware of how much she stuck out, Harry took a few steps into the alley, allowing the shadows to cloak her. She would knock on the door of number 25 and ask for Mrs Cartwright, she decided, feigning puzzled embarrassment when told no such person lived there. What appeared to be an innocent case of the wrong address might allow her the opportunity to spy inside the house. Surely no one could take offence at that. But just as Harry was reaching a decision, she became aware of footsteps approaching. She shrank back further into the shadows as a figure loomed in the entrance of the alley, blocking out what little light there was.

'Who's there?' a sharp female voice called in a distinct London accent.

Harry said nothing. Could the woman see her? She didn't know. 'Come out here and show yourself,' the speaker went on. 'Only thieves and guttersnipes hide in dark alleys and we have ways of dealing with them you don't want to find out about.'

Harry's heart thudded in her chest as she considered her options. There was nothing for it – she would have to do as the unseen woman instructed. Perhaps she could claim to be lost. Steeling herself, Harry stepped forward. 'I think I'm a little off course. Could you help me?'

There was a gasp and a loud curse. 'You!'

Frowning, Harry moved clear of the alley. And then she understood. The woman staring back at her in furious disbelief was Mildred Longstaff. 'Hello again,' Harry said, once she'd mastered her own surprise. 'I've been looking for you.'

Mildred's lip curled. 'Why? You don't look like the police.' She eyed Harry's outfit in suspicion. 'You from Selfridges? I didn't steal nothing – you can search me if you like.'

Harry had no doubt that any stolen goods were long gone, perhaps stashed somewhere safe along the way home. But that wasn't her business. She took a breath and did her best to smile. 'No, I've been sent by your family, Mildred. They're desperately worried about you.'

Whatever Mildred had been expecting Harry to say, it clearly wasn't this. Her jaw dropped. 'You what?'

Her astonishment was so complete that it gave Harry a moment's pause. 'Your sister, Esme, wrote to – wrote to me after you disappeared and I agreed to see if I could find you.'

The girl shook her head. 'Well, you'd best keep looking, Miss Nosy Parker, 'cos I don't have a sister and I ain't called Mildred. Never heard of anyone who was.'

It suddenly occurred to Harry that Mildred's current accent held no trace of the Surrey village she'd grown up in. Moreover, her reaction to the news of her family's distress was not what Harry had expected either. Clearly the girl had been badly traumatised by her treatment at the hands of Lady Finchem and had adopted a whole new persona to deal with it. That she had fallen so far into a life of crime was testament to the depth of her desperation.

'You don't have to lie to me,' she said gently. 'All your family want is to know you are safe, and for you to understand that you are always welcome to return home.'

Mildred laughed. 'Quite the do-gooder we have here. I'll say it again, I ain't Mildred.' She stepped nearer and thrust her face into Harry's. 'And if you know what's good for you, you'll scuttle out of here sharpish and forget you ever saw me. You won't like what we do to nosy parkers, either.'

With that, she turned on her heel and strode towards the corner. Harry hurried after her. 'Mildred, please, if you've fallen in with a bad lot then I can help you.'

It wasn't until they were level with number 25 that Mildred spun round to face her. 'This is my last warning – go away and never come back. No one here needs your help.'

Before Harry could respond, she had pushed back the warped front door and was gone. Harry curled her fingers into fists, and stared up at the house in frustration. She hadn't expected to be met with open arms by Mildred but she certainly had not anticipated that the girl would deny her very name. But there seemed little more she could do here – at least she could let Esme Longstaff know her missing sister was alive, if not exactly well.

With a discouraged sigh, Harry stepped back and was about to turn away when she saw movement in the topmost window of the house. Squinting, she peered up. An indistinct figure hovered behind the dirt, pale-faced and unmoving as it gazed down at Harry.

Optimistic that Mildred had changed her mind, Harry raised a hand to wave but the figure did not respond. A second later it vanished. She waited as long as she dared but no further movement came and, eventually, Harry gave up.

By the time she reached Elephant and Castle station, she had almost convinced herself the figure at the window had been a figment of her imagination. But the unhappy truth about Mildred had not been imagined. Harry could only wish she had better news for the Longstaffs, although she was sure it would bring them a measure of relief. Even so, the first letter she composed on Monday was going to be a difficult one.

7

Mr Sherlock Holmes
221b Baker Street
London
NW1 6XE

5, The Cottages
Foxley
Surrey

21st November 1932

Dear Mr Holmes,

I must offer you my sincerest apologies for wasting your time but I know you will be glad to hear the happy news I am about to share, which is that my sister, Mildred, has written at long last. She has not shared much of her experiences since she left Lady Finchem's employment but assures us she is well and has secured a new position in a good London household.

I am certain more details will be received in due course but I wanted to write to you post-haste to release you from any obligation to us and allow you to lend your remarkable skills to others. We are, of course, grateful and honoured for your attention, and most thankful to Miss Moss for her visit.

Yours faithfully,

Miss Esme Longstaff

Harry read the letter at least three times before it sank in. Her first thought was that she was glad she had thought better of sending the letter she had written immediately after her visit to Tea Cutter Row. The encounter with Mildred had troubled her for days and she had been reluctant to heap more misery on the Longstaffs by revealing her current situation. But now it appeared Mildred's conscience had been jogged by Harry's words and she had written to set their minds at rest. Quite how much of her letter had been true was not for Harry to decide – she found it a little difficult to believe the savage girl she had encountered could have secured a domestic position in one of the city's doss houses, let alone with a respectable family, but she decided that was neither her nor Sherlock Holmes' concern. The maid was no longer missing: the case was closed.

Over the weeks that followed, letters continued to arrive demanding the help of Sherlock Holmes.

Dear Mr Holmes, I suspect my lodger is a German spy…

Dear Mr Holmes, I fear my sister's husband is under the thrall of a witch doctor…

Dear Sherlock Holmes, I am convinced my budgerigar has been stolen and replaced by one that is almost identical…

Harry was not moved by any of the desperate entreaties. With her usual diligence, she read each one, typed the standard response in duplicate, and sealed the original in an envelope for Bobby to collect on his rounds. There was no further correspondence from the Longstaff family and Harry tried not to think about them too much. Her short-lived career as a detective had not concluded entirely to her satisfaction, even though the mystery had been solved, and she preferred not to allow her misgivings space to grow, especially when there was nothing she could do to resolve them. Finding herself in need of distraction, she reluctantly accepted her brother Sebastian's invitation to dinner with the Honeywells.

'Oh, do come, Harry. Mama has set me up and I can't get out of it,' he'd begged on the telephone and she'd felt honour-bound to accept, even if it did mean enduring Eugenia Honeywell's clumsy attempts to matchmake. She sat through it with polite but determined resolve, while trying not to make eye contact with either the poor unfortunate Philip or her visibly amused brother.

The only interesting point in the evening occurred when the conversation turned to the mystery posed in the latest Agatha Christie novel, featuring the detective Hercule Poirot. 'I don't know how she does it,' Mrs Honeywell said, her cheeks flushed as she took a generous gulp of wine. 'I can never work out who the killer is, even when little Mr Poirot has explained it all.'

Julian Honeywell patted his wife's hand. 'It's always the most unlikely person,' he said loftily. 'Work out who couldn't possibly have done it and they'll be the guilty party.'

'But if they couldn't have done it, how can they be guilty?' Eugenia asked, her forehead creasing in puzzlement. 'I don't understand.'

'Does it really matter if you don't understand?' Philip asked from across the table. 'Just enjoy the story.'

Eugenia sighed. 'Oh, I do. It just makes one feel so dull, that's all.' She took another mouthful of wine and brightened. 'I found myself in the middle of a mystery of my own a few weeks ago. I received a letter from an employment bureau asking about a maid we used to have.'

Philip yawned. 'Nothing mysterious about that.'

His mother gave him a reproachful look. 'I haven't finished, dear. The peculiar thing was that the maid never worked for us.'

'Mistaken identity,' Julian harumphed but Harry stiffened in her seat. She had all but forgotten her visit to Mrs Haverford but it couldn't be a coincidence, could it? 'How strange,' she said, after a moment. 'Did you ever solve the mystery?'

Eugenia Honeywell shook her head. 'Not to my satisfaction, no. I rang the agency and spoke to someone, who insisted the girl had worked for me. I insisted I'd never heard of her and things got somewhat heated.' She glanced around, her expression almost imploring. 'Domestic staff come and go, of course, but I do try to remember their names.'

The sentiment might have been more convincing if she hadn't slurred her words. Once again, Julian patted her hand. 'No real mystery,' he said kindly. 'Either the agency got it wrong or you did. Both fairly common events, in my experience.'

Eugenia consoled herself with more wine and grew a little tearful as she insisted she remembered who had worked for her. Harry squirmed in her seat, unable to shake the feeling that she was responsible for some of the other woman's distress. By unspoken agreement, she and Seb made their excuses not long after and left. As they shared a taxi back to Mayfair, Harry shook her head. 'Remind me to say no next time you try to drag me into a dinner Mama has arranged.'

Her brother laughed. 'Only if you remind me to do the same. Philip isn't a bad sort but his parents are fairly awful and he's no match for you.'

That was half the trouble – Philip was nice enough, if a little condescending, but not the least bit attractive to Harry. 'Do me a favour and tell Mama that when you see her,' she told Seb. 'She's determined to marry me off to the first man with a decent income.'

Seb stretched and sighed. 'Ah, the perils of being female.' He gave her a sidelong look. 'Do you think you'll ever marry?'

'No,' Harry said, with some force; too many conversations with her mother had made her dislike even the thought of giving up her independence to become someone's wife. Then she softened. Thousands of people got married every year – they couldn't all be wrong, could they? 'Maybe, if I met the right person at the right time. But not now.'

'The right person,' Seb repeated thoughtfully. 'Who might that be, I wonder? You wouldn't have already met him, by any chance?'

Harry felt her cheeks grow warm and was glad of the darkness surrounding them. He meant Oliver Fortescue, of course, the lawyer son of their father's best friend. He was four years older than Harry, had gone to university with her eldest brother, Lawrence, and there had been a summer when she'd followed them both around like a puppy. But Oliver had been bright and brilliant and destined for greatness at the Inns of Court. He'd had little time for teenage Harry and she imagined he would have even less time now. 'No,' she said firmly.

Seb held his hand up in mock surrender. 'Okay, just thought I'd ask. You know the only way to stop Mama's meddling is to find someone yourself.'

There was a kernel of truth in his words that Harry preferred not to examine. 'Like you have?' she parried.

'I am a confirmed bachelor and plan to enjoy that happy situation for as long as I can,' Seb answered, with equal firmness. He leaned forward to tap the glass window that separated them from the driver. 'And speaking of which, just here, please.'

Harry glanced out of the window to see they were outside the Cosmo. 'Rather you than me,' she said. 'I've got work tomorrow.'

'I haven't,' her brother said cheerfully, and planted a kiss on her cheek before opening the car door and climbing out. 'Sweet dreams, Sis. See you soon.'

* * *

LORD ROBERTSON BURGLARY

Deanery Street Theft An Inside Job

Maid Held For Questioning

The headline was splashed all over the newspaper sellers' stands as Harry made her way to work on Wednesday morning, their cry of 'Read all about it!' strident over the buzz of traffic. She didn't make a habit of paying attention to the morning editions, preferring to buy an evening paper on her way home to flick through as she ate her supper, and there were several publications she would not touch under any circumstances, but on this morning there was no escaping the story. Every newspaper being held aloft and rustled on the Underground bellowed the crime from the front page and, as Harry's vision drifted along the wall of newsprint, she felt her curiosity catch. What had been stolen from Lord Robertson, she wondered, and by whom?

With a subtle shift, she began reading over the shoulder of the man seated beside her and felt her blood run cold before she had finished the first paragraph. The burglary had resulted in the loss of a significant amount of jewellery and money, but it was not the list of stolen goods that made Harry read the words all over again. It was the name of the maid, the girl who had been detained on suspicion of masterminding the crime: Mildred Longstaff herself.

Harry bought a paper of her own the moment she left Baker Street Underground station and absorbed the details as she walked to the bank. The theft had taken place the night before, while Lord Robertson and his wife were enjoying a trip to the theatre. They came home to find their butler incapacitated and items of considerable value missing. Mildred had been arrested on the spot, even though she proclaimed her innocence, and was being held at Vine Street Police Station.

Harry found it hard to concentrate on her work that morning. When Bobby arrived with the day's deliveries, he whistled disapprovingly through his teeth as he eyed the folded-up newspaper on the floor beneath her hat and coat. 'What's the world coming to?' he asked, shaking his head for sorrowful emphasis. 'But I'll tell you this for nothing – if I was going to steal some jewellery, not that I would, I wouldn't stash the loot under me pillow. Asking to get caught, that is.'

Harry brooded on his words long after the post boy had continued on his rounds. The similarities to the tale told by Lady Finchem were not lost on her and she had to admit her faith in Mildred's innocence was almost gone. It seemed long past time to face the fact that she was not the girl her family thought her to be. But Harry had not considered her unintelligent when they had met – why would she repeat the same crime in her new position, with exactly the same mistake in hiding the stolen loot? It didn't make sense.

The evening newspapers added more lurid detail. Mildred had appeared at the Magistrates' Court on Marlborough Street and tearfully protested her innocence, declaring she hadn't even been at the house when the burglary happened – a claim disproved by several witnesses. She had not been able to explain the presence of stolen jewellery under her pillow, either, and had simply insisted she hadn't put it there. The magistrate had taken a dim view of her protestations; bail had been denied and she had returned to prison to await trial. Police suspected she was not working alone and had appealed for anyone who might have noticed anything unusual on Deanery Street between the hours of eight and eleven p.m. on the night in question.

Harry shook her head sadly. Things did not look good for Mildred, which made her feel even more sympathy for her long-suffering family. She doubted they could bear the expense of a lawyer.

By the following morning, the headlines had moved on to a tragic mining accident in Wales that had drowned twelve men, and Mildred had been consigned to lower down the page. Harry bought *The Times* on her way into work, hopeful that Mildred had been exonerated but the evidence of her guilt did not seem to be going away. It made for depressing reading and Harry could only imagine what the Longstaffs were going through. Things were likely to get much worse before they got better, for both Mildred and her family.

Doing her best to put the matter out of her mind, Harry spent the morning responding to the latest pile of letters to Sherlock Holmes. She telephoned Mr Babbage to request another filing cabinet, as the one she had was very nearly full, and she requisitioned some new typewriter ribbons. But although she undertook her work with the same attention to detail as always, she found herself restless and irritable. More than once she was tempted to tell Mr Holmes' correspondents exactly what she thought of their wild accusations and frankly insane stories.

Rubbing her temples in an effort to shift the headache that lurked there, she gazed around the small office and sighed. Perhaps it was time to stop cutting off her nose to spite Simeon Pemberton, who had probably forgotten she even existed. Perhaps it was time to find a new job.

Deciding she was sorely in need of fresh air, Harry took her lunch to Regent's Park and spent a restorative thirty minutes feeding the ducks her leftover crusts. As she made her way along Baker Street towards the bank, she was surprised to see a young woman waving at her from the other side of the street. 'Miss Moss!' she cried, hurrying across the road and eliciting angry shouts and toots of horns as she did so. 'Goodness, I am so relieved to have found you.'

Harry stared at her in astonishment. Esme Longstaff was the last person she'd expected to see. 'Good afternoon, Miss Longstaff,' she managed, having glanced both ways along the street to see if Mr or Mrs Longstaff were nearby. 'What a pleasant surprise to see you again. Are you well?'

Clearly flustered and a little out of breath, Esme took a moment to compose herself. 'I am in good health, thank you, but I must confess to finding Baker Street most confusing. I have walked its entire length searching for 221b but cannot find it. Either I am very stupid or the numbers are muddled.' She tipped her head. 'But now you are here, you can relieve my bewilderment. Where are the consulting rooms of Mr Holmes, please?'

Harry kept her gaze firmly averted from the entrance to the Abbey Road Building Society, where she was sure the doormen were watching her curiously. 'Mr Holmes is not currently in residence at Baker Street, as I'm sure you recall.' She paused. There was only one reason she could imagine for Esme's presence in London and it was not something she was in a position to help with. 'I'm sorry to disappoint you.'

To her horror, Esme Longstaff's green eyes swam with tears. 'I suspected you would say that but I don't know where else to turn. It's my sister, Mildred. She's – she's been arrested.'

Harry felt a swell of sympathy. 'Yes, I saw it in the newspaper and thought of you immediately. It must be terribly distressing. But tell me, where are your parents? Surely you didn't travel to London alone?'

'I did. My mother has taken to her bed and Father does not know what to do.' Esme clutched at Harry's arm. 'Mildred didn't do it – I know she didn't.' The tears that had been brimming in her eyes spilled over. 'You have to help her. You and Mr Holmes.'

Harry gazed at her in dismay. The evidence against Mildred, coupled with her previous crime and Harry's own encounter with her, made it hard to see what could be done. 'Are you so very sure of her innocence?' she asked gently. 'This is the second accusation your sister has faced, perhaps even the third, if Mr Blunt is to be believed. Is it possible there might be a side to her personality you don't know?'

'No.' Esme's reply rang with confidence. 'Even if what you say is true, I have reason to believe she was not acting under her own volition.'

Her refusal to accept that Mildred might be guilty was not a surprise but the second part of her statement was. Even so, Harry was reluctant to encourage Esme's belief. 'I must tell you that I met Mildred some weeks ago, before your letter arrived to advise me – that it to say Mr Holmes – of her new position.' She met the girl's gaze with frank honesty. 'The encounter did not suggest she was unhappy with criminal activity.'

'That cannot be!' Esme cried, loudly enough to cause passing pedestrians to look their way. 'You must be mistaken. My sister is not a thief. Please, let us go to Mr Holmes' rooms and I will explain further.'

Acutely aware of the interest Esme's distress was attracting, Harry weighed her options. Abandoning her in such a state was unthinkable, especially when she was unaccompanied, but she certainly could not invite the distraught young woman into the bank; that would raise a host of questions Harry preferred not to answer. Yet neither could they continue their conversation on the street. Things were further complicated by the fact that her lunch break was over and she had been due back at her desk a full five minutes ago. But would anyone apart from the bank's doormen notice if she returned late? She thought not.

'What we both need is tea and there is none at 221b Baker Street,' she said. 'Happily, there's a café just around the corner. If you will join me there now, I will listen to what you have to say.'

Esme pressed her lips together in a tight smile, her green eyes glistening. 'Thank you.'

They spoke little on the short walk to the café. Harry selected a quiet table near the back. In her experience, café society was much about seeing and being seen – few customers wanted to sit where they would not be noticed. Esme sank wearily into the chair, reminding Harry of the emotional toll her sister's arrest must be taking on her, and she ordered teacakes along with a large pot of tea. 'It must have come as a great shock to hear of Mildred's fresh troubles,' she said, once the waitress had gone. 'How did you find out?'

Esme sighed. 'Through the newspaper. We hadn't heard from her again, following the letter telling us of her new position, but assumed she must be settling in.' She looked down at the table. 'It was quite a blow to discover she had been arrested instead.'

Harry regarded her compassionately. 'Have you been able to see her?'

'I tried. I went to Vine Street Police Station yesterday but they told me she had already been taken to Holloway Prison.' She gazed at Harry in horror. 'Prison! I've heard such terrible things about the conditions for inmates. The thought of my sister suffering there is too much to bear.'

Her fears were understandable, Harry thought – the poor conditions in all prisons were no secret, although reformers were doing their best to improve matters. It was possible family visits might be allowed at a later date but the Longstaffs might find that more distressing than their imaginations. 'You said you believed Mildred was not acting freely. What makes you think that?'

The young woman reached into her bag and withdrew an envelope. 'This,' she said, pushing it across the table towards Harry. 'It's the letter she sent but I don't believe she wrote it. Or at least, I don't think she wrote it willingly.'

Intrigued in spite of herself, Harry opened the envelope and scanned the letter. There was no address at the top, merely the word *London* and the date. It was simply written, apologising for her long silence but advising them not to worry as she had a new position as a general maid with a wealthy family. When Harry had finished reading, she looked up at Esme. 'Is this not Mildred's handwriting?'

The girl hesitated. 'It is. As you can imagine, I have any number of examples to compare it to and I confess I am not able to deny it. But this letter is so very different to the others. The detail is sparse; she makes no effort to explain herself. Most importantly, she does not ask how we are.'

Once again, Harry recalled her own encounter with Mildred. 'It is possible she has changed,' she said quietly. 'From what I understand, her departure from the Finchem house was very distressing.'

Esme shook her head. 'Mildred is a sweet and loving girl. No amount of distress would prevent her from worrying how her disappearance affected us.'

Sweet and loving were not words Harry would have ascribed to Mildred but she kept that to herself. 'Then why didn't she write to you before?' she asked.

'Shame,' Esme suggested. 'Embarrassment? But perhaps you

know more than you are saying, Miss Moss. Why do you think she didn't write?'

Thankfully, the tea arrived at that moment, which bought Harry some thinking space. By the time the tea was poured and the teacakes buttered, she had an answer prepared. 'I fear Mildred may have fallen in with a bad crowd,' she said tactfully. 'I wasn't able to trace her once she left the Finchems – in fact, it was only by extreme luck that I located her at all – and then your letter arrived so I assumed she had turned over a new leaf. But I must admit that while I was saddened to see the news of her arrest, I was sadly not entirely surprised.'

Esme leaned forward, her expression intent. 'But don't you see? This matches my suspicions – that Mildred was somehow coerced into writing this letter. If she was keeping the company of criminals, might they not have put her up to stealing Lord Robertson's valuables?'

'Possibly,' Harry conceded. 'But the fact is there's no evidence anyone else was involved. Some of the stolen jewellery was found in her bedclothes.'

'Pffft,' Esme puffed in disgust. 'My sister is not stupid. If she had turned to crime, she would have found a better place to hide her ill-gotten gains. Twice in the same place? Ridiculous.'

There wasn't much Harry could say to that – she had thought exactly the same thing and hearing Esme observe it somehow made it seem even more nonsensical. And there was also the timing of Mildred's last letter, the date of which was just a day after Harry had met her in Tea Cutter Row. Was that significant? Had she managed to jog Mildred's conscience somehow? But she still didn't see how any of that pointed to the girl's innocence – there were witnesses who placed her squarely in the centre of the crime, despite her claim that she had not been at the house that evening.

'What does Mr Holmes think?' Esme asked suddenly. 'I appreciate we dispensed with his services but dare I dream he might have retained an interest in my sister? Her need is most dire and I am certain his legendary powers of deduction would save her.'

The earnestness of her expression brought home the weight of Harry's subterfuge. What had initially seemed like a worthy undertaking had now escalated into something of the gravest importance and she was reminded all over again that she did not have the skills or intelligence of the great Sherlock Holmes. He would doubtless have proved Mildred's innocence in an instant – revealed some insignificant detail only he had noticed that unravelled the case against her immediately – and a grateful Esme would be reunited with her sister. But this was not a work of fiction, Harry reminded herself unhappily. Esme might expect Holmes to work miracles but Mildred's very real peril could not be resolved with a flourish of Arthur Conan Doyle's pen. She swallowed an inward sigh. 'I will consult with him,' she said reluctantly, wishing she had ignored the foolish impulse to answer Esme's letter. 'Perhaps he will have some insight.'

Esme clasped her hands together. 'Thank you. With all my heart, I thank you.'

Harry spent the remainder of the afternoon typing her usual humdrum correspondence but her mind kept returning to Mildred's case. Her meeting with Esme had only reinforced how many aspects of the crime did not fit together, as though she was trying to complete one jigsaw puzzle with the pieces of another. How had Mildred been able to obtain the position in Lord Robertson's household after leaving Lady Finchem's in disgrace? Who had coerced Mildred into writing to her family about it? Why had she risked her newfound role by committing the exact same crime that had seen her sacked before? And strangest of all, how had she gone from being the sweet, loving girl Esme described to a spitting, snarling wretch who denied even her own name?

Nothing made any sense and Harry was starting to feel very much out of her depth. What she needed more than anything was to speak to Mildred again, in the hope that desperation might shake some sense into her, and the idea spurred her into action. She might not be able to call on Sherlock Holmes for help but she was not without friends and acquaintances. Perhaps it was time to call in a favour.

8

Oliver Fortescue had not changed much in the year or so since Harry had last seen him. She stole a glance sideways from the passenger seat of his car, watching his brow furrow in concentration as he navigated the streets of North London on Saturday morning. His hair was as black as ever, flopping slightly over his forehead the way it had always done. His nose was perfectly straight and noble, as though carved by Michelangelo himself, and his skin was lightly tanned, even in November, which reminded Harry of his fondness for impromptu trips to the Côte d'Azur, although she doubted he had much time for that now he was a celebrated City lawyer.

'Tell me again how you got caught up with this girl,' he said, steering them onto Camden Road. 'I'm not sure I quite caught the connection when you rang yesterday.'

Harry took a breath. She had anticipated this question and had her explanation ready. 'You know how it is,' she said carelessly. 'Mildred is originally from Foxley, which is a village on our estate. Her plight caught my eye, that's all. I wanted to help.'

Oliver raised a dark eyebrow. 'Very decent of you. Although I must warn you, I'm not sure how much help either of us will be. I reviewed the police report this morning, and the court records, and I'm afraid it looks like an open-and-shut case.'

'Perhaps,' Harry said. 'But as I said to you on the telephone, there are one or two things that don't add up. I think it's worth hearing Mildred's side of the story, which is why I came to you.'

'Naturally,' Oliver said, smiling. 'You'd have had trouble getting into Holloway otherwise. Now, don't forget you're masquerading as my legal clerk. Keep your eyes and ears open but for God's sake don't drop me in it. The deputy governor is a friend of my father.'

'I won't,' Harry said fervently. 'And thanks for doing this. I really appreciate it.'

He drummed his fingers on the steering wheel. 'I wouldn't do it for just anyone, you know,' he said, and glanced across at her again. 'You owe me.'

'I know,' she said. 'Thank you.'

But Oliver's attention had shifted to the road ahead. 'Okay, there it is.' He frowned at her. 'I hope you're ready for this, Harry. It's not going to be a pleasant experience.'

She looked out of the window at the grey, forbidding monster that loomed in front of them. Inside, hundreds of women were serving sentences for crimes she did not want to imagine. Rumours abounded of rats in the kitchens and canteens, seldom-emptied buckets instead of toilets for bodily necessities, and globules of porridge or thin pea soup for every meal. Of course it was not going to be pleasant. 'I'm ready,' she said quietly, as Oliver manoeuvred the car through the iron gates and parked in the shadow of the prison.

Up close, Holloway was even more intimidating. Built in 1852, it was a Gothic monstrosity designed to strike fear into the heart of Victorian criminals, in the hope that it might deter them from doing wrong. Heavy stone walls rose up around a vast arched door, topped with hulking crenellations and dotted with leaded windows that were barely wide enough to admit light. Beyond the door, towers rose to dwarf the outer walls and Harry would not have been surprised to see archers patrolling the battlements. 'It looks like a fortress,' she said, unable to suppress a tremor of trepidation.

'It is a fortress,' Oliver said grimly. 'But it's designed to keep people in rather than out. Come on, let's get this over with.'

He rang the bell and gave his name through a small grate in the huge wooden door. A smaller door cut into the wood creaked open. Oliver showed his identification, and they were let in. There was no need for him to remind Harry to say nothing as they followed a guard across a small courtyard to reach the inner door – the greyness and misery of the place pressed down on her as they walked, and made her feel as insignificant as the lichen that stained the walls. The next door employed the same architectural style as the outer gate, although some concession to aesthetics seemed to have been made – a pair of rearing carved griffins faced each other on pillars to either side of the arch – but they did little to lift Harry's sense of dread. How awful it would be to pass through this door knowing it would be your home for the foreseeable future, she thought with a shudder.

Once inside, they found themselves in a large entrance hall with a wide staircase and a number of doors that Harry guessed led to visiting rooms. Her prediction was proved correct when she and Oliver were shown into one of these rooms; it was small, cold and smelled as though someone had left a bowl of rancid cabbage in a corner for a week. The floor was covered with black and white tiles, the walls were a grimy beige and the only furniture consisted of a table and two chairs. The grim-faced prison guard who had accompanied them to this point surveyed the room impassively then sniffed at Harry. 'Looks like you'll have to stand.'

'She will not,' Oliver snapped, with a crisp authority that took Harry by surprise. She wasn't sure she'd ever heard him sound so commanding. 'Unless you want me to report your insolence to Deputy Governor Short, have another chair brought here immediately and get someone to open a window. It smells like something died in here.'

To his credit, the guard snapped to attention. A few busy minutes later, there were three chairs at the table, the narrow, high windows had been opened and the floor had been liberally mopped. The smell lingered but it was now masked by the eye-watering stench of bleach. 'Almost satisfactory,' Oliver declared, wrinkling his nose. 'Bring Mildred Longstaff, please.'

They waited in silence, a fresh, even more sullen guard observing them from just inside the door. Harry didn't know what strings Oliver had pulled to get access to Mildred and now that they were inside the prison, she was slightly concerned that the girl might react with hostility to the sudden arrival of a stranger. Moreover, she was not at all sure how Mildred would respond to her presence. Harry had seen her on the run for shoplifting, after all. It was likely she might consider Harry a threat instead of an ally. But it was far too late for such considerations now. Time was of the essence and she would just have to hope the girl recognised a lifeline when she was thrown one.

Their original chaperone reappeared. 'Mildred Longstaff,' he announced, and waved towards the table. 'Sit there.'

Oliver and Harry both stood as a red-headed young woman reluctantly approached, head bowed. She wore a black, shapeless skirt with some sort of tunic over the top and Harry could not tell whether the clothing had been provided by the prison or belonged to Mildred; the part of her that loved fashion could not imagine anyone wearing such items willingly.

But all such trivial considerations were washed clean away when the girl looked up. At that moment, Harry's world tilted on its axis and it was all she could do not to gasp. The hair tied back in a severe bun might be the exact shade of auburn, and the features of the face were similar enough to fool a casual observer, but this was not the same girl Harry had encountered first in Selfridges, and then again at Elephant and Castle. She gaped, utterly flabbergasted, as Oliver offered a brisk smile, oblivious to Harry's confusion. 'Mildred, I'm Oliver Fortescue, your lawyer, and this is my assistant. Won't you take a seat?'

The girl stared at him. 'My lawyer? I didn't – I can't afford a lawyer.'

There was no trace of the harsh London accent she had used before, Harry observed, feeling faintly dizzy. Her voice was totally different – softer and considerably more deferential. In fact, she sounded very much like an older Esme Longstaff.

'Your costs are being met in this case,' Oliver said. 'Please, sit down. We're here to help you.'

Mildred's eyes flickered between Harry and Oliver, as though she couldn't decide whether to trust them. 'Met by who?' she said, the words little more than a whisper. 'Please, I need to know.'

Oliver frowned. 'This meeting is being offered *pro bono*. That is to say there is no charge. Where we go from here depends very much on you, Mildred. Now, if you'll sit down, we can make a start.'

Still distrustful but evidently realising she had few options, she slid into the empty chair facing them. The door closed, leaving the three of them alone. Harry took the opportunity to study Mildred, taking in the pallor of her skin and the bloodless lips, both of which contrasted vividly with her coppery hair and green eyes. And then Harry could have slapped herself because she had been so utterly, unforgivably stupid. Of course Mildred Longstaff had green eyes – her family had told Harry so at their first meeting and she had forgotten. Perhaps if she had taken the photograph Esme had shown her all those weeks ago – but no, that had been of Mildred as a much younger girl. Even so, Harry felt dull and senseless. She had been a fool – a slapdash idiot unworthy of the title detective. For hardship and fear could do much to change a person's appearance but they could not change the colour of their eyes. Whoever the girl in Selfridges had been, she was not Mildred Longstaff.

Oliver was talking but Harry did not register much of what he said. She was too busy reviewing everything she knew in light of this enormous revelation. The two young women looked alike – bore more than a passing resemblance to each other, in fact. Did that have some relevance to the case? That the girl Harry had met was not Mildred certainly explained the bewildering differences in personality between Esme's descriptions and Harry's own experience. It might even explain the park keeper's supposed sighting of Mildred in Hyde Park, where she had been accused of picking someone's pocket. What if that had been Mildred's lookalike too? Once again, Harry could have kicked herself. It was all so obvious now and made Mildred's innocence much more believable as a result. And yet... there must be some connection. The young woman in Tea Cutter Row had known Mildred's name – Harry was sure of that. But how?

Still turning the puzzle over in her mind, she tuned back in to the conversation in front of her.

'I didn't steal anything,' Mildred was saying, her eyes swimming with tears. 'Not from Lady Finchem and not from Lord Robertson. You have to believe me.'

'That's why we're here,' Oliver soothed, offering her a clean white handkerchief. 'Why don't you begin by telling us what happened at Lady Finchem's?'

There was little Harry didn't already know. Mildred had been horrified when the missing bracelet had been found in her bed and had vehemently denied taking it. Her cries of innocence had fallen on deaf ears, however, and none of the other staff had stood up for her. Harry stirred, recalling her conversation with Dobbins in the hall of the Finchem house. Leaning towards Oliver, she murmured a question. He nodded his understanding. 'If I may just interrupt, Mildred. Am I right in thinking you shared a room with another member of the domestic staff?'

'That's right,' Mildred said. 'It was a girl named Polly. I thought she was my friend. Turned out I was wrong about that.'

'I see,' Oliver said thoughtfully. 'And Polly also had access to Lady Finchem's jewellery?'

'Oh no.' Mildred's reply was firm. 'None of us did. Only the housekeeper looked after Lady Finchem's things.'

'But they were not locked away,' Oliver pressed. 'In a drawer or a safe, perhaps?'

'In a drawer, I think,' Mildred said, frowning. 'I only went in there to clear out the ashes and lay the fire. Like I said, it was Mrs Rivers who took care of Lady Finchem.'

Harry knew what Oliver was getting at: who had the opportunity to steal the bracelet in the first place? Unfortunately for Mildred, it appeared that she might have but it was important that others could have taken it too. Any of the household staff could have hidden it in Mildred's bed but Harry was inclined to suspect Polly, the maid. Another question occurred to her. Oliver dutifully asked it. 'Tell me, how did you come by your position with the Finchems?'

'I placed an advert in the *Morning Herald*,' Mildred answered. 'The housekeeper replied.'

Harry regarded her, crestfallen. She had hoped there might be a link to the employment agency Dobbins had mentioned. She whispered to Oliver again. 'And you have never heard of Mrs Haverford's Bureau of Excellence?'

Mildred's expression was blank. 'No. Should I have?'

Oliver glanced at Harry, who gave an almost imperceptible shake of her head. 'Not at all,' he said smoothly. 'Tell us what happened after you left Lady Finchem's employment. You did not return to your family in Surrey. Am I correct?'

Mildred agreed that she had not. Once she had been unceremoniously escorted from Farm Street, she had been at a loss what to do. 'I was in a terrible state – crying and shaking. I sat on a doorstep for a while, then I walked for a bit – I don't remember where. And then, somewhere around Piccadilly or Oxford Street, this girl stopped and asked me if I was all right.' She dabbed at her eyes with the handkerchief. 'Of course I blurted out the whole story and she told me she had some friends who could help. I was so fuddled that I didn't think to question it – I just went with her.'

'Perfectly understandable,' Oliver said, as Mildred hung her head. Harry whispered to him. 'You didn't go to Hyde Park at all? Have an argument with someone?'

'I—' Mildred's brow wrinkled in thought. 'I don't think so. At least, I don't remember going there, or any argument. Is it important?'

Again, Harry shook her head. 'No,' Oliver said. 'Now go on – what happened next?'

'We took the Underground to Elephant and Castle.'

'Elephant and Castle,' Harry repeated abruptly, earning her a reproachful glance from Oliver. 'Are you sure?'

Mildred nodded. 'Positive. Dora bought my ticket, said I could pay her back once I was back on my feet.'

Harry's head spun. It couldn't be a coincidence that the Mildred's lookalike had also turned up in Elephant and Castle, could it? But how could it be anything else? Mildred was speaking again. 'We ended up in this house. It wasn't the nicest place but what choice did I have? Dora said I could stay for the night and she would take me to the station so I could go home to my parents the next day.' She picked at a grimy fingernail. 'I didn't mind that. I was scared to go home.'

Harry wanted to tell her how much she had been missed, how diligently her parents had searched for her, but Oliver's instructions still rang in her ears and she stayed quiet. There would be time for that once they had extricated Mildred from this nightmare.

'One night became two, and then three,' Mildred went on. 'They said they'd find me a new job, so I wouldn't have to tell my family what had happened. All I had to do was stay indoors and be patient, they said, while they sorted everything out.'

'Who do you mean by "they"?' Oliver asked.

Mildred shifted uneasily. 'Dora, mostly. But she wasn't always there. Other people came and went – there was a lady called Mrs Goodfellow, and another one whose name I never knew. She seemed to be important.'

'How long were you there?'

'I – I don't actually know. The days blurred a bit and I lost count – mostly I stayed in one of the rooms upstairs. One day Dora said they'd got me a job in a fancy house. She said I was lucky, not many girls got that chance.' Mildred laughed softly. 'I should have known it was too good to be true.'

Harry shook her head. It was beginning to look as though Mildred's only crime had been being too trusting but she said nothing. 'So you went to Lord Robertson's house. What happened then?'

'At first, everything was fine. The work wasn't too bad and I had every second Friday off. Then Dora appeared one evening, told me I had the night off. I knew that wasn't right – it was a Tuesday, not a Friday. But she insisted, said I should take myself to the cinema – I deserved it.' Mildred's lip wobbled as she looked from Harry to Oliver. 'When I got back, everything was fine. And then the master and mistress came back and all hell broke loose. A gold ring was found in my bed and the police were called.'

Oliver shuffled through a pile of papers he had taken from his briefcase. 'This was at approximately ten-thirty in the evening – is that right?'.

The girl shrugged. 'I suppose it must have been. I told them I'd been at the cinema but they didn't believe me. The butler said he'd seen me in the kitchen when he couldn't have done because I wasn't even in the house then. Nobody listened to me.'

Oliver consulted the paperwork once more. 'I see from your statement that you told the police about the house in Elephant and Castle.' He rifled through the pages again. 'It says here they sent an officer to investigate your claim. He found a family of nine living at the address you gave, including five children and a babe in arms. Neighbours confirmed they had been there for years.'

'That can't be!' Mildred burst out. 'There was no family when I stayed there, I swear to it. Are you sure they went to number 25?'

'Hold on,' Harry cut in, before Oliver could reply. 'This isn't 25 Tea Cutter Row, is it?'

Both Oliver and Mildred stared at her in astonishment. 'Yes,' Mildred said. 'How did you know that?'

'A very good question,' Oliver said, eyebrows beetling together. 'Perhaps one we shall come back to later.' He returned his gaze to Mildred. 'It appears the police officer did all he could to corroborate your story but there was simply no evidence to support it.'

Harry was only half listening – in her mind's eye, she was replaying her own visit to Elephant and Castle. She had stood almost on the doorstep of the house. Had there been any sign that a cluster of children lived there? She couldn't remember seeing any toys strewn outside. And then another recollection hit her, of glancing up at the first-floor window and seeing a figure watching her. 'It was you!' she gasped, eyes widening as she looked at Mildred. 'You were at the window when I visited the house in Tea Cutter Row. I saw someone watching me – it must have been you, Mildred.'

The girl's expression went from puzzlement to elation as she considered what that might mean. 'Then you can tell the police that – they'd believe a respectable legal assistant like you.'

Oliver cleared his throat meaningfully, just as Harry realised the error she'd made. 'It's certainly something to consider,' he said, giving Harry a hard look. 'But in the meantime, why don't you finish telling us about the burglary?'

Mildred did not argue. 'There's not much to tell. They kept me overnight in a cell at Vine Street and in the morning I was up before the magistrate. I told him everything I told the police – about the theft at Lady Finchem's and how it was the same as Lord Robertson's but he didn't believe me either. He sent me here to await trial and I've been here since.'

Oliver considered her thoughtfully. 'When I first introduced myself, you seemed fearful of who was paying for my services. Why was that?'

For a moment, it seemed she would not answer. The silence grew thick and heavy around them. Then Mildred swallowed. 'I thought you might be working for them.'

'Who do you mean by *them*?'

Her gaze slithered left and right, as though she was worried she might be overheard. 'By the people who put me in here – Dora and Mrs Goodfellow and anyone else who pretended to help me.' She shook her head. 'They used me to steal a lot of money and jewels and other things. I don't – I don't know who to trust any more.'

Oliver started to speak but Harry cut across him. 'You can trust us,' she said quietly, reaching across the table to squeeze Mildred's cold fingers. 'I will do everything in my power to prove your innocence.'

Mildred let out a ragged sigh. 'You believe me then?'

'I believe you,' Harry replied and she meant it. She did not understand how everything fitted together – not yet – but she was determined that she would. And when that happened, she would use what she knew to get Mildred Longstaff released from prison.

Beside her, Oliver was gathering up his papers. 'That concludes our visit,' he said, not unkindly. 'Thank you, Mildred. I'll see you again soon.'

After pushing back his chair, he crossed to the door and rapped once on the metal. There was a disconcerting scraping sound that made Harry wince as the key turned in the lock and the door opened to reveal the same guard as before. 'Finished?' he asked Oliver.

'For now,' Oliver said. 'Until next time, Miss Longstaff.'

As the guard led her away, Mildred turned to call over her shoulder, 'My family – will you tell them you've seen me? They must be so worried.'

'I will,' Harry called back.

Oliver said nothing as they were escorted back to the outer gates and seen through the door within a door to stand on the concrete outside the prison. In fact he did not speak until they were sitting side by side in his car, gazing at the rain that had begun to mist the windscreen. Without looking at Harry, he started the engine and put the car into gear. 'I don't think you've been entirely honest with me, Harriet White,' he said as he reversed carefully backwards and turned the car towards the road. 'You didn't ask me to bring you here out of a philanthropic desire to help a village girl, did you?'

Harry fought the urge to squirm in her seat. There was no way she could deny it – she'd let slip too many things she ought not to have known. 'Not exactly, no.'

He nodded. 'Are you going to explain?'

She didn't want to. At present, no one knew of her efforts as a private detective – she hadn't even told her family about the letters to Sherlock Holmes – and she felt the fewer people who knew, the better. But Oliver was unlikely to let this go unless she gave him some sort of explanation, no matter how mild his expression currently was, and he would see through a lie in a heartbeat. There was also the incontrovertible truth that Mildred's predicament was much bigger than she had realised – Harry could not help her or catch the real culprits alone. Sooner or later, she would need help. Wasn't it better to come clean with Oliver now so that she could call on him again in the future? She sighed. 'Okay, but you must promise not to tell anyone.'

He applied the brake, bringing the car to a stop. 'That depends on what you're about to say. Are you in some way mixed up in the crimes Mildred described?'

'What?' Harry stared at him in dismay. 'Of course not – it's nothing like that.'

He raised his hands. 'Sorry. I had to ask.'

'I'm not sure you did,' Harry grumbled. 'But you must also promise not to laugh at me when I tell you.'

Now it was Oliver's turn to stare. 'Laugh at you? This is a serious case, involving theft, coercion and organised crime – the last thing I expect to do is laugh. But I do confess myself intrigued. What on earth have you been up to?'

'Promise,' Harry demanded.

'Okay, I promise,' he said. 'Now tell me.'

She took a deep calming breath and rehearsed the words in her head, preparing to say them out loud. *I'm working for Sherlock Holmes. I'm secretary to Mr Sherlock Holmes. I'm investigating on behalf of Sherlock Holmes.* It was no good. Every possible permutation sounded utterly ridiculous. Harry shook her head. 'It all began with a letter,' she said slowly. 'Actually, it began with a lot of letters, more than I've ever seen in my life, in fact. But before we get into that, I need to tell you about Simeon Pemberton.'

9

To his credit, Oliver did not laugh. Harry hadn't wanted to relive the moment Mr Pemberton had first advanced on her as she'd been placing some documents for signature on his desk. She spared Oliver most of the detail but the memory of hot, fetid breath on her neck as her employer had loomed behind her had made the windscreen of Oliver's car swim out of focus for a moment. She could still feel the sudden panic as Mr Pemberton's arms had encircled her, the slick warmth of his moist moustache as it swamped her mouth in a clumsy, unwanted kiss. Most of all, she remembered the soft crunch as her knee rose up to drive into his groin, and the agonised howl of pain as he crumpled to the floor.

Harry hadn't waited for him to get up. Stiffly, almost robotically, she'd gathered up the unsigned papers and taken them back to her desk, where she'd continued with her work as though nothing had happened. The next morning, she had found herself reassigned to the post room.

Oliver's expression hardened into fury at her description but he didn't interrupt, not when Harry went on to explain her well-meaning deception of the Longstaffs, nor when she described her visit to Mrs Haverford's, and not even when she revealed the circumstances of her journey to Tea Cutter Row. He listened in attentive silence as he drove her home, refraining from asking even the simplest of questions even though she knew he must be bursting with them. And when she had finished, he didn't speak for several long minutes. 'I don't know whether to congratulate you or have you arrested,' he said at last, shaking his head. 'Secretary to Sherlock Holmes indeed. I'm almost jealous.'

'Don't be,' Harry said. 'You should read some of the things people demand of him. There's at least one work of fiction in them and probably several.'

'I can imagine,' Oliver said dryly. He glanced briefly across at her. 'You know, I'm surprised and somehow not surprised at the same time. I knew there was more to your interest in Mildred Longstaff than you were telling me but I would never in a million years have guessed what it was.'

Harry smiled but something he had said earlier was troubling her. 'You don't really think I'm doing something illegal, do you?'

Oliver considered the question. 'I don't think so, no. You aren't taking payment so you're not obtaining money under false pretences, and you aren't impersonating a real person, or even a fictional one since you've invented your own pen name under which to investigate.' He paused to navigate a tricky junction. 'The bank might take a dim view of things if they ever find out but I don't suppose you're going to tell them and I imagine you've sworn the Longstaffs to secrecy as a condition of investigating.'

She hadn't, Harry realised with a flush of mortification, and made a mental note to rectify that as soon as she was able. 'Mmmm,' she said noncommittally. 'Something like that.'

'It wouldn't stand up in court, of course,' Oliver went on, 'which brings me to an important point. You cannot become officially involved in Mildred's case. Questions would be asked that put both you and her at risk, legally and physically.'

'Oh,' Harry said, her cheeks growing warm at the thought. 'What do you mean?'

'The people who burgled Lord Robertson are not opportunistic thieves,' he said soberly. 'They are organised and they're playing a long game. I think they chose Mildred quite specifically for the job they had in mind and set up her dismissal from the Finchems to facilitate a bigger crime.'

'I think so too,' Harry agreed. 'Clearly, she was chosen for her similarity to the girl I saw in Selfridge's, although I don't totally understand why that matters. Unless – oh!'

He frowned. 'What?'

'It all makes sense,' Harry exclaimed. 'Mildred said Lord Robertson's butler claimed she had been at the house all evening but we know she was actually at the cinema. What if it wasn't Mildred the butler saw but her lookalike?'

Oliver followed her line of reasoning. 'Mildred said it was Dora who gave her the night off. Perhaps the lookalike you saw is the girl Mildred knows as Dora.'

'They must be the same person,' Harry said, clicking her fingers. 'There's enough similarity between Mildred and Dora to fool someone who wasn't looking too closely and we know Dora isn't afraid to break the law. Those shoplifting gangs are as bold as brass.'

'They've been around a long time, in one form or another, although I agree they're getting more ambitious,' Oliver said. 'They dress well, fool the shop assistants into thinking they're ordinary customers and then make off with a fortune in jewellery and furs. I'm surprised the thieves in Selfridges didn't have a fast car waiting to whisk them away.'

If they had, it hadn't been obvious, Harry thought. But although she agreed some of the shoplifters had been well-dressed, Dora had worn a shapeless coat and floppy hat that screamed potential thief.

'She was probably there to distract the guards,' Oliver said when she mentioned the anomaly. 'They're clever, these women. Most of them are members of a gang called the Forty Thieves, also known as the Forty Elephants, because they started life in Elephant and Castle. I've seen plenty of them on trial for their crimes, including the old matriarch, Alice Diamond, and some of what they get up to is worse than their male counterparts.'

'Elephant and Castle again,' Harry observed. 'It can't be a coincidence. You don't think Alice Diamond could be the one behind the Robertson burglary, do you?'

'Not likely. She retired years ago, after a stint in prison. There's a new queen in charge of the gang now but I'm not sure they're the power they once were.'

Harry filed the information away for future consideration. 'Well, someone is definitely pulling the strings,' she replied. 'The whole thing has the feel of a set-up, going right back to the supposed theft of Lady Finchem's bracelet.'

He nodded. 'Planted under Mildred's pillow by a member of the household staff, probably the maid, Polly.'

'Who came from Mrs Haverford's Bureau of Excellence,' Harry finished triumphantly. 'I knew there was something fishy about that place. The girl I chatted to in the waiting room tried to tell me something about working in Mayfair. I wonder if this was what she meant.'

'Impossible to know for sure. But if what you suspect is true and the agency is a front for something more sinister, it sounds as though you had a lucky escape,' Oliver said as he pulled up at the entrance to Harry's apartment. 'Thank goodness you had the presence of mind to use a fake name.'

Harry thought guiltily of the story Mrs Honeywell had told

about being contacted by the agency. 'Mmmm,' she said again, deciding it was probably better Oliver didn't know about that. 'So what do we do now? Should I warn Lady Finchem about Polly? What if she robs her for real next time?'

'Absolutely not.' He fixed her with a stern look. '*You* are not going to do anything. Whoever is pulling Polly's strings must be smart enough to know things are way too hot to try another robbery, so Lady Finchem should be safe enough. But I will think of a way to pass what you've told me over to the police, so that they can pursue further enquiries.'

'But—' Harry began, staring at him in consternation. 'The police won't do anything. As far as they're concerned they've caught the culprit. Mildred will take the blame and the real criminals will get away scot-free.'

'I think you underestimate the fine upstanding members of the Metropolitan Police,' he disagreed. 'They want to see justice done and they've been fighting these criminals a long time. They're not in the business of prosecuting innocent people.'

Harry snorted. 'Come on, Oliver, you're a lawyer. That's exactly what happens sometimes. The police don't have the imagination to see past the ends of their noses.'

'In books, perhaps,' he said mildly. 'But in real life, they're a lot more diligent. We do try not to let the wrong person go to prison, on the whole.'

She had to admit she couldn't imagine someone as conscientious as Oliver letting that happen. 'You might not,' she allowed. 'But I'm not sure other people are so scrupulous.'

'Either way, it doesn't matter,' he said firmly. 'Your involvement ends here, Harry. No more undercover adventures and definitely no more trips to Elephant and Castle. You've taken too many risks already.'

'But the Longstaffs—' she objected.

'I will contact them, let them know I've seen Mildred and she seems well, if understandably upset and confused,' Oliver said. 'I can arrange a family visit, if you think that will set their minds at rest.'

Harry remembered the way the forbidding grey walls had loomed over her and shivered. 'Maybe. It could make things worse.'

'I'll make the offer, at least,' Oliver said. 'But you're going to have to trust me to handle this the right way, Harry. Can you do that?'

She looked at him then, with his serious dark eyes and stern expression, and tried to forget how many times she'd dreamed of sitting this close to him as a teenager, when he'd barely known she was there. She certainly had his attention now, although she could do with a little less severity; he wasn't actually her employer. And now she had been staring at him so long that she struggled to remember what the question had been.

'Um, yes. I trust you, Oliver.'

'Good,' he said. 'Apart from anything else I'd hate to have to explain to Lawrence that I'd let something happen to his little sister.'

Just like that, the spell was broken. For a moment, she'd felt as though Oliver was seeing her as an equal – a partner in solving the crime. Now she realised he had only gone with her today out of a sense of responsibility to her brother. Even worse, he viewed her with the same maddening protectiveness as Lawrence, with no understanding of how stifling that could be. She was a grown woman, perfectly capable of looking after herself. She was not an ornament that needed to be wrapped in cotton wool and kept safe when it was not being admired. Disappointed in him, she reached for the door handle. 'Thanks for taking me to see Mildred. I really appreciate it.'

'You're welcome,' he said.

'And I appreciate you feel a responsibility to Lawrence but I'd rather he didn't know about what happened at the bank.' She paused. 'With Mr Pemberton, I mean.'

Oliver was quiet for a second or two. 'I understand. Although I still think he got off lightly.'

'Perhaps,' Harry said as she got out of the car without waiting for him to come round and open the door. 'But if there's one thing I learned from growing up with three brothers, it's where to place a knee to cause maximum pain.'

He winced. 'I'll let you know if there are any developments in Mildred's case.'

'Please do,' she called over her shoulder, and thrust her key into the lock of the front door. 'Goodbye, Oliver.'

She didn't wait to watch him drive away – the adrenaline from the visit to Holloway was starting to fade and her irritation over Oliver's overbearing attitude was prickling beneath her skin; she was suddenly very tired. It had been an eventful morning and she could still smell the stench of the prison hanging around her. What she wanted was a cup of coffee to pep her up and a long, hot shower, and she didn't much care which order they came in.

* * *

Harry spent the rest of the weekend making notes and jotting down thoughts about possible connections in Mildred's case. She might have promised Oliver she would not undertake any more physical detective work but that didn't mean she had to stop thinking about it. The idea of an all-powerful female gang intrigued Harry, even as the extent of their crimes shocked her, and she wanted to know more.

Late on Monday afternoon, she detoured to the London Library and spent several hours scouring the newspaper archives for stories about the exploits of the Forty Elephants. There were plenty to be found, stretching back decades. At first they had concentrated on theft and blackmail, trading on society's belief that women were the fairer sex and therefore incapable of such audacity. As their confidence grew, they took advantage of the more relaxed attitudes of the 1920s to expand their criminal activities and travel to cities other than London in search of fresh targets.

But Oliver had been right – their reign of terror had faded with the imprisonment of Alice Diamond in 1925. While they were undoubtedly still active, with a new queen stepping up to take Diamond's crown, they no longer appeared to rule London's underworld and Harry couldn't help wondering whether another gang had stepped in to fill the vacuum they had left. One with even more sinister intent...

The second item on her to-do list was to find the advert Mildred had placed in the *Positions Wanted* column of the *Morning Herald* newspaper. It wasn't that she doubted the girl's story, more that she wanted to see exactly how she had worded the advert. Domestic staff very often listed physical characteristics when seeking employment and that might have been the very thing that set Mildred on the path to disaster. Harry had to go back months to find it – the tiny print was blurring in front of her eyes when at last she saw Mildred's name. Squinting at the paper, she forced herself to focus and saw with a whoosh of elation that her suspicions had been correct: Mildred had included her height and hair colour in the advert, as well as mentioning her diligence and ability to work hard, and her home address for contact.

Sitting back, Harry gave herself a mental pat on the back. This was how the criminals had selected their mark. And right in the middle of the page, dwarfing the columns around it, was an advert for Mrs Haverford's Bureau of Excellence. Harry knew it didn't mean anything but the juxtaposition made her frown. She was sure there was more to the employment agency than met the eye.

Perhaps they were simply involved in getting thieves past the front door of wealthy households in order to rob them, but if that was the case, they were very selective in their work. If what Harry suspected about the supposed theft at Lady Finchem's was true, the gang was not averse to a complicated set-up to net a bigger haul at a later date. She could see why some people admired them.

While researching the Forty Elephants, Harry had kept an eye out for old articles about burglaries in Mayfair – she had found no mention of the agency in any of the reports. Whatever Mrs Haverford was about, she was managing to stay under the radar of the authorities and the press.

Weary and hungry, Harry was about to close the last copy of the *Morning Herald* when a name she recognised jumped out at her. It was another advert by a young woman seeking a maid's position – a Beth Chamberlain. Harry stared at it for a moment, unable to believe her luck. She had given up on ever finding the young woman she had met in Mrs Haverford's waiting room – it was clear she could never risk going back there – but it seemed providence had brought Beth to her. Listed at the bottom of the advert was an address in Camden Town.

Carefully, Harry copied the house number and name of the street into her notebook. Oliver had forbidden her from going under cover, and instructed her not to go back to Elephant and Castle, but he had not told her to stop investigating and it was just possible Beth had information that would help Mildred. As soon as Harry was able, she would take a trip to Camden and cross her fingers that Beth was there.

* * *

The telephone in Harry's office was ringing. The sudden shrillness made her jump; the telephone never rang. In fact, she used it so rarely that it was kept on top of the filing cabinet instead of her desk. After staring at it for a few seconds, she got up to lift the receiver. 'Miss White speaking. How may I help?'

There was the sound of a throat being cleared. 'Ah, Miss White. It's Mr Babbage here. Do you think... that is to say, would you mind coming down to the post room? There's a matter we need to discuss.'

Harry's heart thudded. He sounded uncharacteristically formal. 'Of course. Right away?'

'If you can manage it,' he replied. 'I'll get Fergus to put the kettle on.'

This last sentence only increased Harry's unease. She'd had little reason to visit the post room since starting her new position – Bobby delivered any new stationery or equipment she requisitioned – but there had never been any suggestion of refreshments when she had needed to venture into the basement. It must be serious if Mr Babbage was providing tea.

As always, the sounds and smells of the post room overwhelmed her as soon as the service lift opened and the sensory overload only increased as she got nearer the machines and men who kept the bank's business flowing. One or two of them tipped their caps respectfully as she approached, others nodded and a couple stared at her in the same way they always did, as though she was a mythical creature that had appeared from nowhere. Harry picked her way around the edge of the room, avoiding the monstrous machine that whirred and clanked in the centre, and knocked on the door of Mr Babbage's office.

He had not grown any less gnome-like in the months she had known him. His cheeks were ruddy, his beard neat and his waistcoat showed signs of strain around the middle. If he'd been carrying a fishing rod, Harry feared someone might pick him up and plant him beside their garden pond. But the cloth of his waistcoat was not the only thing about him that was tight at that moment – his smile was constricted too. 'Come in. Take a seat.'

Harry did as he asked. A thick brown mug awaited her on the desk, gently steaming, and she knew without asking that Fergus, the post room's youngest member, had made sure he gave her an unchipped cup. She didn't reach for the tea, however. Instead, she folded her hands in her lap and waited for Mr Babbage to sink into the chair opposite her. Then she fixed her employer with an enquiring gaze.

'Well, now,' he said, with an attempt at joviality that did nothing to reassure her. 'How are things in the office of Mr Holmes? Behaving himself, is he?'

She managed a polite smile. 'I have no complaints so far.'

'Good, good,' Mr Babbage said heartily. 'You have everything you need?'

'At present,' Harry responded. She was still waiting for the additional filing cabinet she had requested but it didn't seem like the right time to mention it.

Mr Babbage clapped his hands together and rubbed them. 'Excellent, excellent.' His gaze roamed the room, passing over the smudges of grime on the walls and the tattered papers and posters stuck to them, before returning to Harry. He coughed. 'I'll get to the point, Miss White. It's come to my attention – that is to say it has been *brought* to my attention – that your attitude towards your position here has been somewhat less than professional.'

Harry stared at him, feeling her face start to burn. He couldn't know what she'd been doing. He couldn't. 'I beg your pardon?'

He blinked several times and tried again. 'More specifically, it's been observed that your timekeeping has been lax, Miss White.' Mr Babbage glanced down at the desk in front of him, where a sheet of paper she recognised as an internal memo rested. 'There was an occasion last week when you took an hour and forty-two minutes for lunch.'

So that was it. Harry could have laughed with relief. 'I see. May I ask whether my work is otherwise in any way unsatisfactory?'

Mr Babbage spread his hands. 'How would I know? I don't have two sacks of unanswered letters any more so you must be doing something.' He let out a heavy sigh. 'Perhaps this is my fault – I've left you alone to get on with things too much. But it's so busy down here and you seemed very capable. I thought I could trust you.'

His expression was so wretched that her heart went out to him. She had no doubt who had reported her extended lunch to him, although how Simeon Pemberton had learned about it she couldn't say. He must have one of the doormen spying on her, she thought indignantly. But she couldn't deny that she had been late, which had put Mr Babbage in an awkward situation and for that she was sorry. 'You can trust me. I can't deny the transgression you describe but I assure you it is the only time it has occurred. I am usually very punctual and I'm sorry I wasn't on this occasion.'

'Yes, but even so...' He glanced down at the paper once again and his rosy cheeks became even more florid. 'Was there a good reason for it? Were you unwell, for example?'

She hesitated, her mind racing through the possible answers. There were any number of fabrications she could invent and she was sure he would accept them gladly. But she did not want to lie. 'A friend met me in some distress – a young woman of my acquaintance – on the street outside the bank,' she said, choosing her words with care. 'I took her to a café to comfort her, then returned to work as soon as I was able.'

'Perfectly understandable,' he exclaimed, and she thought he might clap his hands again. 'A most generous and compassionate action on your part. And is the young lady now well?'

Harry pictured Esme Longstaff, who was undoubtedly wracked

with anxiety for her sister's welfare, and crossed her fingers beneath the desk. 'Much better than she was.'

'Capital,' Mr Babbage said, beaming at her. 'I'll make a note that I am satisfied with your explanation and that will do. It is a first offence, after all.'

Feeling her jangling nerves start to settle, Harry reached for the mug and took a long draught. It was good tea, strong and bitter and somehow more restorative when drunk from such a no-nonsense receptacle. 'Thank you, Mr Babbage. I'll make sure it doesn't happen again. Is there anything more?'

Now it was his turn to hesitate. His smile faded as he regarded her. 'Not as such, no. But perhaps a word of warning.' He glanced through the window at the bustle of the main room. 'I don't know the circumstances behind you being sent down here and I'm not sure I want to. But clearly there's more to the story than I've been told. In short, Miss White, someone with power is watching you and it appears he's out for blood. I think you know who I mean.'

It was Mr Pemberton, of course, but Harry knew better than to confirm it. She waited, her eyes fixed on Mr Babbage as he went on. 'We're a tight-knit lot down here and we look out for each other but there's only so much I can do against someone like that.' His troubled gaze met hers. 'Try not to give him the means to hang you.'

Gratitude warmed her heart. Mr Babbage, Bobby and the men of the post room were a world away from the floral scents and hidden sneers of her previous colleagues and for that she was becoming very glad. 'I'll try,' she said quietly. 'Thank you.'

Mr Babbage sat back in his seat. 'That's settled, then,' he said, and flapped a hand. 'Off you go. Give Mr Holmes my regards.'

As Harry made her way back to her office, she settled on two courses of action. One, that she would give Simeon Pemberton absolutely no reason to remark upon her work or punctuality again, and two, she would do everything in her power to find out which doorman had ratted her out. As she was rapidly coming to appreciate, knowledge was power and there might come a time when she was able to turn such information to her advantage. Her conversation with Mr Babbage had made one thing clear: while it was reassuring to know he was in her corner, it was time for Harry to take steps to protect herself. If that meant a little digging around at the bank, so be it.

e deprivation was just as bad. The windows were clean – as far as he could tell under the dim glow of the street lamp – and each oorstep bore clean white edges, as though they had been freshly crubbed and marked with the donkey stone just that evening. These people might be poor but they had standards. She checked her notebook: Beth had given 4 Caroline Street as her address. Harry raised her hand and knocked on the door.

As much as she hoped Beth might be at home, Harry did not expect her to open the front door. The young woman peered out at her, frowning. 'Can I help you?'

Harry concentrated on reproducing Sarah's accent. 'I hope so. Don't suppose you remember me but I was at Mrs Haverford's a few weeks back, looking for work.'

A faint glimmer of recollection dawned on Beth's face. Her frown deepened. 'I do remember, as it happens, but I don't see why you're standing on my doorstep. There's no job here.'

'It's you I came to see,' Harry replied. She glanced over her shoulder. 'Look, it's a bit delicate. Is there somewhere we can go and talk?'

Instantly, Beth scowled in suspicion. 'What about?'

Harry took a breath. She had considered a number of stories to persuade Beth to share what she knew of Mrs Haverford's business and each one had sounded flimsier than the last. Part of the trouble was that she had no idea how loyal Beth was to the shadowy Bureau; in fact, she was risking much based on a whispered half-sentence and a gut feeling she could be trusted. 'About what's going on in Mayfair,' she said, pausing to gauge Beth's reaction. 'I think you know what I mean.'

'I'm sure I don't,' Beth retorted, folding her arms. 'And even if I did, I wouldn't go blabbing about it on the street where anyone could hear me.'

'So invite me in,' Harry urged. 'Tell me what you know.'

10

Harry turned herself into Sarah Smith for her trip to Camden Tow on Thursday evening. Once again, it was not an area of Londo she'd had reason to frequent, but she'd heard of the market and knew it was a place of considerable poverty. Much the same as Elephant and Castle, the junction outside the Underground station was bustling and congested, despite the later hour. Buses jostled with lorries and cars; a horse and cart was slowing everything down and a policeman was trying to hurry the driver along. Mindful of her near miss with the bus on Oxford Street, Harry took extra care in making her way across the roads; her mother would be mortified if she were run over in such unfathomable clothing. But she made it to Caroline Street without risk to life and limb, although there were some suggestive comments from a drunk man as she passed the Mother Red Cap public house that made her grit her teeth.

The dull grind of traffic faded as she got further away from the junction, although she could still hear the sharp blare of horns. Caroline Street was narrow, one of several back-to-back roads packed with dingy houses, although Harry felt more domestic pride was shown by those who lived there than in Tea Cutter Row, even if

Still the younger woman looked unconvinced. 'What's it to you?'

This was it, Harry sensed. Whatever she said now would determine whether Beth invited her inside or slammed the door in her face. 'The first time we met, I told you I was looking for a friend who'd been accused of stealing. Do you remember?'

Beth's gaze narrowed. 'I remember.'

'You asked if she'd been working in Mayfair,' Harry went on. 'And then you warned me about working in the fancy houses round there.'

'Did I?' Beth said carelessly, but Harry caught a gleam in her eye that told her the girl knew where the conversation was going. 'Can't think why.'

Harry ignored that. 'My friend's name is Mildred Longstaff. She's currently in Holloway Prison, awaiting trial for the robbery of Lord Robertson.'

The door moved fast but Harry was faster. She stuck her foot into the gap, wincing a little at the impact but grateful for Sarah's no-nonsense boots. 'She didn't do it, Beth. Someone set her up and I mean to find out who.'

'You're mad.' The other woman shook her head.

Harry couldn't really argue with that – there was a small part of her that was wondering whether she had taken leave of her senses. 'Probably. But I'm going to find out all the same.' She fixed Beth with a frank stare. 'Because this time it was Mildred who caught the blame, but next time it might be you or me or any of a hundred other innocent women and girls who work in the city. And I don't think any of us want to go to prison.'

Beth hesitated as though torn. Her gaze bore into Harry until finally she sighed. 'Wait here,' she said, making to close the door again.

Harry wedged her foot more firmly in the gap. 'Not a chance. How do I know you'll come back?'

Beth smiled. 'You'll just have to trust me, won't you? Like I'm trusting you.'

There wasn't much Harry could do, short of forcing her way inside the house and she wasn't about to try that. Reluctantly, she pulled her foot free and allowed the door to close. Minutes ticked by. Harry waited, listening to the distant rumble of the traffic and wondering if Beth was even now sending a message that would summon the criminals behind the Robertson burglary. But then the door opened and Beth appeared again, wearing a hat and coat and what looked suspiciously like lipstick. 'Look lively, then.'

'Are – are you inviting me in?' Harry asked in confusion.

Beth rolled her eyes. 'Not unless you want the whole conversation to be overheard by my mother and three younger sisters.'

'Then where are we going?'

'The pub,' she said, and grinned at Harry's startled expression. 'Don't worry, they know me in there. No one will mistake us for prostitutes.'

'Oh good,' Harry replied faintly. On the rare occasion she went out drinking in London, she met friends for cocktails in chic hotel bars. But she was not Harry White now, she reminded herself. Sarah Smith could certainly visit a public house. 'How far is it?'

Beth stepped onto the street, closing the front door behind her. 'You probably passed it on the way here. The Old Mother Red Cap, opposite the station.'

She should have guessed, Harry thought, her heart sinking as she hurried to catch up with Beth. With a bit of luck, the drunk she had encountered on her way to Caroline Street would be long gone.

The saloon bar was less dingy than Harry expected but the air was still thick with smoke, tempered by the sweet smell of hops. A bar lined the back wall, with shelves lined with stacks of Woodbine cigarettes and bottles that reflected in mirrored glass behind them.

Yellowish china pump handles stood tall above the polished wood of the bar itself, presided over by a burly man who looked to Harry as though he was one impertinent comment away from a good brawl. Sawdust covered the floor, to soak up spilled beer, she supposed, and tables had been dotted here and there, with chairs and benches that were mostly occupied. Other drinkers were standing in clusters, men in caps with scarves knotted around their necks and a pint pot in their hands; the buzz of conversation was constant, interrupted every now and then by a burst of laughter or loud exclamation.

It didn't seem like the kind of place women would be drawn to and yet, to Harry's mild surprise, she and Beth were not the only ones; she guessed that perhaps a third of the drinkers were female, mostly middle-aged or older. Several of the men looked across as Beth and Harry entered, one or two nodded in greeting as they edged inside, but there was no repeat of the raucous comments Harry had endured earlier. At least, not yet.

'There's a table over there,' Beth said, craning her head over the crowd. Employing a judicious elbow here and there, she cut her way towards the corner. Harry followed and couldn't prevent an involuntary flinch at the rough wooden seats surrounding the sticky-looking table. The reaction did not escape Beth's notice. 'Sorry, were you expecting a cushion? You won't get no airs and graces in here – this is a drinker's pub.'

'I can tell,' Harry said, looking around her. Now that she was adjusting to the environment, she was beginning to appreciate the novelty of being somewhere so different from her usual world. Her brothers would not approve of what she was doing, although for wildly differing reasons. Lawrence would be concerned about her reputation and would insist that she hurried along home, Sebastian would show some initial amusement that would eventually be replaced by caution, and Rufus would ask her to buy him a drink before borrowing whatever cash she had and abandoning her to join the house gambling ring.

Beth grinned at Harry. 'Speaking of drinks, I'll have a pint of mild, thanks.'

Harry supposed that was only fair, since she was the one who had caused Beth to go out. Edging her way through the crowd, she delved into the pocket of her skirts and withdrew a handful of coins, inspecting it anxiously. She hadn't brought much money, mindful of the fact that Sarah Smith was meant to be poor, but now she was concerned she wouldn't have enough to buy Beth's drink and get the Underground back home. But the prices chalked above the bar were mercifully cheap, some way short of those Harry would expect to pay in a hotel bar. She bought two pints and carried them back to the table.

Beth took a healthy draught of beer and smacked her lips together. 'So, Sarah Smith, how did you know where to find me?'

The question wasn't unexpected. Harry had dismissed the idea of claiming George Newlyn had told her as a lie too easily disproven. Once again, she told the truth. 'From the newspaper. I was looking for information about Mildred, trying to work out how she came to be in such a mess, and I saw your advert.'

The young woman raised her eyebrows. 'Quite the little detective, ain't we?' she said, although Harry thought she sounded slightly impressed. 'So what is it you want from me?'

She leaned forwards. 'Something is rotten in Mayfair, maybe even in the whole of London. What do you think it is?'

'You don't need me to tell you about that,' Beth said, shrugging. 'Thieving isn't a new thing.'

'No, but this is different,' Harry said. 'The thieves didn't just break in when the house was empty, they put someone on the inside.'

'Your friend,' Beth pointed out. 'Maybe she's not as lily-white as you think.'

'Or maybe someone has gone to a lot of trouble to make it look that way,' Harry argued. She paused, wondering how much to trust Beth. 'Like I said, next time it could be you or me or even one of your sisters. None of us is safe.'

Beth was quiet for a moment. 'All right. What do you want to know?'

Harry marshalled her thoughts. Beth had already told her she didn't know Mildred, which wasn't a surprise given Mildred had said she'd never visited Mrs Haverford's Bureau. But Polly was another matter. 'There was another maid at the first house Mildred worked in – a girl called Polly. Do you know her?'

Beth's forehead crinkled. 'I know a few Pollys. Got a description?'

Harry cast her mind back to her visit to Lady Finchem. The maid had not made a strong impression and it was only afterwards that her interest had been aroused. 'Small,' she said vaguely. 'A bit mousy, in looks and in personality.'

'Could be any of them,' Beth snorted dismissively. 'But I think I know the one you mean. Works for some old politician, right?'

It couldn't be a coincidence, Harry thought. 'That's right. Friend of yours, is she?'

'Nah. I've seen her at the agency from time to time, that's all. Not since she got that job, mind you.'

Harry tucked the information away. She'd known from Dobbins that there was a link between Mrs Haverford and the Finchems but it was satisfying to have it confirmed. 'I thought she might have seen something that could help Mildred.'

Beth gave her a shrewd look. 'Leave off. You think she's in on it.'

There was no use in denying it: Beth was sharper than a dressmaker's needle. 'Possibly,' Harry conceded. 'Someone must have planted the stolen bracelet under Mildred's pillow and they did share a room.'

'No idea,' Beth sniffed. 'It wouldn't surprise me, though. She's from south of the river. Some very light-fingered families in those parts.'

'South of the river?' Harry echoed.

The other woman tipped her head. 'Southwark, Camberwell, somewhere like that. A thieves' paradise, my old dad calls it, although he says the East End is worse. Steal the shirt off your back without you even noticing in Bethnal Green, he reckons.'

Harry was only half listening. 'Could it be Elephant and Castle Polly comes from?'

Once again, the look Beth fired her way was sharp. 'Could be. I see you've been reading more than just the *Positions Wanted* column in the newspaper. You think the Forty Elephants are behind that robbery.'

'It makes sense,' Harry said. She scanned Beth's face and decided to take a risk. 'Think about it. Mrs Haverford finds staff for a lot of wealthy families. What if someone at the agency is part of the gang? They pick a house, put someone on the inside and then set up one of the other domestics to take the blame.'

'The police would catch on,' Beth scoffed.

'Only if they heard about it,' Harry argued as another thought occurred to her. 'Jewellery's not the only thing worth money in houses like that.'

'Blackmail, you mean?' Beth considered this fresh suggestion, her eyes never leaving Harry. 'I go to Mrs Haverford's,' she said at length. 'How do you know I'm not one of them?'

Harry puffed out a long breath. 'I don't.'

The other woman lapsed into thoughtful silence. Noticing the full pint on the table in front of her, Harry raised her glass, caught a whiff of it and hastily lowered it again. She had no idea what went into a pint of mild and she had no interest in finding out. Carefully, she glanced around the bar to see if anyone was paying attention but Beth had been true to her word; as far as Harry could tell, no one had even noticed them.

'You might be right,' Beth said, stirring to reach for her own drink. 'There's a few domestics that get work through the agency that shouldn't – lazy or downright nasty types you wouldn't trust with tuppence, let alone the silverware. I've always wondered why Mrs Haverford puts up with them but maybe there's a good reason she does.'

'Do you know where Polly lives?' Harry asked, hoping she might be able to track the girl down but Beth shook her head.

'Can't help you there,' she said, and drained her glass with a speed that caused Harry's jaw to drop. 'But her surname is Spender.'

It wasn't much but it was more than she'd known before. 'Thank you,' Harry said. 'I really appreciate you talking to me.'

'Don't mention it,' Beth replied. She eyed Harry's untouched drink. 'You going to finish that?'

Harry got to her feet. 'No. It's all yours.'

Beth grinned. 'You can come again, Sarah Smith.' She slid the drink across the wood until it sat in front of her. 'A word of warning, though. That toffee-nosed accent of yours creeps through every now and then. You should work on that before you do any more snooping.'

Dismay twisted in Harry's stomach. 'I don't know what you mean. I'm from Poplar.'

'And I'm from Buckingham Palace,' Beth said with a cackle. She looked up at Harry and her gaze softened. 'All I'm saying is have a care for your safety. There are dangerous people around. People who don't like the kind of questions you're asking. If you're going to pretend to be one of us, do it better.'

The words sent a shiver down Harry's spine. 'I will. Thanks.'

With a final nod, Beth turned her attention to her drink and Harry knew she was dismissed. Outside the pub, she took a deep breath of the cool night air, blessedly free from cigarette smoke, and reviewed her evening's work. It had been a risk coming to Camden Town but she was certain it had been worth it. All she had to do now was ensure Oliver never found out.

11

It was with some trepidation that Harry took the train to Abinger Hall on Saturday morning. Her mother had telephoned on Friday to inform her of a dinner party and had made it very clear that it was not a request Harry was expected to decline. 'Sebastian is coming back, and Lawrence. If they can tear themselves away from London then I'm sure you can too.'

Being summoned home was not the issue, although Harry had planned to spend the weekend considering her next investigative move. Her mother was not, by and large, especially demanding of her children and the truth was it had been some time since Harry, Seb and Lawrence had all been there at the same time. She loved being at home when her brothers were there; it reminded her of the golden summers of their youth when they'd conspired to escape the nanny and play hide-and-seek in the woods around the estate. But there was no getting away now and the mere thought of a dinner party dampened Harry's spirits.

Children had been banished from dinner parties when she'd been young and she'd loved sneaking out of bed to spy through the bannisters at the glamorous visitors as they arrived. That was when she'd first seen Baroness Campbell von Laurentz, and she'd been astounded to see her driving her very own Rolls-Royce. Today's guests would have no such appeal. They would probably be friends of her grandfather or father; she would have to make small talk and listen to endless stories about topics she cared nothing about, when what she really wanted to do was catch up with her brothers in the comfort of the library, with a dog on her lap and a glass of really good port in her hand.

But her heart really plummeted when she walked into the vast hallway and learned from her mother who the weekend guests were. 'Lord and Lady Finchem,' Evelyn said, in answer to her question. 'And their sons, of course. I understand from Phyllida that you didn't meet either of them during your visit to her so now is your chance.'

Beside Harry, Seb covered a smile. 'Lucky you, Sis.'

Evelyn turned a severe expression upon him. 'I've also invited the Goldsworthys, with their two girls. You could do a lot worse than charm one of them up the aisle.'

Sebastian sighed. 'I can certainly charm them, Mama, but the chances of me marrying either are slim to none.'

'Never say never,' Evelyn said encouragingly. 'And don't look like that, Harriet. If either of you showed the least care for your futures, I wouldn't have to go to all this trouble.'

Harry and Seb exchanged a look. This was a well-worn topic of conversation and neither had any inclination to suffer it again. Thankfully, the sound of an engine outside caught their mother's attention. 'Ah, that will be Lawrence and Oliver, I expect.'

Harry froze. 'Oliver? As in Oliver Fortescue?'

'Of course,' her mother said. 'How many other Olivers do we know?'

'Several,' Seb put in mildly. 'It's quite a common name.'

Evelyn tutted. 'Don't be so rude. There's nothing common about

Oliver.' She made for the door, shadowed by a silent Chesterton. 'You can both say hello, then make yourselves presentable. Our guests will be arriving soon and I want you both to make a good impression.'

Seb nudged Harry. 'Oliver Fortescue. Looks like it really is your lucky day.'

Harry felt her cheeks grow warm but she said nothing. She'd had one unsatisfactory update from Oliver since their visit to Holloway – he'd written to confirm he had been in touch with Mildred's family, and he was awaiting a trial date but that was all. Perhaps it wasn't such a bad thing that he was at Abinger this weekend. It might give her an opportunity to find out if there was any progress.

Conscious of Seb's eagle-eyed attention, Harry had to remind herself not to stare as Oliver entered the hall. Half a head taller than Lawrence and utterly at ease in the grandeur of Abinger, she watched him bend to kiss her mother's cheek, smiling at something she had said, and was instantly seventeen years old again. When she had seen him in London, it had felt like neutral territory but here she seemed to have been ambushed by a jumble of emotions she hadn't felt for years. He straightened up and saw her. She nodded warily, hoping her face wasn't glowing the way she imagined, and he nodded back. And then Lawrence was sweeping her into a hug. 'And how's my favourite sister? You look as wonderful as ever, all rosy-cheeked charm and mischievous twinkle.'

'You make me sound like a Christmas ornament,' she grumbled indistinctly, her face somewhat squashed into his overcoat.

'Could be worse.' Releasing her, Lawrence tossed a glance over one shoulder. 'You remember Oliver Fortescue, don't you? My old university pal.'

Grinning widely, Seb opened his mouth to reply but Harry beat him to it. 'Of course. I didn't realise he was joining us.'

Her eldest brother raised his sandy eyebrows. 'He wasn't. But we're members of the same club. I ran into him yesterday, mentioned I was coming down here for Mama's blasted dinner party, and he suggested joining me.'

A frown began to dig into Harry's forehead and she forced herself to look unconcerned. Had Oliver invited himself before or after discovering Lady Finchem would be at Abinger Hall? Surely he wouldn't come all the way here to make sure Harry didn't raise the subject of Mildred. 'Did he?' she said with a faint smile. 'How splendid.'

Once again, she felt Seb was about to interject but this time she was saved by Oliver himself. 'Seb, you old rascal,' he said, extending a hand to shake. 'It's been too long.'

'I should say,' Seb replied. 'Last December, wasn't it? One of Mama's festive shindigs.'

'Probably,' Oliver agreed. 'I have a hazy recollection of some excellent cheese and rather too much champagne.'

'I'm not sure it's actually possible to have too much champagne,' Seb said. 'But here I am waffling away when Harry is simply burning to say hello.'

He turned an impish gaze her way and she returned it with narrowed eyes that told him she would deal with him later. 'Ah, Harry,' Oliver said. 'I hope you're well?'

'I am, thank you,' she said, matching his formal tone. 'Although I confess I'm a little surprised to see you. What brings you to Abinger this weekend?'

He knew what she was getting at, she was sure, but he did not take the bait. 'Lawrence mentioned a family party and I couldn't resist gatecrashing.'

Evelyn appeared at his side. 'None of that, Oliver. As far as I'm concerned, you are family. Lawrence, why don't you show Oliver to his room? The rest of you can hurry along too – Chesterton will organise your bags. The Finchems will be here at any moment and I'd rather the hallway didn't resemble Paddington station when they arrive.'

Harry's eyes flashed to Oliver's at the mention of the Finchems but he was following Lawrence towards the grand staircase and seemed not to have heard. She still wasn't sure how his unexpected presence made her feel. On one hand, it gave her an opportunity to grill him about developments in Mildred's case but, on the other, she didn't like the idea of him breathing down her neck every time she so much as blinked near Lady Finchem. And then there was the matter of her brother's relentless teasing. She would have to speak to him about that.

In other circumstances, Harry would have made an excuse to avoid joining their guests for welcome drinks in the drawing room but she suspected Oliver might do exactly that, which might give her the chance to approach Lady Finchem. She had no idea how she would raise the subject of Polly Spender without incurring the wrath of her mother but she hoped an opportunity would present itself. Unfortunately, it seemed Oliver had anticipated her intentions: when Harry entered the drawing room, he was already there, standing beside the fireplace with a glass in his hand, deep in conversation with her father. Swallowing a disgruntled sigh, she started towards the drinks trolley. If she was going to be bored, she may as well do it with a gin and tonic to numb the pain.

Almost immediately, Evelyn was at her side and steering her towards the window. 'Harry, darling, do come and say hello to the Finchems.'

'Can I at least get a drink first?' Harry asked plaintively.

'Your father will mix you one. You know how much he enjoys playing bartender,' her mother said and Harry knew better than to argue.

Phyllida Finchem was sitting in an armchair in the bay window that looked out across the lake. Three men stood near her. One was older, bearded and grey at the temples, and she assumed this was Lord Finchem. The other two were younger, both dark haired and good-looking; Harry guessed they were somewhere between twenty and twenty-five. These must be the sons her mother was so desperate for her to meet. Lady Finchem rose graciously as Evelyn and Harry approached. 'Miss White,' she said. 'How charming to meet you again.'

'And you,' Harry replied. 'I trust you are well?'

'Tolerably so,' Lady Finchem replied. 'Allow me to introduce you to my husband, Lord Finchem. Henry, this is Miss White, Baron Abinger's granddaughter.'

The grey-haired man nodded. 'How do you do?'

'Very well, thank you,' Harry said. 'I hope you had a good journey.'

'Awful, to be perfectly honest. The roads were dreadful and my driver seems to have forgotten what the accelerator was for.' Lord Finchem glared at her as though she were personally responsible for the traffic. 'Still, we're here now.'

Harry smiled politely. 'You are indeed and we are very glad to have you.' She turned to her mother, who was hovering at her elbow. 'Did you mention a drink? Gin would be lovely.'

As Evelyn left her, Harry risked a glance across at Oliver. He was now talking to her uncle, since her father was busy mixing drinks, but she could see his gaze flicking towards her every now and then. She turned to Lady Finchem once more. 'Won't you introduce me to your sons?'

Perhaps it was her mother's constant match-making efforts but Harry always felt the dragging weight of expectation when meeting eligible men of around her own age and, from the slightly pained smiles of James and Percy Finchem when they were introduced, she guessed they felt the same. James was the elder, although Harry doubted there was more than a year or two in it. He took her hand and kissed it, a gesture that was so extravagantly suave it took all Harry's self-composure not to laugh. 'How charming to meet you, Miss White. I've heard so much about you.'

'And I you,' she replied, omitting to add that most of what she had heard concerned his future income. 'Such a pleasure to meet you at last.'

He smiled. 'And may I say, the reports of your beauty don't do you justice. I'm quite captivated.'

His brother groaned. 'Don't mind James. He thinks he's the hero in a Jane Austen novel.' He held out a hand. 'I'm Percy. Pleased to meet you.'

And now Harry did laugh. 'Lovely to meet you too, Percy.'

She was spared from any further displays of sibling rivalry by the arrival of her mother with a tall gin and tonic. 'Here you are, Harry. Now, I must just go and attend to the Goldsworthys.'

She bustled off, leaving Harry once more with the Finchems. James was regarding her curiously. 'Are you really called Harry or is it a nickname?'

'My birth name is Harriet but everyone calls me Harry,' she explained, and took a long sip of her drink. 'Are you always James or might your friends dare to call you Jim?'

Lady Finchem made a faintly horrified sound. 'We do not abbreviate our names as a rule.'

Percy sighed. 'I can't help wishing you'd gone for the longer version of mine, though. Percival sounds terribly noble, don't you think, Harry?'

'Quite Arthurian,' she agreed, and turned to James. 'Whereas yours is more royal.'

A movement by the fireplace caught her eye. It appeared Oliver had concluded his conversation with Uncle Tobias and had now turned to watch the scene in the window. Suspecting he would come over in a moment, Harry fixed Lady Finchem with a puzzled look. 'I do believe your housemaid had an unusual name. What was it now – something Shakespearean, I think. Paulina?'

There was a frozen silence. 'Are you referring to Polly?' the older woman replied at last, her tone dripping with disapproval. 'I hardly think that is a name worthy of Shakespeare.'

'Oh, yes,' Harry exclaimed with a tinkling laugh. 'How silly of me – of course it was Polly. Just like in the nursery rhyme.'

Percy shook his head. 'Polly doesn't put the kettle on any more,' he said. 'She left a few weeks ago.'

The revelation was so unexpected that it almost made Harry choke on her gin. Hastily, she covered her mouth, arranging her features into an expression of polite sympathy. 'How inconvenient. I do hope your housekeeper has been able to find a replacement?'

But whether she had or hadn't was overshadowed by Oliver's jovial greetings. He shook Lord Finchem's hand, then those of his sons, and Harry was entirely unsurprised to note he seemed to be well acquainted with the family. 'Has Harry been keeping you entertained?' he asked.

'She certainly entertains me,' James said, with an admiring glance that almost made Harry blush.

'See?' Percy complained in mock-embarrassment. 'I can't take him anywhere.'

On another occasion, Harry might have been tempted to flirt back but her mind was too busy unravelling the Finchem household gossip. So Polly no longer worked for them... Had she served her purpose there and been moved on by Mrs Haverford? she wondered. Or was there another reason for her sudden departure? But she could hardly ask with Oliver looming over her. She would just have to wait for another opportunity to find out more.

'Will the baron be joining us?' Lord Finchem asked loudly. 'I've got some important parliamentary matters to discuss with him.'

'And I would like to speak with the baroness,' Lady Finchem added. 'They're seen so rarely in London these days. Are they both well?'

Harry thought of her grandparents, both in their early eighties and showing no signs of slowing down. It was true that they were not regular visitors to London, however; Baron Abinger attended the House of Lords when duty required but had long since delegated the family's society obligations to Harry's father. 'If old age is good for anything, it's not having to suffer fools prattling on about nothing,' he had declared on more than one occasion.

Baroness Abinger was more gracious in company but was kept busy by her charitable endeavours. She was content to let her daughter-in-law fly the Abinger flag in London, which Evelyn did with enthusiasm. Harry had sought each of her grandparents out not long after arriving at the hall that morning, only to learn from their housekeeper, Mrs Pilbeam, that her grandfather had gone clay pigeon shooting on the west side of the estate. When she'd remarked upon his absence to Seb, he'd smirked. 'Grandpapa's no fool. He can't stand Henry Finchem, says he's a dreadful old bore.'

She'd had better luck with her grandmother, whom she had found in the cluttered but cosy room the baroness used as a study. 'It's always lovely to see you, Harry,' she had said, barely glancing up from her desk. 'But I simply must finish these letters. Be a dear and tell your mother I'll see our guests at dinner.'

In answer to Lady Finchem's nosiness, Harry adopted a diplomatic smile. 'They are both very well, thank you, but unfortunately taken up with unavoidable estate business at the moment. I'm sure you will see them this evening.'

'Where's Rufus?' Percy asked suddenly. 'He's always good fun. I rather hoped he'd be here.'

It was a good question, Harry thought, glancing around the room. Where was her youngest brother? Lawrence was sitting on the arm of the sofa beside Sebastian, chatting amiably with the Goldsworthy girls. Her mother was deep in conversation with Mrs Goldsworthy and her father was mixing Mr Goldsworthy another whisky. How had Rufus managed to wriggle out of their mother's summons? 'I have absolutely no idea,' Harry said truthfully. 'Are you friends?'

She'd appraised her original opinion of Percy's age as they'd been talking and now estimated him to be older than she'd thought – nearer her age than her youngest brother's. But perhaps they had attended the same school, although Percy must have been several years above. 'Acquaintances more than friends, I'd say,' Percy explained. 'He was quite the character at school. Never a dull moment when Rufus was around.'

'The boy needs a purpose,' Lord Finchem rumbled. 'Like Fortescue here. No chance of him scandalising the neighbourhood with brawls and other damnable behaviour.'

Harry stiffened at his evident disapproval. 'I know Rufus is a little wayward but I hardly think—'

'Wayward,' Lord Finchem repeated incredulously. 'He was arrested for being drunk and disorderly in Piccadilly last week. Fortescue had to smooth things out.' He rounded on Oliver. 'Didn't you? Come on, man, speak up.'

It was news to Harry. She gazed at Oliver in consternation. 'Did you?'

'It was all a misunderstanding,' he said soothingly. 'Youthful high spirits. No charges were brought.'

'All the same—' Harry began, wondering why no one had thought to mention it to her. Being arrested was no small thing.

'It was nothing,' Oliver reassured her. 'He'd got in with an excitable crowd – that's all. No harm done.'

Not this time, Harry wanted to say, but she was aware that Lady

Finchem once again seemed to be radiating ice. 'I'm glad you were on hand to help,' she said to Oliver. 'Thank you.'

'Indeed,' Lady Finchem observed, eyeing Oliver as though he was somehow mixed up in Rufus's disgrace. 'So useful to have friends in the legal business to call upon in times of need.'

Harry had heard enough. 'Will you excuse me?' she said, summoning up a smile that she hoped was less brittle than she felt. 'I've just remembered something I need to discuss with Mama.'

Without waiting for a reply, she went to stand near her mother, who was regaling Mrs Goldsworthy with an apparently hilarious story about a mutual acquaintance. For the sake of form, Harry loitered for five minutes, nodding and smiling in the right places while Lord Finchem's accusations whirled round and round her head. The moment she felt she could slip unnoticed from the room, she made good her escape. Briefly, she contemplated hurrying from the hall and running all the way to the woods, the way she had as a child, but the sun was beginning to dip below the horizon. Perhaps a lie-down in the silence of her bedroom would help.

She was halfway up the stairs when she heard Oliver call her name from below. Glancing down, she saw with mild exasperation that he was following her. 'What is it?' she asked as he started up the stairs. 'I've got a headache.'

'I wanted to make sure you weren't upset by that rubbish about Rufus,' Oliver said once he was nearer. 'He was never in any danger of being charged, you know.'

Harry rubbed her temples wearily. It hadn't been a lie – she did have the start of a headache and she suspected it was about to get worse. 'But he was drunk?'

Oliver pursed his lips as he considered the question. 'He'd probably had more than he should. But it was the others he was with who were the instigators. They tried to climb up the statue of Eros in Piccadilly Circus but ran for it when a policeman caught them. Rufus didn't run fast enough, unfortunately.'

She couldn't deny it sounded very much like her little brother. 'He's lucky you were able to sort everything out.'

He shook his head. 'They knew they didn't have enough to show the magistrate. At worst, they'd have let him sleep it off in a cell overnight.'

'A cell!' The thought made Harry's stomach clench. 'I didn't even know he was in London. Where had he been?'

'One of the new nightclubs in Soho,' Oliver said. 'But don't beat yourself up – your brothers had no idea he was in town, either, until I turned up at Lawrence's apartment with a very chastened Rufus in tow.'

'That doesn't make me feel any better,' she said, sighing. 'How did Lord Finchem find out? I don't imagine he was one of the revellers.'

'No, but Percy Finchem was in the crowd – he saw everything.' Oliver shook his head. 'Watch yourself around those two. They're not quite what they pretend to be.'

If Harry's head hadn't been thumping, she might have asked what he meant by that but all she wanted now was the quiet of her room. 'Well, I hope the experience scared him into behaving better. I bet Mama was livid when she found out.'

Oliver grimaced. 'So I believe. That's why he's not here this weekend; she's packed him off to your great-uncle in Scotland to contemplate his actions.'

The thought almost made Harry smile. Great-Uncle Douglas lived in a ramshackle castle in the heart of the Highlands. There was no danger of Rufus running afoul of the law there, unless he took up poaching. 'Rather him than me,' she said.

'Absolutely,' Oliver agreed, then fixed her with a direct look. 'So what was all that about Lady Finchem's household staff? I hope you haven't been digging around.'

'Of course not,' Harry said, raising her chin. 'Well, maybe a bit but it was worth it.' She glanced at the empty hall below and lowered her voice. 'Polly doesn't work there any more. Don't you think that's odd?'

He frowned. 'Maids move on all the time. I expect there's a perfectly good explanation.'

'Or perhaps she's done what she went there to do,' Harry suggested. 'Which was to set Mildred up for the considerably more substantial Lord Robertson job.'

'We cannot know that,' Oliver said flatly. 'Anyone could have planted the bracelet.'

'But Polly is the most likely suspect,' Harry insisted, wishing she could share what she'd learned from Beth. 'You have to admit it's suspicious that she's left the Finchem household.'

Oliver gave her an impatient look. 'No, I don't. I hope you're not planning to interrogate Lady Finchem about this, Harry. I thought we'd agreed to leave Mildred's case to the police.'

She threw up her hands in frustration. 'Can you at least tell me what's happening, then? Have they found any evidence that she's telling the truth?'

'No,' Oliver admitted. 'Like us, they suspect an organised gang but if it is the Forty Elephants, they've covered their tracks well.'

Again, Harry thought of Beth's observations about Polly's family and their roots in South London. It couldn't be a coincidence but, as Oliver had pointed out, there was no concrete evidence. And Polly's disappearance made it more difficult for Harry to prove the connection. 'So what happens next?'

'I'm in contact with the detectives working on the case,' he said. 'We'll have to wait for them to make a breakthrough. And in the meantime, I'm optimistic Mildred will give a good account of herself at trial. She's polite, well-mannered, and of previous good character, aside from the Finchem matter. I think a jury will like her.'

The idea of poor Mildred having to explain herself in the dock made Harry shiver. 'It can't come to that. We have to find out the truth before then.'

'No, Harry,' Oliver said, his expression darkening. 'I told you before, this isn't something you should be involved with.'

'Why?' Harry exclaimed with a flash of irritation. 'Because I'm a woman? I can look after myself, believe it or not.'

He exhaled sharply. 'You have no idea what kind of people you're dealing with.'

'I'm not afraid,' she snapped, folding her arms.

'Then you should be,' he whipped back. 'Gangs like these aren't afraid to use force to protect themselves. If you cross the wrong person, it won't be just your job you lose. It could be your life.'

The vehemence in his voice made her pause. 'You're trying to scare me.'

'Because you're not listening!' Running a hand through his hair, he softened his voice. 'As I said when we left Holloway, I don't want anything to happen to you.'

'Because you still see me as Lawrence's kid sister when I'm so much more now,' she argued, but even as she spoke, Beth's warning echoed in her head. *Have a care for your safety. There are dangerous people around.* 'And I'm getting better at disguises.'

'You need to let this go, Harry,' Oliver said, as though she hadn't spoken. 'You're not R. K. Moss, or whatever made-up name you came up with, and you aren't working for Sherlock Holmes. This isn't a game.'

The insinuation that she was playing at detective work caused her temper to flare even more. 'Is that why you came down here? To make sure I was being a good girl and doing as I was told?'

He sighed. 'No, I came to see you and your family, because I like being here. Nothing more sinister than that.'

His words took the wind out of her sails. 'Oh.'

'I'm not trying to oppress you, Harry,' he went on. 'I'm trying to keep you safe.'

Deep down, she knew it was true but it didn't make her feel any less patronised. 'Well, I'm glad you came, even if you are being an insufferable prig.' She eyed him reproachfully. 'I do understand how serious this is, you know. An innocent girl's future is at stake.'

'I know,' he said. 'Look, I appreciate you're trying to help and I'm very glad you brought Mildred's situation to my attention. But it really would be best to leave things to the professionals now.'

By which he meant men, Harry thought, but there was nothing to be gained by losing her temper again. Instead, she began to climb the stairs once more. 'I'm going for a nap. See you at dinner.'

Harry lay on her bed for what felt like an age, the conversation spinning in her head, mingling with everything she had learned so far. Oliver's dismissiveness irked her more than anything, even though she knew it was born from concern for her wellbeing. But she had made the link to Mrs Haverford's Bureau and she had uncovered the similarity between Mildred and Dora that was at the heart of the case, details she instinctively felt to be important. And she couldn't shake the feeling that the police did not appear to be trying very hard – if they had made even a modicum of progress, she might have felt more confident in leaving matters to them. But there was no fresh evidence, no hope that Mildred might be proved innocent, and that meant Harry could not do as Oliver demanded. As she had told him, a young girl's future hung in the balance and Harry could not stand by and let her take the blame.

After tossing and turning for a few more minutes, she huffily gave up on sleep. It galled her to admit it but Oliver had not been wrong about everything – she could not risk directly investigating the crime. Her family would be mortified, for a start, and their embarrassment would only be the start of Harry's problems; she would most likely find herself banished to Scotland to keep Rufus company. But it did not follow that she could not investigate at all, however; she simply needed to be cleverer, which meant following in the footsteps of Holmes and expanding her repertoire of disguises. Luckily for her, she had an almost endless supply of costumes at her disposal.

Leaving her room and making as though she was going for a bracing walk, Harry doubled back to the barn where the sacks of old clothes were waiting to be redistributed through her grandmother's charity. She began to sort through the clothing, her mind abuzz with possibilities. Sarah Smith needed a different coat and hat, but not fresh boots, and perhaps there were some black items she could wear when she needed to blend into the shadows. Harry contemplated a pair of men's trousers thoughtfully; with a belt they might stay up and they were certainly more practical than skirts, although her mother would faint clean away at the mere suggestion.

Mindful of the time, Harry made her selections and arranged the sacks exactly as they had been before. The hardest thing was going to be smuggling her finds back to London without anyone noticing – Oliver, in particular, would be watching her closely and might pick up on an overstuffed bag. She would have to leave some of her own clothes behind to make room. But it was a small sacrifice if it helped to set Mildred free, and Harry was more determined than ever to do just that.

12

At dinner, Harry found herself seated between Percy and James Finchem, an arrangement so blatant in its intentions that it made her blush just to think of it. Sebastian had not fared any better – he was squeezed between Maud and Rosalind Goldsworthy. Further up the table, their mother regarded them with matriarchal satisfaction. Swallowing a curse, Harry steeled herself for the charm offensive and tried to ignore Oliver's sympathetic smile from directly opposite. Was it a coincidence that he was sitting well within earshot of everything she might say? Surely he hadn't sweet-talked her mother into seating him nearby?

But it turned out Harry had misjudged the entertainment value of the Finchem brothers. As dinner progressed, she found herself in equal parts charmed and amused. On her left, James took every opportunity to flirt, while on her right, Percy consistently shot his efforts down with deadly humour. They were, she decided as the exquisite main course of pheasant was served by the household staff, quite the double act.

'You will have to excuse my brother,' Percy said, after a particularly earnest compliment had made Harry's cheeks grow warm. 'He tries to make up for his terrible looks by blinding a woman with outrageous flattery.'

Harry laughed. 'I see. So I'm not prettier than a whole garden full of roses?'

She took some satisfaction in seeing Percy hesitate, if only for a moment. 'Even a stopped clock is right twice a day,' he said expansively. 'It doesn't mean you should buy it for your mantelpiece.'

James leaned closer. 'I'm afraid Percy was dropped on his head as a baby. He talks utter nonsense most of the time. Please accept my heartfelt apologies.'

Harry glanced back and forth between them. 'Are you always so terrible to each other?'

Percy grinned. 'Always. He makes it so easy.'

James reached out to top up Harry's wine glass, an action that caused Oliver to frown. Although seemingly engrossed in conversation with Rosalind Goldsworthy, Harry had no doubt he had been following the chatter across the table and she had the distinct impression he didn't like either of the Finchem brothers much. Whereas Harry herself was finding them quite refreshing.

'My mother tells me you work in London,' James said. 'Something to do with banking.'

'That's right,' Harry replied, taking a sip of wine. 'I like to stay busy. Do you work?'

'Only on his golfing swing,' Percy observed. 'But he'll tell you he's in the shipping business to try and impress you.'

James smiled. 'It's the family company, dates back to 1741. We import and export all over the world. If you're ever in need of silk for a dress, let me know.'

'Don't tell my mother that,' Harry advised. 'She will never leave you alone.'

'I'd be happy to help,' James said. 'Especially if it gives me a chance to speak to you.'

There was a snort from Percy. 'I work in the family business too. If you want to avoid my brother's toe-curling efforts to woo you, then take my card.'

Harry wasn't sure whether it was the wine or the effect of being conversationally bounced between James and Percy but she found her head was spinning by the time dessert was served. After coffee, everyone began to drift towards the drawing room for brandy. There was talk of a card game but Harry excused herself and slipped through the tall double doors that led to a paved balcony overlooking the gardens. The night was blessedly cool, sending goosebumps blossoming across her skin even as she drank in the chilly air. The gardens were blanketed in darkness but she knew the view well enough to imagine the topiary hedges and fountain that sat at their heart. Somewhere in the distance, an owl hooted, punctuating the faint clink of crockery from beyond the doors as the staff cleared the dining room table. Harry absorbed the quiet, even as the fresh air intensified the fizz of alcohol in her veins. She couldn't stay out here for long, but perhaps it would soothe her frazzled nerves enough to rejoin the fray.

Gradually, the clinks and rattles subsided and Harry guessed the dining room was empty. She was just about to go back inside when the door creaked behind her and a figure stepped out. At first, they were silhouetted in the light and she couldn't make out who it was. The height told her it was a man – one of her brothers, perhaps, sent to find her? But then the figure spoke and she recognised Percy Finchem's playful tone. 'I wondered where you'd escaped to,' he said, pulling out a silver cigarette case and offering it to her. 'Are you hiding from James, by any chance?'

She shook her head, both at the question and the offer to smoke. 'Not at all. I just needed some air.'

He lit his cigarette, the flare of yellow briefly illuminating his face. He had the same brooding good looks as James, the same straight nose and strong jaw, but she now realised his eyes were blue instead of brown like his brother's. Which of his parents had given him those? she wondered, then realised she was staring. A little flustered, she took refuge in small talk. 'Do you spend much time in the country?'

'Not if I can help it. I don't mind the occasional visit, especially when the company is so captivating.' He paused to blow out a long stream of smoke. 'But I can't see myself ever living in the family pile. There's nothing to do, apart from drink, and I can do that in the city, where at least they know how to make a decent Manhattan.'

Harry couldn't totally disagree – she had left the comforts of Abinger Hall for the bright lights of London when she was only a little over twenty-one. But unlike Percy, she could see herself returning to Abinger when she was older. Her Aunt Valeria had done exactly that after refusing to marry and she seemed perfectly happy with her horses. 'It's not for everyone,' she agreed.

'Luckily for me, I won't inherit the old place,' Percy went on. 'That's my brother's doom and he's welcome to it.' He fixed her with a speculative look. 'Have you ever been to New York? Now that's a city.'

Harry considered the daily newspaper articles about America, where prohibition was causing all kinds of unintended consequences. 'Not much chance of a cocktail there.'

Percy gave her a sly grin. 'Oh, but there is. You just need to know where to go. And there's something deliciously dangerous about a speakeasy. It makes one feel alive, knowing the door could be broken down at any moment.'

There was something in his voice that surprised Harry, a darker edge that belied his amiable exterior. She cocked her head. 'That, and the chance that the alcohol might kill you.'

He laughed. 'Of course. What's the point of living if you always play it safe?'

Spoken by someone who had never had to worry where his next meal was coming from, Harry thought dryly. But she could hardly point the finger there – she'd never had to face hardship either and besides, she wasn't sure it really mattered. You didn't have to be wealthy to understand the thrill of danger. 'I think there's a time and a place for a calculated risk,' she said, as Oliver's insistence that she stop her investigations floated across her mind. 'Sometimes the end justifies the means.'

'You're so right,' Percy murmured and she was startled to realise how close he was. 'I mean, aren't you taking a risk just by being out here alone with me, under the stars?'

Her heart thudded in her chest as she met his gaze and it wasn't only the truth of his words that made it beat faster. She could smell his cologne mingled with the smoke from his cigarette and it belatedly occurred to her that perhaps James was not the most seductive of the Finchem brothers after all. 'I don't know,' she said. 'Am I?'

For a moment, she thought he might kiss her. For a moment, she almost wanted him to. But he simply smiled. 'Not at all, Harry. There's nothing dangerous about me.'

She wasn't sure whether it was the gleam of moonlight on his white teeth, or the breath of wind that blew his dark hair across his forehead, but there was something lupine about his expression then that made her shiver. 'But you're cold,' he said, with sudden concern, and shrugged off his dinner jacket to drape it around her shoulders. 'Come on, let's get you back inside.'

After finishing his cigarette, he pulled open the door and ushered her into the dining room. Warm air embraced Harry as she made for the drawing room but before she could push the door back, it was pulled open and Oliver was there. 'Harry,' he said, frowning in surprise. His eyes took in the dinner jacket hanging from her shoulders and his frown deepened. 'I was just coming to look for you.'

She was suddenly conscious of Percy's solicitous hand on her back. 'Here I am,' she said. 'No need to launch a search party.'

Oliver's gaze narrowed a little as he glanced at Percy, who offered a nonchalant smirk. 'Wasn't there a mention of poker? Something tells me Fortescue here is a card sharp on the sly.'

Harry saw Oliver's expression darken and his dourness made her tired and cross at the same time. Shrugging off Percy's jacket, she handed it over. 'Oliver never gambles,' she said. 'Goodnight, all.'

She didn't look back as she climbed the stairs, unable to decide who she was avoiding most – Oliver and his evident disapproval, or Percy and his undisguised interest. Perhaps it was both, she decided as she closed the door to her bedroom and let out a long slow breath. For very different reasons.

* * *

Harry woke early on Sunday morning, after a restless night full of unsettling dreams. She lay still for a minute or so, listening to the birds outside her window, and then rose to throw open the curtains, gasping a little at the cold against her feet. The fire in the small hearth had been lit, so the room was not as chilly as it might have been. Making a mental note to thank Lucinda the maid for her soundless efficiency, Harry pulled on her dressing gown and returned to the window. Outside, the lawn was white with frost, sparkling in the first rays of the freshly risen sun, and Harry felt a sudden urge to feel the grass crunch beneath her feet, to watch her breath plume against the peaches-and-cream sky. It was not yet eight o'clock – she doubted any of the house guests would have risen at this hour, especially not if the threatened card games had materialised. It should be safe enough for her to venture downstairs without any danger of bumping into anyone.

She dressed quickly, rummaging in her wardrobe for jodhpurs and riding boots. The stable hands would have been up for hours, she thought, feeding the horses and mucking out. She was sure no one would object if she took one of her aunt's horses for a crisp morning ride.

'I recommend Duchess, Miss White,' Caleb the stable boy said, when Harry asked which horse she might take. 'She's steady but enjoys a gallop if you fancy it.'

'Perfect,' Harry replied appreciatively. 'Exactly what I need this morning.'

She knew as soon as they left the yard that she had chosen well. When she'd lived at the hall she'd had her own horse but Duchess was a pleasure to ride. She was a dappled grey mare of around four or five, placid but responsive when Harry urged her into a canter. It wasn't long before they had left Abinger Hall behind and were deep into the woodlands on the western estate. Autumn was in the last of her glory – the trees wore magnificent shades of gold and russet and bronze, but many had shed their treasure onto the woodland floor to create a carpet that glimmered in the speckled morning light. Harry gave Duchess her head and marvelled at the power the horse exuded. The exhilaration of the ride, together with the rush of wind across her cheeks, combined to scour her restlessness away. Last night's encounter with Percy in the garden felt tame by comparison and even Oliver's po-faced disapproval had lost its power to irk her.

She returned Duchess to the stables some two hours later, refreshed in spirit and ravenously hungry, with a plan for the rest of the morning. If Oliver wouldn't tell her what was happening with Mildred, perhaps the Longstaff family would.

Once Harry had rubbed Duchess down and thanked her for a most enjoyable ride, she went inside to wash and change. Obeying her rumbling stomach, she found Sebastian alone at the dining room table, nursing a tall glass of tomato juice and a plate of poached eggs. 'Just the person I was looking for,' she said cheerfully, helping herself to a thick slice of toast.

Her brother winced. 'Not so loud, please.'

Harry eyed him sympathetically. 'Late night?'

'Early morning,' he replied, grimacing. 'Do you know, I think I was hustled by Maud Goldsworthy. The girl has a poker face that could break the bank at Monte Carlo.'

'Oh dear.' Harry tried not to laugh.

'The other one wants to play me at tennis and I can only imagine she'll win.' Seb let out a morose sigh. 'They're monsters.'

'Don't let Mama hear you say that; she's got high hopes for wedding bells,' Harry said. 'Do you mind if I borrow your car?'

Instantly, he perked up. 'Going anywhere exciting? Give me half an hour and I'll come with you.'

She glanced at the clock and shook her head. The last thing she wanted was a companion. 'I'm only going to Foxley. But I'm heading there now, I'm afraid.'

Sebastian cocked his head. 'What are you up to? Don't tell me you've gone all Lady Chatterley and have a lover stashed away in the village.'

'Of course not. It's a lovely morning, I just feel like taking the MG for a spin, blowing the cobwebs away.'

'You were in bed by ten – you shouldn't have any cobwebs,' her brother observed, subsiding back into his slumped position. 'In point of fact, you look disgustingly well, if a little overdressed for a drive. Are you sure there isn't a man involved?'

'Positive,' Harry said firmly. 'Now, where are your keys?'

'On the dresser in my room.' He eyed her curiously once more. 'There's more to this than you're letting on but luckily for you, I'm too hungover to pursue it.'

Thank goodness for late-night poker games, Harry thought, even as she summoned up another sympathetic smile. 'Get Mrs Pilbeam to mix a raw egg into that Bloody Mary,' she advised as she left the room. 'Good luck with the match.'

It wasn't until Harry reached Foxley that she thought to wonder whether the Longstaffs might be churchgoers. The service appeared to have ended; villagers stood in clusters in the churchyard and on the pavement outside, passing the time of day. The grass verges were all taken up with cars and Harry was obliged to circle round three times looking for somewhere to park. The MG garnered plenty of admiring looks as she drove, its cherry-red paintwork vibrant in the sunshine, and she cursed her stupidity. Why hadn't she realised the villagers would be at church? It would only take one person to observe her walking from the car to the Longstaffs and her cover might be blown. At least she'd had the sense to wrap a scarf around her hair.

The fear of discovery was so great that, in the end, Harry parked by the side of the road three-quarters of a mile from the village. Patting the gleaming bonnet and whispering a prayer that it would still be there, undamaged, when she returned, she set off back the way she had come. The crowds had thinned by the time she reached the row of cottages where the Longstaffs lived. Pausing to compose herself, and checking right and left to make sure she was not observed, Harry knocked at the door of number 5.

It took a moment or two for Esme Longstaff to answer. As Harry waited, she couldn't help noticing that the roses framing the door were in need of serious pruning; the flowers had long since shed their petals and rosehips hung from the too tall stems. Vicious-looking thorns drooped over the lintel, putting Harry in mind of Sleeping Beauty's castle. If she'd had a pair of secateurs on her, she might have been tempted to do the job there and then but as she had no such tools, she simply waited.

When at last the door was opened, Esme was still wearing what Harry guessed to be her smart coat and best hat, and her expression was one of perfect surprise. 'Miss Moss! We hardly dared hope – that is to say, my letter can barely have reached you.'

Harry cycled through her possible responses and settled on honesty, at least for that moment. 'Your letter?'

Esme blinked, her green eyes even more puzzled. 'Yes. I wrote to you on Thursday, begging you and Mr Holmes to intercede once more on Mildred's behalf. Is that not why you are here?'

No doubt the letter would be waiting for her on Monday, Harry thought. 'I'm afraid we have yet to receive it,' she said. 'I was simply in the area and thought to see how you were faring.'

Esme clapped her hands together. 'Then my prayers have been answered.' She stepped backwards. 'Please do come in. You find us just home from the morning service but if you give me a moment, I will bring some tea.'

Harry held up her hand. 'Don't trouble yourself on my account. But tell me, is there a reason you wrote again – a development of which I'm not aware?'

The young woman reached for her hat pin. 'Why don't you wait in the living room? My parents will join you shortly and we can tell you everything.'

Left with no option, Harry did as she requested. The room was unchanged from her last visit, although the fire had burned low during the family's absence. She added a log, stirring the embers until they flared bright, and topped it with a few lumps of coal. There were not many in the scuttle, she noticed, and made a mental note to have some sent from Abinger Hall. Once flames had begun to lick the wood, she left the hearth and perched on one of the faded sofas, listening to the creak of floorboards overhead. At last, the door opened and Mr and Mrs Longstaff came in.

They had aged in the weeks since she had last seen them, Harry observed as she greeted them. Mr Longstaff's hair seemed greyer, his eyes more sunken. Mrs Longstaff had lost what little colour she had – her face was unnaturally pale, her skin waxen. Her mouth was pinched with worry and her eyes were surrounded by dark circles that suggested sleep had been a stranger. Harry felt a surge of compassion as she considered them and she was glad she had followed the impulse to call upon them before returning to London.

'Have you come with news?' Mr Longstaff's voice was gruff with barely suppressed hope as he addressed Harry. 'It has been some time since we heard from Mr Fortescue. Has there been a breakthrough?'

Harry wished with all her heart that she did not have to disappoint him. 'Nothing substantial, I'm afraid. Enquiries are continuing, of course.'

Upon the sofa, Mrs Longstaff made a restless motion. 'Enquiries. What use are they when our girl languishes in hell?'

Her husband placed a hand on her shoulder. 'You must forgive us our impatience. We had hoped, given Mr Holmes' famous powers of deduction, that he might have solved the case by now.'

Harry felt the hot burn of shame. Of course they would expect a speedy resolution – in the stories, Holmes knew from the speck of dirt on the toe of a boot who had committed the crime, as well as the how and the why. His superhuman intellect allowed him to leap to conclusions that amazed the more pedestrian Dr Watson, and ran rings around Scotland Yard. Not for the first time, Harry felt the heft of what she had undertaken. Detective work in real life was not like fiction at all – she had bitten off far more than she could chew and she had nothing to hide behind now, apart from the character in whose name she had come. 'As you know, Mr Holmes is not in London, which makes his investigations somewhat slower. But please rest assured we are on the trail of the real criminals and hope to clear Mildred's name soon.'

The door opened again, and Esme reappeared. Harry was unsurprised to see she carried a tray of tea. She waited until the girl had placed the tray on a table and took her notebook from her bag. 'You mentioned a letter, Miss Longstaff. What was your reason for writing?'

Esme busied herself handing out the teacups. 'It was an act of desperation,' she said quietly.

Mr Longstaff harumphed. 'You have been to visit Mildred just as we have, seen the dreadful place where she is being held.' It was not a question but, even so, Harry nodded. 'Then you understand the depth of our concern. Mildred does not belong there, among the common criminals and debtors.'

Esme's eyes flashed at him. 'I have told you, Papa, that not everyone sent there is guilty. Mrs Pankhurst was confined there a number of times while campaigning for the vote and I am sure no one would describe her as common, nor a criminal.' She paused and seemed to recollect herself. 'But you are right that it is no place for my sister. Her letters to us confirm that.'

Harry felt a quiver of interest. 'Mildred has written to you?'

'A number of times,' Esme replied. 'With each letter, she grows more despairing.'

'May I see them?'

'I thought you would ask,' Esme said, and pulled a bundle of thin envelopes from her pocket. 'They are difficult for us to read, loving Mildred as we do, but I have nevertheless pored over them. Perhaps you will understand our impatience better after reading them.'

The paper was cheap, almost translucent, and Harry had to concentrate hard to read the words scratched out in blunt pencil. In each letter, Mildred's fear bled from every line, although it was clear she had made some effort not to worry her family. Nevertheless, she made mention of the food, which tasted of nothing, and the lack of sanitation, of the disinterest among the guards and the rats that scuttled along the corridors at night. Her reports of Oliver were favourable – it was clear she set much store in his advice – but Harry could see what Esme meant: Mildred was losing hope.

The most recent letter was postmarked Tuesday and it made Harry frown almost before she had finished the first few lines. It comprised of a single page and, unlike the others, which had evidently been composed with care, the sentences were painfully long and their meaning harder to define. They still made sense in a jumbled sort of way but Harry had to read several sections over again to understand them. *You three will doubtless think that I am confused and sometimes I fear you are right, although not always completely right for as you, Esme – my heart and my conscience – well know that is not life.*

Harry stirred uneasily and glanced at Esme, who was watching her. 'Naturally, you appreciate our concern.'

Harry studied the letter again. 'It certainly seems as though she is struggling. Are you fearful for her state of mind?'

'Wouldn't you be?' Mrs Longstaff cried, clutching at the frill of her blouse.

'Of course,' Harry said heavily. 'Is that why you wrote to me – to Mr Holmes? To see what we could do?'

Esme nodded. 'In part, yes. We hoped you might visit with Mr Fortescue, set our minds at rest. Family visits are only permitted every second Wednesday but lawyers may go at almost any time.'

'But then the woman from the Prison Reform Society came,' Mr Longstaff interjected suddenly. 'She was very interested in Mildred's letters and we thought perhaps she might arrange a visit.'

'The Prison Reform Society?' Harry repeated, frowning. The newspapers were full of such earnest organisations, those who felt prisons should not be places of humiliation and degradation and campaigned to improve conditions. Harry's grandmother had friends who were members but she had never heard of them making house calls. 'How did she come to find you?'

He shrugged. 'She read about Mildred in the papers and came to see if she could help.'

The explanation only increased Harry's confusion. Reformers tended to focus on conditions in general rather than the experience of individual prisoners, and the newspaper reports had given few details about Mildred's family and certainly not their address. 'Did she give her name?' she asked. 'Leave a card, perhaps?'

'She called herself Mrs Jones,' Esme said. 'I don't believe she gave us her card.'

It didn't make sense, Harry thought, perplexed. Why should a prison reformer be interested specifically in Mildred Longstaff? 'When was this?'

'Thursday,' Mrs Longstaff said.

'And she turned up out of the blue?' Harry pressed. 'She didn't write to make an appointment or introduce herself?'

'Well, yes,' Mr Longstaff said. 'That is to say no, she didn't write beforehand. But we thought nothing of that – she must have other families to visit.'

Harry thought of Holloway, with its many inmates. 'Hundreds, I should think,' she said slowly. 'Tell me, what did she want to know?'

'How Mildred seemed to be doing, if she had written with any complaints,' Mr Longstaff said. 'That's when we showed her Mildred's letters. Then she asked how she came to be in prison, and we saw no reason not to tell her the truth.'

Mrs Longstaff leaned towards Harry. 'She was particularly pleased to hear that Mildred had a lawyer. She wanted to know how Mildred came to find him and who was paying for his services.'

An unsettling suspicion was forming in the pit of Harry's stomach. 'What did you tell her?'

'Again, the truth,' Mr Longstaff answered. 'That Mr Fortescue had seen Mildred's case in the newspapers and had offered to represent her free of charge.'

Harry exhaled. It was exactly the explanation Oliver had said he had given. 'Of course.'

Mrs Longstaff smiled. 'And naturally we mentioned Mr Holmes.'

Harry almost groaned. Why hadn't she sworn them to secrecy from the very first? 'Ah.'

'Not by name,' Esme hastened to put in. 'I assumed, since he is in retirement, that he would not want to be inundated with fresh cases. We merely mentioned that the matter was being investigated by a great detective whose identity could not be divulged.' She eyed Harry with some uncertainty. 'Was that wrong?'

'Not at all.' Harry did her best to sound reassuring. 'Would you be able to describe Mrs Jones for me?'

Esme looked thoughtful. 'Blonde hair, not natural but fashionably styled. Fairly well spoken and smartly dressed, although I thought her red lipstick a little misplaced.'

'I found her very striking,' Mr Longstaff said, which earned him a glower from his wife.

'How old would you say she was?' Harry asked.

'Mid-fifties,' Mrs Longstaff said, with some feeling. 'Perhaps even sixty.'

Mr Longstaff opened his mouth to argue, then appeared to think better of it. 'Do you know her?'

A picture was forming in Harry's mind. While it was true that many women had blonde hair, whether from a bottle or from nature, and plenty wore red lipstick, even during the day, she couldn't help recalling her interview with Mrs Haverford. Could it be coincidence? The description was inconclusive and there was always the possibility that there really was a prison reformer called Mrs Jones. Even so, Harry's suspicions were aroused. No matter which way she turned, it appeared everything led back to Mrs Haverford. 'I don't believe so,' she told Mr Longstaff.

Esme was watching her carefully. 'But there is such a thing as the Prison Reform Society and they do plan to help Mildred. Why else would Mrs Jones come all the way from London?'

'Why indeed?' Harry murmured. Her frowning gaze came to rest upon Mildred's letters. 'That last one – may I read it again?'

Wordlessly, Esme handed it over. There was something off-kilter about it, Harry thought as she pored over the words once more, and she didn't think it was as obvious as Mildred losing her senses. The discrepancy became more pronounced when comparing it to the previous letters but Harry couldn't put her finger on what exactly it was that was nagging at her. After a few more minutes, she gave the letter back to Esme. 'I'll see if I can contact Mrs Jones,' she said. 'And of course Mr Fortescue and I will check on Mildred as soon as we can.'

'Thank you,' Esme said. 'And thank you for taking the trouble to visit today. We appreciate your time.'

Once Harry had said goodbye to Mr and Mrs Longstaff, Esme showed her to the front door. With a backward glance as though fearful she might be overheard, she thrust Mildred's most recent letter into Harry's hands. 'Seven, ten, six, nine, seven,' she hissed.

'Sorry?' Harry said, unsure whether she had heard correctly.

'The code,' Esme whispered urgently. 'Mildred and I used it when we were children. Apply it yourself and you'll understand why I'm so afraid for her.'

'Can't you just tell me?' Harry asked, but Esme was ushering her across the doorstep.

'My parents don't know the truth – it would kill them.' Her green eyes blurred. 'Please help my sister, Miss Moss. Time is running out.'

With that, she closed the door, leaving an astonished Harry

staring at the plain black paint. She stood there for a moment, Mildred's letter in her hand, then she turned and walked away. What were the numbers Esme had mentioned? Seven, ten, six, nine, seven. Harry repeated them over and over as she hurried to where she'd left the MG but it was only when she was safely behind the wheel that she unfurled the thin paper and began to scan the words. After several minutes had passed, she took out her notebook and began to scribble furiously.

Dear Mama and Papa, and dearest Esme,

Firstly, please believe that I am quite well and I want for nothing but I am tired. The weather continues wet but also is being sunny at times. I have often watched the floating clouds in the sky; they make me feel less like I have no hope, although the truth is found in my eyes. The clouds float outside, free everywhere. Sometimes the food is better but the porridge takes so very very much longer, but I still try to eat it so that I am not hungry but I am. When you three last visited me you were here and I try to hold on to the memory but it gets harder as more days go by.

You three will doubtless think that I am confused and sometimes I fear you are right although not always completely right for as you, Esme – my heart and my conscience – well know that is not life. But as long as I have you inside me they shall never be able to mean more to me than our dear hearts mean to us all, for nothing could ever kill what you three all mean to me but most especially, my dearest and most beloved sister Esme. I try my hardest to please you all, but there are moments I cannot help even though your endless trust in me is all I need to pray before God and I can only hope that He has it in his heart and He is merciful, as all of you three are merciful too, or it may be just too late.

Your daughter and sister,
Mildred

Harry stared at the deciphered message for another full minute. Then she started the engine of the MG, threw it into a three-point turn and drove towards Abinger Hall as though all the demons of hell pursued her.

13

Harry was somehow surprised and not surprised to find Oliver waiting for her on the steps of the hall when she drew up in the MG. Of course Seb would have blabbed about where she was going, she thought as she climbed out and crunched across the gravel. And of course Oliver would have known why. But she had the perfect defence in her notebook – the desperate message Mildred had encoded in her letter – and she intended to use it before he could attack.

'I thought we decided you were going to stay out of this,' Oliver growled the moment she was within earshot.

'No, you decided that,' Harry retorted. 'In the meantime, I've been gathering some very interesting information about your client. Do you want to hear it or should I go straight to Scotland Yard?'

For a moment his scowl wavered and Harry supposed his anger at her was doing battle with his desire to do right by Mildred. In the end, he shrugged – a tight little gesture that told Harry his annoyance was only temporarily at bay. She held out Mildred's letter. 'Read this.'

To his credit, he didn't argue. Once he had finished, he looked up, clearly puzzled. 'Are you sure Mildred wrote this? It doesn't really make any sense.'

'That's because you don't have the cipher,' she said, with some satisfaction. She held out her notebook and the message she had decrypted.

'Esme, I am being watched,' he read aloud. 'They have eyes everywhere. The longer I am here, the more I fear for my life. They mean to kill me. Esme, please help me before it is too late.' Oliver looked up at Harry, his gaze suddenly troubled. 'When did this arrive?'

'Last Wednesday. But that's not all.'

Tersely, she told him about the Longstaffs' visit from Mrs Jones. He considered the news thoughtfully. 'There is a movement to improve conditions in prisons but they tend to write long reports and petition Parliament.'

'Exactly,' Harry said. 'They don't make house calls. I don't think Mrs Jones was interested in prison reform at all. I think she wanted information.'

'About Mildred?'

Harry folded her arms. 'About you. Someone is unhappy that Mildred isn't as helpless as she seems.'

Oliver eyed the letter again, his expression grim. 'She's telling us they have someone inside the prison. If that's the case—'

'Then Mildred's life really is in danger,' Harry finished. She fixed him with a meaningful stare. 'We have to do something, Oliver.'

He nodded. 'I'll take this to the police. Maybe they can—'

'We can't leave this to the police any more,' Harry exploded. 'They're too slow. By the time they work out what's going on it could be too late.'

Oliver threw his hands up in the air. 'So what do you suggest?

We go and stake out the gang's headquarters, bring the criminals in ourselves?'

Harry stared at him. 'Well, why not? We know where Dora lives—'

'No, we don't!' he exclaimed. 'The police checked the house in Tea Cutter Row and found nothing.'

'Then they didn't look properly,' she snapped. 'I went there too, remember? I know what I saw.'

He opened his mouth to answer and she knew – just knew – he was going to suggest she was mistaken.

'Don't,' she warned.

Oliver ran a hand through his hair. 'Harry, we cannot do this alone. It's too dangerous.'

She held up her notebook. 'And it might cost Mildred her life if we don't.' They glared at each other for a moment, locked in a battle of wills, then Harry sighed, suddenly weary. 'Just think about it, Oliver. That's all I ask.'

He pressed his lips into a hard, thin line. 'Fine, I'll think about it. As long as you promise you won't go tearing off to Elephant and Castle without me.'

Grudgingly, she nodded. 'I promise.'

'I'll speak to the prison first thing tomorrow, arrange a visit for early evening, if you're free?'

'Oh, I'm free,' Harry said, remembering the pinched anxiety on the faces of Mildred's parents, the fear in her sister's eyes. 'Just tell me when.'

Oliver nodded at the message she held. 'That's good work, by the way. Credit where credit is due.'

As much as she hated herself for it, his praise made Harry feel warm inside. 'I knew there was something there but I'd never have figured it out without the code,' she said. 'As you keep reminding me, I'm not Sherlock Holmes.'

Oliver gave her a lopsided smile. 'Well quite,' he said as he began to walk up the stone staircase. 'You actually exist, for a start.'

* * *

Harry found it almost impossible to concentrate at work on Monday. Her fingers were clumsy on the typewriter keys, meaning she had to start each letter several times, and her thoughts kept returning to Mildred's hidden message. Had Oliver been in contact with the prison yet? The telephone remained stubbornly silent, which was not unusual, but Harry's nerves thrummed with expectation, creating the almost oppressive sense that the room was holding its breath. When Bobby knocked at her office door, mid-morning, she jumped so violently that the peace lily on her desk was sent clattering to the floor. 'Blimey,' Bobby said when he poked his head around the door and saw the mess. 'You having a smashing time in here or what?'

'Ha ha,' she said, kneeling down to gather up the plant. 'I knocked it over – that's all.'

He shrugged. 'Accidents happen.' He placed a bundle of envelopes on her desk. 'I reckon you're getting on top of things now. Sherlock Holmes should have had you as his secretary when he was doing his detecting, instead of that boring doctor.'

Harry looked up, surprised. She was under the impression that Bobby wasn't much of a reader but his comment suggested he knew a little bit about Sir Arthur Conan Doyle's books. Perhaps he'd been visiting the library. 'Dr Watson wasn't really his secretary,' she said, straightening up. 'He was more of an assistant.'

'Same thing, innit,' Bobby said, wrinkling his nose. 'He wrote down everything that happened. I reckon you'd be good at that too.'

She settled the lily back on the desk, patting the soil back into place. It was an extraordinary thing, the way people half believed, or in some cases fully believed, that the adventures of Holmes and Watson had been real. Even Bobby was not immune, it seemed. And yet wasn't she embroiled in a real-life investigation of her own? The Case of the Missing Maid. Perhaps Bobby was onto something. Maybe she ought to chronicle events the way Watson had – the way the police must do now. It would not be for publication, of course, but it might help her spot something she had missed – the tiny detail that cracked the case and won Mildred her freedom. 'Thank you, Bobby,' she said thoughtfully. 'That's very kind of you.'

The boy nodded at the bundle of envelopes beside her typewriter. 'You'd never be short of ideas.' He stepped back, patting the brass trolley in the doorway. 'Anyway, I'd better get moving. This lot won't deliver itself.'

Once she had opened the latest batch of envelopes, Harry opened the notebook she always kept in her handbag and began to skim its pages. Before long, she had a rough timeline of events, along with a list of persons and places of interest. Arrows bisected the paper, linking Mildred to the Finchems, the Finchems to Polly, Polly to Mrs Haverford, Mrs Haverford – or Mrs Jones, as Harry suspected she had called herself – to the Longstaffs. There was no doubt of the connections; Harry could sense the strands binding everything together like an invisible web. But who was behind it all? she mused as she tapped her pen on the paper. Who was the spider tugging on the silk?

When the telephone rang, Harry leapt again and almost sent the peace lily crashing for a second time. Thrusting out a hand, she caught it as it teetered on the edge of the desk and steadied it, before getting up to answer the shrill cry of the phone. No sooner had she said her name than Oliver's voice was in her ear. 'Harry, we've got trouble,' he said, without preamble.

Her heart sank into her shoes. His tone was so grim that it could only be bad news. 'What is it? Is there more evidence against Mildred?'

'It's worse than that,' he said. 'She's been attacked. I don't know how bad it is yet.'

'Attacked!' Harry gasped, clutching at the filing cabinet as the room lurched. 'By who?'

'I don't know,' he replied grimly. 'Another inmate, I think, but there aren't many details.'

'Is she...' Harry trailed off, unable to say the words.

'She's alive,' Oliver said. 'They've got her in the hospital wing and Deputy Governor Short has agreed to keep her under guard.'

'Can we see her?'

'Not tonight,' Oliver said. 'I'm hoping for tomorrow, if she's conscious and able to talk about what happened.'

The thought of Mildred hurt and vulnerable made Harry's stomach churn. 'But what if they try again? She said they have eyes everywhere. What if that includes the prison authorities? What if the guards are part of the gang?'

There was a brief silence. 'No, that can't be the case,' Oliver said, his tone firm. 'Bridget Short is a very respected professional – she wouldn't stand for that. She cares about the welfare of the inmates.'

The fact remained that Mildred had been attacked on this woman's watch, Harry thought pensively. Her gaze came to rest on the notebook lying open on her desk, the pages scored with interconnected strands, with the shadowy spider at its heart. She'd assumed the mastermind behind the burglary must be Mrs Haverford but what if the web went deeper than she or Oliver guessed? 'Someone tried to silence Mildred, Oliver. This can't be a coincidence.'

'No,' he conceded. 'I don't think it can. Let's see how she is in the morning. With a bit of luck she'll be able to tell us who did this to her.'

Harry stood with the telephone in her hand for a long time after he had rung off, staring at nothing. Mildred's worst fears had come true, she thought dully, and she was trapped inside a prison with someone who might want her silenced for good. Slowly, Harry replaced the receiver and went back to her desk. It was going to be a long night for them all.

* * *

Harry wasn't sure if it was her imagination but the clouds that hung over Holloway on Tuesday afternoon were ominously dark. Thunder had rumbled during the drive from Holborn, punctuated by the occasional jagged spark of lightning, but the storm that was threatening had yet to break. Dusk was falling earlier than usual; Oliver had managed to make an appointment for three o'clock and Harry had not hesitated. She had called Mr Babbage and advised him she had an appointment with the dentist. Shortly after that, she was sitting beside Oliver and speeding through North London.

Neither of them spoke much, not when they were waiting beside the enormous wooden doors and not when they were being shown through the maze of grey corridors that led to the prison hospital wing. By the time they reached Mildred's bedside, the journey had blurred in Harry's memory. She hoped they were not expected to remember their way back.

Mildred was the only patient in this section of the ward and somehow managed to look paler than the bandages that swathed her head. She lay with her eyes closed as they approached, an ugly black and purple bruise peeping out on one temple. The guard stationed at her bedside stood up as Harry and Oliver approached with their escort. 'Oliver Fortescue,' he said, by way of introduction. 'How's she been?'

'Asleep, mostly,' the guard said. 'No one's been near her, apart from the doctor and the nurses.'

'Good,' Oliver said. 'I'd like to consult the doctor – where is he?'

The guard pointed to an office in the furthest corner. 'You might find him in there.'

Oliver eyed Harry. 'Do you want to stay here, in case she wakes up? I won't be a moment.'

Harry nodded absently, unable to take her eyes off the girl on the bed. Guilt surged through her. If only she'd done something – anything – to prevent this from happening. But what could she have done? The chain of events had been set in motion long before she'd ever heard the name Mildred Longstaff and yet she still felt she had failed the young woman. Her thoughts strayed back to another conversation she'd had with Oliver on the journey to Holloway. 'I spoke to the Prison Reform Society,' he'd told her. 'You won't be surprised to hear they don't have a Mrs Jones working for them, and nor do they visit families at home, at least not without an appointment. The woman I spoke to sounded faintly horrified at the mere suggestion.'

He was right – it wasn't really a surprise and yet Harry had still found it shocking. It was the brazenness that sent her reeling. It shouldn't have – everything she had read about gangs like the Forty Elephants suggested these were people who were supremely confident in taking risks. But Harry hadn't fully appreciated how many of its members seemed to be hiding in plain sight, unafraid of getting caught and perhaps even prepared for it. It was that boldness that had culminated in the attack on Mildred, just as the girl herself had predicted, with little apparent fear of repercussions. Harry had no doubt the gang had people on the inside of the prison. The question was who those people were.

They were dependent on Mildred for answers, Harry thought now as she gazed at the supine figure. Oliver had been given the green light to visit, which suggested Mildred had been conscious at some point, even if she was not awake now. And then Harry saw her eyelid flicker as the girl stole a glance at her. The eye closed fast but not before Harry understood her meaning: she wanted the guard to leave before she would speak.

Oliver returned with the white-coated doctor in tow. He checked Mildred's charts, took her pulse and shone a light beneath her eyelids. At length, he gestured to a pair of chairs on the other side of the bed. 'Her vital signs are as good as can be expected but I couldn't say when she might wake up. I hope you're prepared to wait.'

'As long as it takes,' Oliver answered as he and Harry took the empty seats. Once the doctor had gone, Harry nudged Oliver and whispered in his ear. Oliver fixed the guard with a purposeful look. 'I'd like a moment alone with my client, if you don't mind.'

The man looked mutinous. 'What, now? I'm not supposed to leave her.'

Oliver smiled. 'I'm sure I don't need to remind you of her entitlement to confidential consultation with legal representatives.'

The guard threw Mildred a disbelieving look. 'She's not even awake. I don't think she's consulting with anyone, except maybe Mr Sandman.' He chuckled at his own joke.

But at that moment, Mildred opened her eyes. She blinked several times. 'Oh, Mr Fortescue,' she said, in a voice that was little more than a hoarse whisper. 'It's you.'

The guard's demeanour changed. He scowled first at Oliver and then at Mildred. 'There you are, she's awake,' Oliver said. 'Now give us some space, please. You're not here to protect her from us.'

While clearly disgruntled, the man did as Oliver demanded, going to lurk a short distance away where he could keep his eyes upon them. Harry rose from her seat and poured water from a jug on the bedside table. 'Here,' she said. 'Drink this.'

Wincing, the girl sat up a little and took a sip from the glass. She lay back immediately, as though the effort exhausted her. 'Thank you for coming.'

'Of course we came,' Harry said, forgetting once again that she was meant to be a lowly assistant. 'You've been attacked.'

Beside her, Oliver cleared his throat. 'We learned from your sister that you feared for your life. Do you know who is responsible for hurting you?'

Mildred looked away. 'No.'

Harry and Oliver exchanged glances. Did she genuinely not know or was she still scared about who might be listening? 'Why don't you tell us what happened?' Oliver said gently.

'I don't remember much,' Mildred said. 'I was in the kitchen, helping to scrape the plates – some of us get to do that if we've behaved ourselves. There weren't many people about; most of the women had gone back to their cells, and I suppose I must have been alone.' The girl lifted a hand to touch her bandaged head. 'I was bending down to pick up the bin when I heard footsteps but before I could turn around, there was this blinding pain in my head and everything went sort of grey.'

She trailed off, as though reliving the moment, and Harry felt for her. 'Go on,' Oliver encouraged. 'You were struck on the head. Then what?'

'I fell, I think,' Mildred said uncertainly. 'They were kicking me – all I could think of was getting away.'

'How frequent were the kicks?' Oliver asked but she did not understand the question. 'Did it seem to you that there was one person or two?'

'Oh, I see,' Mildred replied. 'One, I think. It's hard to be sure.'

'Of course. And the footsteps you heard, was the tread heavy, like a man's? Or lighter, like a woman's?'

'Lighter, I think,' she said, after a moment's consideration. 'But the kicks were heavy like a man's.'

A strong woman, then, Harry surmised. Or a man who was light on his feet. The former seemed more likely, since a fellow inmate was suspected, although there were plenty of male prison guards. 'And you're sure you didn't see the face of your attacker?' Oliver pressed.

Mildred's lips were bloodless, as pale as the rest of her. Her auburn hair was hidden beneath the bandages; the whiteness of her complexion only made the green of her eyes more intense. She blinked, hesitated, then closed her eyes. 'I'm sorry.'

'There's no need to apologise,' Harry said. 'You've been through a terrible experience. Perhaps you'll remember more in a day or two.'

The girl did not answer, although Harry thought she caught a minute shake of her head. They waited, in case she was gathering her strength, but it became clear after a few minutes that she had fallen asleep once more. 'Come,' Oliver murmured. 'We can visit again tomorrow.'

With a reluctant nod, Harry got to her feet. It was then that Mildred's lips parted, although her eyes remained shut. 'I hope you admired the flowers at the cottage,' she said slowly. 'They must be quite arresting at this time of year.'

Harry's brow furrowed. Did she mean the cottage in Foxley? As far as she could recall there hadn't been much in the way of flowers, just the treacherous climbing roses that threatened to behead anyone walking in and out. Perhaps there was a garden behind the house, although quite why Mildred would expect either Oliver or herself to have seen it was a mystery. 'I'm sure it is lovely,' Harry said kindly. 'Try to get some rest.'

Mildred's fingers twitched against the white bedlinen as though she was fighting to stay awake. 'Arresting,' she whispered feebly. 'The flowers...'

Oliver shook his head. 'That blow to her head must have shaken her more than we realised.'

But Harry wasn't really listening. She was watching the approach of two guards, who stopped to briefly confer with the man who had been guarding Mildred. He gestured towards the bed and the new guards approached Oliver and Harry. 'Deputy Governor Short would like a word before you leave,' one said, unsmiling.

A stab of unease needled Harry's insides. 'Why?'

The guard turned a dead-eyed stare her way. 'Because she's in charge here and what she says goes.'

'Of course,' Oliver said smoothly. 'It will be our pleasure. Lead on.'

The deputy governor's office was up two flights of curving stone steps in one of the prison's peculiarly Gothic turrets. Harry half expected it to be cold – the rest of the prison had a dank chill to the air – but the room was warm, almost cosy. A fire burned in the small grate and thick rugs covered the floor. The deputy governor herself was seated in an armchair facing the flames. She stood as they entered and turned to face them.

Harry wasn't sure what she'd been expecting – a figure of some stature, perhaps, like most of the guards she had encountered during her time in Holloway. But the woman before her now was small, almost birdlike. Her dark brown hair was pulled into a neat bun and she wore round, black-rimmed glasses that put Harry in mind of a librarian. A neat, cream blouse sat beneath a grey pinstripe jacket, which matched her skirt. She looked like the kind of fussy spinster to be found between the pages of an Agatha Christie novel, Harry thought. She did not look like she should be in charge of a terrifying women's prison but Harry was well aware appearances could be deceiving.

'Oliver Fortescue, have you grown since I last saw you?' she said, her voice warmed by a soft Irish burr, but it was the words themselves that caused Harry to swallow a sudden, wildly inappropriate snort of laughter. This was not at all what she had been expecting.

'I don't think so, Bridget,' he said, stepping forward to embrace her. 'How are you?'

'Tolerable,' she said, then turned a bright-eyed gaze to Harry. 'And who is this? A new clerk?'

Oliver hesitated. 'A temporary assistant,' he said, his tone dismissive.

Harry wasn't surprised he hadn't introduced her. He had been careful to smudge her name while signing in on both their visits and she guessed he was protecting them both, in case anyone asked questions.

Bridget cast a quick, curious eye over Harry but if she thought it strange that Oliver hadn't given her name, she did not say so. Instead, she waved them to the chairs beside the fire. Oliver declined, saying he preferred to stand, but Harry took the seat opposite Bridget and warmed her hands in the heat from the fire. 'So you've been to see Mildred Longstaff,' Bridget said, but it was more of a statement than a question. 'How is she?'

'Awake,' Oliver said. 'Slipping in and out of lucidity, however. I'm afraid we didn't learn much.'

Bridget shook her head. 'A bad business. Conditions here are improving every day. We're introducing sports and handicrafts to keep the women busy but there's always a few bad apples.' She eyed Oliver shrewdly. 'She wasn't able to identify her attacker, then?'

'No,' Oliver said. 'I'm hopeful she might remember more in the days that follow.'

Harry let her gaze drift around the room. An oil painting hung above the fireplace – a rather fine still life that she decided was probably worth a significant amount of money. Bookshelves lined one wall. Photographs adorned another, mostly group shots of women who were clearly also prisoners, dressed in sporting outfits and standing together as teams. That wasn't a surprise, Harry thought as she considered the pictures. Hadn't Bridget said the prison had introduced sport as a way to keep the inmates occupied? 'Do you have a football team?' she asked suddenly, interrupting Oliver mid-flow.

Bridget blinked at the incongruity, then nodded. 'Quite a successful one, as it happens. Why do you ask?'

'I was just admiring your photographs,' Harry said, but her mind was whirring. Mildred had mentioned her attacker had light footsteps but a strong kick. Did that suggest a footballer?

'That's the current team in the centre,' Bridget said, as Harry stood up to take a closer look. 'They've won a trophy or two.'

Harry studied it thoughtfully, taking in the set expressions and proud tilt of the women's heads. Mildred had been too afraid to reveal much about her attacker but what if she had tried to give clues? The football hint was one – what else had she said? Nothing of any note. The flowers had been an arresting sight, which was an odd way to put it but she'd begun to ramble towards the end. Except – Harry almost snapped her fingers – what if she hadn't been rambling? What if she had been speaking in code? 'Tell me,' she said casually, even though her heart was suddenly racing. 'Are any of your players called Rose?'

Bridget's eyebrows shot up. 'Yes, as a matter of fact that's our goalkeeper's name. Rose Blackburn. She's very good.'

'I'm sure she is,' Harry replied. 'I imagine she has a good strong kick, too.'

'She does,' Bridget agreed, then frowned and appeared to recollect herself. 'But as pleasant as this is, I didn't invite you here to discuss our football team. Oliver, I want you to know that I'm taking this matter extremely seriously. If you learn anything from Mildred, you must bring it straight to me. Do you understand?'

Oliver nodded. 'Of course, Bridget. I'm still hopeful I can clear Mildred's name.'

Harry watched the older woman carefully. Was it strange that she insisted Oliver bring the name of Mildred's attacker to her instead of the police? It was hard to tell. 'I know you will,' Bridget said. 'Having talked to the girl myself, I find it hard to believe she's anything more than an innocent caught up in someone else's crime but of course we must all follow the evidence.'

Her gaze strayed to Harry then, still beside the framed photographs, and seemed to linger on her with cool interest. Harry returned her gaze with inquisitiveness of her own. Was Bridget Short a kindly professional who simply wanted the best for the women under her care? she wondered. Or was there a cold heart lurking beneath her spinsterish appearance?

'Thank you for your time, Bridget,' Oliver said. 'I'll be sure to let you know if we uncover anything.'

'Give my regards to your parents,' Bridget replied. She turned a shrewd gaze upon Harry. 'And it was a pleasure to meet you, Miss—'

'Wilson,' Harry said, without missing a beat. 'Good to meet you too.'

Harry didn't speak until they were outside the vast door of the prison. Dusk had turned to night while they had been inside, shrouding the turrets and crenellations in heavy black shadow. She glanced up and shivered. 'Mildred is not safe in there.'

Oliver bowed his head. 'I know.'

'At least she told us who did this to her,' Harry went on. 'I'd bet my inheritance that Rose Blackburn is connected to Dora and Mrs Haverford.'

He frowned. 'Who is Rose Blackburn? Not the goalkeeper Bridget mentioned?'

'Exactly her,' Harry said with satisfaction. 'Don't you see? Mildred told us her name without seeming to. Even from a hospital bed, she's a smart girl.'

'I don't follow,' Oliver said, firing a confused look her way.

Harry shook her head impatiently. 'First of all, she said her assailant had a strong kick. And then she mentioned how *arresting* the flowers were at her parents' house. I thought her mind was wandering but she was actually giving us the second clue.' She smiled at him. 'The only things I noticed growing when I visited the Longstaffs were the roses around the front door. And that's what Mildred was counting on, along with the odd use of the word arresting.'

Oliver considered this. 'You might be right. I can certainly look into this Blackburn woman, find out what she was put away for.'

'You can,' Harry agreed. 'But that doesn't help Mildred now – her life is hanging in the balance. She said her enemies have eyes everywhere and that means we can't trust anyone. Not even your friend the deputy governor.'

He opened his mouth to speak but Harry held up a hand. 'I mean it, Oliver. The only person I trust right now is you. Next time, they might kill Mildred. I'm done waiting for the authorities to do their jobs. It's time we took matters into our own hands and solved this case once and for all.'

'Harry—'

'No!' she snapped, rounding on him. 'The answer has been staring us in the face for weeks. We don't need to catch the entire gang; we only need to find the girl, Dora, and confront her with everything we know.'

Oliver growled in frustration. 'This isn't a crime novel, Harry. If Dora is truly a hardened criminal then she'll laugh in our faces and I can't say I'd blame her.'

Harry folded her arms. 'Then we bring her in ourselves. Let the police deal with her.'

He stared at her, ashen-faced. 'You can't be serious.'

'I am,' she insisted. 'And if you won't come with me, I'll go to Tea Cutter Row on my own and wait all night if I have to.' Harry took a deep uneven breath and met his incredulous gaze. 'This ends tonight, Oliver. Are you with me or not?'

There was a long silence. Then Oliver groaned. 'I can't believe I'm agreeing to this.'

'We have to do it before it's too late,' Harry urged. 'There's no other way we can prove Mildred's innocence in time.'

He ran a hand across his face. 'Fine. If we have to. So what's the plan – we turn up there and knock on the front door, demand to speak to Dora?'

'Of course not – that would be suicide,' Harry snorted. 'We'll go in disguise.'

'Disguise?' he repeated, his jaw dropping a little. 'What kind of disguise?'

'I'll leave that up to you,' Harry said. She began to walk towards his car. 'Just make sure it's convincing – something that blends in. We'll meet outside Elephant and Castle station at eight o'clock; that should give us enough time to get home and change.'

Oliver followed, shaking his head. 'I can't believe we're doing this.'

Harry felt something similar, although her disbelief mostly stemmed from the fact that he'd finally agreed to act. She smiled at him, feeling the blood sing in her veins. 'I know. Exciting, isn't it?'

14

The trousers took some getting used to, Harry decided as she loitered near the entrance of Elephant and Castle Underground station. It wasn't that they were uncomfortable, exactly, more that the material felt strange swishing around her legs, but she had to admit they were practical. More to the point, they gave her a degree of anonymity she had never experienced before, not even when she was dressed as Sarah Smith. No one had given her a second look on the Underground, although several people had moved downwind of her. No one had called out to her as she walked, or told her to smile beneath her flat cap – she felt entirely disregarded and the freedom thrilled her. Dressing as a man was a revelation, she concluded with a considerable thrill of satisfaction. She might have to do it more often.

She spotted Oliver the moment he left the station. It wasn't that his disguise was no good – he had kept things simple with a pair of dark trousers and a scruffy tweed jacket that had definitely seen better days, and he wore a flat cap that was not dissimilar to her own. But she had spent so much time watching him over the years that she thought she would probably recognise him anywhere. She did not think he had noticed her, however, so she sidled up to him and rattled the old tin cup she held. 'Spare some change, guvnor,' she said in a gruff, guttural tone.

'Not now,' Oliver said, barely glancing at her. He scanned the busy junction, eyes narrowed.

Harry rattled the cup again. 'A fancy gent like you can spare a coin or two. Come on, have an 'eart.'

Irritated, Oliver did look down then and his reaction almost made Harry laugh out loud. 'It's you!' he said, gaping at her. 'But who – what—' He took a deep breath and got hold of himself. 'What on earth are you wearing?'

'It's my disguise. Do you like it?'

He opened his mouth once or twice. 'It's certainly effective. I'm not sure your own mother would recognise you.'

Harry grinned. 'I sincerely hope not. Didn't I tell you I was getting better?'

'You did,' Oliver said and the look he gave her was almost admiring. 'I'm starting to think I've underestimated you in many different ways.'

In other circumstances, the words might have made her heart skip with a mixture of pride and something else she didn't want to examine too deeply, but she was acutely aware of where they were and what they were about to do. 'Drop a coin in my cup,' she said in a low voice. 'Then cross the street and walk down London Road. Turn left into Garden Row and wait by the pub there. I'll meet you shortly.'

She knew he must have questions but he refrained from voicing them. Instead, he rummaged in a pocket and tossed a penny into the tin mug. 'Now be off with you,' he said loudly, before striding away. Harry picked out the coin and tested it with her artfully blackened teeth, fighting the urge to grin. Oliver might have resisted coming here tonight with all his might but she had to admit he was learning fast.

She waited ten minutes, approaching one or two strangers as they left the station and earning a few coins for her trouble. Eventually, she took herself in the direction Oliver had taken and found him lurking near the Albert Arms public house. 'What took you so long?' he asked irritably.

She shrugged. 'This is enemy territory. I wanted to make sure we weren't being watched.'

He sighed. 'So where is Tea Cutter Row?'

'That way,' Harry said. 'But first, we need to get a drink.'

'Are you mad?' Oliver said, staring first at Harry, then at the pub. 'I'm all in favour of a bit of Dutch courage but we'll never get out alive.'

Harry shook her head. 'I've done this before. We go in, we order a pint of mild each, and we listen to what's being said.' She shook her mug, causing the coins to rattle. 'Don't worry, I'm buying.'

The beer did not smell any more inviting than the last time Harry had held a pint but she forced herself to drink it as she eavesdropped on the conversations around her. For the most part, there was nothing in particular of note – a man called Victor had lost his job and was drowning his sorrows. Another had argued with his wife and had come to the pub to escape her sharp tongue. Voices were often raised and the language was colourful. In the darker corners, shady business was undoubtedly being conducted but if Harry's last meeting with Beth had taught her anything, it was that her disguises had limits. The last thing she and Oliver needed was to get caught up in something that had no bearing on Mildred's innocence. Instead, Harry kept her mouth shut and watched the door, hoping the girl called Dora might appear, but at length, she nudged Oliver. 'Time to go,' she said. 'Bring your glass.'

The air was cool after the fug of the bar. Slipping her arm

through Oliver's, Harry raised her half-empty glass and began to weave along the pavement. Oliver caught on quickly and matched her movements. Together, they staggered onwards, looking for all the world like a pair of drunks weaving their way unsteadily home. Tea Cutter Row did not look any more inviting under cover of darkness. As they approached it, Harry tugged at Oliver's shoulder so she could whisper in his ear. 'We'll walk to the end of the street first. There's an abandoned house opposite number 25 that we can double back to, as long as no one spots us.' She squinted along the narrow road with some anxiety. 'Or at least there was.'

Her heart began to thud as they neared the house where she'd confronted Dora. But all seemed quiet. A faint light shone in one of the ground-floor windows, suggesting someone was in there, but she did not get the sense they were being watched. And then she noticed the number was missing from the flaking front door. 'That's odd,' she murmured to Oliver, without slowing their unsteady pace. 'The number is gone.'

'No, it hasn't,' Oliver replied. He nodded at the house next door. 'There it is. Number 25.'

Frowning, Harry followed the direction of his gaze. Sure enough, the house beside the one she had followed Dora to bore a scratched and dirty two and five. 'But that's not—' she began and realised in a flash what had happened. 'They switched the numbers! When I came here last number 25 was the house next door. They must have changed it so the family there weren't lying when they claimed they'd been there for years. No wonder the police didn't find anything Mildred claimed they would. They went to the wrong house.'

'But they'd have checked,' Oliver objected doubtfully. 'Wouldn't they?'

'Would they, though?' Harry said. 'No, don't stop. Let's cross the road; we need to get out of sight.' She scanned the houses opposite and let out a sigh of relief – the abandoned squat still appeared to be empty. Zigzagging across the road, she and Oliver lurched inside and Harry forced herself to ignore the indignant screeches of the rats as they scattered. She let go of Oliver's arm and placed her beer on the floor. 'Would the police have counted the houses? I know I wouldn't.'

Oliver nodded. 'You're right. I bet they took it at face value that the house bearing the number 25 was actually the one they wanted. How simple.'

'Simple but brilliant,' Harry said grudgingly. She peered out of the shattered window. 'There's a light on, anyway. Somebody is home.'

Removing his cap, Oliver scratched his head. 'So now what?'

Harry settled into a crouch by the window. 'Now we wait.'

It was cold and uncomfortable and the stench of decay and mould made her want to gag. It must have been a shock to Mildred's system to come here after the grandeur of the Finchem house, or even after her parents' home in Foxley. It wasn't just the dirt or the neglect that troubled Harry; perhaps it was just a fancy but beneath the rotting leaves and rubbish she thought she detected an air of hopelessness about Tea Cutter Row. 'Do you ever wonder what it would be like to live somewhere like this?' she asked Oliver quietly, after they had been there for around an hour.

'I'm trying not to,' he said gravely. 'I think something hairy just crawled up my trouser leg.'

Harry shuddered. 'That's not what I meant. Can you imagine what it's like to grow up in a place like this? Without heating or hot water or money for food?'

There was a brief silence. 'It's no accident that many of the criminals I see in the courts come from deprived areas. It's easy to do the right thing if you've never had to worry about where your next meal is coming from.'

She couldn't argue with that. But her grandmother's charity work had shown her it was possible to give hope and opportunities to communities like these. Oliver expected Dora to react to their approach like a hardened criminal but perhaps there was a small chance she might see the error of her ways if Harry explained how desperate Mildred's situation was. Only time would tell.

They waited mostly in silence, moving only to shoo a rat or restore blood flow to numbed limbs. If Harry hadn't been wearing a watch, she might have guessed it was the small hours of the morning when Dora eventually appeared. But a quick glance at the dial told her it was just before eleven o'clock when the girl's slight figure came into view at the end of the street. 'Oliver,' she whispered and felt him stir beside her. 'There she is!'

'Are you sure it's her?'

Harry watched the figure move along the street. It was impossible to make out much detail but she thought whoever it was had the right height and build. 'I suppose there's only one way to find out.'

'She'll run,' Oliver predicted, straightening up.

'Then we'd better hope we can keep up with her,' Harry said. 'Ready?'

She sensed rather than saw him nod. 'Ready.'

The figure was almost at number 25 when Harry and Oliver burst out of the empty house and charged towards her. 'Dora! We want a word with you,' Harry challenged gruffly. 'Or should I call you Mildred Longstaff?'

For a second the girl froze, her face a mask of startled indecision. Then she was off, darting like a hare for the safety of number 25. But Oliver was faster. He reached out a hand to intercept her. She danced past him into the middle of the street and paused to bare her teeth. 'Who are you?'

Harry held up both hands. 'We don't want any trouble. In fact, we want to help you. All you have to do is tell us what you know about the Lord Robertson burglary.'

Dora stared at her. 'You've come to the wrong place if you don't want no trouble.' She glanced at the window of the house. 'You're already in it, up to your necks.'

'It's you who's in trouble, Dora,' Oliver said. 'We know you brought Mildred here when she lost her job with Lady Finchem. And we know you took her place at Lord Robertson's on the night of the burglary.'

The girl laughed. 'Have you two just got out of the loony bin or something? I've got no idea what you're on about.'

Harry narrowed her gaze. 'I think you do. And I'm sure Mildred would be able to pick you out of a police line-up as the person who set her up.'

'Mildred?' Dora snarled, suddenly ferocious. 'She ain't going to be picking nothing. Not long for this world, from what I hear. Such a shame but like they always say, if you can't do the time, don't do the crime!'

With a sudden lunge, she tossed the bag she held at Oliver, who caught it with a grunt of surprise. Then she was running, dodging between Harry and Oliver and speeding back the way she had come. 'After her!' Harry roared, cursing the weight of the misshapen boots that were part of her disguise. What she wouldn't give for her white tennis shoes, she thought as she panted after Dora, trying to keep her in sight. Oliver sped past her. 'Stay with her,' Harry called. 'I'm right behind you.'

The girl was swift, and she had the advantage of knowing the streets. She led them on a torrid race, dodging left and right down alleyways and cut-throughs, twisting down shadowy side streets in an effort to shake them off. Harry thought her lungs might explode with the effort of keeping pace but she stuck at the task with breathless determination. Sweat dripped down her face as they tore past the Albert Arms. It was closing time – clusters of burly men stood on the street, clapping each other on the back as they said goodnight.

'George! Sammy! Help me!' Dora cried over her shoulder, and Harry glanced back to see a pair of bulky figures detach themselves from the crowd.

'What's going on, Dora?' a deep voice called.

'Debt collectors,' she cried and the crowd let out an ugly rumble. A second later, the noise erupted into a roar and it seemed as though the whole company was thundering after them. Oliver looked over his shoulder with grim resignation. 'You stay with Dora. I'll keep them busy.'

Harry stared at him. 'You can't fight them all – they'll kill you!'

Oliver grimaced. 'They'll have to catch me first.'

He peeled off to the left and the crowd howled in response. The thunder of feet on the street lessened but Harry knew she was still being pursued. Sucking in as much oxygen as she could, she redoubled her efforts to reach Dora. Soon the girl would be at the Elephant and Castle junction, with many different roads to choose from and the possibility of leaping aboard a bus or tram. Harry had to keep her in sight until then.

Thankfully, the men behind her had the disadvantage of having spent the evening drinking; when Harry dared a look back, she saw only a few were still chasing her. She could only hope Oliver had been so lucky. Dora seemed to be slowing too – the distance between her and Harry was shortening. But even so, Harry knew she would not catch her before the bright lights of Elephant and Castle came into view and, sure enough, Dora reached the junction well ahead of Harry. She glanced back, caught sight of her pursuer, and danced desperately out into the traffic. Horns blared and brakes screamed but miraculously Dora was not hit.

A tram rolled past, temporarily blocking Harry's view. Cursing loudly, she hopped up and down on the spot until she could dodge around the end. It took her a moment to locate Dora once more – the girl was faster than Harry could believe. Praying that the vehicles surrounding her would be able to stop, she followed, taking as direct a route as she dared and ignoring the furious cacophony she left in her wake.

Ahead, Dora dodged around a corner, disappearing from view for several long seconds. When she reappeared, Harry guessed she was making for the railway arches on the far side of the junction. She had only given the area a cursory glance while she was waiting for Oliver, not wanting to miss him if he had arrived early, but suspected it must be a rabbit warren of dingy alleyways and places to hide. Forcing her legs to move faster, Harry ran as quickly as she could. If she lost Dora now, she might never find her again.

But luck was on Harry's side – it appeared Dora was winded. Next to the towering bridge that carried the railway over the streets, the girl paused to look back, clutching at her side. Harry used a bus as cover, hiding behind its bulk as it trundled by and darting into the shadows at the edge of the road to creep nearer to Dora. The girl was still scanning the traffic, catching her breath but ready to fly at a moment's notice. Even so, she didn't see Harry until it was almost too late but, right at the very last second, she caught sight of her and took off beneath the arches. Muttering another curse, Harry made chase.

There were no street lamps here. Harry slowed her pursuit, her sense of self-preservation suddenly screaming. The road was gravelly underfoot, littered with holes that would turn an ankle in a second. Beyond the uneven, narrow road, the arches were dark and shadowy, pitch-black in places. In some, fires burned, roaring from metal bins and surrounded by hollow-cheeked men Harry was certain she did not want to meet. Not for the first time that evening, she was glad of her disguise; the trousers had been easy to run in and her overall appearance meant she should go untroubled by those lurking in the shadows.

Peering ahead, she tried to pick out Dora but saw nothing. If the girl had any sense, she would have gone to ground, burrowing into one of the arches or alleyways until Harry gave up. Breath pluming, Harry tried to second-guess where the girl would hide; she couldn't be too far away. She crept forwards, eyes straining against the darkness, ears pricked for the slightest sound above the rumble of traffic from the junction. Rounding a corner, she found herself in a dead end. Sheets of corrugated iron leaned against wire fencing that stretched far too high for Dora to have climbed. Harry gazed around in frustration, fighting a rising sense of panic. Where was the blasted girl hiding?

And then she caught a blur of movement from the edge of one eye – a sheet of metal flying through the air and a shape bursting towards her. Before she could move, Dora barrelled into her, hammering the air from her lungs as she bore her to the ground.

For a moment, Harry saw stars. Her head rang from its impact on the dirt and her lungs would not work. She fought desperately to breathe, winded by the brutal collision. A whining rasp escaped her. Black and white dots bloomed before her eyes and she thought she might faint. Then her locked muscles relented and air whooshed into her chest again. She croaked in a breath, blinking in pain as her vision cleared. The dead end swarmed into view again.

Dora was on her in a second, fists and feet lashing out. Purely on instinct, Harry rolled left and stumbled agonisingly to her feet. Her ribs hurt. Her head ached. There was a trickle of something she suspected was blood on her chin. And her cap was on the ground, along with the brown scarf she had tied around her hair. Dora stopped, staring at her in amused disbelief. 'What have we here? If it isn't Little Miss Perfect, getting in my way again.'

Harry blew out a breath, willing her ringing head to clear. 'Give yourself up, Dora. There's nowhere to run.'

The girl laughed. 'You got me cornered all right. I hope you know how to fight.'

Harry squinted at her opponent. She would fight dirty, that was for sure, but Harry anticipated she would underestimate her. It might give her an advantage, although it would be a slender one at best. Raising her chin, she pushed the sleeves of her threadbare jacket up her arms. 'I grew up with three brothers,' she said, shifting her weight to her toes. 'I'm no stranger to fighting.'

'Better hope they taught you well,' Dora snarled. 'I'm going to grind you into dust otherwise.'

She lunged forward but Harry was ready for her this time. Dancing aside, she thrust out a fist and let out a cry of triumph when it connected with the side of Dora's head. The girl stumbled but stayed on her feet, wheeling round to wrap her arms around Harry's waist. Once again, Harry anticipated her move. She spun out of reach and snatched up a handful of dirt, which she threw into Dora's face. The girl retched and coughed, clutching at her eyes. Harry did not wait for her to recover. Tearing across the yard, she hauled the sheet of iron into the air and launched it at her opponent. Crying out, Dora crumpled into a heap.

Warily, Harry circled just out of reach. She had been fooled by this move before; in the past, Seb had been known to feign injury before sweeping Harry's feet from under her. Sure enough, Dora waited until she judged Harry was near enough before kicking out. 'So predictable,' Harry said as she skipped backwards. 'Haven't you got anything else?'

'I got plenty,' the girl snarled. Thrusting one hand into a pocket, she pulled out something dark and small. Harry heard a sharp click and saw a silvery glint. A knife, she thought, and her blood ran cold. She'd never faced a weapon before. She would have to concentrate.

Grinning, Dora swiped at her. 'Scared, are ya?'

Harry shook her head. 'We don't have to do this, Dora. Even now, it's not too late. Hand yourself in and we can help you.'

The blade glinted again. 'I don't need your help, Miss Goody-Goody. I was doing fine before you started getting in my way.' Dora lunged forwards, swiping wildly and missing Harry's cheek by inches. Harry gasped as it whistled past. Next time she might not be so lucky.

'We know you're not working alone,' she called, watching the girl's movements intently. If she timed it right, she might knock the knife out of her hand.

'Of course I'm not,' Dora sneered. 'We've got people everywhere. You've got no idea what you've stumbled into.'

She leapt again, slashing viciously, but this time Harry anticipated the attack. Stepping aside, she brought her own hand down in a sharp chopping motion, connecting with Dora's forearm with a hefty crack. 'Aaargh!' Dora bellowed as the knife tumbled from her nerveless fingers. Before she lost momentum, Harry whirled around and stuck out a boot to trip her. Dora hit the ground with a painful-sounding thud.

'Last chance,' Harry offered as she kicked the knife into the shadows. 'Give up now, before one of us gets really hurt.'

The offer only seemed to infuriate Dora more. With a howl of incoherent rage, she got to her feet and charged towards Harry. Poised on the balls of her feet, Harry waited until the very last second to dart aside. Unable to stop, Dora's roar became a scream as her own momentum carried her hard into the metal sheets that lined the fence. Her cry stopped abruptly as she made contact and collapsed. Corrugated iron clattered all around her, raising the kind of cacophony that would only attract more attention.

Panting, Harry waited, watching Dora for any movement even as she kept one eye trained on the blackness beyond the clearing. The girl lay still. Cautiously, Harry edged forward. Playing dead was one of Lawrence's old tricks, although she fervently hoped he had grown out of it now. But Dora did not reach out to wrestle her to the ground. She did not move at all. Harry held a hand in front of the girl's face, relieved to feel the steady warmth of her breath. With luck, she would not be badly hurt, although she would have an almighty headache when she woke up.

Slowly, wincing at the sudden onslaught of a hundred aches and pains, Harry glanced warily around. Still no one came. Retracing her steps to the entrance of the dead end, she bent to retrieve her hat and scarf. The hat went back on her head but she used the scarf to tie Dora's hands together, testing the reef knot to make sure it was tight enough to secure the girl but not so tight that it would stop the flow of blood to her fingers. Once she was satisfied, Harry sat back on her haunches, wondering what to do next. If she left Dora here, she could probably find a policeman but she was loath to leave the girl unprotected somewhere so dangerous. No one had come to investigate the sounds of fighting but that did not mean they hadn't been heard.

But a few minutes later, the dilemma was solved for her: the thunder of running feet on the road outside was followed by the desperate sound of Oliver's voice. 'Harry! Harry, where are you?'

With a weary glance at the unconscious Dora, Harry limped out of the yard. 'I'm here.'

A shadowy figure at the end of the alleyway came hurrying towards her and Harry was relieved to see it was Oliver. He took one look at her appearance, swore loudly and pulled her into a deep hug. 'I thought I'd lost you.'

Trying to ignore the protests of her bruised ribs, Harry allowed herself a brief smile. 'And I thought I'd lost you. How did you escape?'

'Ah, they were all drunk,' Oliver said, stepping back and releasing her. 'But you're hurt.'

She shook her head, and immediately wished she hadn't. 'Just cuts and bruises.'

Frowning, he reached out to gently tilt her face to the light. 'You're going to have a lovely black eye tomorrow.'

Gingerly, she reached up to feel the skin around her eye socket. It had already started to swell. 'Could have been worse,' she said, remembering how close the knife had been.

Oliver shook his head. 'And Dora? Don't tell me she got away.'

At that, Harry managed a weak smile. 'Of course not. Follow me.'

He did as she demanded, eyes widening as he took in Dora's crumpled form. Once he had satisfied himself that Dora did not appear to be seriously hurt, Oliver gazed at Harry with a troubled expression. 'So now what do we do?'

'Hand her over to the police,' Harry said, puffing out a long breath. 'It's the best way to help Mildred.'

'Yes,' Oliver said patiently. 'But how do we do that?' He adopted a singsong voice. 'Oh, excuse me, Officer, here's a criminal who is wanted in connection with a burglary that I just happened to find?'

Harry stared at him. 'Why not?'

Oliver huffed impatiently. 'Because *you* are not supposed to be here, Harry. You are the granddaughter of a baron – you have a reputation to protect, not to mention a job that would take a dim view of you getting involved in street fights with gangsters.' He paused to glare at Dora. 'And so do I, as a matter of fact.'

He had a point, Harry supposed, but it was too late to back off now. 'Don't you have contacts?' she asked, throwing her hands in the air. 'Those pals at Vine Street or wherever who help you out every now and then?'

He shook his head. 'In case you hadn't noticed, we are not in Mayfair. Things work a bit differently around here.'

'Call in Scotland Yard, then,' Harry said, thoroughly exasperated. 'Isn't there a real-life Inspector Lestrade who would love to take the credit for clearing up a notorious burglary and nabbing the real culprits?'

Oliver opened his mouth to argue then paused, looking thoughtful. 'Actually, you might be onto something there. Not Inspector Lestrade but there is someone who might be able to help.' He fixed Harry with a determined stare. 'But you cannot be here. I'm going to insist on this, Harry – it's time for you to go home.'

She thought about refusing. Now that the chase was over, she wanted to stay and see Dora taken into custody. Only then would she believe they had prevailed. But Oliver was right – it was not prudent for her to stay. Her presence could not be easily explained, especially not dressed the way she was. 'Promise you will tell me everything the moment you are able,' she said, with extreme reluctance.

'Of course,' he answered. 'If you'll promise you will go straight home.'

Grimacing, Harry rolled her shoulders. 'Believe me, I'm not going anywhere else. There's a bath with my name on it.'

He shook his head again but she thought there was a touch of admiration in the way he looked at her. 'Put some cream on that bruise. I don't know what your mother is going to say when she sees it.'

Harry pulled the flat cap down to cover her hair once more and began to limp towards the bright lights of Elephant and Castle. 'We'll just have to make sure she doesn't, then. Won't we?'

15

ROBERTSON BURGLARY ARREST

Police Raids in Elephant and Castle

Original Suspect Released

The newspaper sellers were enthusiastic about the headlines that had developed overnight; Harry could hear them bellowing from her apartment. She had planned to wake up early to buy a copy of *The Times* and find out exactly what Oliver and his contact at Scotland Yard had cooked up, but her weary body had other ideas. When she did finally wake up, it took her twice as long as usual to do her make-up and she still suspected her black eye would give the game away. She certainly received a few curious looks as she hurried along Baker Street, trying to read the paper at the same time as buttoning up her coat.

Danny the doorman tutted as she dashed up the steps to the bank. 'Four minutes to spare, Miss White,' he said, then did a double take. 'Strike a light! You been in the ring or something?'

Harry did not stop. 'I walked into the cupboard door,' she said blithely. 'So clumsy of me.'

She kept her head down as she crossed the marbled lobby of the bank and it wasn't until she reached her office that the significance of Danny's comment on her timekeeping dawned on Harry. He had always been ready with a smile and a joke when she arrived and left each day but she wouldn't be surprised to find that he was the one who had reported her to Mr Pemberton. The other doorman, Patrick, had always been polite and deferential – more of a hat tipper – but she had no idea what his personality was like. Sooner or later, she would establish which of them was Simeon Pemberton's spy but it was unlikely to be today.

After swiftly removing her hat and coat, she sank into her seat at the desk to pore over the main story on the front page. Dora Grubb, of Tea Cutter Row, South London, had been arrested by Inspector Archibald of Scotland Yard after an extensive undercover police operation to find the real culprits of the Lord Robertson burglary, the article claimed. The diligence and hard work of the police had paid off, Archibald was reported to have said, and an innocent girl had been saved from an unjust punishment. Efforts to catch the other criminals involved were ongoing, the story went on. Bridget Short, Deputy Governor of Holloway Prison, welcomed the news and praised the efforts of Scotland Yard 'to right a terrible wrong'. Inspector Archibald's comments caused Harry to raise a wry eyebrow but she supposed she should be grateful that her role in the case remained a secret. And since no one other than Dora knew the truth, her involvement was likely to remain hidden, as was that of Sherlock Holmes, which was most definitely, indubitably, as it should be.

'I am glad my client's innocence had been proven,' City lawyer Oliver Fortescue said in a statement. 'She has suffered most egregiously but will now be restored to her family to recover from her ordeal.'

True to his word, Oliver rang Harry just after midday to confirm Mildred had been released without charge. 'Scotland Yard were very apologetic,' he told her. 'They arranged for an ambulance to drive her to a hospital near her parents' home. I daresay we could visit once she's on the mend, if you'd like?'

'I would like,' Harry said firmly. 'I'd like that very much indeed.'

'I also passed on your suspicions about Rose Blackburn to Bridget Short,' he said. 'She took the matter very seriously and promised an immediate investigation.'

'Good,' Harry said, frowning. 'I want Rose to pay for what she did to Mildred.' Her gaze came to rest on the newspaper on her desk. 'But tell me, how did you persuade Scotland Yard to take the glory?'

On the other end of the phone, she heard him snort. 'Have you seen the papers today? That was the easy part. Covering our tracks was much harder. I'm afraid I've had to tell an awful lot of not-so-little white lies to the authorities, and in particular to my friends at Scotland Yard.'

It had all been necessary, of course, but his words still caused Harry no small measure of discomfort. 'Ah. I'm sorry about that. I know you pride yourself on your honesty.'

There was a brief silence. 'I do, in normal circumstances but this case was anything but normal.' He paused. 'Besides, being a lawyer is all about knowing which inconvenient facts to leave out. And all's well that ends well – Mildred is safe and neither of us got seriously hurt. I'd say we acquitted ourselves pretty well, wouldn't you?'

'Not too badly,' Harry said, smiling into the phone.

Oliver coughed. 'In fact, now that the dust is beginning to settle, there is something I wanted to ask.' He hesitated, as though steeling himself and Harry thought that she'd never heard him so unsure. 'I wondered whether you might like – if you have time, that is – whether you would like to—'

But what Harry might like to do was interrupted by a frenzied knocking at her office door. Frowning, she placed her hand over the receiver. 'Come in.'

Bobby peered in at her, an odd expression on his face. 'Telegram,' he said, holding out a thin white oblong.

'Sorry, I've got to go,' Harry said hastily to Oliver. 'Catch up later.'

'Of course,' Oliver said, although he sounded oddly deflated. 'I owe you a pint of mild, if nothing else.'

Smiling, Harry rang off and turned her attention to the telegram. It wasn't unheard of for the fastest method of written communication to make an appearance at the bank but it was the last thing Harry expected to land on her own, inconsequential desk. Telegrams were notoriously expensive too – who on earth needed to contact her that badly? 'Are you sure it's for me?'

Bobby shook his head. 'That's the thing – it ain't. It's for Sherlock Holmes.'

'Oh!' Harry exclaimed, although she really ought to have known. She gathered her wits. 'Thank you, Bobby. Leave it on the desk, if you don't mind.'

He stared at her. 'Ain't you going to open it? The boys in the post room are desperate to know what it says.'

Harry smiled. 'All in good time, Bobby. I expect it's just another misguided invitation to investigate a murder. The usual thing.'

'Ah, got you,' the post boy said, winking. 'Say no more.' He stepped back, about to leave, when he noticed her bruised face. 'Blimey, look at that shiner. You been in the wars, Miss White?'

She shook her head. 'Just a fight with a cupboard door,' she said, cheerfully repeating the lie she'd used earlier that morning. 'You should see the state of the door.'

He grinned. 'Gave it hell, did you? Good for you.'

It took several more minutes for the post boy to give up hope that Harry would open the telegram in front of him. Even so, she gave it a further five minutes once the door had closed before she slit the thin paper open, despite the fact that it was practically burning a hole in the surface of her desk. She expected it to be from the Longstaffs, thanking Mr Holmes for his sterling work. But it was not from Esme Longstaff, nor had it been sent by her parents. It was from Mr John Archer, of Thrumwell Manor and it read simply:

Sherlock Holmes. PHILIP ST JOHN at death's door. Time of the essence. Reply immediately.

Harry stared at it for a moment. The sender was unfamiliar but she knew the name Philip St John – he was a celebrated author, one of her father's favourites, and a darling of the English literary scene, even though it had been some years since he had been seen in public. What did it mean, *at death's door*? More importantly, what did that have to do with Sherlock Holmes? Frowning a little, she set the telegram to one side. Emergency or no emergency, John Archer would have to wait his turn. She had other work to do before she could reply.

Rolling a sheet of paper into her typewriter, Harry took a moment to compose her thoughts and tipped her head at an imaginary Sherlock. 'A new addition to your casebook, Mr Holmes,' she murmured, recalling Bobby's observation that she would make a better assistant than Dr Watson. 'I'll try to do it justice.'

Resting her fingers on the keys, she took a deep breath and began to type. *The Further Adventures of Sherlock Holmes*, she wrote, the keys clattering at speed. *The Case of the Missing Maid by R. K. Moss.*

AUTHOR'S NOTE

In 1932, the rapidly expanding Abbey Road Building Society moved into their new headquarters in the heart of London. The offices spanned numbers 219–229 Baker Street, which any fan of crime fiction knows includes a very famous address, and sure enough, the bank immediately began to receive letters addressed to Mr Sherlock Holmes. There were so many that they were forced to employ someone to reply – a secretary to Holmes who played along with the belief that the great detective was a real person – and the role continued for many decades, perhaps even until the bank left Baker Street in 2002. It's not too much of a stretch to imagine that a bright and enterprising secretary might be tempted to investigate one of the alleged crimes on Sherlock's behalf, even though the mere suggestion was enough to cost them their job... And so The Baker Street Mysteries was born.

Harry White is, of course, as fictional as Holmes but I had great fun envisioning her following in his footsteps, albeit it many years on from the cases he solved. I hope you've enjoyed *The Missing Maid* as much as I enjoyed writing it. The game is most definitely afoot.

Holly Hepburn
January 2024

ACKNOWLEDGEMENTS

Like most authors, I live in genuine fear of forgetting someone who helped shape each of my books but here is a non-exhaustive list of those who contributed to *The Missing Maid*.

First and foremost, my thanks go to Jo Williamson of Antony Harwood Ltd, for being a constant champion of my writing for over 15 years now. We've come a long way and I hope there's still plenty of road to travel. Boldwood Books is a new publishing home for me, so I hope you will forgive me for failing to thank you all individually but my most heartfelt appreciation must go to my lovely editor Rachel Faulkner-Willcocks, whose enthusiasm from the first moment she heard the Baker Street Mysteries concept has been uplifting and refreshing. It's been a joy to work on the first story with you, Rachel, and I really value your advice and suggestions to make Harry's inaugural adventure a better book. I can only hope you've held some patience back for Book 2.

Massive thanks to Helena Newton for her excellent copy-editing skills, and Rachel Sargeant for her brilliant proof reading. Your attention to detail is very much appreciated. A grateful tip of the deerstalker to the Boldwood design team for coming up with such a cracking cover. Thank you to Nia Benyon and Jenna Houston for sprinkling their marketing and PR magic over this book, and to Amanda Ridout for building such an incredible team of inspired publishing professionals. I am thrilled to have joined Team Boldwood.

Thank you to my very lovely author friends – to Rowan Coleman, who encouraged me to develop my Sherlock-But-Not-Sherlock idea several years ago (I did finally get around to it, Rowan) and Miranda Dickinson who has frequently listened to me stumble through plot problems and never failed to suggest truly excellent solutions. And as always, my thanks and undying love go to T and E, as well as to Luna for many many writing day cuddles. It is time to go for a walk now, yes.

Last of all, I want to thank the readers who have embarked upon this fresh new voyage in uncharted (for me) waters. I hope you've enjoyed reading this book at least as much as I enjoyed writing it.

ABOUT THE AUTHOR

Holly Hepburn writes escapist, swoonsome fiction that sweeps her readers into idyllic locations, from her native Cornwall to the windswept beauty of Orkney. With *The Missing Maid*, her first book published by Boldwood Books, she turns her hand to cosy crime inspired by Sherlock Holmes himself. Holly lives in leafy Hertfordshire with her adorable partner in crime, Luna the Labrador.

Sign up to Holly Hepburn's mailing list for news, competitions and updates on future books

Follow Holly on social media:

x.com/HollyH_Author
instagram.com/HollyH_Author

Milton Keynes UK
Ingram Content Group UK Ltd.
UKHW041848050424
440692UK00006B/42

BREAKER OF BONES

BREAKER OF BONES

DAVID PENNY

190604.1630

THE THOMAS BERRINGTON HISTORICAL MYSTERIES

The Red Hill

Moorish Spain, 1482. English surgeon Thomas Berrington is asked to investigate a series of brutal murders in the palace of al-Hamra in Granada.

Breaker of Bones

Summoned to Cordoba to heal a Spanish prince, Thomas Berrington and his companion, the eunuch Jorge, pursue a killer who re-makes his victims with his own crazed logic.

The Sin Eater

In Granada Helena, the concubine who once shared Thomas Berrington's bed, is carrying his child, while Thomas tracks a killer exacting revenge on evil men.

The Incubus

A mysterious killer stalks the alleys of Ronda. Thomas Berrington, Jorge and Lubna race to identify the culprit before more victims have their breath stolen.

The Inquisitor

In a Sevilla on the edge of chaos death stalks the streets. Thomas Berrington and his companions tread a dangerous path between the Inquisition, the royal palace, and a killer.

The Fortunate Dead

As a Spanish army gathers outside the walls of Malaga, Thomas Berrington hunts down a killer who threatens more than just strangers.

The Promise of Pain

When revenge is not enough. Thomas Berrington flees to the high mountains, only to be drawn back by those he left behind.

The Message of Blood

When Thomas Berrington is sent to Cordoba on the orders of a man he hates he welcomes the distraction of a murder, but is shocked when the evidence points to the killer being his closest companion.

In memory of George Penny
2nd January 1923 - 23rd March 2015
One of this world's true gentlemen

AL-ANDALUS

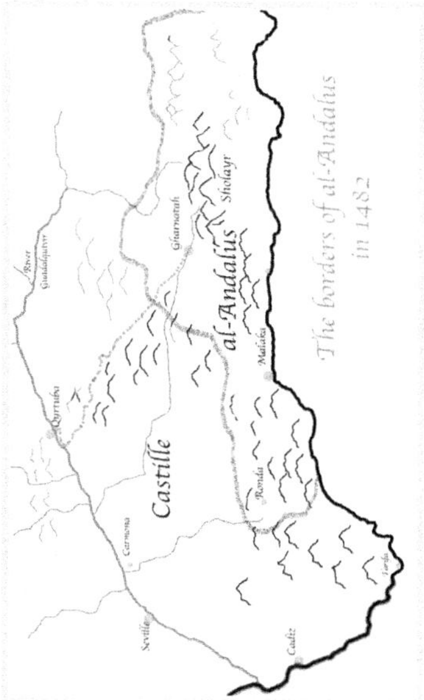

River
Guadalquivir
Gharnatah
Sholayr
al-Andalus
Malaka
Qurtuba
Castille
Ronda
Carmona
Seville
Cadiz
The borders of al-Andalus
in 1482

SPAIN: 1483

CORDOBA, ANDALUSIA

When mania creates a monster,
only one man can stop the killing.

March 1483, and surgeon Thomas Berrington makes a reluctant journey to Qurtuba at the request of his master. He expects only to operate on a Spanish prince and return home to Moorish al-Andalus. But fate has something else in store for him and his companion, the eunuch Jorge.

A warped killer is taking young women to create twisted creatures from their bodies. When Thomas is tasked by Queen Isabel to hunt down the culprit he is propelled into an unfamiliar world of religious mania where it is impossible to tell who is friend and who foe. Meanwhile Jorge is on a quest of his own—to track down the remnant of a family he abandoned twenty years before.

When the Bonebreaker takes a new victim the pair are forced to undertake their most dangerous challenge yet. Thomas and Jorge race to expose the killer before yet another life is taken – this time someone close to them.

CHAPTER ONE

Thomas Berrington came down to the river to wash, the ache in his bones reminding him of every one of his forty-two years. As he approached the water, sufficient light had gathered in the sky to show something floating there and he stopped short. The water roiled slow and deep, stained offerings marring the surface. The object drifted from sight into a mist that obscured the river more than twenty feet from the bank. Thomas shook his head, convinced he had been mistaken. A second look at the water and he decided washing could wait until he entered Qurtuba.

He lifted his robe and pissed into the polluted river. Had it been cleaner he might have relieved himself elsewhere, but he didn't believe his own contribution was likely to make much of a difference.

His companions remained asleep. Pero beneath a blanket on the back of his cart, Jorge curled under his own blanket on the ground, his saddle for a pillow. It was almost the end of March but Thomas had woken to ice on his beard. He knew by noon he would be cursing his heavy cloak. They should have reached the city by now but Pero had insisted they take a detour two days earlier when rumour reached them of a skirmish near Castro del Rio. Now they were south of the Guadalquivir and still fifteen miles from their destination. The breadth and power of the river brought to mind the puny waters of his homeland of England, a place he hadn't seen since he'd left at the age of twelve.

Thomas was adjusting his robe when he heard something out on the water, the source hidden by the mist. He stepped closer to the bank but saw nothing as the sound came again. An oar dipping? A splash as something was dropped into the water?

Perhaps something moved, darker grey against grey, but he couldn't be sure and was reluctant to call out. Even this close to the city brigands might prey on the unwary.

Another splash was followed by two more. A shape pulled away upstream—it might've been a boat containing two figures, it might've been no more than a thickening of the fog. It slid in and out of the mist, never quite becoming visible as the sound of its passage faded. Thomas stared at the water as something drifted past and he took an involuntary step backwards. At first he took it for a child's limb, but then he made it out—the hindquarter of a wolf, the fur matted, the limb angled in a way to suggest it was not human. He watched it drift from sight, spinning slowly in the languid current. When he started to turn away, wondering why anyone would discard such a thing, another floated towards him. This time it caught against rushes beside the bank and Thomas, cursing the curiosity that had got him into trouble many times before, reached out with a stick and drew it close.

"What have you found now?"

He turned to see Jorge coming down the slope, picking his way delicately as if afraid he might tread in something unfortunate, which well he might. Even cold, unkempt and tired his friend still possessed the special aura that had picked him out to be a palace eunuch.

"Nothing."

"It looks like something to me." Jorge moved a few paces downstream to perform his own ablutions.

Thomas avoided looking, studying the severed limb instead. He turned it over with the end of the stick, leaned closer. A frown settled on his brow. Whatever he thought he had first seen it hadn't been this.

"Never seen a wolf's haunch before?" said Jorge, adjusting his robe as he approached.

"Why would anyone toss it into the river? An entire wolf, perhaps, but who would cut it up first?"

"Or torn apart." Jorge crouched beside Thomas, who knew his friend only pretended interest. They were closer now than before the business of last year which resulted in the ousting of one sultan and the ascent of another.

"So why throw it away? And see—this hasn't been hacked. The cut is clean, precise."

Jorge looked and shrugged. "As precise as you would be?"

"Perhaps not, but someone with skill did this."

"A butcher? I expect they have more practice than surgeons. Why should they not also be skilled?"

"They have no need of such precision. And a butcher wouldn't hack up a wolf."

"One more mystery in the world for you to solve," said Jorge, re-arranging his position so he could sit against the bank. "The priest is awake, by the way. He wants us moving. I told him I'd come and find you."

"You've found me."

"What are you going to do if you can't cure this prince?"

Thomas pushed the wolf's leg back into the current and watched it drift from sight. He thought the mist might be lifting a little. He could make out a rocky bluff on the northern bank, perched atop it some kind of fortified structure. "Go home," he said in response to Jorge's question, but the man had already disappeared and Thomas was alone again. He shook his head, both amused and frustrated at the eunuch.

Thomas rose to his feet, was starting to turn away when something else caught his attention, something different, paler, like the first sighting had been. He leaned over the water as the fickle mist chose to thicken at just the wrong moment.

The object drifted into the channel. Thomas took steps along the bank until it turned and approached closer once more. He looked around for another stick, found one, but whatever it was remained stubbornly out of reach. Even so he could make out what it was. This was no portion of a wolf. What he stared at was the headless torso of a young woman.

CHAPTER TWO

Pero de Carracedo had already taken the cart and started down the rutted track by the time they returned. Thomas rolled his blanket and stuffed it into a saddlebag, then lifted both saddle and bag onto his horse and tightened the cinch before mounting. He glanced at Jorge, who was taking longer, and wondered whether to inflict the news of what he had witnessed on him. When he turned back the cart and priest had disappeared into the fog, but the muffled sound of its wheels could still be heard.

"We should simply turn around and ride home," said Jorge. "But you won't do that, will you."

Thomas glanced up from tying his saddle. His mind was still on what he thought he had seen in the water, playing it over and over, each review adding layers of irrationality to the vision. He was starting to convince himself he had been mistaken. It could not have been what he believed. Impossible. He had seen animal carcasses that had been in the water too long, the fur fallen out, the skin grown pale and waxy. Yes, he thought, it had been the body of the wolf that belonged to the limbs, a body too long in the river.

"Will you?" repeated Jorge.

Thomas tugged at the saddle until he was satisfied it wouldn't tip him off. He glanced around at the campsite to make sure nothing remained behind.

"You know we can't," he said. "Besides, a few months away from Gharnatah might prove healthier for both of us."

"It's almost a year since Muhammed came to power," said Jorge. "Surely a man can hold a grudge only so long."

"He's never going to forget I ousted his father, nor what I know of his part in it. You witnessed his threat at the infirmary where I recovered from my wounds. He only keeps me close so he can torture me further. No—a month or more in Qurtuba sounds good to me."

"They won't want us to stay long. Why would they?"

"As a favour from one king to another?"

Thomas watched as Jorge mounted his horse, the man now comfortable in the saddle, his body straight. Jorge's hood was thrown back to reveal the hair that had grown on his scalp, although the short beard on his face failed to mask the smoothness of his cheeks. Neither the journey nor his travel-stained clothes could hide the beauty of the man. Thomas would have preferred it if he looked worse.

Jorge spurred his horse into a canter and disappeared into the swirling mist after Pero. Thomas remained where he was, the conversation with Jorge reminding him of why he was standing on a stinking riverbank in the cold grey light before dawn. Little more than a year before his life had been settled. That had ended when the first attack occurred at the palace that dominated Gharnatah, and with it the scarring of a beautiful concubine. Helena. She had been gifted him by the old sultan, Abu al-Hasan Ali, because she was no longer considered beautiful. Except Thomas's skills had restored her—not fully, but enough to cause trouble. Before long she was sharing his bed. And then the other killings had started.

He shook his head.

Since that moment death seemed to stalk him. As he had stalked the killer in the palace. Stalked and found him, ending in a confrontation which resulted in the death of the culprit, but also the overthrow of the old sultan by his son, Muhammed. Life since had become complicated. The arrival of Helena's sister Lubna had sparked all manner of emotions in Thomas, even though she was not beautiful like her sister. Instead Lubna was smart, and she was fascinated by his work. Now he shared his life between Helena and his duty on the hill in the jumbled alleys of the Albayzin training Lubna to be his assistant, trying to ignore his growing attraction for her.

He wiped a hand across his mist-damp face and cursed. A few months away from that life might indeed be welcome.

Thomas mounted his own steed and let it carry him at a slow walk, relishing the moment of solitude. There had been precious few on the journey, and there were things on his mind that gnawed at his composure. It was obvious to him Jorge wasn't himself, and not just because of the uncompromising presence of the priest or the uncomfortable journey. Thomas wanted to talk with his friend, to tease out whatever burden he was carrying. They would need each other's support in this unfamiliar land.

He closed his eyes, enjoying the drift of moisture against his face until the horse whinnied and shuffled sideways. Thomas opened his eyes and saw a shape, barely distinguishable from the grey mist. The longer he stared the less convinced he was that anything was there. Tendrils of mist thickened and faded, turning the world unreal.

Then the shape moved, coming closer. Thomas soothed his mount as it skittered backwards.

A wolf approached, yellow eyes switching between horse and Thomas. He looked beyond it, expecting others, but saw nothing. He dropped a hand to his saddle and drew the sword that rested there. The wolf's eyes watched the movement. It stopped and cocked its head at a sound only it could hear. It looked back at Thomas, tensed and emitted a sharp yelp before sprinting away. Mist closed around the creature as if it had never existed. Thomas waited before sliding the sword back into its sheath. The wolf was a disturbing reminder of what he had seen in the river. But the more he thought on it the more convinced he became that what he took as a girl's body could not have been.

"Come on, old man!" called Jorge. "Can't you keep up?"

Thomas smiled. His friend might be carrying some secret burden, but he remained the same beneath it. He urged his horse into a canter until ghostly figures appeared ahead.

Jorge had claimed he couldn't ride when they left Gharnatah. Now he sat at ease on his mare as a seasoned rider. For once Thomas envied him his lack of balls, for his own ached from the constant motion.

Jorge came trotting back, appearing like a wraith through the shifting grey currents.

"I told him to wait but he said no. I don't like the man."

"I expect he wants to get all that gold to his masters. And I doubt he likes you much, either."

"Are we going to catch him up? We can't let Pero enter the city first. There's no knowing the tales he might spread of us."

Thomas dug his heels into the horse's flanks, urging it into a canter. He glanced at the sky. The mist was starting to clear. Already he could make out the circle of the sun. He twisted in the saddle, curious, and caught a glimpse of the structure he had seen earlier. Yes, a castle, perched on the crest of a rocky outcrop. It rose from out of the mist which still cloaked the water, the early sun catching white walls.

"Aren't you curious about those remains?" Thomas asked.

"Not my area of expertise," said Jorge. "Nor yours, I wouldn't have thought."

"They're strange. Not the discards of any hunter I've ever seen."

"This whole place is strange."

Thomas made no reply. He wondered what Qurtuba would make of them—two strangers in Arab dress. They needed the priest to enter the city, he was their promise of a safe passage.

He caught sight of the cart at the top of the next rise. A breeze had started up and the mist trailed away in ragged tatters. Beyond it the air sat heavy, stained with smoke, but the city remained hidden. In the next small valley they caught up with Pero. The track rose, and at the brow the city came into sight, sitting on the north bank of the Guadalquivir. The track brought them back down to its banks, a stench rising from the water even worse than before as it carried the refuse of ten thousand souls. Ahead the roadway turned to follow the banks.

Soon other travellers appeared from side roads, some like them with carts, but drawn by oxen rather than fine horses, others hauling their own goods in home-made barrows. Each of them cast curious, and in some cases fearful glances at the two mounted men. It was the start of another day in Spain beyond the boundaries of al-Andalus, and this land hadn't seen their like in many years.

Thomas had forgotten how different this place was. Gharnatah lay surrounded by fields and small villages, irrigation ditches carrying water from the snows of the Sholayr to grow crops: vines, wheat, mulberry and olives. Here the land was given over to sheep and goats, which grazed it so hard, barely any grass remained. As the breeze picked up with the rising sun, puffs of dust rose from the passage of wheels and feet to carry away a little more goodness from the soil.

Thomas had not ventured beyond Moorish boundaries in twenty years and had little wish to do so until now. There had been no choice in this venture, none at all, as there had been no choice in his life the past year since he had been instrumental in deposing one sultan and raising a new one to power.

The city walls rose higher as they approached. A bridge spanning the river funnelled everyone to the southern gate.

"Is the palace far once we enter the city?" asked Jorge. "My arse aches and I need a bath."

"It's close," said Pero. "But there will be no bath." His face showed how he felt about the application of water to the body. Thomas glanced at him, observing dark hair that hung lank around his face, grey skin that showed little health, and considered the priest might benefit from the application of soap and water. But he knew most in this land distrusted cleanliness. He had even heard Pero call it ungodly.

Thomas shifted his attention to his surrounding, knowing the priest was too set in his ways to change. He noted the lack of trees close to the walls, and pits dug at intervals. In one place the detritus of a destroyed trebuchet had sunk into the ground like some decomposing beast. Only the largest part remained, the rest having been scavenged for firewood. Qurtuba looked like a city used to siege, yet he knew it was not. A city preparing for siege, perhaps.

Thomas pulled the long tail of his tagelmust across his face as a northerly wind carried the stench of the city to him. With time he might grow accustomed to the stink, but the thought of doing so only made the stench worse.

"It's busy," said Jorge. A knot of people were gathered around the gate as they approached.

"It is close to the palace, and the only way across the river from the south," said Pero. He used a whip to make the horses move faster. "And there are always those wishing to petition the king over one matter or another." It was almost his longest speech of the entire journey. His tone indicated his feelings about the petitioners. As they passed through the borderlands between two kingdoms Thomas had seen little evidence that the milk of human kindness flowed through Pero's veins.

"What are they doing?" Jorge's question brought Thomas back to the present and he glanced up.

A crowd gathered at the gate set through high walls, and as they came closer he heard raised voices. A woman rushed towards them across the bridge, vegetables scattering unheeded from the woven basket on her back. She crossed herself repeatedly, muttering a prayer over and over. Thomas rose in his saddle. People were pointing at something that swung from the arch of the gate, but he couldn't make it out. He sat and urged his mount forward.

He still couldn't see what hung swaying from the arch, not until he was almost beneath it. He bullied his horse through the crowd, which parted with reluctance. Here some were praying, other voices raised in fear. Thomas translated the Spanish words awkwardly, no longer used to the language. He cocked his head to one side, unable to interpret what his eyes showed.

A swinging figure ... or not. Something swinging, but it was deformed.

A man leaned over from the top of the wall, his pike reaching out, catching on the rope holding the atrocity to the arch. The tip of the pike caught, causing the figure to swing more. As it came back the man twisted the end and caught the rope. He gave a sharp tug, another, and the rope parted. As the body fell Thomas saw it for what it was. Not human, not animal, but some illogical combination of both. He knew at once what the discarded limbs in the river meant, knew his first impression had been right and the torso floating in the water had been human after all.

CHAPTER THREE

As the body fell to the ground the crowd surged back, cries of horror passing outward like ripples. Thomas dismounted and walked forwards, pushing his way through the throng, hearing the same word uttered from a dozen lips. *Bonebreaker.* The word accompanied by a raw fear on each face.

Nobody challenged him as he reached the figure. He knelt and turned it over, re-arranging the tangle of limbs, the fur-matted torso. A girl. No, he corrected—she *had* been a girl. A pretty girl with blonde hair, perhaps fifteen or sixteen years old, any chance of getting older prematurely stolen from her. The grimace on her face hinted death had not come easily. How could it have been otherwise? Mottled scars showed on her arms and thighs, lesions formed by a hot iron. Her torso was that of a wolf, deep chested, blood-matted fur contrasting with pale limbs. The wolf had been male; it's prick and balls out of place against the girl's delicate thighs. Thomas's expert eyes scanned the body, taking in more than he could evaluate, storing images away because he had no idea how long before someone came to stop him.

Not long.

As Thomas reached to close her staring eyes he was grabbed and toppled backwards. A second hand caught him from the other side and he was hauled away to the side of the gate and flung against a wall. Three soldiers stood in front of him, their faces twisted in disgust.

"What have you done to her, bonebreaker?" A hand slapped his face hard and Thomas tasted blood.

"Don't be a fool. I'm a stranger here, newly arrived from—" He stopped. Telling these men where he was from wouldn't help.

"You're a Moor."

Thomas shook his head, but not in negation. To these men he must appear a Moor, and he doubted they had even heard of England. Not that he could call that place home anymore.

"I am here at the request of your king and queen," he said, his Spanish stilted, awkward on his tongue.

"A Moor?" The soldier spat. His companions, sensing Thomas wasn't anything their leader couldn't handle, returned to the body and started to drag it away.

"What happened here?" As Thomas waited for a response his eyes scanned the crowd. Most were poor working men and women trying to scratch a living from a harsh land. But among them were better dressed folk, and gathered on the edge of the crowd a small group of monks dressed in white robes. One of them stood a head taller than the others, his hood tossed back to reveal long hair streaked with grey, a beard of the same colour. Thomas's eyes moved on and then returned. The man had a scowl on his face, as if the atrocity offended his sensibilities.

He watched Pero approach the monks. It was obvious he knew the men, but from their body language they appeared to be arguing. The tall man was their leader, a second beside him also involved in the conversation. As he watched, Pero turned and pointed towards Thomas, who took in all this information in a moment before returning his gaze to the man in front of him.

"You're asking me what happened?" said the man. He prodded Thomas's chest with a finger. "You tell me. This looks like the work of a heathen."

"If I had done this don't you think I'd be covered in blood? You should be searching the city for the real culprit while the trail is fresh."

"For all I know you're soaked in blood beneath this—this blanket." He grabbed Thomas's robe, tearing the linen to expose his chest, then tugged the tagelmust away from his face.

"Do I look like a Moor?" Thomas said. From the corner of his eye he saw Pero start towards him.

The guard looked Thomas up and down, taking in the pale skin, the scars that crossed Thomas's chest, the long hair and short beard.

The guard nodded. "A spy." He grabbed at Thomas's shoulder.

"Leave him," the priest said using a commanding voice, a tone Thomas had not heard Pero use before.

The guard turned. "And who are you?"

"I am Pero de Carracedo, priest to the royal household."

"Anyone could say that. For all I know you're no more than another spy."

Pero took a pace closer, his dark eyes blazing with anger. The guard stopped scowling and stepped back. Thomas drew his torn robe around himself.

"Perhaps I am," said Pero. "But you recognise that man, don't you?" He pointed to the group of monks. "You recognise Abbot Mandana, I am sure." He cocked his head to one side. "Are you a true Christian, sir? Would you like the abbot to question you regarding your faith?"

The man took another step, his face paling. "I am a true follower of Christ." He made the sign of the cross. "If I misunderstood, I apologise. The killings are putting a fright into everyone."

"Clear this mess up and open the gate." Pero started to turn away, scowling, deliberately not looking at the abomination that lay on the ground.

Thomas glanced towards the guard, but he had already turned away, issuing curt orders, taking his frustration out on the men under him.

"We will take care of this poor girl." The tall man, the one Pero had called Abbot Mandana, came to join them, together with his small group of monks who hung back, all except the other tall one who was dressed differently. He ignored Pero and stopped in front of Thomas. "Who are you to take an interest in this matter?"

"He is with me," said Pero, but the abbot's eyes did not leave Thomas.

"I might ask the same of you," Thomas said. "Why are you interested in this … this thing?"

"She was a child of God, taken too soon from this world. I would offer her a Christian burial. What would you do?"

Thomas glanced at the figure. No blood stained the ground. She had been drained before this was done to her. "I would examine the body to discover how she came to such an end." He looked up at the arch. "Is there some way to gain access to the top of the wall?"

The abbot stepped close, rank body odour encompassing Thomas. "The Hermandad will investigate her dying. This is no business of yours." He glanced sideways. "Is this man with you, Pero de Carracedo?"

"He is, Your Grace. He is the surgeon requested by the queen. A gift from the heathen sultan. I have brought him from—"

A sour grimace crossed the abbot's face. "I need to know nothing of your business. If he is who you say I suggest you take him to the palace and leave us to take care of matters here."

Pero bowed his head and plucked at Thomas's robe. Thomas stayed where he was, a cold anger rising within him. Did nobody care about what had befallen this girl? The guards showed little interest in her fate, and the abbot seemed to care only for her soul.

The monks moved towards where what was left of the girl lay. The second tall man remained where he was, an amused expression on his face as he studied Thomas.

"Come away," said Pero, once more plucking at Thomas's robe, and this time he allowed himself to be drawn away. But he stopped when he rejoined Jorge at the gate and looked back. The monks were busying themselves with the body. Someone had brought a rough length of sacking and they were rolling the girl inside it. Thomas frowned, wondering where the sacking had come from. It seemed a strange thing to have carried, but perhaps it was a common object in the city. He tried to ignore the questions that crowded his head, knowing this was none of his business, cursing the curiosity that would not allow him to let it rest.

"Why can you never stay out of trouble?" asked Jorge, his words mirroring Thomas's own thoughts as a chill ran through him. Was he so transparent? Grim as his mood was, he almost smiled. If this man could not see into him then who could? They had shared so much over the years. Ever since Thomas had turned Jorge from a boy into something less than a full man, and in doing so saving his life, their fates had become intertwined. It wasn't always an easy friendship but, he hoped, friendship it was.

"It's not through my own choosing. Trouble keeps finding me." He wondered if the shadowy figures he had glimpsed at dawn had been involved. There was more than one man, at least two. But not the killers, he thought, only servants tasked with the job of disposal. It would have been impossible for the men to have reached Qurtuba and hung the body from the gate in time.

As Pero led them through narrow cobbled streets Thomas allowed his horse to make its own way and closed his eyes, conjuring up the images he had captured when he had the chance.

There had been marks on the girl's pale limbs. Marks from a brand, but also cuts. Many cuts, most of them shallow, as though whoever made them didn't want to kill, only inflict pain. The sound of their passage, of the citizens of Qurtuba, faded as he drifted deeper into the memory.

There had been something else as well, and he examined it for a moment without knowing what it meant. Then it snapped into focus. Her body had been marked with paint, or ink. Dark blue stains at the neck and shoulders, more on her thighs. Someone had tortured the girl and then drawn marks where her head and limbs were to be severed from her torso. A torso he had seen and which even now most likely drifted down the Guadalquivir in the company of the discard of a wolf.

CHAPTER FOUR

"How many have died?" Thomas pulled himself up to take a seat beside Pero while his horse followed meekly beside the cart. They climbed a shallow incline, wheels loud on cobbles. Citizens moved aside, huddling against walls to allow them room to pass.

"Some," said the priest.

"Since when?"

Pero turned his head, dark eyes studying Thomas. "This is none of your business. You are here for one reason only—to heal the prince and then to leave."

"I can't ignore what I saw."

"Then you should learn to do so. You mock my religion, you and that creature who accompanies you, but it teaches me obedience. A quality you would benefit from acquiring."

Thomas was aware Pero acted as emissary between the Spanish court and that of Gharnatah, and he wondered exactly how much the man knew about him. Perhaps more to the point how much he had been told, and by whom.

"Was that you obeying at the inn two nights ago?" Thomas had not yet mentioned what he had witnessed when he'd returned to their room unexpectedly. Pero had been on his knees, stripped to the waist while he used a knotted flail on his back. Standing in the doorway Thomas had noted older marks.

"A man must scourge his body if he is to cleanse his soul. The body is evil and given to temptation."

Thomas grimaced, imagining what Jorge's response might be to such a sentiment, but he turned his head so the priest wouldn't see his expression. He had been shocked at the discovery, but not surprised. Pero's actions were only one of the reasons he had little sympathy with the trappings of religion. If a man could be made to believe that scourging his flesh was for his own good what was such a belief doing to the society it was meant to serve.

"Who investigates the atrocities?"

"The Hermandad, the city guard, of course. Assisted by a few of my brothers."

"Like the abbot and the others?"

"They have offered their help."

"Why?"

"How would I know? Now look, the palace is ahead. I told you it lay close to the gate. Are you going to change your clothes before you meet their graces?"

"Should I?"

"You are dressed as an infidel."

"I have little to wear that is different." Thomas had brought other clothing especially, expecting a situation such as this, but they remained in his chest which was thrown on the back of the cart with the others. He preferred the looser robes of al-Andalus to the blouses and breeches of Spain.

"Something might be found," said Pero. "I will ask."

"Why would you do that?"

Pero grimaced. "I would not have you insult my masters."

And perhaps he would have helped, but as soon as they approached the entrance to the palace someone took the horses—and the cart they pulled—and the three of them were led inside. Thomas drew the torn edges of his robe together, unwound his tagelmust and wrapped it around his shoulders. His dark hair fell across his face and he pushed it back with his fingers, but the attempt lasted only a moment before it returned. Pero's masters would have to take him as he was, ill-clothed and unwashed.

Although Thomas had passed through Qurtuba many years before he had never been inside the palace. He was surprised to find it still contained many original Moorish features. He had expected them to be torn down and the interior refashioned in a Spanish manner, but other than the presence of tables and chairs it looked as it might have centuries before when a Caliph ruled these corridors. Glancing left as they passed an arched doorway he saw a pool running the length of a courtyard. Mottled oranges from the previous autumn's harvest clung to rows of trees, taller palms rising beyond. He might have been back in al-Hamra, except here he had at least been spared the steep climb.

Perhaps I am *dressed appropriately, after all,* he thought.

"Are you taking me to the injured man?" Thomas asked Pero as they passed rooms and courtyards. Jorge walked a little behind, glancing around with curiosity, a frown touching his normally smooth brow. Perhaps he too was taken aback at the familiarity of the palace.

"Not a man, a boy. I told you—it is the queen's son you are to minister to."

"I assumed..." Thomas shook his head. He knew he should have asked these questions before. "What age is he?"

"He has five years."

Thomas turned his head as raised voices sounded from a side chamber, but Pero bustled on and all he managed to glimpse were three men, one in uniform. Then more voices came from ahead and he switched his mind from the Arabic he had been speaking to Spanish.

A woman's muffled voice, high and cultured. "I will have no more mutilations in my city!"

A reply came from behind the partially open door they walked towards. "The Hermandad do all they can, Your Grace, but there is no sign of who lies behind the atrocities."

"Then tell them to work harder. This has to stop. There will be no more deaths, I tell you, none."

"I cannot guarantee—"

"I will hear no more. Find the culprit and hang him from the gates. Let the people see we care enough to protect them."

"He is young," Thomas said, ignoring the conversation drifting to them.

"Does that make a difference?"

"He will heal better because of it. How did he come about his injuries?"

Pero shook his head. "There's no sense in asking me, there are others with better answers. Here, we have arrived." Pero stopped outside the door the conversation had come from. Ornate carvings were etched deep into the dark wood. The priest reached out to knock on the door just as a figure stormed out, barging into him.

Thomas stepped aside as a short man in soldier's clothing, his face red, brushed past. He glanced their way, but if he was curious what a priest and bedouin were doing within the palace, he didn't reveal it.

Even though the door remained open Pero used the heavy brass knocker and waited. Minutes passed, but he made no move to announce himself a second time. He stood with hands folded beneath his robe, eyes downcast, and Thomas said nothing. Something about the place moderated his usual surfeit of questions. Eventually a sharp command came from beyond the door. "Fetch them."

Footsteps approached and a servant beckoned them inside. Within lay a room smaller than Thomas had expected. Tapestries depicting hunting scenes covered two walls, including the one they had entered through. The third was broken by a staircase. The fourth held a series of small windows. From the lack of sunlight on the glass Thomas assumed they faced north. He had lost all sense of direction as they travelled through the corridors.

A tall man stood beside a table in the centre of the room where a woman sat with papers scattered before her. Both were dressed in rich silks, the woman with a string of pearls at her throat. The man wore his dark hair to the shoulder, a trimmed beard forming a point at his chin. Thomas had not expected to be brought into the presence of royalty.

The woman looked up and addressed Pero. "Is this him?"

"His name is Thomas Berrington, Your Grace."

She surveyed him, her eyes cool, face expressionless. She was handsome rather than pretty, pale haired. Her eyes, a mix between green and blue, showed a keen intelligence.

"Berrington?" said the man Thomas assumed was her husband, Fernando, King of Aragon and Castile. "He looks more like an Arab. Berrington isn't an Arab name, and neither is Thomas. Who are you, sir? Have we been made false promises? We were told the best surgeon Granada had to offer would be sent, not some … some half-caste."

Thomas was unsure if an answer was required. While trying to make up his mind Pero took the decision for him.

"He is an Englishman, Your Grace, but still, so I am told, the best surgeon the Moors have. He saved the sultan's son when no-one else could. It is said he has saved many who would otherwise have died."

The queen turned her attention to Thomas. "Is this true, sir?"

"I repaired a wound to the sultan's son, certainly, but I'm sure another surgeon could have done it equally as well. I happened to be there rather than someone else."

She studied him and Thomas felt as if her gaze could see through all the layers of his being directly to his soul. He glanced at the king then back to her. A shiver ran through him. These were the people who wanted to expel the Moors. Little by little the border of his adopted land was being picked away, and now he saw why. This Queen Isabel was made of steel, and her husband had the hardened look of a man more used to battle than politics.

"So you are not the best surgeon?" Her voice was soft.

"It is not my place to say."

"Your Grace," said the queen. "If you are truly an Englishman you should know how to address a royal presence."

"I apologise, Your Grace. I meant no disrespect. It has been a long time since I have been in such exalted company."

"Are you a heathen?"

Likely worse than that, to one such as you.

"When I was young I attended church with my family."

"And now?" A smile touched her lips, transforming her from plain to pretty.

"There are few churches in Gharnatah, Your Grace."

"So I have heard. A state of affairs we will correct once we are victorious. My predecessors converted the mosque here in Cordoba. It is a place of Catholic worship now."

"In Gharnatah a man is allowed to worship his own God provided he pays his due." Thomas knew he walked a narrow path. If she asked a direct question, could he continue without admitting his lack of any belief?

The queen turned to take in Jorge. "Is this man your assistant?"

"He is, Your Grace."

"Another Englishman?"

"Spanish, Your Grace." Thomas wished Jorge would answer for himself. Instead he stood almost insolently, staring around at the opulence of his surroundings, perhaps comparing them with the harem in Gharnatah and finding them wanting.

"You, sir," said the king. "What is a Spaniard doing living as an infidel?"

Finally Jorge had no option but to speak. "I was captured, Your Grace, and turned into a eunuch. My place is in the harem of al-Hamra now."

An expression of distaste crossed the queen's face and her husband stepped back from the table as though wanting to distance himself.

"What is a eunuch doing assisting a physician?"

"I have more skills than might be apparent from my appearance, Your Grace." Jorge's voice was soft, cultured, but some tone of disrespect remained beneath the words. Thomas saw the queen had heard it but was reluctant to act. Only then did he understand how much she needed him.

"I believe it is your son who is injured," Thomas said. "I would like to see him as soon as possible."

"In the presence of myself and Pero."

Thomas nodded. "As you wish, Your Grace."

The king shook his head, a pained expression on his face. "I don't like this, Isabel, not at all."

"He languishes," said the queen, "and however much our doctors bleed him he fails to improve."

"I have heard Spanish doctors are great believers in the use of leeches," Thomas said.

"And prayer," replied the queen. "Blood and prayer. It is our way. Yet still he gets no better. Abbot Mandana suspects a supernatural cause." She stood abruptly and clapped her hands. "Come then, see if you can make any difference. This way." She turned and walked swiftly to the far wall where the staircase offered ingress to some hidden world. Thomas took a breath, glanced at Jorge and followed.

CHAPTER FIVE

Prince Juan was studying his letters at a desk that might have been fashioned for him, an older man perched on a stool beside to offer guidance. The boy was young to be studying, Thomas thought, but he knew princes lived by different rules to normal men.

The boy rose when his mother entered the room; a slow, painful manoeuvre which favoured his right leg, a stick gripped in his hand taking the weight on that side. He made no move to cross the room. Instead she went to him and knelt as the tutor stood, a familiar choreography of privilege each enacted without thought.

"How is he today?" she asked of the tutor.

"We have been studying the reign of your brother, King Enrique, Your Grace."

It was no answer, Thomas thought, but perhaps the queen had been expecting no other, for she appeared satisfied. She took her son's hand inside her own and looked at Thomas. Jorge and Pero remained in the doorway. The king had made no move to accompany them, perhaps considering the act of healing an unmanly pursuit.

"This is the doctor I told you of, Juan. He has come to repair your leg." She gave no hint of doubt and Thomas felt his nervousness grow. "Will you let him examine you?"

The boy had been looking at the floor but raised his eyes now.

He was painfully young, and even without the obvious disfigurement to his leg he looked sickly.

"You said he was a Moor, Mother."

"He has learned the Moorish ways of medicine, but he is not of them, my sweet. You can see that from his appearance."

"He dresses like a Moor."

"He is from England. You know where England is, don't you? You have studied maps, and English blood runs in your veins."

"But his skin is brown. And I don't like the tall one."

The queen smiled at her son, glanced at Thomas and Jorge. Her coolness of before was gone, replaced by a mother's concern for her child

"His skin is brown because of the sun, no more. And the other is a good Spaniard. They will do you no harm."

"Will you stay, Mother?"

"Of course." Again she glanced at Thomas. "I may stay, mayn't I?"

He nodded.

"So will you allow him, Juan?"

The boy looked at Thomas, at Jorge, finally at the priest. "Pero must stay, too."

"Of course."

One more series of glances, then he nodded and started across the room. He limped badly, leaning hard on the stick in his right hand. His damaged leg was bent, shorter than the other by an inch or more. Each step caused him pain so that by the time he reached a narrow couch beneath the window he was even paler than before, and sweat stood out on his brow.

His mother walked beside him, her hands ready should he stumble, but he'd made the short journey on his own. As Thomas followed from the doorway the boy's tutor moved unobtrusively in the opposite direction. Thomas knelt beside the couch as the boy reclined, his leg held out in front of him.

"I will need to remove his boot and use my hands," Thomas said, glancing at the queen. He wondered if sweat stood out on his brow, too. He might be used to attending royalty in Gharnatah, but here in the Spanish palace uncertainty plagued him.

The queen nodded her agreement and sat beside her son, taking his hand in hers.

Thomas removed the leather boot and touched the prince's leg through his linen breeches, ran his fingers along its length, pressing. The bone had broken below the knee. It was a bad break badly set and he traced the disfigurement where the tibia had broken through the skin. A previous surgeon had attempted a repair but had been too gentle. He pressed as lightly as he could, but still the boy winced, biting at his lip. Thomas had discovered enough. The bone had not knitted properly and he felt it shift when he pressed down hard. Thomas wondered how the prince managed to walk at all. He also wondered what the queen would say when he told her what needed to be done.

"How did this happen?" he asked.

"He fell while running downstairs." The queen's tone indicated a momentary shortness and Thomas imagined Juan had often run downstairs against her orders.

"Do you know exactly what occurred?"

"I know what I was told. I was not there at the time."

"Then who does know?"

"I do," said the boy, and Thomas realised they had both been ignoring him.

"How much do you remember?"

"Everything."

"Even through the pain? There was a lot of pain, wasn't there?"

Prince Juan nodded.

"And can you talk of it?"

He nodded again. "Ask me your questions, Moor. My mother believes in you so I will answer whatever I can."

Thomas was impressed. Sickly the prince might be, but he had inherited a core of steel from his parents. He glanced at the queen. "It would be better if I spoke with him alone."

She shook her head. "No."

It was the response he had expected.

"Then send Pero away. Jorge, too." He didn't bother explaining why. The boy was young, uncertain, the less people in the room the more chance there was of approaching the truth.

"Show the man to his quarters, Pero. Find him some food if he hasn't already eaten."

"There are letters for you from Gharnatah, Your Grace, and gifts," said Pero.

"My son is more important than letters. Come to me after noon prayer. My husband goes to hunt and we will discuss matters of state then."

Pero nodded and led Jorge away. Thomas turned back before they left the room. He touched the boy's leg and glanced at the queen. "I would like to see the leg itself, if that is permitted."

"You are the physician." She rose and went to the desk where her son had been working, returned with the three-legged stool his tutor had been using and set it for him. She arranged her skirts and sat once more beside her son, a short, stocky figure whose sharp eyes missed nothing but now showed worry. A mother's concern for her son reflected upon her handsome face.

"May I ask you to remove your breeches, Prince Juan?"

The boy glanced at his mother, who nodded once. He rose, untied the cord at his waist and tugged them down. His mother moved closer to help. Eventually he sat again, naked from the waist other than for a linen cloth wrapped between his legs and silk stockings on his small feet. Thomas unrolled the stocking from his right leg.

The damage was worse than he had feared. The leg was fractured in three places at least, one a complete break which had punctured the skin. A vivid scar showed testament to the damage.

"When did this happen?" Thomas asked.

Again the queen answered for her son. "At the turning of the harvest last year, so six months."

Thomas nodded. "Good. There is still a chance."

"You can repair it?" asked the queen. Thomas heard the disbelief in her voice.

"And without the help of leeches, Your Grace. But..." He hesitated, leaned back and stood. "Can we talk a moment outside, Your Grace?"

She surprised him once more by immediately standing and striding for the door. Thomas patted the boy's good leg. "We won't be a moment."

"What are you going to talk about? Me?"

"I need to speak with your mother for a moment," Thomas said. "We will be back before you know we're gone. You can practice your letters again if you want, but don't get dressed."

He followed the queen outside but left the door open.

"Tell me true, Don Berrington, can you really repair my son's leg?"

"I can improve it, but by how much is debatable. You need to know it is not a swift process, and there will bc more pain."

She nodded, as if pain was to be expected. "How much?"

"I will do what I can, but there will be some."

"Nothing can be done for pain."

"I believe otherwise."

She stared up at him, a defiance in her eyes and body and Thomas was surprised to find he liked her. Here stood the woman who would destroy his world, yet there was much to be admired.

"What will you do?"

"I need to break the leg again if he is to walk without a limp. Then it will have to be re-fixed, but done properly this time."

"The best doctors were called on. They said the break was too bad. This was the best that could be done."

"I can do better," Thomas said.

"You have great faith in your abilities, physician."

"As do you in yours, Your Grace. You recognise my abilities as I recognise yours. Let us not pretend otherwise. It was you who asked me to come. Now I am here you must let me do my job."

"You are an enemy of Spain," she said. "How do I know I can I trust you?"

"You have no alternative. It is not me who is your enemy but my master, and it is he who has sent me."

"You live with Moors, of course you are my enemy. Their presence is not to be tolerated."

"But their physicians are, it seems. Why else would you have asked for me?"

"Take care, sir, and remember who you are talking to."

"I am talking to a mother who loves her son," Thomas said. "I believe the queen can stand aside for a moment in order to do what is best for him."

She turned aside, her body taut, and Thomas waited. He knew speaking to her this way was a risk, but one he had to take if the boy was to be helped. He disliked politics, disliked even more the intermittent war that grumbled along between Spain and the remnants of the Moorish caliphate in al-Andalus. He understood the strange chivalry that allowed for this woman to request a surgeon. Understood too why the new sultan would send him in response to her request. By doing Spain this favour Muhammed would gain a favour in return, which might keep the battle at bay for another year.

Thomas was still waiting for a response when a commotion sounded at the end of the corridor. He moved quickly to place himself between the disturbance and the queen, spreading his arms, readying for an attack.

A guard appeared, then two men. The first was a surprise—the tall abbot he had seen at the gate, who seemed to have access everywhere. The other he didn't know, a short man dressed in dark clothing. He pushed past the guard, the abbot following in his wake. "You know who I am, fool, let me pass. Your Grace, I am not too late, am I?"

Still Thomas didn't move. He stepped to one side, blocking the man's route to the queen, before he felt a hand touch him lightly on the arm.

"It is all right, this man is my own physician, Don Harras, and the other is Abbot Mandana. He advises me on religious matters. I thank you for your gallantry but I am safe."

"Is this him?" said Don Harras.

"Don Thomas Berrington, yes. He is the one they sent."

The man's mouth curled into a sneer. "And you trust him?"

They formed a loose square, Thomas and the queen on one side, her doctor and Mandana the other.

"Can you repair my son's leg, Don Harras?"

"You know I have done all I can. Your son at least walks now, Your Grace."

"This man claims he will walk without a limp."

Mandana sneered. "How will he do that? Cut off his leg and attach a new one?"

An inappropriate remark, Thomas thought, considering what he had witnessed hanging from the city gate barely an hour ago. He wondered if Pero had scuttled off to tell tales to his master.

"You don't need to know how I will repair him, sir," Thomas said.

"Your Grace, this is unacceptable! This man is a Moor, an unbeliever. Who is going to pray over your son for his recovery? How can a heathen cure him without appropriate prayers?"

Don Harras nodded vigorously.

"I have others to offer prayer. This man is claimed to be the best surgeon in Spain. Would you have me not try?"

"I would have you trust those around you who share your faith."

"Don Berrington comes from England. I believe they share our faith there, do they not?"

"England?" Mandana looked Thomas up and down. "He does not look English to me."

"Speak to him," the queen commanded Thomas.

"Pardon, Your Grace?"

"Speak to him in your language."

Thomas delved deep into his memory. Was he even capable of recalling words he hadn't uttered in almost thirty years?

"See—he is no more an Englishman than am I!"

"Would you even understand English if I spoke it to you, man?" As Thomas uttered the words they sounded guttural in his ears which had grown accustomed to the soft cadence of Arabic.

Mandana frowned.

"He would not, sir, but I do," said the queen in accented English. *"But he will recognise the sound if not the meaning."* She switched back to her native tongue. "You can leave us now. I thank you both for your concern, but your opportunity has passed." She lifted a hand, a mere flutter of the fingers. The guard who had blocked them approached, as did a second who had come to stand beside him.

"Please escort Don Harras from the palace." She turned away, the man already dismissed. "You may remain within the walls, Abbot, but I would ask you not to disturb us again."

Thomas remained a moment while the queen returned to her son. He saw the abbot's face stiffen, his pride injured by her curt dismissal. A guard grasped Don Harras's arm. The man shook it off, but a hand gripped him on the other side and he was pulled away. The abbot returned Thomas's stare, his pale grey eyes cold.

I have made another enemy today, Thomas thought. *But what is one more to add to an ever growing list.*

CHAPTER SIX

"I need my instruments from the cart," Thomas said.

He discovered Jorge making himself comfortable in their quarters, a large room on the south of the palace not far from the prince's rooms. A window afforded a view across a formal garden to the Guadalquivir, where a water wheel turned. Just beyond lay the old bridge they had crossed that morning.

"I took this bed as it's the bigger," said Jorge. He reclined against an ornately carved headboard, ankles crossed. After their adventures the year before and Jorge's restoration to the harem, he had returned to shaving his head, but on the journey from Gharnatah his hair and beard had grown out, affording him a roguish air.

"And you, of course, will need a large bed." Thomas was pleased to see a small return of Jorge's usual good humour. For two days now as they approached the city he had been unnaturally quiet, growing more so the closer they came.

"A man always lives in hope. I caught a glimpse of several ladies in waiting who reside not far from here, one beautiful enough to grace the sultan's harem."

"Perhaps Muhammed would welcome new blood." Thomas knew that since coming to power the year before the young sultan had made few changes. It was beyond time for him to stamp his own mark on the palace.

"She is too good for Muhammed," said Jorge. He stared off into space, still a sense of distance about him.

"Where are they?" Thomas said.

"Your instruments? In your trunk, still on the back of Pero's cart I expect."

Thomas was tired. He had slept little and travelled far and doubted he would find anywhere to bathe in this forsaken city. He was in no mood for verbal sparring.

"Where's Pero, then?"

Jorge only shook his head.

"What's the matter with you?" Thomas sat on his own bed. Smaller than Jorge's, but he had grown used to the narrow cot in his workshop and this felt like luxury.

"Nothing's the matter with me. I'm tired, 'tis all. We're all tired. When do you operate on the boy?"

"He's a prince. And I'll operate as soon as I get my instruments."

"He's young," said Jorge, "and he looks weak. Is he up to what you're going to put him through?"

"Do you even know what that is?"

"I've been around you long enough to know it's bound to be painful."

"But necessary if he's to walk again."

"And the queen—does she know what's involved?"

"I told her."

"But does she *really* know?"

"She will."

Jorge rolled from the bed. "I suppose we'd better find your instruments of torture then. I don't know, it seems all you ever bring me is trouble. I should go home to my women."

"I thought you had your eye on a new one."

"And pleasing to the eye she is, too. Do I really have to pretend to be your assistant?"

"You're the only one I have."

"You should have brought Lubna."

They left their room and entered the corridor. "She wouldn't have come, you know she wouldn't." Thomas had considered bringing her. He had been training Lubna for a year now and she was quick to learn, but he was still uncomfortable with the feelings he felt for her while still ostensibly sharing a house with her sister.

"Not even if she was with you?"

"Not even then. Remember we only look like Moors, but she is one." He didn't want to discuss the matter. Jorge was always far too interested in the emotions of others. "Where do you think the cart is? Are we even going in the right direction?"

"We are."

Jorge, it turned out, had no idea where the cart they had accompanied for the past week had been taken. But he knew someone who did, or at least someone who could find out.

The sound of female voices came from ahead and they entered a spacious room, a large table set in the centre. It held a tapestry which stretched beyond the table's edges to fold onto the floor. Five women clustered around it, needle and thread in hand. Three of them looked up as they entered. One smiled. Jorge had been right, she was indeed beautiful, with dark hair, almost black eyes, and a sultry mouth that hinted at sin. Exactly the sort of woman Jorge would notice. She told them the cart would be in the courtyard and offered to show them the way.

"If you can direct us that will be sufficient," Thomas said.

"It's no trouble to take you, no trouble at all." The voice was as redolent of mischief as the face and body. She laid the needles of her craft on the tapestry and told her friends she would return soon. Once in the corridor she fell into step beside Jorge while Thomas followed.

He knew he should be thinking of the young prince, but instead the image of the atrocity which hung from the city gate nagged at his mind, as well as what he had seen in the river. He would have liked longer to examine the body and wondered what had become of it. The more he thought of the two events the more convinced he grew they must be linked.

The cart stood alone in the centre of an open courtyard, forlorn without its harness. Thomas climbed onto the flat bed and began searching for the trunk that contained his instruments, his drugs and the other equipment he thought he might need when they'd left Gharnatah. Nothing had been removed from the cart, and he dragged aside a brass-strapped case and dropped it heavily into a free space. Jorge remained on the far side of the courtyard talking with his new friend. Thomas could do with help but refused to ask, a little annoyed Jorge hadn't offered. They had been in the city only a few hours but already the man was recruiting a new harem.

Thomas pulled and tugged and dragged but still couldn't find what he sought. He started to worry it had not been packed at the other end of his journey. He and Lubna had taken the trunk to the palace and had seen it stacked with the others ready to load. On the journey the whole of the cargo had been covered tightly by layers of oiled cloth designed to keep out water and dust. Thomas stepped down and strode across the courtyard.

"I can't find my trunk. We need Pero. Does your friend know where to find him?"

"I have a name, Thomas Berrington," said the woman, her voice filled with a sultry amusement.

"Then you have the advantage of me, my lady."

"Esperanza." She offered no more.

"Has Jorge given you my entire life story? Or only the highlights?"

"He told me you are a mystery, which is what you remain to me. If you want Pero I can take you to him."

"Take Jorge," Thomas said, "and bring him here."

He returned to his labours. Some of the cargo was too heavy for him to move on his own however much he strained. He started to think he shouldn't have sent Jorge away when the eunuch re-appeared accompanied by the dark-robed priest. There was an expression of annoyance on Pero's face. Esperanza was not with them.

"I can't find my trunk," Thomas said. "I need it to prepare for the prince."

Pero pulled himself onto the bed of the cart beside Thomas. "Can you truly help him?"

"I believe so. If I can find the trunk."

"Wait here." Pero jumped down and rushed through an archway.

"She is indeed lovely, isn't she?" said Jorge. He leaned against a wheel of the cart, eating a pomegranate he had managed to acquire from somewhere, slowly picking individual berries from within and sucking them against his tongue. The sweet scent filled the air and Thomas realised how hungry he was.

"I should have taken your cock as well as your balls, but I doubt even that would stop you."

"Ah, true love always finds a way, my friend."

"More like true lust. Does she know what you are?"

"She will. Already she senses my difference, and I hers."

"And what is her difference, other than her beauty?"

Jorge smiled, his lips wet with the juice of the pomegranate. Before he could reply Pero came bustling back accompanied by three men.

"Off." He waved at Thomas, then jumped onto the cart and started issuing commands. The men dragged and tugged and lifted, placing boxes and trunks and cases in separate piles under the priest's command. As they lifted a hank of fine cotton sent as a gift, Thomas caught sight of his small wooden trunk tied with a leather strap.

"Take care, it contains delicate instruments."

The men dragged the trunk roughly, and would no doubt have let it drop to the ground if Pero hadn't said, "Do as he asks." His voice was soft, but carried a sure sense of command. Two of the men dropped to the ground while the third heaved the trunk to the edge of the cart. They deposited it to one side of the pile of goods intended for the palace.

"Is that everything?" asked Pero.

Thomas shook his head. "No, not all. I would talk with you a moment." He glanced at Jorge. "Can you show these men where to take the trunk?"

Jorge raised a shoulder. Thomas ignored him, knowing his indifference was all show.

"It is almost time for noon prayer," said Pero. "I have been looking forward to visiting the cathedral again."

Thomas walked to the arch which led to the outside world. "I would know more of these deaths."

Pero shook his head, a sour expression on his face. "What makes you think I know anything?"

"Because you were talking to the men who were to take care of the body."

"We are all men of God, of course we talk to each other, and they were doing no more than their duty, as was I. It is a lesson you would be wise to learn, Thomas Berrington."

"I would speak with one of them," Thomas said. "Or the city guard."

Pero barked a laugh. "The Hermandad know nothing."

"Then who does?"

Pero sighed. "You refuse to turn away? In spite of this not being your city and this matter none of your business?"

"I do." Even as he spoke Thomas wondered why he felt the need to investigate. Pero was right—the matter had nothing to do with him. Yet he couldn't ignore what he had seen.

CHAPTER SEVEN

Pero and Thomas bustled through streets that were far busier than when they'd arrived. Sun filled the narrow alleys, dust hanging in the air from the traffic of hundreds of feet. Open doorways gave into shops selling all manner of fish, fowl and game. Fruit lay arranged on stalls while urchins ran between people's legs, impeding progress.

"Where are you taking me?" Thomas was breathless from the speed of their passage. He jolted against a man who cursed him, but by the time the stranger turned Pero had led them onwards.

"To someone who knows more than I do. Perhaps then you will allow me to pray?" He took a sharp turn into an alley barely wide enough for them to walk side by side. It rose steeply, the ground beneath their feet roughly cobbled, until they emerged into a square. To one side stood a church so small it looked as if it had been shrunk in the sun like a raisin. On the other a wall contained a single faded door beyond which lay a two-storey house. It was to here Pero led them.

He pushed at the door without knocking and called out. "Lawrence! Are you here?"

A figure appeared in the doorway of the house. It was no priest but a woman dressed in the robes of a servant. "He's in his study."

"Then fetch him," said Pero. "This man would speak with him."

He turned to Thomas. "You will have to introduce yourself, I am late already. I am sure you can manage."

The woman disappeared and Thomas found himself alone in the small courtyard. Two orange trees stood in a corner, their trunks emerging from between rough slabs. Old fruit hung mottled from the branches while fresh white flowers filled the air with scent. A wooden table and two chairs were set in the shade of the trees.

Voices sounded from within the house and a tall man appeared. Thomas recognised him as one of those he had seen at the gate that morning, the man who had dressed differently to the other monks. He had stood next to the abbot, not sullying his hands with the work of moving the body.

"Laurita tells me Pero brought you." His voice carried a faint accent Thomas had not heard in many years. "You want to ask me something?"

"If I can."

The man stared at him without expression, then turned abruptly and called into the house. "Laurita, bring us wine and food." He walked to the table and sat, kicking out the other chair with his foot. The seat appeared flimsy. Thomas pulled it all the way out and lowered himself carefully.

"You were at the city walls this morning," he said.

The man held a hand up. "Before we start, tell me who you are."

"My name is Thomas. Thomas Berrington. You, I assume, are Lawrence."

The man laughed. "So *you* are my countryman."

"I'm sorry?"

"I'm an Englishman, like you," said Lawrence, using Thomas's native tongue. The words sounded odd in his ears and he struggled for a moment with their meaning, the syntax strange to him now. Had the queen not made him use it earlier that day he might not have managed at all, but at least it explained the hint of accent he had heard.

"Yes—an Englishman," Thomas replied in the same language

before switching back. "But I would prefer we use Spanish, if we may. Unless you have Arabic?"

"It's been a long time for me, too. And no, no Arabic I'm afraid." Lawrence leaned to one side as the woman emerged with a tray. She set down a jug of wine, two beakers and a bowl of bread and meat. As she turned to leave Thomas saw Lawrence's hand trace the curve of her rump before she slapped at him.

"You're the surgeon come to cure Prince Juan, aren't you. What brings an Englishman to such a place and such a profession?"

"It's a long story," Thomas said.

Lawrence poured wine for them both, plucked a chunk of meat from the bowl and wrapped it inside bread. He glanced at the sky. "It is only just past noon. We have all afternoon to talk. If you want me to answer your questions I think an exchange of information is called for."

"I don't have all afternoon," Thomas said. "I shouldn't even be here. I have two nurses to train before tomorrow."

"You operate so soon? Here, eat something. Whatever this meat is it's delicious."

Thomas ignored the offer. "I want to know more about this morning," he said. "How many deaths have there been?"

Lawrence raised a shoulder. "Are you sure you're not hungry?"

"No, I'm not hungry," Thomas snapped. "Tell me—how many and when?"

Lawrence lifted his gaze. The man's eyes were a dark blue, a cold calculation there that belied the benign expression on his face.

"It's your turn now. Tell me how you came to Spain. Although," he said smiling, "I hear it is not in Spain you live."

"You would waste time in gossip when people are dying?"

Lawrence sighed and wiped his fingers on his robe. "I see you are not to be distracted." He leaned forward, placing his hands on the table top. "Why are you so interested? Surely this is none of your business."

"I saw something at dawn this morning, before we arrived in

the city. Something I believe now to be related to the woman's death."

"Barely a woman," said Lawrence. "She had little more than fifteen years, I judge."

"How could you tell from what was left?"

"A man can tell if he knows how to look. I am sure you can tell, Thomas. What did you see?"

"The limbs of a wolf. In the river."

"Where?"

Thomas shook his head. "I don't know the place. Three hours east of the city. There was some kind of castle on a bluff."

"And you think it connected? Why?"

"There was something else. When I first saw it I took it for the body of a child. Then I saw it wasn't a whole body. And afterwards I convinced myself I had been mistaken. Except now I don't think I was."

"Did you see anything else?"

"There was someone on the water. A boat. Two people. At least two people."

"Can you identify them? We should go to the Hermandad."

"The mist was thick. All I saw were shapes and the sound of something tossed into the river."

"Nothing more?"

"Nothing I can be sure of. If I told you anything else I would be making it up. This girl isn't the first, is she?"

Lawrence sat back. "No, not the first."

"How many others?"

"That I know of? A dozen."

"Over what period?"

"The first was almost exactly a year ago." Lawrence reached out and took some more meat. "Are you sure you won't have some of this? It really is excellent."

"Why is the perpetrator called the bonebreaker?" Thomas asked. "I saw the body this morning. The girl's limbs were attached to the wolf's body with much skill."

"It hasn't always been so. The first body was discarded in the middle of the old bridge. It was a mess. The arms and legs were smashed. The legs of a goat were simply laid against the stumps of hers, the arms replaced with the wings of a crane, as if she was being turned into some kind of angel."

"You know a lot about the matter."

Lawrence scowled. "Everyone in the city knows about the murders. We live with fear every day. Laurita refuses to go to the market anymore unless I accompany her."

Thomas glanced at the shadows cast by the trees, aware of how far they had moved while they talked.

"I should be going. I'm expected at the palace, but I would like to return and talk again if I can."

Lawrence smiled. "I'm usually here. And you still owe me your story."

"Are you a priest like Pero?" Thomas thought about his caress of the woman—although he knew it meant little. He had known priests who were married and priests who juggled a half dozen mistresses. The church had changed its laws some time since, but the old ways took a long time to fade.

"No-one is like Pero. I was a priest once, but then I have been many things. Now I am a caretaker and recorder of facts. I write down the names of those who are born and die within the city, the names of fathers and mothers and children. It's the reason Pero brought you to me, because I know things. The way I dress is an affectation, nothing more."

"Do you know what happened to the girl's body?" Thomas asked. "I would like to examine her if I can."

"She's been taken for burial. All the victims are treated with as much dignity as can be provided."

"Where has she been taken?"

"The Monastery of Almodovar del Rio. Too far for you to visit, but I suspect you've seen it already. It's a few hours ride east of the city. It sits on cliffs above the river."

CHAPTER EIGHT

Thomas walked down steps into a small square. An inn lay on the far side, empty tables outside waiting for customers once noon worship ended. He was expected at the palace soon but needed time to think over the revelation Lawrence had provided—whether deliberate or not he couldn't yet tell. Did it mean anything or not? He smiled and shook his head. Of course it meant something, but was it something significant? However much he teased at the memory Thomas knew he had seen nothing identifiable on the river. A shape, nothing more. What had floated past could have been the torso of the murdered girl or it could have been something else entirely. Memory played tricks he was familiar with, and Thomas took care to draw conclusions only from facts he knew to be true. And the body could have been from a pig, or a small calf from which the water had denuded the coat. Or it could have been that of a young girl.

He sat on a raised ledge which ran around the base of the cathedral, hoping the warm air might clear his mind, but thoughts continued to tumble and swirl however much he tried to tease them into sense.

He was still sitting when he heard voices behind and turned to see a small group enter the square. Nobody looked in his direction as he watched them stroll across the roadway and disappear, jealous of their carefree laughter. A single figure emerged behind them and Thomas recognised Jorge immediately. His height, the way he carried himself, his air of difference. Except something else was different now. His friend walked down the roadway with gaze lowered. He walked right past Thomas without glancing at him and continued on.

Thomas refrained from calling out. He more than half expected Jorge to cross the square to the inn, but instead he continued onto the bridge. He had barely seen his companion since their arrival, and they had talked little. It wasn't like Jorge to talk little.

Thomas wondered where his friend was going—was there some destination on the far side of the Guadalquivir? But Jorge appeared to have no destination in mind. Three quarters of the way across the bridge he stopped and looked down into the water.

Thomas waited, but Jorge made no move to either go on or return, so eventually he rose and followed.

Jorge only turned at the last moment, even though Thomas's boots were loud on the cobbled surface.

"I've been looking for you." He turned back to his study of the water.

"I was searching out information. Why?"

"What?"

"Why were you looking for me?"

"To confess."

Thomas indicated the building behind him. "The cathedral's there, not that you'd know it was one."

"Strange place, isn't it?" said Jorge. Finally he looked up and met Thomas's eyes. "I'm about to tell you something I've never told anyone before."

Thomas waited, worried by the pain on Jorge's face. He had never seen the man look this way, not even when they had been locked in a dungeon waiting for their executioners.

"It was here," said Jorge, waving a hand vaguely in the air, "that I killed my brother."

"Say that again?" Thomas knew Jorge was no killer.

"He fell," said Jorge, "and I couldn't save him. He died down there, and that's how I came to be who I am." His face twisted into a snarl. "How I became what you turned me into."

"You told me you were captured."

"I was."

"That you were with soldiers and you were captured."

"When did I ever say I was with anyone? You assumed. Everyone assumes. I was alone. Starving. Looking for a way to die without killing myself. I still believed killing myself was a sin then. But so is murder."

A wind rushed up the river, rattling the trees growing on the islands and along the banks. Thomas shivered and pulled his robe closer, reminded that winter hadn't yet loosened its grip altogether.

He glanced back along the bridge. He knew the queen would go to Juan's room soon and wonder where he was, but nothing was more important than the man standing before him.

He put his arm on Jorge's shoulder, expecting it to be shaken off, but Jorge only turned to him, his face reflecting an inner turmoil. When Thomas led him away Jorge followed as though he possessed no will of his own. He led him to the inn where there was warmth and light and conversation. He found a table set apart and called for food and wine. A lot of wine, but none of it for him.

Thomas listened as Jorge spoke. He knew it didn't matter who sat across the table, the words were meant for Jorge himself, but still he listened.

He ate the food when it came without tasting it.

"We were boys," said Jorge, staring across the small square, but Thomas knew he was seeing nothing.

"What age?"

"I was ten, almost eleven. Daniel was thirteen."

"That was his name? Daniel?"

"Daniel Olmos. As I was Jorge Olmos."

"Who else in your family?"

Jorge's gaze came back to Thomas. He shook his head. "My father, my mother, three sisters, another brother." He waved a hand. "But they don't matter. They never did. Only Daniel and I mattered."

"You were close."

"We had to be. Our father beat us and our mother ignored us. They drank. They were feral. We weren't all my father's children. I don't think Daniel and I even had the same father."

"Tell me what happened," Thomas said. The inn had grown busy and he hoped they wouldn't be overheard. Confessions of murder would not go down well in a city febrile with talk of a killer.

Jorge laughed, but the sound lacked any trace of humour. "We were going to catch fish. They fill the river in spring. You can stand on the bridge and watch them leaping the rapids. Great silver fish. One would have fed us for a week." He wrapped a hand around his cup of wine but didn't lift it. "What have you been doing?"

"Nothing." Thomas knew his own discoveries could wait. Right now Jorge needed to unburden himself. "Tell me."

"Do you know how hard this is?" said Jorge.

Thomas looked at him. No, he didn't. He tried to think what Jorge would say if their roles were reversed. Jorge was always better at this kind of thing—emotions.

"You'll feel better if you tell me," Thomas said.

Jorge shook his head. "No, I won't. But I'm going to tell you anyway." He took a breath and started. "We climbed down to the water. I was always a good climber, Daniel not so much, so I went first. We were right next to the fish but every time we grasped at one it was too slippery and got away.

"So we climbed back up and tried the next buttress along. There was a loose stone at the top so I avoided it. I should have told Daniel, but all I was thinking about was getting down and catching something." Jorge lifted his wine, stared into it then put it back on the table. "I should have told him. I was stupid not to."

"You were ten years old," Thomas said.

"I was a street kid," said Jorge. "To someone such as that ten is as good as being an adult. I didn't think and I should have."

"What happened?"

"What do you think? He swung over the edge and the stone came away. I saw him fall, still gripping it. Heard him hit the rocks. Heard the sound it made. Saw his blood flow into the river. The fish swam through it, excited. Those damn fish." He finally raised the cup to his lips and drained the contents. Thomas reached across and refilled it.

"Did you check to see if he was dead?"

"He was dead. How could he not be?"

"So what did you do? Did your father throw you out when you told him?"

Jorge drained his cup a second time and once more Thomas filled it.

"How could I go home and tell him? How could I tell anyone? A man came along the bridge and saw us. He yelled at me, called me a murderer. I knew they wouldn't believe me." He shook his head. "No—I panicked, that's what I did. I had to get away. I flung myself into the water and let it carry me away. Past the fishermen's huts, past their nets, past the islands. Fish banged against my legs, so many of them, and I let the river take me, hoping it would swallow me up and kill me too, but it didn't."

"Why did you run?"

"Because I killed him!"

"You said you were boys. Boys play, they get into trouble, they—"

"Trouble? This was more than trouble."

"No-one would blame you."

"My father would. He'd have beaten me until I was dead like Daniel."

"You said he was older than you. So he was in charge, wasn't he?"

"It makes no difference who was in charge. I killed him."

Thomas sat back and eyed the wine. He wanted to drink but

had much yet to do. His head throbbed with fatigue and a thousand thoughts, but he knew he couldn't abandon Jorge.

"Was Daniel the reason you agreed to come with me?"

"I was asked." Jorge's eyes avoided Thomas's.

"You were—but nobody expected you to say yes. Nobody would have blamed you if you refused. It was me they wanted."

"I couldn't let you come alone."

"Thank you. So was he? The reason?"

"I..."

Thomas waited.

He gave in and drained his cup of its contents, poured more from the jug and took a second mouthful.

"I came..." Again Jorge stopped. He drank, refilled his cup, drained it, drank more.

Thomas raised a hand and called for a second jug. "You should eat something," he said.

Jorge looked at the congealed stew in front of him and pushed it away.

"Did you come to make retribution?" Thomas asked.

Jorge reached for the fresh jug of wine and filled his cup, half draining it.

"I don't know why I came. Only that I had to."

"You can't bring him back."

"You think I don't know that? But I may be able to—" Jorge stopped abruptly.

"What."

"I had a younger brother and three sisters," said Jorge, and Thomas saw his shoulders loosen. Either the wine was doing its work or they were getting close to some answer.

"All younger than you?"

Jorge nodded. "And one more on the way. There were others but they died."

"It's a harsh world."

"Even harsher when you're at the bottom of the dung heap."

"Not any longer."

"Which makes the memories all the worse. It isn't right for there to be such wealth alongside such poverty."

Thomas only shrugged, waiting for Jorge to get to the real point.

"They would have found it hard without Daniel. Between us we managed to earn a little extra, enough to help out. Enough to keep from starving."

Thomas didn't say that this only made it all the worse to have abandoned them. He didn't think he needed to. Jorge already knew what he had done.

"I sometimes wonder what happened to them," said Jorge, his voice barely audible.

"It's natural."

"I don't suppose my parents are still alive."

"It wasn't so long ago," Thomas said, working it out. "If you were ten at the time, that makes it nineteen or twenty years. It's possible they're still alive."

"Not them. People don't live much over thirty when you come from where I do."

"Your sisters or younger brother, then. And you said your mother was expecting again. There might have been more after that. Have you—"

"What do you think I've been doing all day?"

"Other than feeling sorry for yourself?" Thomas knew it was a cruel jibe, but seeing Jorge this way disturbed him. He had never known the man to examine his own feelings so deeply. Jorge's emotions were always fire-quick, flaring to white heat one moment then dying to embers the next.

"Yes, other than that," snapped Jorge. He drained his cup, placed it on the table but did not refill it.

"Did you discover anything?"

"Nothing of any help."

"Where did you go?"

"Where do you think? Back to the slum."

"Perhaps they rose above that."

Jorge shook his head. "Not my family. My father was a drunk and a bully. My mother ... well, I told you what she was like."

"Even if your parents died your brothers or sisters might have risen. You should keep trying. Go out again tomorrow. I would come and help but I operate on the prince in the morning, and will need to be close for a week after, at least."

Jorge finally allowed his gaze to rise to meet Thomas's. "Do you think they might still be here somewhere?"

"It seems to me you have to know one way or another."

"Yes, I do." Jorge pushed at his bowl containing the congealed food. "I am so hungry."

Thomas laughed, the sound louder than he'd intended, relief making it so. "They won't have eaten in the palace yet." He stood and dropped coins onto the table. They were coin of Gharnatah with the old sultan's face stamped into them—despite it being against the law of Islam—but they were copper and silver and would be as readily taken here as anywhere else in Spain.

As they walked towards the palace Thomas said, "Will you continue your search today?"

"And tomorrow," said Jorge. "Until either I find them or discover they don't exist. But it's hard work. People are afraid of strangers. All the talk is of this bonebreaker."

Thomas slowed and stopped. Jorge walked on a moment then he too came to a halt.

"Go ahead," Thomas said. "I've just remembered something I must do. I might have news for you later."

Jorge shook his head and began to walk again. Thomas watched until he entered the palace, then turned and began to walk faster, aware he was expected elsewhere, but he would risk being late if it meant he could help his friend.

CHAPTER NINE

By the time Thomas returned to Lawrence's house the man was nowhere to be seen, but the door was open to let a breeze blow through, and he heard noises from upstairs. He rapped on the doorframe and waited. The voices grew hushed and he rapped again, impatience overriding politeness.

Lawrence's head appeared through the upper window, his shoulders bare.

"You again! What do you want now? Don't you know people rest at this time of day?"

"I apologise. You can return to your slumber in a moment. I know we have only just met, but as a fellow countryman perhaps you can do me a kindness."

Lawrence's face showed how slight the likelihood of that was.

"You said you are the keeper of births, marriages and deaths in the city."

Lawrence nodded, his eyes wary. "I maintain some records, yes."

"I arrived here with a companion. I thought he came with me to assist, but in truth he is seeking his family."

"Yes?" A voice sounded from within the room and Lawrence turned away and said something, his voice muffled.

"I have a favour to ask on his behalf."

"Yes?" said Lawrence again.

"You keep records, don't you? Are they in order? Organised?"

Lawrence's expression was answer enough.

"Then can you look something up for me? Olmos is the family name. Daniel was the brother's first name, he died in..." Thomas worked out the dates. He had to calculate using the Islamic calendar and then convert. "In 1464, I think. Is that enough information?"

"When do you want this?"

"As soon as you can. Today would be good."

Lawrence shook his head. "I will look for you later, if I have time. After I have rested."

"I have another task calling me. I'll come back."

"Don't come hammering on the door again. If I find anything I'll leave it on the table for you. If there's nothing there it means I found nothing, understood? No knocking."

When Thomas entered the room he had no idea who anyone was. He had expected two women who were to act as nurses. Instead there were six people present, one a man, one a youth of no more than ten. There was no sign of the queen, which was to be expected, but he had hoped Pero might have been there to make introductions. The room was on the ground floor of the palace and had rough walls and a dirt floor. It was not ideal, but would suffice for what he needed. He was pleased to see a clean table had been brought in, together with a second, larger table.

Only two of the room's inhabitants turned when he entered. They were the nurses, he hoped.

"Names," Thomas said, aware he was being abrupt but his mind was hardly on the current situation. He crossed to the smaller table and set down a box containing glass bottles and a jumble of other items.

"I am Sancha," said the younger of the two, family names obviously not required, "and this is Theresa. We are to assist you."

The older woman was close to Thomas's age, with a pleasant face, the hair pulled back behind her head starting to grey. Sancha was half her age, handsome and red-haired, her loose clothing unable to hide a buxom figure. There was a knowing look in her eyes and Thomas hoped she would perform her duties when asked and not cause trouble.

"What experience have you?"

It was Theresa who replied first. "I have worked in the infirmary for eight years."

"And you?"

"I have assisted Don Harras, the prince's doctor, for a year."

Thomas made a sound through his nose. He wasn't convinced the younger woman would be of much use, but he would have to work with what he had. He wished again he had brought Lubna instead of Jorge, but knew that would have been impossible.

"And these people," Thomas said, his eyes scanning the motley group. "They are all here willingly? They have been told what to expect?"

"They know only what you told them to expect," said Sancha.

"Then they know all they need. I'm not ready for them yet, is there somewhere they can wait?"

Sancha shook her head. "They can go outside to the street. There is nowhere else." Despite her youth she appeared to be the senior member of the pair. Perhaps her work with Don Harras gave her some additional status.

"Then ask them to wait but not to stray far. We will call them in when they are needed, one at a time."

"The boy is my son, sir," the man said. "I was told you needed a young male, but he will be afraid if left alone outside."

Thomas was surprised a youth, even one as young as the boy, would be afraid. Then he remembered the killings and understood. As he returned through the streets conversation was of little else, a sense of unease hovering over the population.

"Bring him with you, then," he said. "I will call you last. It will be for the best, anyway." Although, in truth, he would have preferred to start with the man.

Theresa led the first woman inside and helped her onto the long table, where she lay her head on a rough pillow.

"Have you eaten since you broke your fast?" Thomas asked.

"We were instructed not to."

Her eyes were wide in fear, but it was no bad thing, for Thomas knew when they repeated the operation on the prince tomorrow he too would be afraid. Their appearance didn't help. They all wore masks fashioned from leather which covered their noses and mouths. Beneath each mask lay a thick layer of linen and cotton wet with water. It made breathing difficult but would filter out the worst of the fumes.

Almost an hour had passed since the test subjects had been sent outside. Thomas had used the time to instruct the nurses in their duties. It had taken longer than he hoped because the methods they needed to learn were alien to them. But now they knew the contents of the bottles were volatile and highly dangerous if incorrectly used. He had placed a little of the liquor onto a cloth and held it beneath each of their noses. Only for a moment, but he saw their eyes lose focus and quickly drew it away.

He and Lubna had been developing the substance for the past six months for use on his own patients. There had been successes and setbacks, but nobody had died—not quite. Thomas didn't think he could have developed the liquid so quickly without Lubna's help. She was sharp, quick to learn, and had a natural gift when it came to dealing with patients, a skill Thomas knew he lacked. It was Lubna who had found the clue to the liquid's development as she read the books Thomas recommended. He had read them himself a long time ago, but the significance of what she found had passed him by.

The base for their work was oil of vitriol, a clear liquid which gave off a heavy vapour. On its own, given time, it could cause unconsciousness. But time was the problem. Often twenty or thirty minutes were required. Both Thomas and Lubna knew something faster acting was needed. So they had experimented with adding different substances. Both opium and hashish were tried, and the liquid Thomas now used contained small quantities of each, together with a number of other distillations. He had written the exact quantities of each in his journals, not wanting the knowledge lost to future generations.

It was in the use of this new liquor he had instructed both Sancha and Theresa, but for the first patient he applied the anaesthetic himself while they crowded close, watching. He poured a small amount of the liquid onto a cloth stitched into a leather pad which would retain the effect to some degree, then stoppered the bottle.

Immediately fumes filled the air. Thomas could smell them even through the thick wetted pad beneath his mask, and he stood back as he turned the leather piece and placed the cloth over the woman's nose and mouth.

"Try to breathe normally," he said, his voice calm. "It will be like falling asleep, nothing more."

The woman's eyes showed wide above the mask, and despite his instructions her chest rose and fell rapidly as panic set in. She started to sit up.

"Hold her," Thomas instructed, and Theresa went to the far side while Sancha gripped the woman and held her down. For a moment she fought, but then the fumes had their desired effect. Her eyelids fluttered, came open again, then closed. Thomas withdrew the mask at once, dropped it into a jar and covered it with a lid. "Always remove the pad the moment they fall unconscious," he said. "Leave it on too long and they may never wake. See how her eyes move beneath the lids. She is put out, but only just."

He went to the table and picked up a needle, one he used when stitching wounds.

"Watch," he said, and pushed the needle into the flesh of the woman's arm before extracting it. He pressed down on the bead of blood that gathered. The woman made no move to draw away.

"She will feel it when she wakes," said Sancha.

"Yes, she will, but not at the moment, and a moment is all we need. I have not put her under far. See, even now she is waking."

And he spoke the truth. The woman's eyelids fluttered open, closed again. She groaned.

"She will have a headache. And she may vomit, so Sancha, let her go now and fetch a bowl."

Thomas helped the woman sit up as her eyes came fully open. She breathed deeply and her lips worked as saliva filled her mouth.

Sancha held the bowl close, but she shook her head and pushed it away.

"I am all right."

She swung her legs from the table, but when she tried to stand she staggered and Thomas and Sancha held her arms until she steadied.

"Can you walk?" Thomas asked.

The woman nodded. "I'm fine." She put a hand to her head. "But I dreamed of the bonebreaker. He was coming for me. I ran as fast as I could but it wasn't fast enough…" She shook her head violently, as though that would expunge the image. When she took a step away she stumbled and Thomas reached for her, but she slapped his offer of help away. "I am all right! Where is my payment?"

"Who has it?" Thomas asked.

"I do." Theresa went to the table where a purse lay. She extracted a silver coin and handed it to the woman, who nodded and walked towards the doorway, still weaving slightly.

"Now," Thomas said, "Theresa, go fetch the next woman. And Sancha, this time you will apply the liquor."

Thomas found Jorge in their room, stretched out on the bed he had chosen as his own. "Did you discover anything?" he asked.

Jorge shook his head. "The few willing to talk to me knew nothing. I should have stayed in Gharnatah and not even thought about returning. It was a foolish notion. There's nothing here for me anymore."

Thomas placed half a dozen sheets of paper on the bed beside Jorge. "Perhaps these will help."

Jorge looked at them. "You know I can't read. What are they?"

"I met a man today who keeps records of the city. I asked him to look for the name of Olmos. These are the results of his search."

Jorge sat up and snatched at the papers. He stared at them as though concentration alone would decipher the script there. He held them out to Thomas. "Tell me what they say."

Thomas read out names and addresses, and when he was done placed the papers on the table. "Do you know any of these places?"

"Some are familiar," said Jorge. "But the last one is odd."

Thomas consulted the last sheet of paper. "There's a note at the bottom I didn't bother reading. It's in latin and says *extra muros urbis.*"

"Oh, of course, that helps a great deal."

"It means beyond the city walls. The last person lives outside its protection. Are you going to visit all these people?"

"I'd rather you came with me." Jorge stared at the drapes above his head, avoiding Thomas's gaze.

"You know I'm going to be busy."

"Not all the time." Jorge sounded sullen.

"I'll see what I can—" He was interrupted by a knock on the door, which opened without the visitor being invited in.

A slim man in servant's clothing entered. "Are you the physician and his assistant?" His eyes scanned between Thomas and Jorge, made some decision and came back to Thomas. "I have a message."

"Give it then." Thomas was annoyed, but knew it was only due to his own tiredness and apprehension about what he was going to do to the young prince.

"You are invited to eat in the great hall this evening, sirs. Both of you."

Thomas was tempted to refuse the invitation but before he could do so Jorge said, "We would be delighted."

CHAPTER TEN

Thomas blamed their lateness on himself. He had fallen into a deep sleep almost the moment he lay on his small bed in their room. Jorge had disappeared again but when Thomas woke his friend was sitting in the shadows. Which is why the great hall was already packed by the time they entered, loud with the sound of voices and redolent with the smell of food.

Some hierarchy existed here, but exactly what it might be came to Thomas only slowly. He stopped in the doorway but Jorge went ahead, only slowing when he found himself alone.

He stopped and turned back, impatient. "Aren't you coming?"

Thomas shook his head, not yet ready to commit himself to the niceties of court protocol.

At the far end of the hall a wide table sat on a raised platform. Richly attired men and women—but mostly men—sat to either end. The two seats in the centre remained untaken. A young woman, simply dressed, sat immediately to the left of the empty places. Thomas assumed she was the queen's eldest daughter, Princess Isabel, named after her mother. He knew there were two other children younger than Juan, but the prince was the only male heir.

Below the raised table other benches radiated outward. It appeared the higher your rank the closer to the royal table you sat.

"I see Esperanza," said Jorge, starting forward again, not stopping this time when Thomas failed to accompany him. Thomas let him go, knowing where he was headed.

He examined the tables closer to him, at the far edges of the room, where he knew he would feel more comfortable. Spaces existed here and there but he made no move yet. Instead he waited for Jorge's inevitable return once he had been rebuffed. So it was with surprise he saw Jorge greeted like an old friend instead of the new one he obviously was. People rose and someone was despatched to a lower position. Jorge took a seat beside Esperanza, with an empty seat to her right which Thomas ignored even as Jorge waved him towards it.

He hesitated, reluctant to associate himself with the group of nobles. Jorge's life as harem eunuch had accustomed him to mixing with royalty. Thomas's relationship with them had always been difficult, sometimes dangerous. He had no wish to ingratiate himself. These weren't his people, and he didn't want to become their kind. Jorge motioned him again and this time Esperanza rose, waving him across the room. It seemed he had no choice. As he made his way through the throng he became aware of eyes on him. He might have put the attention down to his form of dress, but knew in this instance it was not. They were all no doubt wondering who the interlopers were, and where they had obtained such sudden privilege from.

As he drew closer it became apparent that his place was not the empty seat beside Esperanza, but one on the far side of the table and a little further down in status. The only spare place was one he didn't wish to take but would have to. On one side sat his companion from Gharnatah, Pero, on the other the tall thin figure he now knew as Abbot Mandana.

"I didn't expect to find you here." Thomas had to raise his voice to be heard above the noise. A servant pushed against him and he leaned aside to allow a bowl of broth to be placed on the table.

"Nor I you," said Pero, who leaned over to examine the broth in front of him. He pulled a face. Thomas studied his own but saw nothing untoward. He tried a spoonful. Not as spiced as he was used to, but fresh and substantial. He tore off a chunk of bread and dipped it into the liquor.

"Shouldn't you be with the prince?" said Abbot Mandana from his other side.

"I saw him earlier today, but he needs rest now."

"When do you perform your alchemy on him?"

"In the morning."

"I will come to his room if you give me a time," said the abbot.

"I need no assistance."

"I do not offer any. You need a man of God for the prayers. The queen will insist on it."

"If you must. But don't get in my way, and don't interfere." Thomas knew he needed no prayers, but this was a different city with different customs. He turned to Pero whose broth remained untouched. "Are you not hungry?"

"You know I do not eat meat."

Although Thomas was not sure he did. The priest had avoided them at meal times as they travelled, always furtive, always secretive. Pero avoided his gaze now, seeming uneasy in his company still, as if he had used up his stock of civility—not that much had been evident on the journey. Or perhaps it was the presence of the abbot, whose hood was thrown back to reveal a mane of thick hair, as much white as grey, with only dashes of its original brown showing at the sides. His face was long, that of an ascetic, and he looked as if he rarely ate. A false impression, obviously. If Pero didn't wish to engage in conversation Thomas wondered if he could tease any information from the abbot.

"Have you taken care of that poor girl in a fitting manner?"

The abbot had almost finished his broth and reached to refill his glass from a pewter flagon. "She will be afforded a Christian burial."

"Have your monks done the same for the other victims?" Thomas was curious as to why they would do such a thing.

Mandana cast him a glance. "They might be victims, but they are all worse than vermin. If we do not care for them nobody else will."

"Vermin? Surely they are all children of God in your eyes, are they not? Do they have no family?"

"None that would claim them. So they are taken to the monastery to be afforded a burial with full dignity. It is the least can be done." Mandana wiped the last of the bread around his bowl. "Are you as good a doctor as people say?"

"I'm *a* doctor," Thomas said.

"Don't get clever with me. Everyone knows you're here to heal the prince. I want to know if you're up to the task."

"If he can be healed then I will heal him," Thomas said.

The abbot wiped the bowl with the last of his bread. He looked meaningfully at the barely touched roll in front of Thomas, who pushed it towards him, then in turn reached out and stole the bread from Pero's plate.

"We will see the truth of that in the morning," said Mandana.

"The prince will need no prayers," Thomas said.

The abbot made a show of looking Thomas up and down. "Are you a heathen?"

"I'm an Englishman."

"Is that meant as an answer?" The abbot leaned around Thomas. "Pero, do you intend to eat that broth or not?"

"You know I will not, Abbot."

"In that case." He reached across and took the bowl. He returned his gaze to Thomas even as he spooned Pero's broth into his mouth. "Why do you live in Granada with the Moors and not somewhere more Christian?"

"Because I like it," Thomas said.

"Do you ever miss your home?"

Thomas shook his head. "It's wet and cold and you can't pick oranges from trees. I prefer it here."

"In Spain," said the abbot.

"In Gharnatah."

"That's still Spain."

"I know those who might argue against such sentiment," Thomas said.

"Argue all they like. It is all Spain, and soon there will be no doubt. No doubt at all. Have you visited the cathedral yet?"

"I only arrived this morning—you saw me do so."

"Mass is performed every noon and again at sunset. Do you celebrate mass in England?"

"They did when I left."

"Hmm." A dismissive sound. "Will he be able to walk again?"

"I believe so." Thomas found he could follow the abbot's random train of thought without too much difficulty.

"He'll be king one day."

"God willing," Thomas said, suppressing a smile.

"Yes, of course." The abbot sat back. His pristine white robe showed streaks of brown where he had spilled broth. "How do you celebrate mass in Granada? Surely it's difficult if not impossible, isn't it?"

"There are places. If a man is willing to pay the tax he can worship in whatever way he wishes." Thomas felt no need to enlighten this man about his own complete lack of faith.

"I've heard the Moors are lax in matters of religion. It wouldn't be allowed here. Have you met Tomás de Torquemada yet?"

"As I said, I only arrived today, and I have been busy. Should I meet him?"

"He's the king's inquisitor. Sounds to me as if you need someone like him in Granada. He'll sort out your unbelievers."

"I think they are all believers in their own way," Thomas said.

The abbot laughed. "You see, that's what's wrong. There is only one true religion. Pretenders are not to be tolerated. It's why we are going to defeat you."

"Not me." Thomas smiled. "I'm from England, remember."

"Will there be much pain?" The abbot's swirling mind had returned to the prince.

"Some, but I believe I can control it."

"Pain is good for the soul. Let Prince Juan experience the cleansing fire of pain. Our Lord died on the cross in agony for us—who are we to turn our backs on suffering? The more we suffer the closer to heaven we will attain."

"Pain can kill on its own," Thomas said. "I will relieve as much as I can."

"No wonder your people are weak." The abbot shifted on the bench, his side pressing against Thomas as a slim girl reached for their empty bowls. For a moment Thomas saw the man's hand explore beneath her shift. She scowled, but she would not dare say anything. The abbot's gaze moved beyond Thomas and all at once he stood, as did everyone else in the room.

Thomas followed their example and turned to see Isabel and Fernando enter through a doorway. They moved to take the empty chairs at the raised table. The chatter of voices stilled, starting up only slowly once the king and queen had taken their seats. A third man who had entered with them walked around the edge of the room and made his way to sit beside Esperanza. Her husband, Thomas assumed, wondering exactly what his position was to be so close to the seat of power. A bad feeling came to him, and he feared Jorge's silly infatuation could prove dangerous. He studied the man, who spoke briefly with Esperanza before turning away. He was of medium height and medium age, at least twenty years Esperanza's senior, his hair long and thin, his beard neatly trimmed into the latest fashion.

Thomas felt a tugging at his robe and turned to find Pero trying to get him to sit. He was the only person to remain standing. When he took his seat he continued to watch the small group on the other side of the table, fascinated as some item of news travelled outward from them, excitement spreading.

"What's going on?" said the abbot. "Has something happened?"

"Perhaps they've caught the bonebreaker," Thomas said.

The abbot shook his head, knocking into Thomas again as the girl brought meat to the table. He smiled. "They won't catch him. They haven't yet and I see no sign they will."

"You can't be happy to allow the deaths to continue?"

The abbot cut a slice of meat and lifted it to his mouth in his fingers and started to speak as he chewed. "People die all the time. What difference do a few more fallen women make? They'll not be missed."

Thomas was jostled as the girl pushed against him. He glanced across to find Pero had been brought fish.

He turned back to the abbot. "Even that girl this morning? She was too young, surely."

"The Hermandad will discover who she was, and I wager she will have worked in a brothel somewhere. Or is a thief. There are still too many in the city."

"Don't you consider the deaths unusual? Are all the bodies dis —" Thomas stopped abruptly as Pero dug an elbow into his side. "What?" he asked, turning impatiently.

"You should not discuss these matters with the abbot," whispered Pero.

Thomas leaned closer, lowering his own voice. "Why not?"

"Those in power consider them a failing."

"Why? And how much power does the abbot have?"

"Oh, he has a great deal of power. Torquemada might be the public face of the Inquisition, but Abbot Mandana considers himself its architect."

Thomas glanced at the abbot, who seemed to have lost interest in him, occupied with his hunk of boar and the man to his left, who was passing on the news which had now reached their side of the table.

"What is this Inquisition? I heard the name today but don't know what it means."

Pero almost laughed. "Do you truly not know?"

Thomas shook his head. "How could I? I don't live in Spain. I'm a citizen of al-Andalus."

"Oh, you live in Spain, sure enough. And you could do with a dose of Inquisition in this al-Andalus of yours. I hear rumours when I visit that people are turning away from their God, heathen God that he is."

"We live in difficult times," Thomas said.

"No—*you* live in difficult times."

"So tell me—what is it?"

Pero sighed. It seemed he had eaten all he wanted of his fish, which now cooled on the plate, more than half remaining. "The king and clergy such as the abbot are concerned there are too many foreign elements in Spain. Jews and Arabs who stayed behind when we defeated them. Then there are defectors from al-Andalus. They are not trusted. For all we know they are spies or agents of destruction. The abbot came up with a plan to bring such people into the fold of Christianity."

"And if they don't want to come into the fold?"

"There is no choice."

"There is always a choice."

"Not in Spain." It was obvious from Pero's expression this was not a matter for discussion.

"What do you do if they refuse?"

"There are measures in place."

Thomas turned away, his meal turning sour in his stomach. His eyes scanned the crowd. Around him people laughed and ate and drank, an atmosphere of excitement building.

"Do you hang them from the city gates? Is that why these murders are taking place? Some kind of—"

"They are burned alive to sear the sin from their souls."

"More pain," Thomas muttered.

"What?"

"Something your abbot said. The pain of Christ and it's cleansing effect on the soul."

Pero met Thomas's eyes and, although nothing was said, Thomas knew what they were both thinking. The priest too believed the ecstasy of pain would bring him closer to God.

Thomas could listen to no more. His stomach roiled and he thought he might be about to throw up. He pushed away from the table and headed for the door, uncaring if he broke protocol. He had managed to reach it when a hand caught at his robe and he spun around, ready to attack whoever had stopped him, but it was only Jorge.

"I see you've been enjoying the company of the wolf," he said.

"I've what?"

"The wolf. Abbot Mandana. It's what he is called by the mob and others. Esperanza has been telling me all about him."

Thomas turned and looked over the throng of heads until he found the man, a space still between him and Pero. He could see why the name fit. He had a lupine quality to him, the white-grey hair, the beard, his sharp eyes and hollow cheeks. Yes—the wolf was appropriate. He thought of the animal he had seen that morning slinking through the mist and shivered, annoyed at himself for a moment of superstition.

"Well he eats enough for a bear," Thomas said. "Perhaps he should change his name." He turned away.

"You can't leave yet, not after the news."

"What news?"

"Esperanza's husband brought it to Isabel and Fernando. They have captured Muhammed and are bringing him here."

Thomas stared at his friend, then shook his head. "They can't be. He was in Gharnatah when we left." A fresh wave of unease rose through him. He had spent the last year attempting to avoid Muhammed XII, Sultan of Gharnatah, as much as possible after the man had threatened him, but Thomas's work in the palace meant he couldn't avoid the man altogether.

Jorge laughed, not sensing Thomas's mood as he normally would, the excitement of the room affecting him, too. "How long does it take to ride to battle? You know how headstrong he is."

And how poor a general, Thomas thought. It could be true.

He wondered how the new sultan's capture might affect them, and whether there would be a home to return to. He turned away, weary of rumour and politics, but Jorge grabbed his arm again.

"You can't leave."

"And I can't stay, either." Thomas pulled free of Jorge's grip and walked through the open doorway, the noise of celebration fading as he strode away.

Death and politics—it seemed they were fated to plague him his entire life.

CHAPTER ELEVEN

Thomas found an unwelcome if not unexpected guest in the prince's room when he entered the following morning. Abbot Mandana stood to one side picking at a bowl of cherries. Incense from a censer hooked over a screen curled into the air, thickening it.

"Take that thing out," Thomas said, pleased to find the two nurses waiting, less pleased to see the queen, who would find the next hour hard.

Sancha turned to obey.

"It is to help with the prayers," said Mandana, holding up a hand.

"You can pray later. I need to be able to both see and breathe." Thomas nodded at Sancha. "Leave it outside, and don't allow it back when I have gone."

Mandana opened his mouth to protest, but the queen rose from her seat beside Prince Juan and nodded at Sancha, who unhooked the gold chain and carried the smoking censer from the room.

"Him, too," Thomas said, staring at the abbot. He had not liked the man the evening before and liked him no better now.

"He is here to pray for my son," said the queen.

Thomas leaned close and whispered into the abbot's ear. "Have you a strong stomach, sir?"

Mandana turned his head and stared at Thomas. "I was a soldier before I took the cloth."

"As was I," Thomas said, his voice still low. "Have you seen a young man scream in agony?" He glanced up, but the queen remained at her son's bedside, beyond range of their voices.

"I have seen many things, physician, as I am sure you have."

Thomas straightened. "Then keep out of my way, stay close to the queen and stop eating."

Mandana deliberately popped four cherries into his mouth, his cheeks hollow as he sucked the flesh from them before spitting the stones into the palm of his hand. Thomas shook his head and moved to the bedside.

"How are you feeling this morning, young man?" He deliberately used a casual form of address, hoping to put his patient at ease.

The prince glanced at his mother, back to Thomas. "Well enough. My leg doesn't hurt so much today. Perhaps it is healing."

After he'd finished training the nurses the previous day Thomas had spent several hours with the prince, asking about his interests, trying to entertain him with stories of the strange customs of al-Andalus. As they spoke he'd offered sweetened teas he had made himself which contained herbs and a small amount of opium. It relaxed the boy and eased his fears. After leaving, Thomas had found the kitchen and made sure the head cook knew to send up a stronger draught at bedtime, and a second when the prince woke. It meant the boy was already relaxed, but Thomas knew it wouldn't be enough on its own, which was why he had risen before dawn and made up the mixtures he would use.

"You know your leg won't heal without help," he said, seeing the panic deep within the prince's eyes. "You're not afraid, are you? A brave boy like you?"

"No."

"Of course you're not." Thomas drew a plain earthenware bottle from his bag, unstoppered it and poured half the contents into a silver beaker. "Drink this, Juan."

"These tonics you give me taste strange." He took it anyway and swallowed the contents, pulling the same face as any other five-year-old boy would.

"All medicines do. That's how you know they are good for you. Everyone knows if they tasted pleasant they wouldn't work." Thomas was gratified to see the boy's smile. Already his eyes were losing their fear and starting to turn dreamy. The latest draught was the strongest yet and soon he would sleep. Strong, but not strong enough for the trial that was about to come.

Thomas stepped away and the queen took his place, her hand drawing her son's into her lap. Thomas crossed the room and spoke quietly to the two women.

"Sancha, do you remember what I need of you?"

"To administer the liquid to the prince if he shows sign of waking. And to hold him when you ask."

"I will watch you," Thomas said, "and say when to use more. Apply it only when I say so. It is dangerous to use too much, so be sparing." He turned. "And you, Theresa?"

"I am to hold him down. Hold him down hard." There was steel in her eyes, and Thomas knew from their conversation she was used to dealing with patients who fought back. She had cared for men who were dying in the worst agonies—and, Thomas was sure, helped them in the same way he had on occasion. Sometimes it was better to send a man to his God a little before his time in order to spare him more pain than anyone should have to suffer.

"Good. And you are both prepared?"

They nodded, neither of them showing any sign of reluctance. Thomas was pleased to have them.

"If the queen or the abbot try to interfere you are to keep them away if you can."

This request caused them some doubt. They knew they were in no position to deny either person.

"I will talk to them as well," Thomas said. He glanced at the bed. "I think he is sleeping now, we can start. The sooner the better."

He crossed the room and touched the queen on the shoulder.

She turned abruptly, not used to anyone laying even the lightest of hands on her person, but Thomas's mind had turned to the task ahead and had no room for manners of the court. "Are you sure you wish to stay, Your Grace? This will be hard for a mother to witness."

"Will there be danger?"

"There is always danger, but I will do all I can to minimise it."

She continued to clutch her son's hand. "Is it true, Thomas Berrington, you are the best surgeon in all of Spain? I am placing a great trust in you, sir."

"I am the best in all the lands between here and the East." He said the words to reassure her, but in his heart Thomas believed them. He had yet to find anyone better, and the best surgeons in the world resided within the borders of al-Andalus. He knew of no-one who had created the magic liquids he had fashioned, those that would keep the prince in a deep slumber even through the pain.

He glanced up to ensure both women had put on their masks, then applied his own, tying the string behind his head. He eased one of the bottles free of its padded case and unstoppered it, poured a little of the clear liquid onto a cloth and handed it to Sancha before quickly re-stoppering the bottle.

"Do you remember all we did yesterday?"

She nodded. Thomas hoped she did.

"Your Grace, if you could move to the far end of the room. We need space to work."

The queen remained at the bedside, her knuckles white, and Thomas touched her shoulder again, leaving his hand there, feeling the tremble in her body.

"The fumes will make you unwell."

He increased the pressure of his hand and finally she released her grip and stood abruptly. She cast Thomas a glance, half disdain, half annoyance, before striding across the room to where chairs had been set in the far corner.

Thomas looked around. Everything was in place, everything

ready. There was no excuse not to start. Shutting out the presence of the mother he drew the covers from the prince's body. As requested he lay naked from the waist down, the deformation of his right leg clear in the morning light falling through the tall windows.

"The board," Thomas said. Theresa knelt, and from beneath the bed pulled out a wooden board which had been fashioned according to Thomas's instructions. He took it from her and laid it beneath the boy's leg. "And the rest?"

"Here." She handed him an iron mallet and an object more familiar to a carpenter, a clamp with a spiral bolt to force the jaws together. These were items Thomas hadn't needed to bring with him, knowing he would find them wherever he went. He placed a second, shorter length of wood against the knot of misaligned bone, adjusting everything until he was satisfied. He slid the clamp around the construction and tightened it, then checked again.

He glanced at Sancha. "He is fully unconscious?"

She nodded.

"A little more, but only the slightest amount." He watched as she poured only a small amount of the volatile liquid onto the cloth. "Good. Now remove the cloth and lay yourself across him. Theresa, take his other leg and his feet." He waited. "Are we ready?"

Both women nodded. Thomas tightened the screw, fast to begin with then slower as resistance mounted. He used his fingers to feel around the sides, ensuring the contraption remained in place. He tightened again, his shoulders as tense as the clamp. He had used the technique before, forcing a misaligned bone to snap and shift into place, but this time nothing was happening and he didn't know why. His examination had indicated the break was still not fully healed, but something was causing it to resist.

He slackened the clamp and lifted the top board, felt the prince's leg, tracing the thick knot of misaligned bone. Then he fitted the board once more, adjusting its position, shifting where the clamp fit, and started again. Still nothing moved.

Thomas took a breath, not for courage but because the exhalation caused his mind to still. He reached down and picked up the mallet. He had hoped it wouldn't come to this.

He brought the mallet down sharply on the top of the clamp. There was a snap as the bone in the prince's leg re-broke. The boy screamed. His body writhed but his eyes remained closed, and Thomas knew it was an automatic reaction. He waited for the movement to still. The two women lay across the prince, their bodies rocking as his small frame twisted beneath them.

Thomas took a moment to glance at the queen and the abbot. She sat hunched, tense, biting on a knuckle. The abbot smiled, his eyes bright as though this was all an entertainment laid on especially for him.

Thomas returned his attention to the patient. The boy had stilled and he laid the mallet aside, unscrewed the clamp and lifted the length of wood. Already the leg had started to discolour. There would be damage, certainly, but Thomas hoped any internal bleeding would stop of its own accord. If he had to open the leg it might not be possible to save it. He leaned closer, examining the skin. Beneath the bruising he saw several small scratches caused by the impact of the wood, but the thing he most feared had not happened. The bone had not broken through the skin, which meant infection would be minimised.

Thomas washed the leg with warm water then wiped it with a cloth soaked in pure alcohol from another bottle he had carried in his trunk. He used his hands, feeling for the broken bone within the leg. He closed his eyes, needing to see with his fingertips. He found the end of the bone where it had set badly and pushed it back into place. It would never be perfect. The bone below the knee had snapped in three places as planned. Now he manipulated it, rebuilding a structure that would in time support the prince's leg. He took his time, not rushing, wanting the result to be the best he could make it.

With each grating of bone against bone the prince writhed, sounds emanating from his throat. The queen also moved, her own cries mirroring those of her son, but Thomas was pleased she kept her seat. Every fibre of her being would be urging her to cross the room, but he saw her fight the instinct, once more demonstrating the determination that had brought her the crown.

The leg started to swell, making it more difficult to feel the position of the bone, but his eyes told him he had done as much as he could. He took a linen bandage and began to wind it as tightly as possible below the knee, working upwards, wetting the cloth so it would shrink as it dried and pull the binding even closer. He was half way done when the prince's eyes snapped open and he emitted a high scream. This time his mother could hold herself back no longer and came sprinting across the room, almost knocking Thomas aside. He gripped her waist and lifted, tossing her to one side. Not for a second did her eyes leave her son.

"Let me finish, Your Grace, otherwise this is all for nothing. Sancha, more of the ether, but—"

"Yes, I know, only a little. I'm no fool." Her voice was short, the strain affecting them all.

The queen stood close beside Thomas, her short frame taut with anxiety. He glanced across the room. The abbot remained seated, eating cherries once more. His cheeks were flushed and his breath came rapidly.

The prince stilled as Sancha placed the ether soaked cloth against his nose and mouth. He breathed deeply once and his eyes closed, breathed again and Sancha withdrew the cloth, placed it in a glass bowl and put a lid on top. Thomas nodded and returned to his bandaging.

He finished the first layer of linen, took a length of birch bark he had requested and wrapped it around the existing bandage, easing it into place, using a blade to ensure it fitted as perfectly as he could make it. The bark would form a stiff casing for the leg while the bones knit. He wrapped another wet bandage around the bark to hold it securely in place. The entire time the queen stood beside him as though made of stone.

As Thomas finished applying the second layer of bandage the prince once more stirred. This time when Sancha glanced at him Thomas shook his head. "Let him come awake slowly. When he opens his eyes give him some of this for the pain." He handed her a small vial. "Put three drops in a glass of wine. He can have the same twice an hour today, then no more than once an hour tomorrow."

As Sancha prepared the tincture Thomas took long strips of cloth, tied them around the reset leg, then ran them under the bed and knotted them against the sides. He repeated this with other strips all the way to the boy's waist, immobilising his lower body. Finally satisfied and with the prince rousing and starting to moan, he fetched a straight backed chair and allowed the queen to sit beside her son.

"Don't sit on the bed, not for a week. He must be held rigid until then."

"How long before he can walk?"

"Eight weeks, perhaps a little less."

"And you will stay while he heals?"

"I can't stay months," Thomas said.

"You must. I trust no-one else."

"Don't say that until we know he is going to heal."

"He might not?"

"I think he will, but there are long days ahead yet. He's young, which is good. The young heal faster. Five or six weeks and he can try putting weight on the leg. I will write full instructions for your physicians."

"You will remain. I insist." Her voice gave no hint she would soften on the matter.

Movement drew Thomas's attention and he glanced beyond the queen to find the abbot approaching the bed.

"We should pray, Your Grace."

She looked up. "Yes. We must pray for his recovery. You will join with us, Cousin Thomas?"

He could hardly refuse. He didn't want to leave the prince's side. He would stay all day and through the night and several nights more until he was sure danger had passed. Besides, he recognised the honour the queen had bestowed on him by calling him cousin. It offered no indication of familial relationship, he knew, only used when referring to a grandee, a member of the upper nobility.

"I will pray with you," Thomas said. *For what little good it will do.* He preferred to place his trust in science, not some God he had never seen. He went to his knees, eyes still open, studying the prince's leg and his face for any sign of agony.

CHAPTER TWELVE

Thomas stood beside Jorge in the shade of an ancient olive tree while flies buzzed around them. The sun was bright but it was too early in the year to offer much heat. At the foot of the slope a small stream glittered, a tributary of the great Guadalquivir. On the banks of the stream sat a house, beside it a workshop. Thomas crouched and rested his arms across his knees, waiting for Jorge to make a decision.

It was late afternoon and most of the city rested, but below them a figure in the workshop continued to labour. Thomas had remained with the prince for two hours after the queen had left. The boy continued to sleep, uneasily he had to admit, but the nurses knew what to do. He could spare a few hours so had gone in search of Jorge, and they in turn followed the trail of his family. The five locations they had visited so far revealed only poor households eking out a living, which was the only similarity to Jorge's old life. The fifth and last name was for a blacksmith who lived outside the city walls. As they walked through the northern gate Jorge had grown uncharacteristically silent, his face turned down to gaze at where his feet kicked up plumes of dust.

"You're either going to have to go down or turn back," Thomas said. "And if you turn back you're never going to know."

Jorge turned over a stone with his toe. He offered a sour glance but said nothing.

Thomas narrowed his eyes and stared at the figure visible beneath the roof of the workshop. The side facing them was open. Within a brazier burned, glowing bright as the man pumped bellows with his foot. Thomas wondered how anyone could work in the heat that must lie trapped in the workshop.

"Yes—Olmos the smith," the old man had said, who was selling roasted almonds just inside the city walls when Thomas had asked. He too had sat beside a brazier in the sun, his skin dry while Thomas sweated. He'd bought two wraps of almonds and thanked the man, popping the nuts, sweet and bitter together, into his mouth as they'd passed through the northern gate, handing the other to Jorge.

Olmos the smith.

A smith he certainly was. The clash of metal on metal came up the hill, a faint echo returning a moment later from the city walls. At one time this place would have formed part of the larger Qurtuba of three centuries before. Even now abandoned buildings crumbled into the landscape. More recently this place, being beyond the city wall, would have been fraught with danger, but there was little risk of attack anymore. Fernando and Isabel had ruled these lands with an iron fist wrapped in a velvet glove since coming to power. They had set up courts of law, instituted the Hermandad, and driven out the vagabonds, thieves and murderers from all the cities of Spain under their control. Still—the house and workshop lay two hundred paces beyond the protection of the walls.

Houses, hovels and shacks dotted the dry land bordering the city. Built from the stone of abandoned buildings they had been constructed by those who couldn't afford rents within the walls. As the land rose to low hills the ground became covered with olive groves, orchards of orange, lime and lemon, mulberry, and fields of goats and sheep and pigs. The house standing next to the smithy was larger than others in this place, and well built. Perhaps it was the presence of the stream that had brought the man here. A smith needed a plentiful supply of water. Charcoal, too, and there were stands of trees in places, pigs rutting in the ground beneath. This was all a man might need to raise a family.

Within the shadows the smith continued to work. He carried the makings of a sword, the unformed blade glowing red from the brazier as he laid it on the anvil and raised a hammer, striking down. Sparks flew. Thomas winced, thinking of his own strike against the prince's leg that morning—brutal but necessary.

The man turned the blade, struck again, then crossed the workshop to where a vat of water waited.

Thomas watched him work, then glanced at Jorge, who lifted his head at the sound of metal on metal. The smith had repeated these movement a half score times and each time Thomas saw the same thing. His body swayed, leaning at each step as he limped on a malformed leg. Even at this distance the unnatural shape was clear.

He wondered if what he suspected was true. Jorge's tale of seeing his brother trapped beneath the stone, skin without colour while his lifeblood flowed into the river, but the fact of his death had been no more than an assumption.

Steam enveloped the figure as he thrust the sword into water. When he turned and hobbled back to the furnace Jorge took a pace forward and started down the slope. Thomas watched him, nodding in satisfaction, then rose and followed. Had Jorge taken much longer he would have had to abandon his friend.

"I wondered how long it would take you," said the smith as the pair of them stood on the threshold. The man continued to turn the blade without looking up. It wasn't a sword, not yet, but would be when the layers of metals were folded and refolded to add strength and flexibility. "What do you want? I'm busy—can't start a new job for a week at least." Finally he glanced up. "You don't look like fighting men. Show-blades, is it? There are others better for that than me. I make weapons for killing, not show."

"I don't want a blade," said Jorge.

"Then what? A gate? Some trinket to woo a fine lady? You don't look like you need trinkets." Teeth showed in a face almost obscured by a dense black beard. The hair was the same, long, tied up behind to keep it from the flames. Life had been hard and he looked a decade older than Jorge's thirty years, not the two he was meant to be. Thomas wondered if they were making a mistake.

"Don't you recognise me?" said Jorge.

The smith continued to turn the blade, but he studied Jorge a moment longer before shaking his head.

"Is your name Daniel?"

"Who's asking?"

"Daniel Olmos?"

"If you've come all the way out here you already know who I am. But I don't know you, do I?" He looked Jorge up and down, disdain obvious in his eyes. He afforded Thomas a brief glance, but he had said nothing yet and stood further back.

"You know me," said Jorge.

Daniel carried what would soon be a sword to the anvil and laid its glowing length flat. He struck fast, over and over, sparks showering from the metal. Daniel didn't look up again until he was finished and had drenched the sword once more, then he came and stood before Jorge, the blade hanging loose in his hand. He stood leaning to one side because his left leg was shorter than the right. His eyes studied Jorge's face, and perhaps he recognised something there because a frown passed across his brow before being wiped clear.

He shook his head. "Don't think so."

"My name is Jorge. Jorge Olmos."

Daniel looked at him again. Thomas saw there had been recognition.

"My brother's dead," said Daniel. "And good riddance to him."

"No—you were dead. The river carried me away. I lived."

Daniel shook his head, said again, "My brother is dead. I don't know who you are but I don't welcome this poor joke you're making." He waved the partly formed blade in Jorge's direction. "Get out of my workshop—you and the silent one. Go back to whatever palace you came from and let them have their laugh. My brother is dead."

"No—*my* brother is dead."

Daniel turned away to the furnace. Jorge stepped under the roof. Thomas followed, distant enough to give him the space he needed, close enough to step in if the smith lost his temper. The heat of the workshop enveloped him like the breath of a dragon.

"So who are we two standing here?" said Daniel. "Are we ghosts?" His right leg pumped the bellows and the charcoal glowed red then white. The heat increased and sweat burst from every pore in Thomas's body. Even his eyes felt like they were sweating.

"You know who we are."

Before Thomas could react Daniel turned. He was fast—his hand snapping out to grip Jorge's wrist. He turned the hand over and stared at it.

"No—you can't be my brother. Look at you. A real man would be ashamed to have hands as soft as these." He turned his own over, hard with callous and burns. "These are working hands. My brother was a worker, too. And now he's dead."

Jorge pulled his hand free and lifted his shirt.

"Do you remember giving me this scar?" He showed a faint, pale line that ran along his side. Thomas had seen the scar the night before when Jorge stood naked as he washed.

"Many men have scars."

"We were playing tag below the cathedral," said Jorge, "and you had a knife. You always had a knife. I don't think you meant to catch me with it but you did."

"Anyone could have told you that story. My wife knows it. My children, too."

"You're married?" said Jorge. "I have nephews and nieces?"

"Both. If you were who you claim to be."

"You were afraid of what our father would do when he saw you'd cut me. I was, too. He wasn't the kind of man to take sides, was he? We'd both be blamed. Both get a beating. So we bound it up with a piece of cloth we stole from a stall. The stall-holder chased us, further than we expected, and I was slicked with blood before we lost him. But father never did find out."

Daniel shook his head. "I already said—anyone could have told you that."

"Not about the cloth we stole. You would never admit to that."

"I might have said something to Zanita. She could have told someone else."

"No, I was wrong," said Jorge. "You're not my brother. He wasn't stupid."

Daniel went at him, but Thomas was ready this time and stepped into the space between them. Daniel came close, face stained with grime from his work. His chest pressed against his, but Thomas stood his ground and something in his eyes gave Daniel pause. He stepped back and looked beyond Thomas.

"So what if you are Jorge? My question still stands. What do you want with me?"

"I thought it was time we got to know each other again."

"Why?"

"Because we're brothers."

"No—we were brothers. Now we're nothing but strangers." He scanned Jorge up and down. "Perhaps even less than strangers."

"Your children then. I'm their uncle. I would like to get to know them. They might like to meet me, too."

"Not if I don't allow it. They're good kids—they do as I say."

"Why would you do that? I might be the only blood you have left."

"Because you gave me this," said Daniel, punching his left leg. This close the unnatural bend was obvious, both above the knee and below. The knee itself didn't appear capable of bending. Thomas already knew, unlike Prince Juan, this break couldn't be repaired. It had happened too long ago.

"We were equally guilty," said Jorge.

"Except you walked away. Look at you. Rich, handsome, skin like a woman's. What are you now, a merchant stealing money from the poor?"

Jorge smiled. "You would never guess what I am."

Daniel looked him up and down. "What you look like is a waste of space." He glanced at Thomas. "Your companion, too." He turned back to the weapon he was creating and spat on the fire, phlegm sizzling into steam.

"At least think about it," said Jorge, turning away.

"Don't need to think." Daniel carried the glowing sword to the anvil and beat sparks from it.

Thomas remained where he was when Jorge went outside. He watched the man work. Watched the slab of muscle in his back as he beat the sword into submission. Then he turned and followed Jorge, welcoming the cool breeze that had seemed warm before they entered the workshop.

They would come again in a few days, after Daniel had time to come to terms with his lost brother's sudden appearance. Jorge started up the hillside but Thomas waited, reluctant to leave things as they were. He knew searching out family was important to Jorge—more important than Thomas had imagined. His friend never spoke of the past, never showed any indication he had left anyone behind. Jorge appeared content with his life on the hill in Gharnatah. Thomas knew all about regrets, all about a family who were dead. Except, in this instance, they were not.

He pushed hair back from his face and was about to follow when he caught movement from the corner of his eye. He stopped and turned.

A girl—no, a young woman—stood in the open doorway of the house. Two children clutched at her skirts, but she looked too young for them to be hers. She was beautiful, with blonde hair and eyes of bright hazel. Young she might be, but her simple dress did little to hide the shape of the body beneath. And a mischievous look in her eyes told of a knowledge beyond her years.

"I heard you." Her voice was light, pleasant. "Is it true what the other one said? Is he really my uncle?"

"If you are Daniel Olmos's daughter then yes, he is your uncle. Theirs too. Where is your mother?"

"Gathering firewood. She left me in charge." A smile touched her lips and the tip of her tongue came out. It was a lascivious gesture and made Thomas uneasy. "Call him back. I will fetch you something to drink."

"We have business to attend to, but I thank you."

Her gaze went beyond Thomas to where Jorge continued to climb the hill towards the city walls.

"My uncle is very handsome." Her eyes remained on Jorge as she spoke.

"Yes, he is. Perhaps we will see you again in a day or two."

She looked back to him. "I look forward to that. To get to know you both." Once more she smiled and Thomas turned away, uneasy at the response her blatant show of sensuality had on him.

As he walked fast to catch up with Jorge he wondered if it was a family trait. Was it the reason Jorge had been picked to become a eunuch? That same knowingness? That same soft sensuality?

CHAPTER THIRTEEN

"I want to thank you for praying with me," said the queen when she re-entered the prince's room that evening. "Abbot Mandana told me you were a heathen. Is it true you have taken the faith of the Moors?"

Thomas sat upright. His back ached from the tension of watching over the prince. "I have taken no other faith than that I was born to," he said. His words were the truth, although he neglected to say he had given one up.

"Would you pray with me in the cathedral? It is a wondrous place filled with the glory of God."

Thomas had heard the queen was likely the most devout woman in all of Spain.

"I will have little time, Your Grace. Your son needs constant care for several days yet."

She sat in a chair beside him, too close for protocol, but she was a mother and her son lay comatose, his leg bound, sweat standing out on his pale skin. Perhaps she would have taken more care, but Theresa remained in the room, sitting far back in a corner out of earshot of their conversation.

"Yet I heard you left the palace this afternoon."

"The two nurses were here, Your Grace."

The queen reached for her son's hand and took it between her own. Even above the other odours in the room Thomas caught her scent. It was rich, sweet, heavily applied as he knew others at court did. Their silk clothes were impossible to wash. Over time sweat gathered in the cloth and more perfume was applied to mask it. At least she appeared to wash.

"I will sit with him a while, sir. It is a mother's duty."

"There is little you can do, Your Grace. I will send for you when he wakes, but it will not be tonight." He didn't mention that when the prince did wake he was likely to scream in agony. He would only call the queen after he had eased that pain. Thomas was aware of the fine line he needed to tread. Too little opium and the boy would writhe in agony. Too much, and for too long, and he would suffer when it was withdrawn.

"I do not wish to leave him unless I have to."

"Will your husband visit?"

He saw her glance at him, knowing his form of address lacked respect. But they were not his king and queen, and he cared nothing for any expectation placed on him. He knew he had often suffered as a result of the streak of stubbornness that ran through him. All his life it had brought trouble. Even as a boy in Mercia he had never walked away from a fight. It had led to some bad beatings, but gradually he had learned to master the skills nature had given him. In the end perhaps he had learned them too well.

"What are you thinking, Cousin Thomas?" She chose to ignore his question, still using that strange—to him—form of address which he knew indicated great respect. A respect he believed he hadn't earned.

"Nothing, Your Grace. Something a long time ago and far away."

"In England?"

He nodded. On the bed the young prince stirred and Thomas leaned closer. The boy rocked his head to one side, back. Beneath his lids his eyes moved as they followed some vision available only to him. Then he stilled and Thomas sat back, leaning into the chair. He liked chairs. In Gharnatah they were few and far between, but he had several in his house. His old house. More memories. He knew he needed to distract himself.

"Yes, Your Grace, in England."

"Did you know my great-grandfather was an English duke? But I know little of your country. What is it like?"

"Green and wet," Thomas said.

The queen smiled. "Like the north of my country."

Thomas laughed. "No. Far wetter and far colder."

The queen stared into space for a moment, and he thought she was thinking of her son, but when she spoke it wasn't of the prince. "What brought you here, Thomas Berrington? Such a long way from your homeland?"

"War, Your Grace."

She nodded. "Of course. There is always war." She glanced at him. "You know I intend to expel the Moors from this land, don't you?"

He returned her nod, meeting her eyes, a gross abuse of protocol, but there was only the light of intelligence in hers.

"What will you do when that day comes?" asked the queen.

"If I am still alive?"

She smiled. "Yes—if you are still alive. Will you return to England?"

"I don't know." And it was true, he had no idea what he would do. England wasn't his home anymore, hadn't been for many years. He belonged in Gharnatah with those he loved. Except when the time finally came—and it would, he had no doubt of that—both he and the people he loved would be refugees. A scowl crossed his face as he thought of those he had left behind.

He jerked upright as the queen patted his hand, not sure if he had drifted into sleep. What was she thinking? But again that smile, and he wished their positions were not as they were, because he liked this woman, respected her intelligence, and would have enjoyed discussing matters with her long into the night.

"If at the end you live, seek me out. I will find a place for you so you may stay in the land you love. You do love this land, don't you? I see it in your eyes."

"Yes."

"Then come to me." She sat back. "That is if I live, too. War can be cruel."

"Yet still you fight it."

For a moment he thought he had gone too far, seduced by the warmth and closeness of the room.

The queen's eyes were unflinching when they met his, and now he recognised the steel within her. "You know I cannot let the infidel remain within my borders. You, a good Christian, must understand this."

Again the deception of silence, Thomas too weak to correct her. He didn't know how to respond, but she went on, unaware of his thoughts.

"Don't return. You can stay here in my court. You are skilled and my doctors are charlatans." That smile again. "You know they are, don't you? We have no-one like you and would benefit greatly from your presence. Will you not stay?"

Thomas thought of the hatred the sultan Muhammed bore him. This woman wanted him here while his master wanted him gone. He wondered who ruled in Gharnatah now.

"I hear the sultan is captured. Perhaps the war will be over soon."

"That is the message sent. If it is indeed him. My general claims it is, but I won't believe it until I see him." She looked at Thomas. "Even then I will not recognise him. But you would."

He returned her gaze, saying nothing.

"If I asked, would you tell me if it is him or not, when he arrives?"

"When will that be?"

"A week or more yet, perhaps even longer. He was captured at Lucena. There will be no haste to bring him to Cordoba. There are protocols to be followed in such matters."

Thomas knew that more than likely the prisoner was Muhammed. The sultan was young and headstrong. Even as they were preparing to depart there had been signs of soldiers readying themselves. The detour they had been forced to make around Castro del Rio was most likely caused by Muhammed's army pushing into enemy territory. It was typical of the man, Thomas thought, to send him and Jorge to the queen and then attack her at the same time.

The prince stirred and Thomas reached for his free hand, feeling for the pulse in his wrist. It was a little fast, but steady. The boy's eyes continued to move beneath their lids, the opium bringing dreams.

"Jorge can identify him as well as I," Thomas said.

"But it is you I ask," said the queen.

He didn't want to meet her eyes. After the way Muhammed had treated him, after the threats he had made, it shouldn't feel like betrayal but it did.

"Thomas?" There was iron in her voice, and he realised this was a test of something, his loyalty perhaps. Except he was no longer sure where his loyalty lay, if he ever had known.

"Ask me again, Your Grace, when he arrives."

A moment of pain, of anger perhaps, crossed her face, and events might have taken a darker turn if the prince had not chosen that moment to open his eyes and scream.

It took Thomas half an hour to settle Juan. His mother stood to one side, as close as she dare without interfering. Only when her son quietened did she draw close, sit and once more take his hand. For a time he remained awake, and as the pain abated he enjoyed her presence before the opium took him once more.

"You're a brave boy, my angel. Such a brave boy."

The prince offered no words in reply, only a smile. Gradually his eyes lost focus and closed.

"How long will this pain last?" The closeness they had shared was gone. Now she was the queen once more, demanding answers.

"A few days. At the moment he will be in agony each time he wakes. In three days that will fade. I have lotions I will apply to his leg that will help."

She seemed to shrink into herself, leaning back into the chair, and for a moment her eyes closed. She spoke without opening them. "Will he truly be able to walk again?"

"I believe so."

"As well as before?"

"No. Never as well as before. But well enough."

She opened her eyes and Thomas saw the softness of a mother had re-asserted itself. "One day Juan will be king, and a king must be strong. If you had been here when he fell, would you have been able to do a better job?"

"Yes." There was no need for pretence. Thomas never pretended. He knew how good he was.

"You should stay here once he is well." It was a subject she was unwilling to give up. The smile that touched her mouth belied the meaning he heard in her words and he smiled back.

"Would you respect me if I abandoned my homeland?"

"No. I could not do so, and I understand why you wish to return. But when this war is done with..."

Thomas nodded. He understood.

They ate a late supper in the prince's bedchamber. A small table was brought in and a light meal served. The queen drank wine, Thomas water. Theresa left to be replaced by Sancha. She sat in the same corner working at a square of lace and they ignored her as though she was not there.

"Is it true your companion is a eunuch?" asked the queen as they ate.

Thomas looked up, surprised. "Yes, it's true."

"He doesn't look like one."

He smiled. "No, that's also true."

"The ladies of my court are fascinated by him."

"Jorge affects some women that way."

The ghost of the smile that touched her lips told him perhaps the attraction applied equally to queens.

"And is it also true he was born here?"

"In Cordoba? Yes." In deference Thomas used the Spanish pronunciation.

"How did he find himself living with heathens and become what he is?"

What to tell her, Thomas wondered. "He was captured by the Moors. Not in battle, he tells me. He was wandering, lost, and came across a group of soldiers. He tried to hide but they caught him. He says he expected to be killed, but instead they took him back to their camp. He was a beautiful boy and something about him caught the attention of the old sultan."

"So they took him, turned him into what he has become?"

Thomas made no reply, picking at a slice of lamb.

"I have heard the process is barbaric."

Thomas understood her curiosity. Many shared it. "It used to be," he said.

"Did he suffer a great deal?"

Thomas swallowed and wiped his fingers on a cloth, once more inwardly cursing his predilection for honesty. "I know he did not. It was me who turned him into what he is, Your Grace. There was pain, but not as much as there would have been had someone else performed the operation. You are right, the process was barbaric, but I have changed it since."

"You? They..." She turned aside, looking at her son who lay quiet, breathing peacefully. "They allowed you to change their customs?"

"When those customs resulted in a death rate of nineteen in twenty, yes."

"So not so much pain for your friend."

"Not so much pain, no."

Once more the amused glance. "My ladies gossip about him."

"Ladies do," Thomas said.

"Pain...." said the queen, and Thomas thought she was talking about her son, but when she raised her eyes her next words surprised him. "I understand you witnessed the atrocity at the city gate when you arrived yesterday."

He nodded and pulled at his food, needing a moment.

"Someone told me you tried to examine the body."

"I was not allowed."

"I heard that, too. Would it have done any good if you had? Would you have learned anything useful?"

"I don't know, and I never will now."

"This is not the first death," said the queen.

"Pero told me."

She ate for a moment, drained her glass. She smiled as Thomas refilled it.

"Pero also told me what you did last year."

"I did many things last year, Your Grace."

"You know of what I mean. I would be interested to hear the details."

"I will not betray my sultan," Thomas said, and saw her expression change, a moment of anger flashing across her face.

"I do not ask you to betray anyone, sir. But will telling me of how you caught a killer be a betrayal? It was you who tracked the man down, wasn't it? Or was Pero misinformed?"

"No, he was not."

She leaned forward, all anger gone. "I would hear more of the matter. I wish to know what manner of man you are."

"I am a surgeon, Your Grace."

"No—you are more than that. I would not have you speak of confidences, but please, tell me what you can."

Thomas sat back. He couldn't see what harm it would do to tell her some of it. So he told her of the attacks on concubines and sultanas, of the soldier who'd crept through hidden tunnels in the palace of al-Hamra spying on the women of the harem, attacking and killing them. He told her of his own involvement when the old sultan, Abu al-Hasan Ali, had asked him to look into the murders. He told her of a final confrontation with the killer. But he did not tell her of the betrayal of the sultan, the betrayal of the concubine Helena who had been gifted him, nor of the rise to power of Muhammed and the part he had played in it.

"You married this woman, I hear," she said. "The first to be attacked. She was very beautiful and she was scarred, wasn't she?"

"Helena? She is not my wife. But yes, she was scarred, although if you saw her now you would barely know it."

The queen stared at him. "But you live as man and wife, do you not?"

"We did."

"Who do you live with now?"

"I live alone. I have a servant, but I live alone." This woman would not understand the complex web of relationships even if he tried to explain them. Thomas barely understood them himself. What he did understand was that Helena's sister, Lubna, the woman he had called a servant, was far more important to him than that. Even if he had never given her any indication of his true feelings.

"You were there, I understand, when the new sultan ousted the old."

"I don't know what tales Pero has been spinning, Your Grace. I was lucky to be alive, and as for the sultan, perhaps it was simply time to make way for his son."

"Kings and queens do not make way willingly. My own brother did not want me to be queen after him. I have had to fight for my position."

"The old sultan did not make way willingly, either. There was a rebellion in the city. I am sure you will have heard all about that, too." Thomas knew he was giving away no secrets. This woman and her husband would have their spies in Gharnatah, as Muhammed had his own throughout Spain.

The prince sighed and muttered and they both looked towards the bed, but he raised one arm then dropped it back and sank once more into slumber.

"When my son no longer needs your constant presence I want you to do the same for me, Thomas Berrington. Find me the killer that terrorises my city. The people are fearful, and I will not have them think I do nothing to protect them."

"I—"

Before he could object she held up a hand. "Do this for me and you may return to your beloved city. Refuse and I will make sure you stay here forever. No more beautiful concubine. No more Arab lover."

Pero has been talking, Thomas thought. But the queen's threats were unnecessary. She was asking him to follow a course he had already decided on, and a thrill ran through him at the thought of tracking down another killer.

CHAPTER FOURTEEN

Thomas gave up on trying to sleep. He glanced across the room at the still sleeping figure of Jorge. The pre-dawn light washed his friend's features into an unnatural paleness, accenting dark rings beneath his eyes. Jorge had not been there when Thomas came late to his own bed, neither did he hear him creep in, so he must have slept at some time, but he failed to recall exactly when. His mind had been worrying away at the queen's request. His curiosity had been whetted by the murder and its possible link to what he had witnessed on the river. But despite how much he would relish becoming involved he knew the prince would need much of his time. There was also the matter of what had happened the last time he'd pursued a killer. It had ended in a fight that might have taken his own life. Except there were no politics involved this time and little danger he would be putting his own safety at risk.

He threw back the covers and stood, knowing he had already made his decision. He dressed as quietly as he could before taking his boots outside to pull them on. As he strode through silent corridors he hoped Pero was also an early riser. Before seeking him out he went to Prince Juan's room and checked on the boy. Sancha was asleep in a chair but woke when he entered. The boy had spent an uneasy night, she said, waking in the dark hours, and she had given him a small draft of opium which had calmed him.

Thomas knew he should stay and check on his charge, but also knew Theresa and Sancha were up to the task of caring for the prince, and there was little to be done while he healed. Still, he checked the boy's leg before leaving, satisfying himself there was nothing untoward.

He found the priest after making enquiries of sulky servants annoyed to be disturbed from their duties. Pero's accommodation was tucked hard against the north wall of the palace. When Thomas rapped on the door a sharp voice bade him to enter.

Pero was already dressed. He sat at a small desk—indeed it needed to be small, for the entire room had little space free, filled as it was by a narrow cot and the desk.

"What is it you want now? Is it the prince?" Pero continued to write, not looking away from the paper his pen scratched against.

"The prince is as well as can be expected at the moment. I have a favour to ask of you."

"Another one?"

"The queen has asked me to look into the murders."

Pero stopped writing and sat straight. "You? Why?"

"Because of last year, I think. She said you told her of what I did."

"I might have mentioned something. But I know little of it at best."

Thomas knew Pero had been in Gharnatah at the time, requesting his presence. It was that request which turned Thomas and Jorge into outlaws for a few days until the true killer was identified. Thomas didn't believe Pero when he said he knew little. He had been present during the final days when Muhammed replaced the old sultan and would know all about what came to pass.

"Will you help me or are you going to argue until someone else is killed?" Thomas spoke sharply, uncaring if he hurt the man's feelings. Pero had shown little concern for his own, both during the journey or since.

"I should speak with the queen first. How do I know you aren't making this up?"

Thomas sighed, wondering if he should have remained in bed. Another few hours of sleep had been tempting.

"Why would I be doing such a thing? Do you think I *want* to go looking for another killer?" Even as he spoke he recognised his words as a lie. The nature of the woman's death intrigued him. The skill shown in detaching the limbs from her torso and re-attaching that of the wolf, although gruesome, were fascinating.

Pero washed a hand across his face, pushed his thin hair back from his brow. "If I take you to the Hermandad will that satisfy you?"

"For the moment."

Thomas was surprised to see Pero almost smile. "I suppose that will have to do. Come on then." Pero rose and looked around for his boots, found them under his cot and sat to pull them on.

Pero led Thomas through streets just beginning to come alive as men and women walked to their work and merchants began to open shops and stalls. The offices of the Hermandad were set hard against the city wall to the north of the palace. Pero introduced Thomas to the captain of the guard, a florid faced man named Carlo Labrada, who was still eating his breakfast.

"This man would speak with you," said Pero. "Under order of the queen."

Labrada looked up at that, a hunk of bread dipped in gravy half way between plate and mouth. His eyes narrowed as they tracked Thomas up and down.

"You were at the gate two days ago when the latest girl was cut down."

"You have the advantage of me, sir."

Labrada waved a hand. "I wasn't there. My constables described you. There can be no two such men in Cordoba."

"I am pleased to hear it."

"Have you finished with me?" asked Pero.

Thomas nodded. "Thank you." He turned back to Labrada as

the priest made his departure. "Can I speak with the men who were there? I would like to view the body. Where is it being held?"

"She'll be interred by now, for sure." Labrada stood and went past Thomas to the doorway. "Hey, Rodrigo, were you there when they cut the girl down?"

There was a muffled reply Thomas didn't hear.

"Who was then?" asked Labrada. "Come in here, I'm not going to stand and yell all day." He returned to the table, picked up a knife and cut a slice of apple. A young man entered. He looked barely old enough to shave, his cheeks shadowed by dark wisps of hair that were trying to join together to form a beard. He stood to attention just inside the room.

Labrada waved his knife towards Thomas. "This man asks about the killings. Tell him what he wants to know. It is, apparently, by order of the queen." His face showed how little he believed the tale, but Pero's presence had persuaded him he would need to offer at least some token assistance.

Thomas turned to the man. "What can you tell me?"

"Not here," snapped Labrada. "Take him outside and let me eat in peace."

Rodrigo turned and left without a word. After a moment Thomas followed. It was a poor welcome, to be sure, but he knew it would be no different in Gharnatah or any other city in Spain. Men rose to positions of seniority because of who they knew rather than their abilities. It was the same the world over.

"I apologise," said Rodrigo as he led Thomas onto the street. "The captain takes some time to learn manners in the morning, depending on how much he has drunk the night before."

Thomas was surprised to hear the young constable talk so openly. He could only guess Labrada was even worse a master than he had already witnessed.

"You weren't at the city gate?" he asked.

"No. But I know as much as anyone who was. I have made it my business to know."

Thomas was impressed. Young he might be but Rodrigo showed more diligence than his captain.

"How long have you been with the Hermandad?"

"Two years come summer."

"So you were here when the first killing took place."

"It was just a killing then. No-one knew there would be more." He started along the roadway, in towards the melee of the centre.

"It was unusual though? The hacking off of limbs, the sewing on of those of animals."

"The first was less..." Rodrigo hesitated, searching for the right word. "Notable," he said at last. "The limbs were not sewn, merely laid. That is what I heard, anyway. I had not taken an interest at that time, only later."

"I heard that myself," Thomas said, recalling what Lawrence had told him.

"So you know some facts already. Who have you spoken with? There is much gossip and few you can trust."

"A priest—no, a man called Lawrence. But whether that's a christian name or—"

"It's a family name," said Rodrigo. "I know him. And what he will have told you is sound information. He too takes an interest, although he does not always share what he knows. You are privileged."

"I had an introduction, the same one that brought me to you. Where are we going?"

Rodrigo glanced at Thomas. "Are you a brave man?" His eyes tracked Thomas from feet to head. Whatever he saw appeared not to provide the answer he sought.

"I have fought," Thomas said. "Why?"

"Where we are going is not a place for men of culture. I would not take a doctor of Cordoba where I am about to take you."

"Tell me what you know."

Rodrigo smiled. "Now you are asking a lot, Don Berrington."

"Call me Thomas." He did not remember telling Rodrigo his name, but was getting used to the notion that everyone in Qurtuba seemed to know who he was. "And tell me what you can before we get to where we are going."

"There's not much to tell. They have all been women apart

from a single boy of ten." Rodrigo grimaced. "That was a hard one to take. What was done to him."

"I saw what was done to the woman two days ago. Her death can't have come easily, either."

"Indeed. But the boy was worse." Rodrigo glanced at Thomas, and he saw the man judging how much to say.

"I am a surgeon who has attended men on the battlefield. There is little you can say that will shock me."

"Well it shocked me. Someone had opened his chest and removed his heart. I pray he was already dead when they did so. An entire crow was placed in the cavity in its place."

"Does that have some significance?"

"I don't know. I'm not a clever man like you, Don Berrington. At the time I believed it was no more than cruelty. Now?" He raised a shoulder. "Who knows…"

"What ages were the women?"

"Between fifteen and thirty, I suppose. But there was only one of that age. Most were twenty or less."

"Innocents?"

Rodrigo laughed. "You will discover that for yourself. We are at our destination."

Thomas had taken little note of their surroundings as they walked. Now he looked around to discover they were in a narrow alley. There was nobody else in sight and the air hung fetid between walls that leaned together as though to close them in from the sky.

Rodrigo hammered on a door. There was no indication it offered entrance to anything other than one more hovel amongst many, but when the door opened the air that billowed out was scented and sweet. A woman beyond the flush of youth stood in the doorway, her dress cut low to openly display her full breasts.

"You again," said the woman, before turning her attention to Thomas. "Have you brought me a new customer? He looks better than most."

"We have questions for you."

"More questions? Why always questions when I have so much

more to offer? Or perhaps the Hermandad don't pay enough for you to afford the services of my girls. But your friend looks like he can." She smiled, revealing three teeth, the rest having fallen out of love with her gums long since. "Is this about the bonebreaker? You know I have taken precautions. His latest victim is not one of mine."

"So nobody is missing?"

"All accounted for."

"You would not lie to me?"

The woman scowled. "Why would I? The sooner you catch him the sooner people will stop being afraid to walk the streets. Death is not good for business. No—I have nobody missing."

It was the same tale at the next three establishments. At the fifth they were invited in, the madam of the house standing aside to allow them entry. She was younger than the crones Thomas had seen so far and most likely continued to work her profession as well as look after her younger charges.

Rodrigo led the way into a surprisingly large room. The interior had been refashioned at some time, extending into the buildings on either side, almost certainly into those of the street behind as well. Three women lounged on ornate cushions in the manner of the harem, and Thomas realised that was the impression that was meant to be given. One of the women was dark skinned and reminded him uncomfortably of Lubna. Except Lubna would never disport herself in such a manner. All three, seeing Rodrigo's uniform, began to rise, but he raised a hand.

Thomas stood to one side, aware no action was required of him.

"Stay where you are," said Rodrigo. "I have questions for you."

"We know what your questions relate to," said the senior woman. "Answer Rodrigo honestly, girls. We all want this killer caught."

"You are all accounted for?"

"My charges come and go. Some might stay away for a night or two. But so far as I know we are all safe."

"Christabela is missing," said one of the girls. It was a reply

Thomas had heard before. Five girls had been missing from the other establishments but none of them matched the description of the latest victim.

"Did she have an appointment?" asked Rodrigo. "When was she last seen?"

"Monday."

"And today is Tuesday, so she is not who we seek."

"Monday last," the girl said. "A week ago and more."

Rodrigo turned to the madam of the house. "And you did not know this?"

"As I said, girls come and go. Some have their favourites. It is not unknown for them to be gone a week."

"What did she look like?" Thomas said. Their eyes turned on him as if only now noticing his presence. He was not uneasy in this place. Before Helena had come to share his life he had used such establishments himself when the need came on him. Although he doubted he would have wanted to frequent any of the houses they had so far visited, and this one was no exception.

"Small, blonde hair."

Thomas glanced at Rodrigo. The victim had been small and blonde. But so had two of the other girls who were supposedly missing.

"Eyes?"

"Blue," said one.

"Green," said another.

"Which?" said Rodrigo.

"Green," confirmed the madam.

As were the eyes of one of the other missing girls.

Thomas closed his own eyes a moment, bringing back the image imprinted on his memory.

He raised a hand. "Did she have a mark on her face, here?"

When he opened his eyes they were all staring at him.

One girl raised her own hand, the mirror image of Thomas. "It was the other cheek."

CHAPTER FIFTEEN

The sight that greeted Thomas when he entered the prince's room two hours later than planned caused him to stop short, before a fierce rage engulfed him. Abbot Mandana knelt at the foot of the bed, hands raised in prayer. A censer of incense burned, copious amounts of smoke tainting the air. A second man leaned over the prince with a bowl in his hand. Sancha stood in the corner, her face fearful.

"What are you doing to my patient!" Thomas sprinted to the bed and grabbed the man's arm, recognising him only as he turned. It was Don Harras, the doctor who had tried to gain entrance before.

"The boy must be bled."

"And prayed over," said the abbot.

Thomas stared down at the young prince. Sweat beaded his brow and beneath his lids his eyes darted left and right. The doctor had removed the bindings from the boy's leg to reveal the skin—mottled, dark blue, black in places. A bowl lay against the prince's leg to catch blood as it poured from a cut in his thigh.

Thomas picked up the bowl and threw it across the room. Then he picked up the doctor, not a light man, and threw him after it. Don Harras slipped on the spilled blood and went onto his side.

When Abbot Mandana rose and came around the bed Thomas turned on him, his anger flaring even brighter.

"Out!" Thomas shouted.

The abbot looked into his eyes, holding his ground. "I don't expect an infidel to understand."

"Sancha, fetch the queen. Now!" Thomas half expected the nurse to refuse, or at least hesitate, but was pleased to see her rise and hurry from the room. "Have you asked her permission, either of you?"

"I don't need permission when it is a matter of the soul."

"It's his leg that's broken. His soul is perfectly healthy."

"What do you know of the soul?"

"Oh, I know what men like you say, but let me tell you something." Thomas punched the flat of his hand against the abbot's chest, rocking him on his heels. In his peripheral vision he was aware of the doctor rising and gathering up the tools of his trade. "Let me tell you what I know of the soul." He slapped the abbot's chest again, sending him backwards a step. "I have seen everything there is of a man, from the contents of his belly to the inside of his skull and every other part of him. I've seen how his heart beats and his blood flows, how his stomach works and his lungs and liver and kidneys. But I tell you what I have never seen. I have *never* seen a man's soul."

"You lack faith—the Lord would not reveal such a wonder to you."

"I have faith in what I can see. Are you going to wait for the queen? Will your faith protect you from her anger?"

"The queen is a holy woman."

"I'm sure she is. With a soul, no doubt. And a great love for her son. Which will be the greater today, do you think—her respect for you as a man of God, or the love of her son?"

The doctor had recovered his sense of importance and bustled to the doorway. He turned back, and for a moment Thomas thought he was going to speak, but the anger the man saw on his face persuaded him otherwise and he hurried from the room.

"Go join your accomplice, Abbot. Find some other innocent to kill."

The abbot shook his head as if Thomas's heresy caused him great sadness.

"One day you will remember how you treated me, and on that day it will be too late. The fires of hell will be waiting for you."

"Then I will warm my bones on them. Out. Now!" Thomas pushed again, sending the abbot stumbling. It was all he could do not to throw a punch. Instead he contented himself with slapping at the man's chest until he forced him from the room.

"I am not without friends and influence in this city," said the abbot. "You would do well to remember that and not make an enemy of me. The queen will hear of this."

"Indeed she will," Thomas said, slamming the door in his face.

When he turned back into the room Sancha was standing at the foot of the bed, her face pale, blood streaking her dress. In his anger he had not seen her return.

"I left a message," said Sancha. "The queen will come as soon as she can. I told them not to touch him, but they said I must not interfere."

"It's not your fault. They are important men—you had no choice."

"It is all our doctors know. They bleed everyone and the priests pray."

"You are a good Catholic, are you not?" Thomas went to the prince and examined the leg. Indeed it did look ugly, but he was pleased at the sight. The colour was coming to a peak and would begin to fade in a day or two. "Fetch me more bandage, we need to bind the leg tight again."

Thomas leaned close, examining the point at which the so-called doctor had sliced into a vein. He hadn't even used a small blade such as those Thomas carried in his bag, but a knife. Likely not even a clean knife, and almost certainly not sterilised with flame.

Thomas took the bandage from Sancha when she returned.

"And my bag. I need to clean the wound. Those foolish men."

He tore a strip of the linen loose and soaked it in water, cleaned around the wound. Bending close he looked for any sign of contamination. As soon as Sancha brought his bag he opened a small bottle of alcohol and poured a little into the wound. The prince rocked his head and moaned.

"How long since his last draught?"

"He has had none since that you gave him this morning."

"He can have more now, then. Sit him up and get him to drink. The rebinding will cause him pain."

Sancha obeyed, leaning the prince's pale head against her bosom.

"I don't understand how he doesn't scream or cry when you touch him." She stared down at the leg. "Our doctor's have no such method to control pain."

"And mine is little better," Thomas said. He wrapped a thin layer of bandage around the leg and laid the bark splint against it before wrapping more bandage, trapping the wood against the prince's skin.

"No—your methods are far superior. Are all doctors in al-Andalus like you?"

Thomas smiled, but when he saw Sancha's reaction he stopped. When he was angry he knew his smile didn't always have the effect he intended. "No, not all. We have many I wouldn't trust, but many I would." He thought of his friend, Dau'd al-Baitar, who had treated him after his injuries the year before. He had trusted him with his life.

"There are few here I would trust," said Sancha. She managed to get the comatose prince to swallow some opium mixed in wine and laid his head back against the pillow. "Will he really walk again without a limp?"

"I don't know. He may. But this certainly hasn't helped, damn them."

Sancha came to stand beside him as he worked. He could pretend she was observing, but knew it would be delusion. She stood too close, her breasts pressing against his shoulder. He had observed the behaviour before, and would discourage it as soon as he was done with the leg. Jorge would understand it better, but Thomas had grown accustomed to the reaction. There was something about his skill, and also strangely his lack of empathy, which attracted some women. Had he been unskilled, or skilled and kind, it would not have been the same. He wondered if they wanted to change him, to soften him, but didn't believe so. It was simply because of what he did, and the lack of emotion when he did it that triggered their reaction.

But not all women.

He thought of those he had left at home, at their different responses to him. He shook his head. They were far away and he had other matters to concentrate on.

As he finished binding the leg rapid footsteps sounded from beyond the door. Sancha moved away and made a pretence of packing instruments into his bag as the queen strode into the room.

"What happened here? I was told you needed my presence."

"Your palace doctor and the abbot have been trying to cure your son with suspicion and prayer. I threw them out."

She came to stand beside the bed. Thomas saw she wanted to hold the boy but was afraid of hurting him.

"Has any harm come to him?"

"Nothing lasting, I hope. Did you know they were coming here?"

She finally glanced at him, tearing her eyes from her son. "Do you believe I would allow someone else to treat him?"

"I don't know. Would they have come here without your knowing?"

"It was not of my doing."

"The guards must be told to allow no-one in without my permission."

"Or mine," said the queen.

Thomas hesitated, deciding how far he could press her. "All right, our permission."

"Or my husband's."

"I don't know him."

"He's my husband." She spoke as though that was enough reason. "Where were you when these men came? Why did you not stop them?"

Thomas glanced at Sancha. She was on her knees cleaning up the last of the spilled blood.

"I was attending to the other task you gave me, Your Grace."

The queen frowned. Thomas didn't want to mention the name, but before he needed to the frown faded.

"Of course. Have you discovered something?"

"I know more than I did yesterday, but there are others I need to speak with yet."

"There is a month if the pattern remains the same." She sat on the edge of the bed and took Juan's hand. The boy slept peacefully now, his breathing slow, calm. "Perhaps you should spend more time here and leave your investigations until he has improved."

"The time to search this killer out is now, Your Grace, while events are fresh in people's minds. And the pattern could change."

"There is no reason to think it will." She stroked her son's brow, all at once looking exhausted herself. "There are matters I must attend to. Your sultan arrives within weeks and will need suitable accommodation prepared. Will you stay with Juan for a while?"

"Until he is settled."

"Should I post guards on the door?"

"It will do no harm," Thomas said. "Although I would be surprised if they try anything again."

She hesitated a moment longer, then nodded and strode from the room, her back straight. Thomas felt a wave of sympathy for her, understanding the conflict between love and duty. And, like him, she had allowed duty to rule her. As soon as it was only the two of them and the prince again Sancha came close.

"I knew when they came I should have sent for you." Her voice was so soft he barely heard it.

"It's done now. And it won't happen again. I'm going to ask for a cot to be brought in. I'll sleep here until he's safe from any tampering."

"Abbot Mandana is a powerful man. He won't like it you threw him out." Sancha wetted a cloth and wiped the prince's face.

"Let him take it up with the queen. We should wash the rest of him, too."

"Why?"

"It will help stop infection."

Sancha laughed. "Who told you that?"

Thomas glanced at her, uneasy at the sense of closeness that was growing between them. He had noticed it with Theresa as well, but more so with this woman, perhaps because she was young and attractive. And if that was so then it must have something to do with his own attitude as well.

"No-one told me. I observe and I read. What makes you think it doesn't? What causes infection if not for being unclean?"

"Humours. Everyone knows infection is caused by bad humours."

Thomas smiled. "We'll wash him anyway."

"As you wish. But I was taught dirt seals the skin and keeps disease at bay."

"Then you have been taught wrong." Thomas helped her remove the prince's blouse and the cloth wrapped at his waist. Naked he looked tiny and defenceless.

"Can you find hot water?"

"I'll go ask in the kitchens. Will you be all right on your own?"

"I think I can manage."

"I didn't mean—" Then Sancha saw he was joking and smiled.

After she was gone Thomas felt guilty for being pleasant to her. She needed little enough encouragement, and there was never going to be anything between them. He knew little about either of the women that had been chosen to nurse the prince. What were their lives like outside the palace? Were they married? Did they have children of their own? Did it matter? And even if it did matter, did he care?

He was relieved the queen didn't appear to blame him for what had happened to Juan, but knew it was going to be difficult to give enough attention to both of her requests without cutting back on the other. While he waited for Sancha to return he stared at the prince and knew he had already made that decision even before the task was given him. The boy had two nurses to care for him. The other matter was more important if lives were to be saved.

CHAPTER SIXTEEN

Jorge was alone in bed when Thomas returned the next morning from his own disturbed night in the prince's room. At least the boy himself had slept peacefully, and Thomas decided he could escape for a few hours.

"Have you not bedded that woman yet?" he asked as he sat down on his own bed. He had half expected her to be here when he returned.

Jorge's only reply was a knowing look.

Thomas started stripping out of his clothes. He needed to wash and dress in a clean robe. Then he wanted to get out of the palace for a few hours to clear his head.

"Do you want to make yourself useful today?" he asked as he padded across to the table where a bowl and jug had been laid. There was soap, and not bad quality either, and he started to wash.

"That depends on what you want. Is it dangerous?" Jorge studied Thomas, but he was used to the attention by now and ignored him.

"I'd like you to come with me and talk to some whores. I thought you'd be better with them than me."

Jorge laughed. "When have I ever had need of whores? Although I recall that used to be your pastime once."

"You are better with women than me, you know you are. Will you come?"

"Are any of them pretty?"

Thomas finished washing and dried himself on a length of dense linen that had been draped over the corner of the table then walked back across the room to dress. "Why don't you come and tell me? You can rate them—treat it as an entertainment, if you wish."

"I might as well," said Jorge. "Esperanza won't see me until this evening, and it would be good to get out of the palace for a while."

"That's what I thought." Thomas glanced at Jorge while he pulled on a pair of trousers. "You're still living dangerously, then?"

"She fascinates me," said Jorge. "I've never met anyone like her —a woman who understands the ways of love in the same way I do."

"You told me before she was different. Is that what you meant?"

Jorge only looked at him.

"You haven't..." Thomas shook his head. It was none of his business what they might have done while he was elsewhere. At least he hoped it didn't become any of his business. And he knew warning Jorge would be a waste of time.

"Tio Jorge?"

They stopped walking, jostled by crowds that flowed in the direction of the cathedral. In the distance the sound of drums and horns carried to them. Preparation for the Easter parade at the end of the week continued to grow hour by hour, excitement driving away some of the tension the killings had caused among the population of the city.

Thomas had intended for them to visit establishments he hadn't spoken with yet, to see if other girls had been approached. If someone was seeking them out as victims he was sure there would be some who had escaped their fate.

But they were interrupted before even starting by the young woman who stood in front of them, a woven sack on her back containing fruit and vegetables. Thomas looked at her a moment before he recognised her as the girl he had spoken with outside Daniel Olmos's workshop.

"Adana," said Jorge, embracing her. Thomas knew Jorge had visited his brother's house since, and it appeared he might have been made more welcome than the first time. Unless it was only by the women. Being Jorge that would make sense, of course.

Adana accepted the embrace willingly, lifting on her toes to kiss the corner of Jorge's mouth.

"This saves me a trip. I was to bring a message to you. Mama wants you to come for dinner." She turned to include Thomas. "Both of you. I have been shopping for food. She says to come—"

A burly man knocked against her, almost sending her to the ground, and Jorge reached out and grabbed the man by the collar, stopping him mid-stride.

"Take care how you treat my niece, sir," said Jorge, for a moment his stare locking onto the man who, at first full of bluster, backed off when those eyes met his. Thomas smiled. Jorge released the man, who hurried away. "Are you hurt?" Jorge asked Adana.

"It happens all the time, Tio. I can take care of myself." She went on one knee and started to retrieve the fruit the man had jostled from her basket. Jorge went down beside her and they started to repack it.

"You didn't finish your mother's message."

"Oh, of course." She flushed. "You are to come to eat with us." She glanced at Thomas. "Your friend as well. She told Papa off for doubting you. She is keen for us to sit around the table and catch up on your missing history. She would hear more from this brother she knew nothing of."

Jorge stood and took the basket when she tried to swing it onto her back again.

"We were on our way to find something to eat. Why don't I carry this for you and we come now?"

"Today?"

"Of course. Thomas here is in great demand. He might not be able to come tomorrow." He glanced at Thomas. "You can spare a few hours, can't you?"

"Perhaps a few."

"Then it's settled. Have you finished your chores?"

"I need meat if you are coming now. Mama says we must have meat for you, Tio, and you too, sir." She glanced at Thomas, and he saw uncertainty on her face. He wondered if a smile would ease her, but knew often as not his smiles alarmed more than they calmed.

"You don't understand," said Jorge, emphasising his words with the point of a knife on the table. "It was the Moors who dragged this country screaming into enlightenment. Not the other way round."

Daniel shook his head, a look of stubborn patience on his face. "They took what belonged to Spain."

"But it wasn't! When they came across the narrow sea this country was under the rule of the northern vandals. There was no Spain. Even a hundred years ago there was no Spain, only warring principalities each trying to carve out its own piece of land."

"And you are missing the most important point." This time it was Daniel's turn to use his knife, pointing the tip in Jorge's direction. "They are infidels. Whatever else you claim, they worship a false god and follow a false prophet. This country belongs to the one true God."

Thomas watched the argument in silent amusement. On the occasions he glanced at Daniel's wife, Zanita, she had been keeping her own counsel. The children were oblivious, apart from Adana, who at fifteen believed herself an adult and acted like one. Thomas noticed her scrutiny of both himself and Jorge, still with that knowingness in her eyes he had caught when he'd first met her. He wondered how much trouble she was to her parents. If not now, then certainly in the future.

He shifted his attention as Jorge joggled his arm. "Tell him everything the Moors have given Spain." Jorge turned his attention back to his brother. "Thomas is a clever man—far cleverer than me. I can't even count high enough to know how many books he has in his house. Tell him, Thomas, tell him."

"Don't involve me, I'm an Englishman."

"Coward," said Jorge.

"How do you know if we had been left to develop on our own Spain wouldn't have made the same discoveries?" said Daniel.

Jorge scratched at his head. "Why do you think Thomas is here? Is it because Spanish doctors are so wonderful he has come to learn from them?" Jorge slapped his hand down on the table, his knife, still clutched, clattering away. "He came to repair the prince's leg because no-one else could. *That* is the knowledge of the Moors right there."

"I don't deny the knowledge," said Daniel, "I deny their right to live in our land."

"Who wants fruit?" said Zanita, rising and gathering the empty plates, rough hewn pottery but serviceable. The meal had been good—mutton bought by Adana that afternoon, onions, root vegetables and spices. Spices which had first been brought across the narrow sea by the Moors and introduced into this land so conducive to the growing of them.

She brought a bowl filled with apricots and figs, dates, apples and pears, pomegranates and blood oranges, walnuts and almonds and olives soaked in oil. A second board held cheese and sausage and a loaf of bread made from white flour.

When Daniel put his fingertip on the table and leaned across it towards Jorge, Zanita put her hand over his.

"Enough of this talk. I want to hear tales of my brother-in-law's life in the harem."

Daniel looked at her. "Then the children should go to bed."

Zanita smiled. "The young ones. Adana can stay if she wants."

"And I will temper my language," said Jorge.

"Not on my behalf," said Adana. "I am old enough to marry now."

Jorge stared at her. "I am sure many will want you, Adana. You are as radiantly beautiful as your mother."

Adana's cheeks glowed, still innocent enough for the compliment to please. Zanita pursed her lips, but Thomas saw she too was flattered.

"Is that how you speak to the women of the harem, brother?"

"Only the pretty ones."

Thomas helped himself to a pear and bit into it, juice running into his beard. He studied Adana while she listened to Jorge, her attention rapt. Despite their father's order the younger children remained and Jorge adjusted his tales and language appropriately, regaling them with stories of opulence and wonders, of riches and hardship and water that ran constantly throughout the city of Gharnatah. And of bathing. The children turned their noses up at the notion, but leaned close, fascinated.

Daniel lowered his voice as he turned to Thomas, ignoring the other conversation as fit only for women. "Is it true you are repairing the prince's leg?"

"Does the entire city know my business?"

"Jorge mentioned it," said Daniel. His gaze locked on Thomas, who saw the unasked question there. He would not force the man to overcome his pride and ask it.

"The prince is young," he said. "His bones had not fully set in their new position so I was able to break them again. The young heal quickly. Quicker than someone my age would."

Daniel nodded. It was all the answer he needed.

"I had to ask, you understand."

It was Thomas's turn to nod, and he felt bad he couldn't help. He glanced towards Zanita, who sat with hands resting across her extended belly. There was another child due soon.

"I can help your wife when her time comes."

Daniel shrugged. "It's only a baby. She's had plenty of practice. As for me, I manage as I am. Jorge said to ask, that you might be able to do something."

"I might be able to do something for the pain."

"The pain I can put up with."

Thomas nodded. "We could help in other ways then, if you would let us."

"I take no charity," said Daniel, lowering his dark brows.

"Recompense then, for the hurt Jorge did you."

"I need no recompense, either." Daniel glanced at his brother. The others had formed a knot at the far end of the table, hanging on Jorge's every word. "It was as much my fault as his. More, probably. I was the older, I should have taken more care." He continued to stare at Jorge, his expression changing. "It's my fault what happened to him. His current state."

"He enjoys his state," Thomas said.

"How can a man live being such as he is? He has no…" Daniel waved a hand, indicating his groin. "I hear the process is agony. Butcher's knives and hot coals and many deaths."

Thomas stared at Daniel and made a decision. "It is me who made him what he is."

Daniel returned the stare, all friendship that might have once been there gone. "You did that to him?"

"Not the way you said, but yes, I made him what he is today. Except there was no butchery involved, nor hot coals. It was a wasteful practice."

"Whereas taking his manhood isn't?"

"Your brother still retains his manhood. It is the other two items I took from him, and which he claims he misses not at all."

"He can never father children though, can he."

"Jorge claims that as a benefit."

Daniel shook his head, turned to watch his family. "I don't understand that."

"No, and Jorge wouldn't expect you to."

"Do you have a wife? Children? A man in your position must have both."

"I have neither. Only a calling."

"Is it true what Jorge was arguing?"

"Which parts?"

"The knowledge."

“Gharnatah possesses much knowledge. As did Qurtuba, once. Three hundred years ago the greatest library in the west resided here.”

Daniel looked at him. “I can't read, but I respect those who can. Zanita is teaching the children, all of them. The world is changing, and a man or woman needs knowledge.”

“You will get no argument from me on that,” Thomas said.

“Spain is changing, too. You must see that. With Isabel and Fernando we will be a single nation again—for the first time in a thousand years. Is it true you have met her?”

“I am healing her son.”

“What is she like? All we see is the pomp. All we hear are the laws handed down by priests and Jews.”

“She cares for her country and her people.”

Daniel stared at the tabletop as he ate nuts off its surface one by one. “That's what I heard.”

“And she respects knowledge. She is willing to ask for the best help when she needs it and not rely on superstition.”

“Spain will be great again.”

Thomas laughed. “Again?”

“All right—Spain will be great. Do you believe that or not?”

“I think I may.”

“And what will you do? When we defeat the infidel? Will you return to this England you come from?”

“I will be an old man before you defeat us,” Thomas said.

“Us? Do you consider yourself a Moor, then?”

“I can never be a Moor. But Gharnatah is my home. I have grown accustomed to its heat and the scent of its flowers in my nose.”

“So will you stay in the new Spain?”

Thomas shook his head and picked a fig from the bowl. The fruit was sweet on his tongue, the flesh soft and grainy. “I don't know. I can't see beyond this moment.”

“You should make plans. A man with plans always has a better chance of success.”

Thomas smiled. “You have a good life here, Daniel. A beautiful wife, beautiful children, and now a brother you thought was lost.”

Daniel didn’t return the smile, but Thomas saw it was hard for him not to as he watched Jorge entertaining his family. “At least they seem to like him.”

CHAPTER SEVENTEEN

Thomas found the captain of the Hermandad in the same room as before, set hard against the city wall. He imagined the man spent most of his time there, making some pretence at managing his men. It wasn't the captain Thomas wanted. He had hoped the man might be able to tell him where to find Rodrigo, but the only information he gleaned was that the young constable would be in the city somewhere and was meant to be working until midnight.

"Don't you know this is an important week?" said the captain. "My men have more important things to do than seek out a killer of women who won't be missed."

Thomas left the man while he was still talking and struck out east through the city. The wider streets were busier than in previous days, an air of gaiety on the faces of people and in the way they walked. Here and there he caught sight of men dressed in strange costumes and once he heard the sound of a horn and drum. As he made his way further into narrow alleyways normal life resumed. At least normal for this place. The inhabitants were less well dressed, dirtier, not meeting his eyes as he searched for Rodrigo. Eventually he saw a familiar alley and ducked into it. He hammered on the door of the brothel as Rodrigo had done the day before.

The aged madam of the house opened it and recognised Thomas.

"Why can't you leave us alone?" She shook her head. "The other one's inside. You might as well come in too, trade's already ruined." She turned and strode away.

When he entered the large room Rodrigo was standing over a girl slumped in a worn chair. He turned at the interruption, the expression on his face one of frustration, which faded the moment he saw Thomas.

"Were you following me?"

"No. Your captain said you were assigned other duties."

"As I am, but this is more important. I arrived only a minute since. I've barely asked a question yet."

Thomas joined him. "Does the girl know anything?"

"She says not."

Thomas turned to the madam. "How many are here at the moment?"

She raised a shoulder. "Six? Ten?"

"Which is it?"

"How am I meant to know? They come and they go. I'm not their keeper."

"For which they are no doubt grateful." Thomas glanced at Rodrigo. "We should search the rooms, question everyone. If—" He snapped his fingers. "What was her name?"

"Christabela," said Rodrigo.

"If this Christabela is the one who was killed someone here will know something."

"You can't just wander where you like in my house!"

Thomas reached into his robe and pulled out a purse. He rummaged within and drew out a handful of coin.

"This should cover our time." He tossed the coins onto the low table. The girl Rodrigo had been questioning darted forward and grabbed at them. The madam pushed her away, sweeping the coins into her skirts.

Rodrigo gave a short laugh. "You could buy this entire establishment for a week with what you've given her."

"I think I can resist the temptation." Thomas pushed the girl away. She had turned her attention to him at the sight of his money, her hands reaching beneath his robe. "Do you think they will talk to us?"

"I doubt it. These girls know how to keep their mouth shut unless it's being used for a different purpose."

"Go first," Thomas said, giving Rodrigo a push. He followed the young man through to a corridor. Rooms sat to either side. There were no doors, only thin drapes that revealed a filmy view into each.

The chambers on the right were empty. To the left only one room contained a girl who reclined on a bed which almost completely filled the space.

"Name?" asked Rodrigo.

She sat up, pulling a transparent robe around herself, her eyes switching backwards and forwards between Rodrigo and Thomas.

Thomas reached into his pocket and opened his purse without withdrawing it. His fingers searched by touch, withdrew a low value coin. He held it up, saw the girl's eyes widen. When he tossed it her hand snatched out like a snake striking.

"How well did you know Christabela?" he said.

"Who?"

"Take it back," he said to Rodrigo. The Hermandad grabbed the girl's wrist and twisted. She cried out and dropped the coin. Rodrigo picked it up and handed it to Thomas.

He held it out once more. "How well did you know Christabela?" he repeated.

She stared at the coin. Thomas had a score of similar value in his purse, the lowest denomination he carried, but this girl would have to lie with a dozen men to earn the same.

"She was new." Her attention never left the coin. "I didn't know her well."

"How new?" Thomas noticed Rodrigo had stepped back against the wall, content to allow him to take over the questioning.

"She came..." Her eyes turned distant as she searched her memory. "Within the month. Two weeks, perhaps three."

"Did she come here from somewhere else?"

"I don't understand you, sir." Her gaze had returned to the coin.

"Another establishment."

She shook her head. "I told you, I didn't know her well."

"Who did?"

Her eyes flickered up to meet his. Thomas saw the internal debate going on. She wanted the money but there remained some trace of loyalty. She didn't want to get someone else in trouble.

Thomas put his hand with the coin back in his pocket and her gaze tracked him in panic. When he withdrew it he held two coins.

"Annalisa," she said, holding out her hand. "Annalisa was her friend."

"Where will I find this Annalisa?"

"Upstairs. End of the corridor. She has one of the good rooms."

Thomas nodded and tossed both coins onto the stained sheets. The girl's hand snatched out, gripping them tight inside her fist. Thomas wondered how long she would manage to keep possession of them.

They passed doors in a corridor identical to that on the ground floor. From one chamber came a grunting noise and a woman's cries of mock pleasure. Thomas kept his eyes on the door at the end of the corridor. It was the only room with a solid door, although at least here the curtains to each side were denser and provided a small measure of privacy.

For some reason he stopped and knocked on the door. He saw Rodrigo cast him a puzzled glance.

When the door opened he saw why Annalisa was afforded the best room. She was tall, exquisitely beautiful, and her skin was as dark and lustrous as polished ebony. She would be an exotic prize in this city.

She glanced at them both and started to close the door.

Rodrigo put his boot out and stopped it.

She glanced down, her eyes cold when they rose. "I don't entertain two." Her speech was awkward, coloured by a strange accent. Thomas wondered how long since she had been captured and brought across the narrow sea.

Thomas held out his hand. Two silver coins lay in his palm. He was starting to wonder whether he had brought enough money with him from Gharnatah.

She glanced at them. "Not even for that much." She tried to push the door again but Rodrigo's boot held it firm. "I will call out. You don't want me to do that. Take your foot away now."

"You were friend to Christabela, I am told," Thomas said.

Her gaze met his. Her eyes were as black as her skin, pupil and iris merging into one, the cornea a pale brown. Her hair was cut short to control its waywardness and she wore an ankle length robe which did little to hide the figure beneath.

"Who wants to know?"

"My companion is a member of the Hermandad, and I am a surgeon. We are investigating her death."

"What good will that do? She was killed by a rich man, and rich men are never punished."

"What makes you say that?"

She shook her head and stopped trying to close the door. "Are you truly seeking her killer?"

"We are."

She studied Thomas a moment. "Are you a clever man?"

"I have been told I am."

She smiled without showing her teeth. "And what do you think?"

Thomas fought with impatience. This woman was different to the others they had seen. Slave she might be but he knew she was afforded a respect they were not.

"Yes, I am clever," he said.

"And your friend?"

Thomas glanced at Rodrigo. "Him, too."

She stepped aside and turned into the room. Thomas followed. Rodrigo came in after him and closed the door. Annalisa sat on the edge of the bed, her feet together, hands in her lap. There was other furniture in the room. Two chairs and a small table. There was also an array of implements of her trade hanging on one wall. Thomas and Rodrigo remained on their feet.

"Put your coin away, sir. I will help you for Christabela, not for money. What is it you wish to know?"

"You were friends?"

Her dark eyes met his and she nodded. "Yes, we were friends. Good friends."

Thomas understood. There was no need to make her explain.

"Even though she was unlike you?"

"Her skin was as pale as the moon's beam, so of course she was unlike me."

"I didn't mean in that way. You have a position here. Respect. She was new."

"And pretty. She had a position, too. Not the same as mine, but she didn't have to work the rooms on the lower floor."

"When did you see her last?"

Annalisa's eyes flickered, staring at something over his left shoulder. "It must be a week. Perhaps eight days. I did not see her every day so I can't be certain."

"Did you wonder why she wasn't around?"

Annalisa shook her head. "She told me she had found someone. A man. A good man." Her eyes tracked Thomas from head to foot, returned to his face. "I didn't believe her. There are no good men."

"Who was he?"

"A man of God," she said." Annalisa's mouth pulled down. " A so called man of God. At least in my land a shaman makes no pretence at morality. If the man was holy why did he want Christabela?"

"Not all priests follow the new customs," Thomas said. "Did she tell you his name?"

"No. I asked but she told me it would be bad luck to say anything. He wanted the relationship kept secret. Did he kill her? A man of God?"

"I don't know."

"She told me she was planning to meet him at a church. Perhaps his church."

"Did she give you a name?"

"Bartholomew? Something like that."

"Bartolomu," said Rodrigo. "The church of San Bartolomu?"

"Yes—that could be it. She was to meet him there at sunset on... I can't remember. One day at the start of last week. Where I come from we do not have days of the week." She snuffed a harsh laugh. "I remember she was so excited. She said there would be a place for me, but I knew that was a lie." She pulled a face. "What would a man of God want with a creature such as me?"

"Men want you," Thomas said, "you know they do."

"But not to live with. I know what my life is. But I do miss her."

Thomas was surprised to see tears well in Annalisa's eyes and track down her cheeks.

He turned to Rodrigo. "You know this church?"

"Of course."

"Then we must go there now. Annalisa, I thank you for your time, and I am sorry for your pain. Here." He held the two silver coins out to her. She stared at them, then her hand came out and slapped them away.

"I told you, I don't want your money! I want Christabela back. Leave me—leave me alone."

Thomas recognised the square as soon as Rodrigo led him into it. Lawrence lived beyond the wall to one side. He wondered if he was the man of God Annalisa had mentioned, but Lawrence already had a wife, or companion, or whatever she was. Then he berated himself for taking what Annalisa had said at face value—whoever committed this atrocity had no intention of marrying a whore.

Rodrigo strode across the square and pulled at the door of the church. It remained closed.

"Churches are always open," said Rodrigo, as Thomas climbed the steps to join him.

"Not this one. But I know who might have a key. What are you meant to be doing rather than helping me?"

"Checking the parade streets for the end of the week. Captain Labrada wants them cleared of traders, pickpockets and whores." Rodrigo laughed, giving his opinion on how likely that ambition was. "Who has a key?"

Thomas nodded towards the house which showed an upper floor and roof above the wall.

"Lawrence? Yes, I suppose he will have. I'll go rouse him from that woman who is supposed to be his housekeeper. Siesta should be over by now."

Thomas laid a hand on Rodrigo's arm. "No, return to your duties. I would not have you get into trouble for failing to clear the streets." He saw disappointment on the young man's face, but preferred to be alone when he talked with Lawrence. He wanted to push the man but didn't want a witness—particularly one who represented the forces of law and order in the city. And he was sure he was more than capable of protecting himself if events turned unpleasant.

CHAPTER EIGHTEEN

Thomas was surprised when the solid oak door set into the wall opened at his touch. He stepped through and looked around. The small courtyard was as he remembered, but there was no-one in sight. A plate on the table held the husk of a pomegranate and an empty cup. Thomas closed the gate and walked to the door of the small house. It too was unlocked but he didn't enter. Instead he rapped on the doorframe and waited.

There was a sound from within, muffled, perhaps voices talking softly so as not to be heard.

Thomas shook his head and rapped harder.

"What!" Lawrence's head appeared from the window on the upper floor. "Oh—it's you. What do you want now?"

"I want you."

"So does someone else. Go away. Don't you know nothing happens for an hour yet? No, of course not. You're an infidel."

Thomas stared up at the man. His hair was tousled and his shoulders bare. From somewhere within the room a voice sounded. Lawrence glanced inside, came back to the window.

"Are you going to stand there waiting?"

Thomas crossed his arms. "If I have to. Don't mind me, I've heard people having sex before. Carry on—I don't expect you'll be long."

Lawrence's mouth tightened into a line and he cursed in English. Thomas smiled and went to sit at the small table. He heard a muffled conversation. A few minutes later feet sounded on the stairs. Lawrence appeared in his dark monk's robe, the hood thrown back as he ran fingers through his long hair.

"This had better be worth it," he said as he pulled out the other chair.

"Yes, please, wine would be welcome," Thomas said.

"The kitchen's at the end of the hallway."

"Perhaps when we finish our business."

"When we finish our business I have *other* unfinished business to attend to."

"You're a strange kind of priest."

"That's because I'm not a priest. Nor a monk, if you were about to ask. I work for the church but am not of it. Tell me what you want before she decides it's time to make supper."

Thomas leaned forward. "I want to look in the church next door. I take it you have a key."

"Of course I do." He pushed his chair back. "You won't need me to come with you, will you?"

"I have questions."

Lawrence sighed. "Wait here while I fetch the keys." He shook his head. "And there I was thinking I was starting to like you, Thomas Berrington."

He was gone a while. Thomas heard him ascend the stairs followed by more argument carried out in whispers. When Lawrence finally re-emerged a bunch of keys jangled in his left hand and there was a scowl on his face.

At the door of the church Lawrence immediately picked out the correct key and turned it in the lock. He pushed the heavy door open and gestured Thomas inside.

The interior of the church was tiny. Thomas didn't think it would be capable of holding more than forty souls. A small altar was set at the eastern end. From the ground to above head height the walls were covered in tiles with geometric patterns in blue. Two narrow columns decorated with familiar Islamic carving rose to support the roof. Above the tiles the walls were carved and set at intervals with heraldic shields. Thomas had never seen anything like it. He turned a full circle, taking in the ornate strangeness. Finally he came back to Lawrence who was waiting impatiently, rattling the keys in his hand so they made an annoying sound.

"You have questions?" Lawrence asked.

Thomas made a quick decision. He had thought of easing into the meat of what he wanted to know, but he didn't have the time and he doubted Lawrence would respond to such a tactic.

"The latest death—the girl who was killed—she came here to meet someone."

"To the church?"

"That is what I have been told."

"Who by?"

"Her friend."

"And who is her friend? Is she reliable?"

"I believe so."

"Well if she came here she'd be disappointed. The church is always locked."

"Why?"

"There are valuable items here. Gold and silver. And the building is empty most of the time. Larger churches have priests."

"So how would she have gotten inside?"

"That's what I'm saying if you listen. She couldn't have got inside." Lawrence spoke slowly, as if to an idiot. "The door is always locked."

Thomas turned away, pressing down a flare of anger. He knew he had disturbed Lawrence but didn't the man know how serious the matter was? He paced the floor, examining the tiles.

"What are you looking for? Some trinket she might have dropped?"

"I won't know until I find something."

"You won't. She wasn't here. If she came I would know."

Thomas straightened up. "Would you? Are you here all the time?"

"No. But I would know. There are only two sets of keys and the others are kept miles from here."

"Who keeps them?"

Lawrence shook his head, letting his frustration show. "Abbot Mandana's monks. Their order owns the church."

"Do they worship here?"

"Of course not." Lawrence started to walk, following Thomas as he moved to a door set in one corner.

"Where does this lead?"

"The courtyard."

"Is it locked?"

"No."

Thomas pushed an ornate handle. The door swung open and he stepped out into sunshine. The courtyard was no larger than the interior of the church. In the centre sat a square cart.

"What's that?"

"It's a pasos. A ceremonial float for the parade next week."

"What parade?"

Lawrence stared at Thomas. "Are you truly as stupid as you look?"

Thomas glanced down at himself. "I hope not. What parade?"

"It is Semana Santa, the holy week culminating in Easter Sunday. Or have you forgotten your Christian calendar as well?" Lawrence spat the words, a scowl on his face that had more to do with bigotry than interrupted intercourse.

Thomas wandered across to the cart. It was large for a cart, sturdy, with an extra set of wheels half way along its length. He walked around the sides examining them, then pulled himself up. There were heavy blocks of wood set into the bed, some with square holes which led down into thick sockets. Thomas knelt and scratched at the boards.

"Is this blood?" He glanced up to find Lawrence standing with his hands on the side of the cart.

"I wouldn't think so. But if it is it's probably from one of the workmen. They're preparing the pasos for the parade. Every holy order has its own display. The monks of Almodovar del Rio always prepare a crucifixion scene. It is much appreciated and they take a great deal of care in its preparation. Had you come tomorrow you would no doubt have met them for they are due to continue work."

Thomas sat on his heels, eyes scanning the bed of the cart. Here and there marks showed where feet had scuffed the wood. In one corner a small heap of sawdust had not been cleaned away. He stood and climbed down.

"Are you finished? Can I return to my siesta?"

"Siesta, is it?"

"Of course. What else?"

Thomas ran his hand along the edge of the cart. The wood was smooth. A lot of time and effort had gone into its creation and upkeep. He moved along the edge. Picked at a splinter. He stopped at the end and ran his fingers through the sawdust he had noticed before.

There was something hidden within.

He brushed at the sawdust, dug beneath to pull out a slim metal chain. As he drew it free he saw a small crucifix attached. It was of poor quality, base metal, the links of the chain uneven and rough. He turned and showed it to Lawrence.

"Could this belong to one of the monks?"

Lawrence studied it. He held his hand out. Thomas was reluctant to let go of his find, but eventually poured the chain into Lawrence's hand. Lawrence ran it through his fingers, examined the cross.

He shook his head. "Too coarse for a monk, and far too delicate. They will all wear a crucifix but not on a chain, always a leather thong. They do not embrace finery. Not that there is anything fine about this trinket."

Thomas held his own hand out. Lawrence stared at the chain a moment longer, at the turning crucifix. Had it not been a base metal it would have glinted in the sun. He closed his fist around it, reached out and placed it in Thomas's waiting palm.

"You might as well throw it away, it's worth nothing."

Thomas slid the chain into an inside pocket of his robe. "Likely you're right."

"Have you seen enough?"

"For now. But I may call on you again."

Lawrence rubbed at his cheek. "And you will be welcome, provided you come at a more convenient time of day."

Annalisa was occupied when Thomas reached the brothel so he sat downstairs, his leg jiggling in impatience, aware of the many calls on his time. The queen's son demanded attention, but the queen had also given him this other task. And then there was Jorge. The meal with his family had been enjoyable and a welcome break from his duties and Thomas would like to visit them again. He knew Jorge had already returned. Was it possible to juggle all of these responsibilities without dropping one? He knew he should have returned to the palace by now instead of sitting in a house of pleasure.

There were more girls than before, and in an attempt to take his mind of his predicament he chatted with one or two, unembarrassed in their company. He had visited such premises himself on occasion before Helena came into his life—although he doubted he would have frequented an establishment as rough as this one. But he knew himself well enough to know, had he come across a creature as exquisite as Annalisa, he would have paid whatever price was asked.

A half hour passed during which he teased out the life story of three of the girls. It was better than sitting amongst them saying nothing. Their tales were all painfully similar. Families who didn't want them. Fathers who'd expressed love as abuse. What Thomas found even more depressing was that they all believed they were lucky to find themselves where they were and being looked after so well.

At last the madam entered and nodded Thomas towards the stairs.

He knocked and entered at her call to find Annalisa with her back to him. She was naked, attending to herself with a bowl of water and a cloth. Thomas stopped but was not fool enough to look away until she had finished. She reached for a robe and draped it around herself before turning.

"What do you want? I hoped never to see you again. Is someone else dead?"

Thomas closed the space between them, catching her scent. It was unusual, something of musk and spice in it. He reached into his robe and drew the chain out.

"Do you recognise this?"

Her eyes went wide. Her hand lifted, wanting to touch the chain but hesitating.

"Do you?"

She nodded. "It is Christabela's." A tear formed in her eye. "I–I wanted to buy her a new one, something to match her beauty, but she said this—this was a gift from her sister." The tear slid down her cheek, followed by a second.

"That is all I need to know. Thank you." He took Annalisa's hand in his and turned it over, coiled the chain in her palm. "If you wish it, it is yours."

"Yes. Very much." Her eyes rose to his. "Thank you, sir."

For a moment Thomas feared she was about to embrace him. He was saved—if indeed that had been her intention—by shouting from downstairs. A voice rose above the female ones, a voice he recognised—Rodrigo's.

He turned and walked fast.

"Thomas, thank God you're here. There's been another one."

"Another what?" Although he knew what the constable meant and a sense of dread settled within him.

"A woman is missing. Today."

Thomas clapped the man on the shoulder. "Come on then, while the trail is fresh. Can you gather some men?"

"I will need to ask the captain."

"Then go. I'll fetch Jorge. I have to return to the palace briefly but then I'll meet you—where shall I meet you?"

"The woman lives in Calleja Noques, close to the river. Ask and someone will tell you how to find me."

CHAPTER NINETEEN

On his return to the palace Thomas found Jorge reclining only half clothed on the large bed. The room smelled of sex, a scent familiar to Thomas, although less so over the past year.

"Is the prince mended?" Jorge asked. "Are we leaving?"

"He won't be mended inside two months. Get up, I have work for you."

"Work?" Jorge's expression showed what he thought of the concept of work.

"The same kind we did last year."

The humour drained from Jorge's face. "Less dangerous, I hope." He swung his legs to the floor and rubbed hands across his scalp, scratching at the month's growth of hair.

"We have a fresh trail for our killer. I have to visit the prince but I'll return directly. Get ready. We go as soon as I come back."

It was meant to take a moment. A check that the boy slept, a fast examination of his leg to ensure there were no adverse effects from the bleeding, but when he entered the room Theresa left in a hurry and Sancha kept him talking. She was worried. The prince had been mumbling in his sleep, rocking his head from side to side.

Thomas felt the boy's neck, checked his pulse, but he showed no sign of fever and his heartbeat was only a little fast. He lifted the boy's eyelids. The pupils were large, but that was to be expected. The eyes showed no movement, no indication of dreaming.

"He looks all right now," Thomas said.

"He wasn't earlier."

"How long ago?"

"It started an hour since, perhaps two. He only stopped moments before you came in."

Thomas sighed and swept a hand across his face. His body ached with weariness but he knew there would be no rest yet. He wondered if he should remove the bindings from the leg and check it again, but that would take too long and carried its own dangers.

"Look, I have other matters to attend to. If he seems worse send for me. Send message to the Hermandad, they'll know where I'll be." He turned, ready to leave, but Sancha put a hand out and gripped his wrist.

"You can't go yet, the queen is coming. She asked to be sent for as soon as you returned."

So that is where Theresa scuttled off to in such a hurry. Thomas knew that meant it was even more important he leave before she arrived. He pulled clear of Sancha's grip and strode to the door, but at that moment it opened and Theresa entered, the small figure of the queen following behind.

"You were not trying to escape me, were you, Thomas Berrington?"

He glanced at Sancha and Theresa. They were servants. He knew they would choose not to hear anything they shouldn't.

"There may be a breakthrough in the killings, Your Grace. A woman has gone missing today and I need to follow while the trail is fresh."

"You go to find our man?"

"If I can." He took another pace towards the door, watching her face for defiance. She took a step sideways, blocking his exit. To continue he would have to move around her.

"A few moments, that is all I ask. For my son."

"I have examined him. He has no fever, Your Grace, and I have left instruction to send for me if there is any change."

"Will you be away from the palace long? I have another matter I would discuss with you."

Another matter? Does she believe me super-human?

"I don't know how long it will take. If we are to catch him now is the critical time, while memories are still fresh and evidence hasn't been destroyed."

She touched his arm, her hand lying there without clutching as Sancha's had. "If you must go then do so, but when you return send a message to me, whatever time of day or night. There are events unfolding I would seek your opinion on." She withdrew her hand. "Good luck, Thomas. Fetch me the killer so I may take his head. I will show this city I do not tolerate murder in my realm."

"What have you found out?" Thomas had done as Rodrigo asked, enquiring for the location of Calleja Noques. Darkness had fallen while he was in the palace and he found the young constable standing with two others outside a narrow doorway, their faces dim in the light that came from a lamp set at the end of the narrow street. A little more light came from a window set beside the door. A stench rose from a channel which ran down the middle of the alleyway.

"Nothing as yet, we only arrived ourselves a moment ago. The captain required persuasion." He glanced curiously at Jorge.

"This is my assistant," Thomas offered. "Is this where she lives? Do you have a name yet?"

"Only for the husband. Arabath. Nuncio Arabath. He trades as a butcher and has a shop nearby."

"Was it he who reported her missing?"

"A neighbour."

"Isn't that unusual? You'd expect him to notice his wife had gone missing. Particularly now with the whole city scared of this bonebreaker."

Rodrigo nodded to one of his companions, who hammered on the door.

"Perhaps we'll discover why now."

They waited.

Rodrigo glanced at Jorge, curious. Thomas noticed people were often curious about Jorge without quite knowing why. It might have been his looks or his easy confidence, or simply the sense of difference that clung to him. Whatever it was he drew attention that was not always benign.

The door was hammered again.

"Someone's coming," said the nearest constable, his ear to the wood.

"Who is going to question him?" asked Rodrigo.

"You have the authority, not me. If I need to I'll step in."

Rodrigo nodded, his face illuminated as the door opened.

A short, square man stood silhouetted, his face invisible.

"Nuncio Arabath?" said Rodrigo.

The man nodded. "What do you want?"

"I understand your wife is missing."

Arabath grunted. "She isn't home, if that's what you mean."

Rodrigo took a step closer, invading the man's space, making him step back.

"I'd like to come inside, unless you'd prefer we discuss your life out on the street."

The man lifted a shoulder as though it didn't matter to him, but he moved aside allowing Rodrigo to enter. Thomas followed, Jorge behind, but he saw the other two men remain in the street, one either side of the door as if guarding it.

It was only a little brighter inside than out. Tallow lamps lacking any glass sat in sconces on the walls. The smell of their burning tainted the air, and Thomas knew as a butcher the man most likely melted down animal fat to burn in them. The small amount of illumination showed a sparse room containing a small table and two chairs. There was no decoration, no rug on the stone floor. A staircase led up to what would presumably be a bedroom. A stained pot hung over an empty fireplace, the wall above marked by smoke.

"Do you know where your wife is?" asked Rodrigo.

"We're not married," said the man. Thomas stood in one corner, listening to the conversation, but Jorge wandered the small room examining what little lay there. Thomas watched him reach out to test for residual heat in the fireplace.

"But you live as man and wife?" said Rodrigo.

"We do."

"For how long?"

The man looked away as though it was a hard question. When his eyes returned to Rodrigo he had found an answer. "Four years. More or less."

"Is it more or is it less?"

"A little more. But not five."

"When did you see her last?"

Again the man looked away. This time when his gaze returned the shadow of a smile passed across his features. "A few days, I suppose."

"Weren't you worried when she didn't come home?"

"She takes herself off sometimes. Visits family. It's not like I own her, is it."

Thomas considered it an odd statement. Most men he knew believed they did own the women who lived with them, married or not. Not just poor men, either. He had seen the same behaviour in kings and princes, too.

"I understand your trade is butchering," said Rodrigo.

"What of it?"

"I expect you are used to cutting up bodies. Cutting up beasts."

Thomas glanced sharply at the young constable, uneasy at the sudden change in tone, wondering if he had been given specific orders by his captain. This man was not the one they sought. He had seen nothing to indicate he possessed the skills evident in what he had witnessed so far.

"It's my trade," said Arabath, too stupid to realise what Rodrigo was suggesting. Thomas wanted to intervene. If they focused on this man the true killer would have time to cover his tracks. He forced himself to relax, shifting his gaze to Jorge who was leaning down to examine a drawer of kitchen implements.

"Where do you conduct your business?"

"I have a shop two streets from here, close to the riverbank."

"Do you butcher animals here?" It was Jorge who spoke and the man turned quickly as though he had forgotten there was anyone else in the room.

"Do you think there is room? Have you seen the size of a sheep, let alone a bull?"

"So why is there blood on the floor here, next to the fire?"

Rodrigo pushed past Arabath to where Jorge stood. He went to one knee and examined the floor, rubbing his fingers across the stone slab.

"That will be Graciana," said Arabath. "We ate a fat hen Saturday. She wrung its neck and cut it up here."

Rodrigo looked up from where he still knelt. "So she was here Saturday?"

Arabath nodded. "I suppose she was, yes. Sunday too because we went to church together." He frowned. "And the day after that. But not the day after that one."

Rodrigo rose to his feet and returned to the man.

Thomas drifted around the edge of the room and stared down at the stain Jorge had found. His friend stood beside him, silent. He was aware of Rodrigo continuing to press Arabath, but knew he was pressing too hard. He was obviously under orders to find a culprit. Any culprit. Thomas was disappointed. He had considered the young constable both intelligent and independent.

He knelt, as Rodrigo had done, and examined the stain. It might be blood, but it could as easily be spilled broth or even fat from the tallow candles. He drew a knife from his waist and dug into the space between the stones. Remnants of food and wood came free, but nothing that offered enlightenment.

"Do you ever visit the brothel on Calle Allejandro?" Rodrigo asked Arabath.

"Why would I do such a thing? I have a companion."

"Many men with wives visit that establishment, or others."

"They might, but not me. What Graciana saw in a man such as me I have no idea. She was beautiful." He puffed his chest out and straightened to his maximum height, which was not much.

Thomas looked up quickly. He glanced at Rodrigo, but the constable did not appear to have noticed Arabath's use of the past tense when he referred to his companion. Perhaps it was a slip of the tongue, perhaps not. Even so, Thomas had difficulty believing Arabath was whom they sought. Unless, he thought, I am patronising the man, judging him by where he lives and how he looks. He might not be the bonebreaker but Thomas believed he had killed his wife. A wave of desolation flooded him. Why had death taken such a liking to him, following wherever he went? He stood and moved across the room.

"I want to see his place of work." He interrupted Rodrigo half way through another question.

"It's too dark. We'll be better off returning in the morning."

Thomas nodded. Rodrigo was right. Arabath wasn't whom they sought, but he couldn't be left at liberty. "Lock him up, then. I believe his companion to be dead at his hand."

Rodrigo laid a hand on Arabath's shoulder, but years of butchering animals had built strength beneath the layer of flab. He pushed Rodrigo, sending him flying to tumble backwards over the table, and fled for the door.

Thomas pushed past Rodrigo's flailing legs. One of the men outside heard the commotion and turned into the doorway just as Arabath reached it. They clashed. For a moment it looked as if the man would escape, then Thomas reached him and spun him around. He ducked as Arabath swung at him. His own punch took the man on the side of the chin, spinning his head to one side, and he collapsed to the floor, his skull making a loud crack against the stone.

"You haven't forgotten how to fight, then," said Jorge, strolling across the room as though this was a normal end to an evening for him.

Thomas scowled at him as Rodrigo righted himself and joined them.

"We've caught him," said the constable, unable to suppress a grin. "We've captured the bonebreaker."

CHAPTER TWENTY

The shop was small and stank of raw meat, blood, and worse. Rodrigo used the key from Arabath's house to unlock the door, which caught on the stone floor as he pushed it open.

"We should have come here last night," Thomas said as they entered the small front room where a stained table sat, no doubt where Arabath sold his cuts. Hanging from a hook to one side were links of blood sausage. A goat carcass hung head down beside it.

"I thought we decided there was no point in the dark," said Rodrigo. Thomas had found him soon after dawn at the offices next to the wall. Arabath had been there, too, asleep in a cell, as Jorge was asleep in his bed when Thomas left.

"I'm pleased your captain hasn't executed him yet."

"He's guilty though," said Rodrigo. "Execution's too good for him. He should be made to suffer like those he killed."

"He's guilty of something, I agree. But the bonebreaker? I'm not convinced."

"Why not? He's a butcher. Look around—he knows how to slaughter a beast. Beast or human, it's all the same to him. Slaughtered and stitched together. What better cover than a butcher's shop?"

"So where is his wife?"

"She won't be here," said Rodrigo.

"Go ask the other shopkeepers in the street if they ever saw her."

"It's a waste of time. He'll have disposed of her body by now. The river's only down there."

Thomas sighed. He had liked Rodrigo in the days before, saw signs of a keen intelligence and an ability to think for himself. Now all that had been put away in favour of simple theories.

"If he is the bonebreaker he won't have gotten rid of her. He likes to display his victims once he has abused them. What is that all about? Why does he attach the limbs of beasts to them?"

Rodrigo raised a shoulder. "Don't look to me for reasons. He's mad, isn't that reason enough?"

"No—he's too stupid to be mad. Go talk to the neighbours."

Once he was alone Thomas looked quickly around the interior of the shop. The drawers contained an array of sharp knives and cleavers. They could be used to remove limbs, but the little he had seen of the body at the gate showed a finer hand than a butcher would possess or these implements were capable of.

Two bolts opened a rear door which gave into a covered yard. It was where Arabath did the slaughtering. The stink of the shop was multiplied ten fold out here. A drain in one side allowed blood and water to flow away, likely straight into the river.

A strong iron bar ran the width of the yard and curved S-hooks hung waiting for fresh beasts. Beneath was a second table, larger than the one inside, its surface also marked from cutting and hacking. The smell that clung in the air was like something solid, the worst of it coming from one corner where bone and soiled meat had been tossed.

Thomas covered his nose and mouth with a sleeve as he approached, but it did little to stop him retching. He knew he had to search the pile, wondered if he could do so without passing out.

It's nothing, he told himself. *Flesh and bone and blood. You have seen enough of that before.*

He knew there was only one way to accomplish the task and that was without hesitation. He stripped out of his robe and shirt and attacked the pile, closing his mind to what he was doing, breathing through his mouth.

It was mostly bone, the marks of a cleaver showing where it had been shattered, the sight bringing to Thomas's mind Daniel's leg, an image he allowed to pass across his vision and away. As he worked his puzzlement grew. The order of the bones was all wrong.

The ones at the top, and the scraps of meat, stank the worst. Marrow oozed in gelatinous stinking ribbons from within, but as he worked downwards the offcuts were fresher. It was when he reached the bottom of the pile, tossing detritus behind him, he found the reason why.

She wasn't whole. Nowhere near whole.

Thomas reached into the mire and withdrew an arm. In the process he uncovered a woman's head. Half her face was missing. Arabath's cleaver had caught her to one side of the nose, splitting the skull. Thomas continued the search, but not all of her was present.

"It's him!" Rodrigo's voice pulled Thomas back from the dark place his mind had fled. He sat on his heels then stood. Only bare minutes had passed yet he felt as though he had been striving for days. His shoulders ached. His legs trembled and he feared they might not support him.

Rodrigo took in the sight, the blood and gore streaking Thomas's arms and chest, and the young man turned to one side and vomited explosively.

"I'm sorry." He wiped at his mouth. "But..." Rodrigo shook his head. "This proves it's him, doesn't it."

"He killed his wife, yes." Thomas picked up his shirt then put it down again. There was a water butt at the back of the shop and he went to it, opened the tap and scooped water into his hands, scrubbing at his arms and chest.

"And the others?" said Rodrigo.

"Not that I know of." Now his task was over Thomas felt nausea rising within him.

"No, look." Rodrigo pointed, and Thomas turned.

He had laid out the body parts as he worked, unthinkingly placing them alongside animal remains. Where her left arm was missing a cow's thigh bone lay. The stump where her right foot should be was set against a hoof.

"There's no meaning here other than what you see," Thomas said. "He killed her and made to hide her remains among the discard of his trade. He would have planned on getting rid of her piece by piece. He's a fool. A stupid fool at that. Did he think we wouldn't come here?"

Rodrigo shook his head violently. "He must have killed the others. It's plain to see. He's been killing for a year and we've proved it!" A grin broke out on the constable's face until he remembered where he was and what they were doing, but it couldn't be suppressed for long.

No doubt he's thinking of the glory coming to him for his part in this.

"Go to the captain and tell him what we've found," Thomas said. "Then bring him here. I'll stay."

After Rodrigo had left Thomas went inside and searched the premises. He knew there would be soap somewhere, if only for cleaning down the tables, and he found it on a ledge, stuck down hard. He took it outside and scrubbed until his skin was raw, but still he felt tainted. They must have baths in the palace somewhere, he would insist one was brought for him.

The afternoon heat was captured within the confines of the small yard, baking his skin and that of the dismembered woman. Thomas stared at her, a sense of completion slowly settling within.

Rodrigo might be right. It was possible the butcher was the man they sought. He had the skills to cut a body up. Would he be able to put it together again, like the one Thomas had witnessed hanging from the city gate? Had his wife discovered his secret and threatened to expose him? Was that why she now lay in pieces on the stinking slabs?

Thomas walked to a corner of the yard where the sun fell on the stone. He squatted against the wall and shut his mind down, closed his eyes and turned his face up to the sun, welcoming its heat against his skin. It would make life easier if all he had to worry about was a healing prince, but something about this didn't feel right. Could he ignore his conscience and say nothing? Soon he would be gone from the city and what happened here would be none of his business. The idea was tempting. He owed these people nothing. They weren't his people. Isabel wasn't his queen nor Fernando his king.

Thomas knew both Sancha and Theresa were staring at him but refused to acknowledge their attention. Prince Juan sat half propped on a pile of cushions. On a side table the remains of a bowl of broth showed he had managed to feed himself for the first time since the re-breaking of his leg.

"It itches," he said.

"It will. But if you scratch it will only take longer to heal."

"Will I be able to run?"

"Most likely." Thomas sat back on the hard chair. His skin was sticky beneath his clothes, but when he had asked about bathing, Sancha told him a hot bath might be found. He had no need to explain why. Word had spread quickly. It always did—faster than it seemed people could carry it. By the time he'd walked into the palace everyone turned to look his way—to look at the man who had captured the bonebreaker.

As soon as he had handed matters over to Labrada, Thomas had returned to the palace. He had given orders that Juan's drugs be reduced over the last day and a half, reduced again today. He had wanted to be present when the boy awoke, but Sancha and Theresa were more than up to the task of taking care of the prince.

Now the two nurses stood close together, whispering.

Thomas felt a sudden urge to get away, anywhere, away from the palace whose air was tainted from constant plot and intrigue. And, he had become aware, a worry over funds. He had realised long ago a person such as himself was all but invisible. He had examined ladies of the harem while they spoke with husbands and lovers; treated kings and sultans as they planned battles and betrayal. Here in Qurtuba he heard news of the crippling cost of the war. Taxes were already high and any demand for more would result in a rebellion. Thomas knew defeat was inevitable for the Moors—what he hadn't realised was how much that defeat was costing Fernando and Isabel. And there were other wars as well. Against Portugal, against France, even in Naples. Fernando wanted the recovery of lands lost by Aragon but his wife was against spreading their resources too thinly.

Perhaps, Thomas thought, I will be able to live my life out in peace after all before Spain is able to consolidate her forces enough to defeat Gharnatah.

"How long will it take to draw that bath?" he said, breaking from his reverie and turning to the two nurses.

Theresa giggled and covered her mouth with her hand.

"Would you like it now?" asked Sancha, brazen, her mouth curled into a smile. Thomas knew he had spent far too much time in their company and likely shown too much kindness which had been misinterpreted.

"Now would be good. Can you arrange it for me?"

Sancha gave a little bow and went to the door, but as she reached for the handle it opened and the queen entered.

She looked at her son, who smiled, then at Thomas.

"I hear I have to thank you again, Cousin. You have succeeded in the other task I set you."

"I would talk with you on the matter, Your Grace, if I am allowed?"

"To what purpose? The man is in the dungeons and will be executed by morning."

Thomas took four paces, closing the distance between them. He lowered his voice. "The man is a killer, I have no doubt of that. But the killer we seek? I am not so sure."

The queen frowned. The perfume she always wore lay thick in the air, it's sweetness reminding him of the putrefied remains he had discovered, and he turned his face aside.

"There cannot be two such as he. My captain tells me he is the man. You worry too much, sir. Are you not pleased the matter is out of your hands?"

"I would be if it were."

"Let the Hermandad take care of it now." She looked beyond him to the prince. "How is my angel?"

"Complaining his leg itches."

She looked concerned. "Is that bad? Has he an infection?"

"He is healing," Thomas said, "nothing more sinister. And he ate some broth earlier."

"Can I sit with him now he is awake?"

"Of course. But would you excuse me, Your Grace?"

"Will you come to supper this evening?"

"If I can."

The queen smiled. "I hear you have been using the bed I sent in. Your duty has not gone unnoticed."

"It was easier than being called for if he needed me."

"Indeed." She could restrain herself no longer and went to her son, taking his hands in hers and receiving a smile in return. Thomas watched for a moment, seeing the love she felt for Juan, wondering how it must feel to experience such deep emotion.

The bath waited for him in his room, its steam scenting the air. He undressed quickly and stepped in, allowing the hot water to rise to his chest. Someone must have searched hard for the bath because it was both long and deep. Or perhaps in a palace such a thing was not unusual.

He closed his eyes, promising himself it was only for a moment, then he would use the soap and scrub himself.

He was startled awake at the sound of the door opening and sat up, expecting Jorge. Instead Sancha entered carrying a steaming jug.

"Ah, good, you've found it already." She showed not a glimmer of embarrassment. "I brought you more hot water."

He nodded and watched as she came to the side of the bath. She knelt and poured the contents of the jug in. Thomas felt the heat of the water against his side and sighed. He caught Sancha examining the scars on his chest.

"Who did this to you?" She touched his shoulder where the skin was pale. Thomas tried to recall where that one had come from and couldn't. It looked old. He might even have obtained it before coming to Spain.

"I don't remember."

"This one, then?" She touched his chest.

Thomas shook his head. "The same." Although with that scar, he did know. It had been in France and the wound had almost killed him.

"And here?" said Sancha, her hand now resting against his belly.

"I wasn't always a surgeon."

"That's obvious. Do you want me to wash you, Thomas?"

He reached up and gripped her wrist as her hand slid down his wet belly.

"I can wash myself."

"I know you can," said Sancha. "What I am saying is you don't have to. Your cock says you want me to."

Thomas glanced down. "My cock and I don't share the same mind. I will wash myself."

After she had gone, with good humour, he reached for the soap and scrubbed at his body, wondering what had brought him to refuse her. She was pretty, her body soft and curved, and not so long ago he hadn't been reluctant to take pleasure when it was offered.

The opening of the door distracted him from his thoughts. He was thankful to see Jorge enter rather than Sancha. He wasn't sure he possessed the resolve to refuse her twice.

"Do you smell sweeter now?" asked Jorge.

"Me too. I hear you're a hero again, and me by association."

"About that," Thomas said as he pulled himself from the bath, water sluicing from his body. Jorge examined him openly, a fact Thomas had grown used to. The man had no filter, and there were times Thomas wondered about his raw sexuality and just how far it might extend. He smiled. Jorge would certainly not have refused

Sancha. No doubt both she and Theresa would be sharing the bath with him now if their roles had been reversed.

"What about it," said Jorge.

"Don't get too used to the idea of being a hero. That man's not the bonebreaker. The real killer's still out there somewhere."

CHAPTER TWENTY-ONE

Carlo Labrada, the captain of the Hermandad—who had done little more than sit in his quarters while his men accompanied Thomas through the city—was taking credit for the arrest of, as he termed it, 'a man who has terrorised Cordoba for near a year'.

Thomas stood in the room the king and queen used for important matters and listened as the self-important fool boasted of his critical role in the capture. The room was plainly furnished, like most within the palace. Isabel and Fernando abstained from the ornate trappings of other courts in Europe, preferring a workmanlike atmosphere.

The fate of Spain—and its friends and enemies both—were decided here, or in other rooms very much the same scattered throughout the country. The lives of the royal household were those of itinerants; the hangers on, the nobles, the servants, kitchen staff and provisioners, following along without complaint. Not public complaint, anyway.

The room was not large but there were only a few people gathered. The king and queen sat on plain chairs at a table. Elegantly dressed nobles—including Esperanza's husband the Duque of Carmona—stood nearby, distance from the royal presence clearly and carefully used to demarcate position.

Thomas stood next to the door, waiting his turn, while the captain finished a speech full of self-congratulation and grandiosity.

"Have the constables who effected the arrest been rewarded?" It was the queen who spoke. Her husband sat at her side, showing interest, but Thomas knew it was Isabel who ran the business of the court, leaving her husband to fight the war against the infidel Moor and the French. It was said he was a charismatic general and popular with his men—although not as popular as his wife. He was also a fearsome fighter, and Thomas's experienced eye took him in, seeing the truth in the claim. The king was a decade younger than him, his face thuggish, body a little more given to fat than muscle, but he knew himself how rapidly that would change when called for. He wondered, in a fair fight, which of them might emerge as victor. A year before Thomas would never have entertained such a thought, but he had changed since, letting some of his old life return—for good or ill was still undecided.

"The constables were doing their duty, Your Grace. They are paid."

"But it was they who caught the man, was it not?" asked the queen.

"Under my command."

Her eyes scanned those assembled in the room until they found Thomas at the back. He was uneasy at her examination, but when she maintained eye contact he finally returned a brief nod.

"Very well, then. You did well, sir, and have our gratitude."

The man seemed to grow half a foot.

"Now clear the room," said the queen, her voice rising, and she clapped her hands. "There are matters of state to discuss."

Thomas remained where he was as men and women trailed past. Finally only five people remained. The king and queen, Abbot Mandana, the Duque of Carmona, and Thomas himself. Isabel waved a hand, calling him closer. She herself rose from her seat and descended a set of steps, the duque offering his hand. Fernando remained where he was, reading papers.

"So what did you think, sir?" She stood directly in front of Thomas.

The killings had been the final topic in a meeting that had gone on for almost two hours. Thomas's head buzzed with matters he didn't understand and had even less interest in, but he admired this woman who had maintained a rigid control throughout the proceedings.

"It is not my place to judge, Your Grace."

"You are right, but I am still interested in your opinion."

Abbot Mandana broke in. "We already know Thomas was instrumental in the capture, whatever that blustering fool claims. And he should be justly rewarded."

"Indeed," said the queen. "Also for healing Juan's leg. But Thomas told me something last night, and I am curious if he still holds to that opinion or has changed his mind now he has time to reflect. So, sir, do you still insist we have the wrong man?"

"What wrong man?" said Mandana. "It could not be clearer he is the culprit. He butchered his own wife. Animal limbs surrounded her. Another day and he would have stitched them together into another abomination hanging from a rope somewhere."

"He has the wrong skills," Thomas said.

"Explain," said the queen.

Thomas surveyed those in the room. The king continued to read his papers, uninterested or feigning such. Abbot Mandana stood close beside the queen, holding himself to his full height. His leanness, his hair and beard streaked grey and white, made him appear even more to match the wolf that gave him his nickname. The Duque of Carmona stood to one side, paring at his fingernails with a small knife, and Thomas was unsure of his purpose here. He took a deep breath, wishing it was in his nature to let things go, but knowing he couldn't.

"He knew how to cut a body up, certainly, but he would never be able to stitch the limbs together with the same skill shown by the true culprit."

"You barely saw the other victim." The duque spoke for the first time, finished with his nails. "The city guard tells me you tried and they expelled you from the scene."

"I saw enough, sir, to recognise the skill present."

"What skill does it take to sew a limb to a torso?" said Mandana. "Ungodly skills." He did not need to add any more, his meaning clear from his expression—*like those possessed by a man of science such as a surgeon*—and Thomas knew the man had not forgiven him for their clash over the prince.

"They are not skills a butcher would possess," Thomas said, aware he was being stubborn.

"I have heard rumour they call *you* the butcher," said Mandana.

"You hear a great deal."

"It is my business to hear. And to judge." Mandana softened his stance and glanced at the queen, who was watching the verbal joust between them without expression. "Your concerns are appreciated and have been noted. But all of us here are of the same mind—the killer has been captured and executed, and—"

"Executed?"

"This morning at dawn. In a manner fitting his crimes. He was sawn. I witnessed his death myself and was glad to see a tiny part of the pain he must have inflicted on others visited upon him."

"I would have liked to question him," Thomas said.

"Why, when he is so obviously guilty? You agree, Carmona?" Mandana looked to the duque for confirmation.

"I agree." He had returned to his manicure, the matter dismissed.

"Your Grace?" Thomas said.

"In this instance I concur with my advisors. It is beyond belief there could be two such killers in the city. You should be pleased you can return to full time care of my son."

"I am, Your Grace, of course." Thomas bit back on the words that wanted to escape him. It went against every fibre of his being to let the matter go, but perhaps they were right and he wrong, difficult as it was to accept.

But as he strode through the corridors of the palace he knew who was correct and who was not. He had been on the killer's trail before he allowed this butcher to distract him. The Church of San Bartolomu was involved, but was Lawrence, too? Thomas found it difficult to suspect the man, but he did live next to the church, and he worked with the monks of the monastery. Thomas tried not to allow his dislike for Abbot Mandana to colour his mind, but the man might also be involved. He knew now what he had seen on the riverbank as they approached Qurtuba had been part of the crime, as was the Monastery of Almadovar del Rio. Now all he had to do was tease out the truth and prove it. He planned to start by definitely ruling out Arabath from any link to the murder of anyone but his wife.

By the time he had visited Juan and instructed Sancha and Theresa in the reduced dosage of opium to administer, it was mid-afternoon and the corridors were quiet as he made his way to his room. He needed to escape from the palace, unsettled by his conversation with the queen and Abbot Mandana. Also because of the change in attitude of the two nurses. He knew he should have been stricter with them. Now Sancha acted as though his seduction was only a matter of time, and Theresa was in on the plot, too, whether as accomplice or active participant only the pair of them were privy to. Well, conspiracy or not, they would wait a long time for him to weaken. Other men perhaps, but Thomas considered himself of stronger moral fibre.

He was half way across the room, intending to rouse Jorge, before he recognised the scene before him for what it truly was, and when he did instead of turning away he stopped in shock.

Jorge lay on his back, his hands gripping the carved headboard. A naked Esperanza straddled him, her head thrown back, eyes closed. Her heavy breasts swayed as she rode him hard.

Jorge opened his eyes and stared at Thomas. A smile appeared on his lips. He slapped Esperanza's rear, and when she appeared to take it as play slapped her harder and she yelped.

She punched Jorge's chest then turned to discover Thomas. This time it was her turn to smile.

"Would you care to join us, sir?"

He turned away and started for the door.

"I'll wait for you by the bridge," Thomas called back, still walking. "We have work to do when you're ready."

But he was still waiting an hour later before Jorge finally appeared.

CHAPTER TWENTY-TWO

"I love her," said Jorge, and Thomas stopped pulling at the section of loose pine walling he was trying to work loose and sat on his heels. They had been in Arabath's house for over an hour and so far he had found nothing to convince him the man was the killer the city sought. That he had killed his wife there was no doubt, but anything else was a fantasy created to placate the queen.

"I take it you're talking about Esperanza."

Jorge gave him a look of exasperation. "For once I'm being serious, Thomas. I love her."

"No think?"

Jorge shook his head. "None."

"What are you going to do about it?"

"What can I do? She's married, a duquessa no less. Her husband's an important man and friend to the king."

"And her?"

"She's friend to the queen."

"What I mean is how does she feel? Have you told her?"

Jorge shook his head. "Of course not—do you take me for a fool?"

Thomas considered comment unnecessary. "Aren't women supposed to know these things?"

"She thinks..." Jorge took a deep breath, the sound ragged. "She thinks what we enjoy is for pleasure and nothing more."

"I don't want to be cruel, but why do you think you love her? Isn't love meant to be reciprocated? I always considered you the expert on such matters."

"So did I." Jorge's gaze rose to meet Thomas's. "I always believed love was rational, but it's not. I don't *know* why I love her, only that I do. She is here," he said, and punched his chest, "inside me."

Thomas stood and crossed half the room before stopping. He didn't know what to do.

Jorge looked up, his eyes bright. "This can't be happening to me. I'm the one meant to be loved, not the other way around."

"You have to stop seeing her."

"I *can't*!"

"You must. If you don't it's only going to make matters worse." Thomas barked a harsh laugh. "This is wrong."

"I know."

"I mean—me offering you advice on matters of the heart. Has the sun suddenly started rising in the west?"

"You're the only person I can talk to. How sad is that?"

"Then we'll talk. But not now."

"There's nothing here," said Jorge.

"I agree. Perhaps they're right and the butcher did kill them all."

"You don't believe that."

"It makes sense to everyone but me."

"Then I know who I believe. Come on, let's find an inn and drink until we can't stand up."

"I have to visit the prince again tonight. And I want to take another look at the butcher's shop."

"You should bed the nurse," said Jorge, starting for the door.

"I should, should I? Which one would you suggest?" Thomas caught him up, fell into step as they descended the alley towards a larger street.

Jorge shrugged. "Doesn't matter. They're both pretty enough, although Sancha is the younger. Both together if you want—I'm sure they're willing."

"So am I."

Jorge slowed. "So what's stopping you?"

"You know what."

"Not Helena."

"Of course not."

"Have you told Lubna how you feel about her yet?"

Thomas said nothing.

"We're both fools, then," said Jorge, and kicked at a stone on the roadway, a scowl on his face.

"It would help if you told me exactly what you're looking for," said Jorge as they traversed narrow streets and alleys. It was early evening and the shops and markets were starting to open again. Men, women and urchins of both sexes crowded the streets. Their unwashed stink no longer offended Thomas's sense of smell, a miracle he both welcomed and feared, wondering if it would ever recover.

"The man we seek has skills Arabath didn't possess. It's true he could have been the killer—he was a butcher, and that meant he knew how to cut up a body, but he needed to reassemble them afterwards. I'm looking for instruments he could use to accomplish that. And books."

"He kept a shop and sold meat," said Jorge. "He wouldn't be able to read."

"So how did he learn?"

"Perhaps someone taught him."

"Who? And why?"

"How am I supposed to know?"

Thomas smiled. They turned into the street where Arabath's shop lay to see a cart outside the door and boxes being unloaded.

"What's happening here?" Thomas asked a burly man who seemed to be in charge. Three boys did the fetching and carrying while a woman stood to one side.

"I'm stocking my new shop. And if you'll let me finish I might even be able to open while there are still customers looking for meat and fish."

Thomas shook his head and pushed inside. The man gave a shout and came after him. The scarred table remained, but shelves had been erected where the boys were unpacking cured meats, sausage and salt fish. Thomas went through into the yard. It had been cleaned, the flagstones wet where buckets of water had been used. The pile of off-cut bones was gone.

"Who did this?"

The new keeper emerged through the door. "I cleaned the place myself. It stank. I'm amazed he had any customers left from the state of the yard."

"What did you do with the detritus?"

"Burned it down on the riverbank this morning, the ashes tipped in the water."

"All of it?"

"No point keeping anything, was there."

Thomas would have asked if the remains of Arabath's wife were included in this cleansing operation, but he already knew the answer. Had there been relatives, what was left behind might have been given a burial, but even then he doubted it.

"Were there any papers in the shop? Or books?"

The man laughed, not bothering with a reply. He returned to his work, no doubt dismissing Thomas as an idiot.

"Now can we get drunk?" Jorge asked.

"You can if that's what you need. I have duties."

"I want to talk," said Jorge.

"We can talk tonight when I'm finished. If you're not rutting again."

Jorge turned away, knocking against Thomas as he went.

Prince Juan had managed more broth, but Sancha told Thomas he had brought it all back an hour ago. The boy's face was flushed, and when Thomas felt his neck it was warm.

"Damn that doctor. Sancha, give him a strong draught." Thomas turned away and searched his bag, returned with scissors and small blade. He dropped the bag at his feet, knowing he would need more from it before he was finished.

"How long has he been like this?"

"He complained of a headache after you left, but said he was hungry. He managed some solids and I remember I was pleased." Sancha helped Juan sit up as he sipped at the beaker.

"Take it slowly. As soon as he gets sleepy give him no more."

She offered a look that said 'I've been doing this for years' and gave Juan a little more.

When the prince's eyes closed Sancha laid him against the pillows.

"Hold him hard in case he moves," Thomas said, and Sancha leaned across the prince.

He snipped the tight bandage. When he loosened the bark and peeled it away a sweet scent rose to greet him and he cursed. The cut where the palace doctor had bled Juan was dark red and weeping pus.

"Damn the man—he didn't even use a sterilised blade."

"Will he die?"

"Not if I have anything to do with it. I need hot water, as hot as you can get, and use the bellows on the fire." While Sancha went off to search out the water Thomas drew a bottle of raw alcohol from his bag. He would need to put the prince deeper still, and started to prepare the same mixture he had when he'd set the leg.

As soon as Sancha returned, accompanied now by Theresa, he had her apply the liquid soaked linen to Juan's mouth and nose. Once the boy was under Theresa held him down and Thomas began to cut. Fresh blood flowed and he wiped it away, cutting deeper, searching out every part of the putrefaction until he was satisfied he had removed it all. Then he poured raw alcohol into the wound, washed it with the hot water and used alcohol again. He searched in his bag and found a metal rod he had used often on the battlefield but little elsewhere. One end had a rough wooden handle hammered onto the metal. He held the handle as he thrust it into the fire, using the bellows until the rod glowed. He pulled it free, moved quickly back to the bedside and without hesitation pressed the dull red metal against the prince's leg.

The boy writhed, guttural cries coming from him, but Theresa and Sancha held him firm. The smell of burning flesh filled the air. Thomas kept the rod held to the wound until he was sure it had sealed. He laid the rod aside and examined the rest of the leg.

Fortunately the infection had not spread, and he checked on the condition of the break. When he palpated the leg it was firm to his touch. The bones were starting to knit. The leg itself was straight. Prince Juan would walk again without a limp, provided the infection had been caught in time. For a moment he had a vision of Jorge's brother, Daniel, only a little older than the boy before him when his leg was crushed. If only someone had been there to tend him then his life would be so much easier now.

He was re-splinting the leg when the queen came into the room. She stopped, observing the scene before her, no doubt smelling the odour of burnt flesh.

"What happened here?"

"Your doctor almost killed him," Thomas said, making no effort to keep the anger from his voice. "The point of bleeding became infected. I have burned it away and he should be all right now, but he will need watching closely."

"You will stay with him?"

"Of course."

The queen glanced at her sleeping son. "Are you sure he will recover?"

Thomas nodded, hoping it was the truth. The queen appeared to harbour a friendship towards him, but he knew that would not continue should her son's condition worsen.

"I have sent Pero to talk with your sultan," said the queen. "I might have sent you with him if not for Juan. I understand he is your friend."

"Muhammed? Not a friend, no."

"Then has Pero misinformed me?"

"He will have told you what Muhammed wanted him to. It

pleases him to pretend a friendship that doesn't exist. I was friend to the father but not the son. When do you plan to bring him here?"

"That is not decided. These things move slowly, and there is a great deal of politics involved."

"What is Mandana's opinion on the matter?" Thomas asked.

The queen looked at him. "I believe you know what he thinks. Why the interest?"

"How long have you known him?"

"The abbot? All my life. He served my brother before he served me. He is a stern man, but clever, and with a great deal of influence. I would not be ruling this land if not for him."

"I understand he was a soldier once," Thomas said.

"Before I knew him, yes. He can still call on an army if need be."

That was what Thomas had been afraid of.

CHAPTER TWENTY-THREE

It was noon the next day before Thomas managed to get away from the palace. He walked fast through crowded streets, taking narrow alleys where he was unlikely to come across men practicing with their parade floats, which might now be expected around almost any corner.

Thomas didn't know if Lawrence would be at his small house backing onto the equally small church he tended, but he needed to see him and the walk turned out worthwhile. Lawrence was sitting outside, as he had been on the first visit, eating a peach he cut into small sections with a sharp knife.

He held the fruit up when he saw Thomas. "You want some?" Then, leaning back, he called out, "Laurita, bring more peaches." He kicked at a chair with his foot in invitation. "So—are they going to execute the heretic?"

"Which heretic?" Thomas took the chair as Laurita brought three peaches out.

"These are all we have left," she said as she turned away. "The storeroom is empty."

"She loves me really."

"I'm sure she does. Do you mean Muhammed?"

"Muhammed? I mean Boabdil."

"We call him by his given name, Abu Abdallah."

Lawrence laughed. "That's what I said, wasn't it? The unlucky one. It's a good name, don't you think—him getting caught that way?"

"It's all politics," Thomas said, reaching for a peach, hungry. He hadn't eaten since breaking his fast before dawn. The prince was improving, his fever starting to lower, and Sancha and Theresa cared for him well. The queen had not appeared today, no doubt in conference with Fernando and her advisors.

"Do you know him?" Lawrence cut another slice of peach. Its juice gathered in his palm and he raised his hand to lick it away.

Thomas scowled. "I have that misfortune."

Lawrence laughed again. "Will you see him? That would be a grand thing, wouldn't it, to observe him in chains? Whipped. Beaten. Oh, a grand thing indeed."

"They ask for my opinion, but I think out of politeness rather than considering it useful."

"So what are you doing here? Apart from enjoying my company, that is, and eating the last of my peaches."

"I don't believe the butcher they caught is behind the deaths. He killed his wife, certainly, but not the others."

"And what is that to me?" Lawrence's good humour remained, but his eyes had turned wary.

"You said you have records of all the religious buildings in Qurtuba. I need to return to the trail I was following before I became distracted. I found the necklace of the murdered girl next door in the church, remember."

"And you have a suspect?"

"Not yet. Which is why I need to look at the records to see who has access."

"I have access," said Lawrence, "you know I do. Am I a suspect, too?"

Thomas stared at him until Lawrence looked away, any friendship that might have grown between them set aside for the moment.

"Will you help me or not?"

Lawrence wiped his hands on a cloth, tossed it across the table to Thomas. He smiled without humour. "If I was guilty I should lure you into the library and kill you while you read my documents."

"You could try."

"Or turn you away and have my compatriots hunt you down."

"True. This is undoubtedly the work of more than one man. But I know you're not part of it."

Lawrence stood. "Then come, I'll show you the papers you want. But watch your back."

"I always do." Thomas rose and followed him inside, through a small kitchen rich with the scent of food. Laurita worked a round of dough, her cheek streaked with flour. She was more relaxed here, pretty.

The kitchen gave on to a narrow hallway where Lawrence led the way to the end. A door stood open to what might have been the largest space inside the small dwelling. A table took pride of place in the centre, piled with documents. All the walls were shelved apart from the doorway and a gap for a single window which looked out onto the square. Thomas realised the room must be built into part of the space occupied by the church next door.

"If I wanted to mislead you I ought to leave you to find what you need alone," said Lawrence. He strode to a far shelf and studied it a moment, then reached for a bound sheaf of papers. "But this is what you seek." He unbound the string and laid the papers on the table, leaning over them. "This one … and this … and this…" He drew papers out with his finger.

Thomas bent over them. "They're in Latin."

"Do you want me to translate?"

"I read Latin."

"Good for you. Pity though, I could have told you anything."

"I already told you, I know you didn't kill anybody."

"Not recently, at least." Lawrence took a chair set against the wall and crossed his long legs. "I was a soldier once. I've killed a few men in my time. Me and the abbot—he was our general."

"Is that what brought you to the cloth?"

"Killing?" Lawrence was amused. "The killing never bothered

me. Those I killed were trying to kill me. Better I live than them. No, I came to my current calling by accident." He offered no explanation and Thomas made no further enquiry, turning to study the papers instead.

He traced the lines with a finger. Despite his claims, Latin was hard for him, and his lips moved as he translated the written words in his head before uttering them softly in Arabic.

Lawrence remained at ease, picking at his nails with the knife he had used to slice the peach. The sound of Laurita beating dough into submission came distantly and the light cast by the sun moved across the floor and touched the edge of the table before Thomas finished reading.

CHAPTER TWENTY-FOUR

"Are you sleeping here tonight?" Sancha asked.

Thomas nodded as he finished checking on the prince.

"Then I'll take the chair." She stood close, her scent enfolding him, and his body responded. For a moment he considered reaching out for her. The prince was asleep and would remain so regardless of what noise they might make, and the temptation of her was strong. He had been away from home long enough for it to fade to little more than a dream. Reality stood less than a foot away.

He had been about to make a decision when a tap sounded at the door. He opened it to find Jorge on the threshold, a second figure obscured in the shadows.

"What do you want? I'm too tired for games." Thomas was short with him, imagining his companion was Esperanza.

"Adana's disappeared."

For a moment Thomas didn't know who he meant, then it came to him. Jorge's newly discovered niece, the family he had been spending more of his time with. Exhaustion fled immediately.

"What do you mean, disappeared? Is that Zanita skulking in the hallway? She can come in, you know."

"Not into a prince's chamber. Adana went to work as usual but hadn't returned by dark. When Zanita went to her place of work they said she had left as normal. She was on her way to the market and then going directly home. Daniel's searching for her now."

Thomas moved away from the bed. He caught Sancha watching. She was listening to the conversation and he felt a flash of anger before recognising it as a displacement emotion. Everyone knew what it meant in this city when a girl went missing. Perhaps in this instance there was an innocent reason. She had met a boy and was even now sleeping safe in his arms. She had run away from home, as her uncle had. But he knew this was little more than wishful thinking.

"Where is her work?"

"A laundry near the marketplace. She starts at dawn and finishes at noon."

"Then we shall go there first."

"Zanita has already been."

"So we go again. It's where the trail starts." He turned to Sancha. "Juan will sleep until morning. I should be back before then, but if not you know what to do."

Sancha nodded and mouthed *Good luck,* but Thomas was already pushing Jorge ahead of him.

He put his hand on Zanita's shoulder and looked into her eyes. "Is there some place she might have gone? A boy? A friend?"

Zanita shook her head.

"Has she been different at home?" They walked fast along the corridor. The hour was late and around them the palace slumbered. Thomas wondered briefly whether Esperanza had been with Jorge when his sister-in-law found him.

"She's been excited to discover an uncle she didn't know she had. Adana's a good girl," said Zanita, as if it was a talisman that might protect her daughter.

Thomas wondered if she believed her own words. Surely he was not the only one who had seen the streak of devilment that lay beneath the girl's pretty outward appearance?

"Take me to the laundry. Will there be anyone there at this hour?"

"Some of the workers live above. They'll be asleep, but we can wake them, I suppose."

Which is what they did, hammering on the door until a lamp showed in a window, a vague pale shape behind it. When it disappeared Thomas banged again until he heard feet descend the staircase.

The door was opened a crack and a face peered out. Thomas held their own lamp high so they could be clearly seen. The face appeared to recognise Zanita because she said, "She hasn't returned here. We are all asleep."

"I have questions," Thomas said, pushing at the door. He met resistance and pressed harder. The slight figure was no barrier and the door opened wide to reveal the woman dressed in nightclothes. She pulled them close around her as if she had been displaying herself, even though they covered her from neck to ankle, only the tips of her toes showing, her nails cracked and stained from her work.

"I answered Zanita's questions before."

"I might have different ones. You know the urgency, don't you?"

The expression on her face was all the answer needed, and he marvelled at how easily the fear had resurfaced. Only days before everyone had been celebrating the execution of the bonebreaker.

"You'd better come in. All of you." She turned and led them through to a large space on the right. Vats of water shimmered under the light of their lamps, tendrils of steam rising from the surface, the air tainted with an acrid smell.

"Was Adana different today in any way?"

The woman shook her head. "She was the same as she always is. Talking too much. I had to scold her."

"You see her every day?"

"Every day but Sunday. I run the laundry and look after the girls who live here."

"So you know Adana well."

"Not as well as some of those who stay beneath this roof but well enough, I'd say."

"Does she ever talk about boys? Or men? Older men? Anyone special?" Thomas heard Zanita start to object, but he saw Jorge place a hand on her arm to quieten her.

"She talks of her family, but I don't think there's anyone special, if that's what you mean."

"She is engaged to be married when she is of an age," said Zanita.

"She is?" It was Jorge who spoke.

"She is not unattractive. And a woman needs the protection of a man."

"Who?" Thomas asked.

"A barber. He has a shop in the north of the city and lives above it."

"Could she have gone to him?"

"Have you finished with me?" asked the laundress.

"Wait, I might have more questions," Thomas said. "Could she have gone to him, Zanita?"

She shook her head. "I don't think so. She barely knows him. They have met only three times, always with me as chaperone."

"What age is he?" Jorge asked.

"Thirty or so."

"And Adana is what, fifteen?"

"It is a good age for a girl to marry. And he has a thriving business. Adana can be wilful. If we don't arrange a good match she might find someone unsuitable."

"He's twice her age," said Jorge.

Thomas stopped Jorge, knowing the matter of the engagement was immaterial unless she really was with this barber, which he doubted. Adana would have to put up with him soon enough. He was certain she would not seek out his bed until she had to. Besides, who was Jorge to cast judgement?

"Might she have gone to him?" Thomas asked Zanita a third time, taking her shoulders and turning her to face him. He needed to be sure.

She dropped her head and shook it, refusing to meet his eyes.

"She would not, I know she would not." It was obvious she too knew the match wasn't appropriate.

Thomas turned to the laundress. "Did Adana say what she was doing when she left here?"

"She was going to buy fruit and flour and then she was going directly home. She was excited, wondering if her new uncle might visit again. Are you he?"

"No, this man is. What was she wearing?"

The woman shook her head. "I don't remember. I never thought to note it."

"I know what she wore," said Zanita.

"Which market would she go to? Oh, you can go now, I've no more questions." Thomas tossed the words at the laundress as he took Zanita's arm and urged her out towards the street.

"It's on her way home. She would have gone there."

"Show me. Does she always use the same merchants?"

"We both do. Some will try to pass off bad goods if you let them. We always buy fruit from the same seller, our meat from another when we can afford it."

"Do you know the owners?"

"A little."

"And where they live?"

Zanita shook her head.

"Who would?"

"I don't know."

"There must be a market supervisor. Who would know?"

"Daniel might."

"It's too far to go to your house." Thomas stopped as they came into the market square. It lay deserted in the night, only a single torch burning on the far side. The tables for the stalls were folded and stacked in the centre awaiting morning. This early in the year the air was chilly against his face and there was an odour of rotting fruit and vegetables. Thomas walked to where a fountain had once stood and turned around, surveying the surrounding buildings.

"We should be looking for her," said Jorge.

"I am."

Jorge followed Thomas's gaze. "You think her held captive here?"

"Of course not. I'm looking for the man who manages the market. He will live in one of these houses."

"You'll never know which one," said Jorge.

"Perhaps not, but look—how many of these are shops, how many inns? At least a half, more than half. And this is a busy market so he will have a large house. Most of these are narrow and poor." Thomas turned again, once more, his eyes tracking, then he stopped. "He lives there." He pointed to a house where a torch burned from a sconce set in the wall, strode out across the market square, Jorge and Zanita moving fast to keep up.

Thomas went directly to the tall, heavy door and knocked. The sound was loud in the confines of the square, rousing several dogs that started to bark.

When there was no reply from within he knocked harder, kept on until a light appeared inside. More lights came on in other houses and to their left a man threw his front door open and stepped out, a length of wood in his hand.

"What are you doing disturbing peaceful citizens?"

"Go back to bed," Thomas said, "this is no business of yours."

From behind the tall door he heard bolts thrown. A key turned in a lock and then a man with a belly hanging over his trousers appeared. He had pulled the trousers on in a hurry and the tail of his shirt poked out through the open front that had been left untied.

"Don't you know it's the middle of the night?"

"Are you the market supervisor?" Thomas asked.

"What is it to you?"

"The stall that sells fruit." He stopped, turned to Zanita. "Which one? Show him."

"An old man and a younger woman, they set up about … there." She pointed.

"Carreras," said the supervisor. "And his grand-daughter. She's twenty and still single, although I'm not surprised. They're not Spaniards even if they have changed their name."

"Where do they live?" Thomas knew this man, now he was woken, would talk for an hour about the comings and goings of his charges in the square.

"Live?"

"Yes. They do live somewhere, don't they? You must have a record of it for their rent. You wouldn't allow them to trade otherwise."

"I might have it somewhere."

"Will you have to look it up, or do you know?"

"Why should I tell you?"

"Because this woman's daughter is missing and the market is the last place she visited. I can fetch the Hermandad if you prefer and get them to search your house in case it's you who took her. Is she inside now?" Thomas made to push past the man, who moved to block him. It was a foolish thing to do.

Thomas's hand shot out and gripped the market supervisor's shoulder, fingers digging in hard through fat and flesh to the bone where a nerve ran. The man's knees bent and he tried to pull away.

"Which is it to be?" Thomas asked, his voice reasonable even as his fingers dug harder.

"Calle Damasco. The fourth door. Now let me go before I call the guard on you."

Thomas released his grip and snapped his hand away, stepping back in case the man decided to make some retaliation, not that he expected any. He turned and walked away without a word, Jorge and Zanita once more running to keep up.

CHAPTER TWENTY-FIVE

The door was answered by an old man who leaned on a stick.

"Do you know what time of night it is?" His clouded eyes moved to take in Zanita and his unwelcoming expression changed, but only a little. "I know you, don't I? You come to my stall."

"Her daughter came to you this afternoon," Thomas said, "and now she is missing."

The man's face blanched and Thomas reached out, thinking he was about to faint.

"What do you know of it?" he said.

"Yes, there was a girl at the stall. She had finished buying her fruit and wanted to talk. Nothing important—she was telling me about her visitors. Then a man approached."

"Approached her directly?" Thomas said. "Did he know her?"

"I don't think so. She didn't know him, anyway. He was berating her for dressing as she did."

"My Adana dresses chastely!" objected Zanita.

The man offered her a glance, perhaps too polite to correct her. Thomas had seen how Adana was when they met in the market place and knew she could be flirtatious. "This man wasn't rational. Your daughter is growing into a woman. Her breasts show beneath her dress, and she is tall and pretty. The kind of girl who excites men who cannot have them. I considered it nothing more than that. It happens all the time, I see it every day."

"What did he say?" Thomas asked. "Do you remember?"

"He talked fast, quiet, leaning close to her. I caught only the occasional word but the meaning was clear. There are men such as him all over the city. Fanatics. Their God talks to them and they hear nothing else. At one point he took her arm and tried to pull her away and she slapped him. His hood fell back and I saw his face briefly before he covered himself again."

"You would recognise him?"

"In a moment. His face is scarred on both cheeks, as if something has clawed at him. His hair was dark, long, and his beard grows oddly, perhaps from the scarring."

"Spanish?"

"Almost certainly. He was no Jew, nor a Moor."

"What happened?"

"He tried to grab at the girl again and she pushed him away. She was disgusted. I went around and stood between her and the man and he came at her a third time. I am not a strong man, as you can see, but others came to our aid and he ran off."

"Where did he go?"

"Into the alleys, through the Jewish quarter."

"But he was no Jew, you said."

The man shook his head. "He was a Spaniard, I'm sure."

"And which way did Adana go?"

"She went towards the northern gate. I think she lives in that direction."

"And you didn't see this monk again?"

"No. Do you think he followed her?"

Thomas glanced at Zanita, reluctant to answer, but he saw she had stopped listening. Instead she stared into space, seeing only visions of mutilation.

"Take her home," Thomas said to Jorge as they stood outside in the alleyway. The stall-holder had closed his door and darkness surrounded them.

"Daniel is out searching for her," said Zanita.

"Then your other children need you. Stay with her, Jorge."

"I'm not going to sit around doing nothing while my niece is missing," objected Jorge.

"You will be doing something. Zanita needs you." Thomas saw the pain on Jorge's face and knew he was wondering why fate was so cruel. He had found a brother he believed dead, a family he didn't know of, only for one of them to be snatched away. "I will find her," Thomas said more strongly, and he reached out and gripped Zanita's arm. "I will find your daughter and return her to you. This is my promise. Now go with Jorge, I have more work to do tonight."

When he was alone Thomas considered returning to the palace for reinforcements, but the palace had its own problems. A single missing girl would not be a priority. He wondered about seeking out the city guard. Perhaps Rodrigo, the young constable, would be on duty. Although Thomas didn't even know if the Hermandad operated during the hours after midnight.

He walked to the market square where their journey had begun. He stood in the middle, turning slowly. The supervisor's house lay dark once more, the man returned to his bed.

He stopped, facing north.

Where would she go from here? He closed his eyes a moment, bringing forth images of the city. Over the time he had lived within its walls he had walked these streets time and again, alone or with Jorge. He had eaten at inns, bought fruit from stalls, fingered cloth and wondered whether to buy some as a gift for Lubna.

There were two streets she could have taken from the market square. Both would lead her to the city walls and through them. From there only one route led home.

If the monk had followed her he would not have abducted her in plain sight. People would come to Adana's help as they had at the market. So it had to be beyond the walls.

Thomas stepped out, walking fast, then started to run, his robe flowing behind as he sped through dark streets.

He found the basket beyond the city walls and knew exactly what had happened there, saw it in the fruit that lay crushed underfoot, in the broken straw making up the handle, in the disturbance of the ground. Larger feet mixed with the scuffs of someone more delicate. A scrap of cloth hung caught on a jagged corner of stone. Thomas pulled it free and slipped it into the pocket of his robe. He picked up the broken basket but left the fruit where it lay, crushed.

Only starlight and the remnants of a quarter moon illuminated this corner of the outer walls. It would have been almost dark when Adana passed the spot, although she would not have been this close to the walls. Her path led from the gate directly downhill to where her father's house stood beside the stream. She had been taken elsewhere and dragged here. Thomas worked his way outwards, searching until he found the expected disturbance in the ground, then tracked it to a spot a hundred feet from the gate. Whoever had taken her must have been confident, because anyone on the other side of the gate would have had a clear view.

He widened his search, found twin tracks where someone had been dragged, their heels digging in. He followed them until they stopped abruptly. He knelt, wishing for a little more light. But when he lay on his side and stared across the ground there was enough contrast to show faint depressions where a small cart had rested. Thomas saw that the trail of dragged heels ended where the cart had waited.

He worked slowly, bent almost double, but lost the trail too soon. He stood straight and looked along the direction the cart had taken. South-west—towards where the Monastery of Almodovar del Rio lay.

The monk had followed Adana here. A white robed monk. The same colour robe as worn by Abbot Mandana. There were others, of course, but the documents Lawrence had shown him pointed in the same direction. Even if Mandana was not complicit, Thomas believed someone at the monastery had taken Adana, and taken other girls before—for almost a year.

He ran again, down to where candlelight glowed in the windows of Daniel's house.

CHAPTER TWENTY-SIX

"Daniel's her father," said Jorge. "We should have let him come."

"He's too involved," Thomas said. "We couldn't trust him not to lose his temper."

"And I'm *not* involved?"

Thomas ignored the comment. Now wasn't the time to get into an argument. He urged his horse along the dusty track as the morning sun cast their shadows ahead of them.

They hadn't said where they were going when they'd left, and it felt like a betrayal to leave the family to deal with their pain and fear on their own. When Thomas had placed the twisted basket on the table where they had eaten together, Zanita uttered a strangled cry, a second following as Thomas laid the strip of cloth beside it.

"Is it from Adana's dress?" he had asked.

Zanita nodded, her hands clutched to her cheeks as if she wanted to rip them off. Daniel had picked up the scrap of cloth and raised it to his face, breathing in its scent. Thomas knew nothing of the girl remained—it smelled of dust and earth, nothing more. It had been cruel to leave the girl's father behind, but he didn't yet know enough about Daniel to be sure of him.

"I wouldn't be surprised if he isn't following us, anyway," Thomas said. The city wall lay two hour's ride behind, the monastery another hour ahead.

He turned in his saddle and looked back. They had ridden up a low hill and Qurtuba sat in a curve alongside the river, the palace and cathedral the tallest buildings, haphazard tiled roofs giving it the appearance of a small town grown out of proportion rather than a once mighty city now shrunk. He saw no sign of anyone on the road behind. They had passed three monks earlier, making their way on foot towards the city. Thomas had asked if they had seen anyone coming ahead of them, but had little faith in their answer when they said no.

It had been dawn before they'd managed to leave. Thomas had gone to the stables and demanded horses. He'd tried to find Pero but the priest had not yet returned from the queen's task, so he had scrawled a quick message saying where he was going and what he suspected. He'd also left a message for the queen apologising for his absence. An hour had been spent with Prince Juan. Sancha had been asleep on the narrow bed Thomas used himself some nights so he'd roused her and left instructions. He'd told her he expected to be back by nightfall.

Jorge had disappeared somewhere for an hour. Thomas hadn't asked where but assumed he had been with Esperanza.

He turned and shaded his eyes, looking ahead to where the monastery of Almodovar del Rio perched on its clifftop. He recalled the morning barely a week before when he had gazed at the shrouded shape rising through mist above the river. He wondered if he had known then what lay ahead would he have turned and fled or not.

"Daniel's better off staying at home," he said. "If we're wrong and she's not been taken he must be there when she returns."

"You don't believe that's going to happen, do you?" said Jorge.

"No. She's been taken."

"By the bonebreaker?"

Thomas rode on for a while, aware Jorge was waiting for a response. Eventually he nodded. "Yes, she's been taken."

"You don't like that name, do you?"

"I have no feelings either way. It's a name, nothing more. It's the man who lies behind the name we seek."

"And you think we'll find him at the monastery?"

"Everyone was distracted by the butcher and his wife. People assumed he was the killer of all the others."

"And you?"

Ahead of them the path rose steeply between rocky outcroppings. Thomas encouraged his horse with his heels, its feet scrabbling up the sudden slope, metal shoes echoing from sheer rock walls on either side.

"I did once. I think I wanted to. I didn't come to this city to solve a crime." He looked around. "You know, this would be a good place for an ambush."

Jorge gave a short laugh. "What do you know of ambushes?"

Thomas glanced at him. "Oh, more than you can imagine, my friend."

Jorge shook his head. "You and your mysterious past again. Are you ever going to stop hinting and actually tell me anything about it?"

The path wound up through a narrow gully. Shards of sharp rock littered the ground and the horses had to pick their way with care. Ahead lay a turn beyond which they couldn't see.

"One day. When we are both old men and have nothing left but time."

"Speak for yourself. I plan on staying young forever."

"As well you might."

"Abdul is old," said Jorge. He spoke of the ancient eunuch who was master of the harem in Gharnatah.

"Abdul claims to be a hundred and ten. He lies, of course, but he might be eighty."

"Older than that. And don't change the subject. How do you know about ambush?"

Thomas twisted in his saddle. He pointed. "There, there, and there. I would place men in those spots. There are rocks to hide behind. They would have bows." He leaned forward. "And just beyond the turn I would place four more armed with swords. A musket if they have one. Yes, a musket would be good, fired as soon as we round the turn. They might manage to take one of us."

Thomas urged his horse into a canter, ignoring the rough ground underfoot. They had to be close to the monastery now even if it couldn't be seen. He smiled as Jorge stayed back.

At the turn there was no ambush. Monks did not lay ambushes.

Ahead the ground fell away towards the river before the sharp bluff rose once more, with the monastery clutching to its summit. The walls had once been white but were now stained and mottled. They rose sheer from the eastern face of the cliff, stepped rock faces protecting it on all other sides. Thomas saw fields carved out on rocky terraces. Beyond to the north the hillside continued to rise, cloaked with ancient olives grown wild, cork oak, pine and birch.

"It doesn't look dangerous," said Jorge as he came up beside him.

"It may not be. But I'm convinced this is where Adana has been brought."

"Is Mandana involved, do you think?"

It was a good question and Thomas thought about his answer before speaking. He shook his head. "He's odd, certainly, but I don't believe so. He's known the queen since she was born and has a position. Why would he risk everything in such madness?"

"Wouldn't he have to know something? He is the abbot, after all."

"He seems to spend most of his time in the palace, so it would be easy enough for a monk to act without his knowledge."

"Except this has to be the work of more than one man."

"Two monks then," Thomas said. "Or three or four. But no more otherwise their secret would be discovered."

"Do you think she's still alive?"

Thomas glanced across to see Jorge's normally benign features drawn into a scowl of anxiety. "For the moment. Past abductions—the real ones—took place several days before any body was found. I believe they are kept somewhere and prepared. The woman we saw when we first arrived had been dead no more than a day."

"What would they do with someone for all that time?" Jorge's expression darkened further.

"I don't know."

"Or don't want to say? I thought you knew everything."

"Not this." Thomas urged his horse on. "If she is there the sooner we find her the better."

"Whoever has her isn't going to just turn her over."

"They will if Mandana backs us. It's his kingdom within those walls."

"Unless he is a part of it."

Thomas glanced at Jorge. "I don't like the man, but I don't see it. It will be one monk or several and we will find out who and bring Adana home safe."

CHAPTER TWENTY-SEVEN

Thomas was surprised when they were met at the gate by Abbot Mandana himself. The roadway that twisted and climbed from the river towards the monastery lay in plain view, the only cover provided by stunted olives and a few stands of mulberry. They would have been seen approaching for a good while, so it wasn't that they were met that caused surprise but that it was by the abbot himself. Thomas had thought him still in Qurtuba.

"What are you doing here?" Mandana stood in the doorway, blocking the way.

"Another girl has been taken."

"What has that got to do with me or my monastery?"

"I believe she was brought here."

Mandana laughed. "Why would you think that? We are monks. We have given up the material world. Our life here is simple. All we wish is to be left in peace to worship God."

"Then you have no objection if we look around. We will be gone inside an hour."

Mandana smiled, his long face unnaturally benign. "It would be ill-mannered to turn you away after you have come so far. Besides, we truly do have nothing to hide." He stepped aside, drawing the sun-bleached door wide.

They entered a courtyard. Mandana pushed the door shut and

threw two heavy bolts across. He made an apologetic face. "We are a long way from assistance here and there are brigands this far from the city, despite the efforts our king and queen make."

Thomas allowed Jorge to make small talk as they crossed to a second entrance framing a door as solid as the one they had just passed through. He glanced around, taking in the stables and buildings to one side. Three small carts stood on the dusty ground. Any of them would have been large enough to conceal a body, particularly one as slight as Adana's. There were fewer people than he had expected. Two monks swept out a covered stable, another repaired the mortar in a wall, his tools scattered on the ground at his feet, the long sleeves of his robe rolled back to reveal sun-darkened arms. Others no doubt worked elsewhere—perhaps within the gardens that Thomas noticed were through an arch—or were at prayer.

When his survey ended he discovered Mandana and Jorge were waiting for him at the second doorway.

"You must be hungry and thirsty after your journey. Come to my rooms and I will send for something." Mandana glanced at the sky. "It will be noon prayers before long and I will have to leave you, but you are welcome to wander wherever you wish. Open any doors and look in any cupboards, there are no secrets here."

Cloistered corridors led them through the heart of the monastery. To their right a large courtyard offered a view to gardens only glimpsed before, each patch of earth enclosed by a low stone wall. There were fruit trees, olives, vegetable plots, chickens and a few sheep. The heat of the day was tempered by blocks of shade thrown by the high walls.

Mandana opened a door and ushered them into what appeared to be his work quarters. Books and scrolls were stacked on shelves and a desk. A large silver cross stood against one wall, with several paintings depicting the crucifixion on wooden boards nailed to the wall. In each the face of Christ was shown in agony. Mandana told them to sit at a table then disappeared, presumably to arrange for the promised food and drink.

Jorge was staring at the icons. "Can you explain to me what the purpose of a religion based on pain and death is?"

"I think it's supposed to make people appreciate the little they have."

"Did you ever believe?" Jorge turned to Thomas, curiosity on his face.

"If we're asked that question by anyone here I suggest we both say yes."

"But did you?"

Thomas gave the question consideration. "When I was young."

"When did you stop?"

"A long time ago."

"When?"

"Why the questions?"

"I'm only trying to pass the time," said Jorge.

"Of course. A long time ago—let's leave it at that, shall we? And you? When you were a boy you would have gone to church."

"Of course I did."

"And believed?"

"I believed something. And the ritual is calming."

"And now?"

Jorge gave him a look but said nothing, and before Thomas could press him the abbot returned carrying a tray. He laid it on the table then moved around to stand on the far side. There were two bowls containing some kind of stew, dark bread and wine.

"Help yourselves. We won't eat until after the sun has set."

Jorge reached for the jug of wine and poured into a large silver goblet. He drank greedily then tasted the stew. He pulled a face, but hunger must have overcome any doubts and he spooned it greedily into his mouth. Watching him Thomas realised he too was starving. He tried to remember the last time he had eaten. It was at least a day.

"Will everyone be at the service?" Thomas asked as he took a small spoonful. He understood why Jorge had pulled the face. The stew was rich and heavily spiced, but there was something sharp underlying the richness. Still, he dipped a hunk of bread into it and ate more, his stomach grumbling.

"We are holding special thanks for the rebirth of our Lord," said Mandana.

"Easter," Thomas said.

"Indeed. This is the most holy week in the Catholic calendar. It holds special significance to men such as us. We will be in the chapel for some time. I apologise for proving such a poor host."

"But we can go where we want, you said?"

"Other than the places where we pray. I am afraid I must leave you now to prepare myself. Remain here as long as you wish. Finish your food and wine. I will come and find you later. If you have gone before I return, then go with God."

Mandana made the sign of the cross, rose and drew his white robe around himself. He pushed fingers through his long hair, settling it behind his shoulders. Once they were alone Thomas rose and studied the papers on the abbot's desk.

"If he comes back and catches you we'll be tossed out," said Jorge. "Come and eat."

"What do you think of the food?" Thomas turned papers over. Land dealings associated with the monastery, edicts from Rome, a letter from the priest Torquemada who Thomas had heard so much about but had yet to meet.

"The stew? There's something bitter in it, but it's good. Stop prying and come eat. You must be as hungry as me."

Thomas relented and returned to the table. He ate quickly and without tasting the food before rising again and returning to scan the documents that sat on the shelves. He carried his mug of wine, sipping at it as his free hand ran across the spines of documents.

From behind Jorge began to hum something under his breath. A minute later his feet started to move, tapping out a rhythm.

"We'd better go search the grounds before you break into dunce," Thomas said, turning. He stopped, sure he had said something wrong, then shook his head. He went to the table and poured more wine, drained the glass, thirsty.

"He should have bought walter," said Jorge.

"What did you say?" Thomas turned his head, a loose confusion starting up behind his eyes. He leaned close and studied Jorge. The man's eyes were bright, the pupils blown wide so no iris showed.

Thomas licked his lips, repeated the gesture when he discovered them numb.

"Jorge—how are you falling—feeling?"

"Fine. In fact..." Jorge's voice trailed away as he stared at one of the icons in fascination.

Thomas blinked. One moment the room was normal. When the blink was over the stone in the walls had turned iridescent. "We've been..." He shook his head, thoughts splintering like dropped glass. He threw his half-consumed bowl to the floor, watching it shatter, the brown stew smearing the tiles. One moment brown, the next red, flowing like blood. He swayed and had to grab onto the table. He thrust his fingers into his mouth, probing until he retched. Nothing came up and he dug deeper, turning aside as he vomited on the floor. "Jorge, do the same—do it now! We've been —" He stopped as the sun came from behind a cloud and lit a square on the wall, in the centre of which sat an image of Christ. The figure seemed to writhe and Thomas heard screams, but when he clapped his hands over his ears the screams only grew louder.

He made himself sick again, then pushed his fingers into Jorge's mouth. Jorge hit him hard, directly on the chin, and Thomas staggered back and fell to the floor. Jorge came at him, moving fast. Thomas watched his friend's foot pull back, swing forward. Without conscious volition he grabbed Jorge's boot and stopped the second blow. Then he pushed, sending Jorge tumbling onto his back.

Thomas straddled him, turned him over. His hands burrowed beneath and his fingers invaded Jorge's mouth. He felt the body trapped beneath him heave, smelled the acrid scent of vomit, but probed again, a third time.

"I'm dying," cried Jorge, his voice shaking.

"We're both dying. The abbot has poisoned us."

"Adana is here, isn't she?" Jorge rolled onto his side and heaved again, but there was nothing left to bring up. "She's here and we've failed her." He banged his head on the stone floor, opening a split in his forehead. He banged it a second time.

Thomas rolled over and got to his knees. He crawled across the room to a table set against the wall. There was a bowl used for washing, with a large jug set beside it. He used the table to pull himself upright and found the jug half full of water. He grabbed the bar of greasy soap and turned, sat down hard. He bit off a corner of the soap, chewed, swallowed, washing it down with water. He felt his stomach heave and held himself in check as he drank more water. When he could hold back no longer he vomited explosively. He waited until the heaving stopped then repeated the operation with the same result.

He felt no better. The room continued to swim, the icons on the walls shone with their own inner light, but he knew he had done all he could. Dragging the jug beside him he crawled towards Jorge.

CHAPTER TWENTY-EIGHT

Thomas opened his eyes and knew he must have passed out. He tried to sit and collapsed back to the floor as the walls of the room folded in on themselves and spiralled away. He closed his eyes again and reached out, found Jorge's robe. He shook the body beneath.

"Don't."

"Why hasn't Mandana come for us?" Thomas kept his eyes shut, unwilling to see reality tortured.

"Why should he? We're meant to be dead."

"Can you move?"

"I don't know. Every time I open my eyes I see something that isn't there."

"Ignore it." When Thomas opened his own eyes again the walls shimmered, tiny specks of crystal embedded in the granite sparking rainbow shards. This time he kept them open as he rolled over then slowly climbed to his hands and knees. His head hung down and drool trailed from his mouth, but the floor beneath him no longer moved like grass in a wind.

"We have to get out of this room," he said.

"Can't."

"Then Mandana will finish what his kitchen failed to do."

"At the moment that has appeal."

Thomas attempted to stand, holding tight to the table. Its surface surged beneath his hands like the flank of a horse but he ignored it, knowing the falsity of reality. This wasn't the first time he had experienced these sensations, but the others had been voluntary and he had been much younger. Those memories called him with a sudden urgency and as he blinked he found himself somewhere else, as though the monastery no longer surrounded him.

He stood on the banks of a river in the border lands between France and Spain. He and Eleanor, the girl he believed he would spend the rest of his life with. They had swum naked in the river and then he had found the fungus growing in damp shade beneath trees. Red-capped toadstools emerging from the ground between birch and pine. He knew what they were, and what they could do. He had used their magic before to escape a life he despised—until he found the girl who stood beside him.

He broke one off and ate half, handed the rest to Eleanor.

"What is it?"

"It will make you feel good," he said.

"I already feel good. I want to fuck again."

"Eat it. The sex will be better."

Eleanor grinned and bit into the bitter cap, her trust almost painful. Neither could wait for the toadstool to work so they had sex first, then again when the effects came and the grass swayed multi-coloured around them and the river ran with fire.

Blink.

Thomas was back in the abbot's room, the pain of what he had lost filling him. He closed his eyes, seeking the moment again, but it was gone, replaced by desolation. She had been with him, her skin silk beneath his rough palms, her hair tumbled, her eyes hungry for more as they moved together… All gone.

Thomas grabbed Jorge's robe and pulled him into a sitting position.

"Get up."

Jorge groaned and worked his way up the table until he stood swaying, his head down.

"We have to leave before they come back from prayer." Thomas glanced at the window, trying to judge how much time had passed, but it was a mistake. The glass splintered light into a million pieces. He ignored it. "We have to find Adana and get out of here."

"Like this?"

"It's not real. Ignore it."

"I know it's not real," snapped Jorge, "but I can't ignore it! It won't let me."

"Then try. Hold onto me if you think you're going to fall."

"How can you manage when everything keeps moving?"

"I told you, it's not real."

"You're not human." Jorge came with him as Thomas moved slowly to the door, but perhaps only so he had something to support him. Thomas expected the door to be locked, but it swung open when he turned the heavy iron lever.

On their way in they had come from the right, so now he turned left. Sunlight cascaded into the cloistered walkway, making the ground appear to rise and fall so at one moment they were climbing a stairway, the next descending a slope.

At the end of the corridor they stopped.

Thomas listened.

He heard the chanting of voices raised in prayer. To their left was a taller building set in a square of grass surrounded by gravestones, and that was where the sound came from. Mandana must be so confident they were dead or dying.

"We were lucky," Thomas said. "I don't think we lost much time."

"We were lucky you knew what was happening."

"It's what I do. Come on, this way." Thomas stepped out across the grass, ignoring the sensation he was walking over the surface of a sea. He almost smiled. Let the abbot make of that what he could. Beyond the square a long wall ran the length of it, studded with narrow openings. They passed through one into a walled garden. On the far side a single monk stood working the soil. He looked up as they entered, his head cocked to one side.

Thomas stopped abruptly but Jorge continued, drifting away as though he hadn't seen the man. Thomas started up, making his way towards him. They had been seen now, and he was curious what the man was doing here while everyone else prayed. He might also offer a clue to where Adana was being kept.

As he came closer it became obvious the monk was a giant. He stood almost a foot taller than Thomas, who was tall himself. What also became obvious was the reason the monk wasn't at prayer. His face showed the benign expression of someone whose brain doesn't work correctly. His hood was thrown back so the sun could catch his face. One side of his head was caved in, a deep circle marking it as if a rock had crushed his skull. It was the kind of blow that would kill most men. Instead it had taken this one's wits.

Thomas shook his head. He had been staring at the depression in the monk's skull too long, the poison working through his system still weaving its subtle magic.

"What are you doing out here?"

The monk grinned, his shoulders rising and falling as he started to laugh. He pointed at Thomas, sounds emerging from his mouth, but they weren't words. Perhaps in his own head they made sense but by the time they arrived in the world they were stripped of meaning.

Thomas glanced down. The man was barefoot, his robe stopping short of the ground by a good measure, obviously meant for someone of normal stature. With his own wits scrambled Thomas had assumed the man was weeding a vegetable plot and indeed, as he approached his mind might have projected a vision of such. Now he saw nothing grew in the patch of worked ground. The soil lay pale and dry, but the man had been doing something.

He made a noise again and grinned. He moved the hoe he held and scraped at the soil, turning the top surface. A small bone rolled over and was reburied.

More conversation, and this time Thomas almost caught a meaning. *I en*. Was he trying to say his name? Or were Thomas's own ears betraying him? At the edges of his vision sparkles of light continued to form, reality blossoming and folding in on itself, so why would his hearing be spared the same treatment?

Thomas stepped away, confused. He looked around for Jorge, who had found a stone bench and sat, his face tilted up to the sun. Perhaps in his mind he had travelled scores of miles and was even now sitting in the gardens of al-Hamra dressed in the silks of a eunuch, with the sound of fountains and the scent of beautiful women perfuming the air. That he had gone someplace else was obvious.

"Jorge!" Thomas called, but there was no response.

"I ends," the giant said, turning over more soil. A finger bone came to the surface and this time was left in plain view

Thomas stared. The bone was small and slender. As he watched it turned purple then faded back to a pale brown. He ignored the vision, knelt and picked the bone up, held it close so he could focus.

"End."

Thomas scrubbed through the loose soil with his hands. There were more bones, small ones at first, then as his fingers worked deeper they encountered something larger. He pulled but the earth held it firm. It felt like a thigh bone. Thick and solid.

"I ends." This time the words coalesced into meaning. *My friends*. The giant was saying *my friends*.

"Where do your friends come from?" Thomas said as he rose to his feet. He glanced across the courtyard. Jorge was no longer on the bench. Thomas looked around but couldn't see him anywhere.

The giant pointed and grunted. He might be saying over there, he might be saying nothing at all.

"Show me," Thomas said, and the giant grinned, nodding his head as if Thomas was all at once his best friend.

He led the way through an arched gateway into another, smaller square. Here grass grew and on the far side lay a tumble of stone where a building had been demolished. Two walls were still standing, but all sign of a roof had gone other than scattered tiles. The monk strode directly to it and Thomas had to trot to keep up. The movement pushed more of the fog from his mind. The visual hallucinations still came, but his thoughts were clearer. As they approached the tumble-down building a smell came to him, unmistakeable, of corruption.

He wrapped a sleeve across his nose and mouth as they stepped over the stump of a remaining wall.

"*Ends*," the giant said, turning around, his arms spread.

Tossed in corners and under stones lay limbs, both animal and human. The discard of a madman. But not this madman, who knelt and picked up a hoof attached to a splinter of bone. He turned it over then tossed it aside as not worthy, or not yet ready, for his attention.

Thomas crossed to where a small pile of remains lay. The top limb was still covered in flesh, tatters of skin and muscle adhering to the bone beneath.

"*O ood.*"

No good?

"Why not?"

The monk put his fingers over his nose and pulled a face. "*Oo esh.*"

"Where's the girl?" Thomas said, and the giant turned away, a look of cunning on one side of his face, the other unmoving. He shook his head and pushed at Thomas, almost sending him over.

"This is where they bring the remains afterwards, isn't it? So where do they keep them before?" But not all the remains, Thomas thought, recalling the limbs of a wolf and the torso of a girl tossed into the river. Only the smaller bones? Or had their method changed and these were from older kills? He looked around, appalled at how many bones lay scattered. Just how many *had* they killed here? This was more than the work of one or two men—the entire population of the monastery had to be involved.

The giant laughed and danced away. He turned, the move deliberate, crossed his arms and stared south through the broken back wall. The land tumbled and fell towards a distant view of the city, the air above it stained with smoke.

Thomas turned and looked in the opposite direction. There the wall had been repaired and an entrance still graced its centre, a scarred door blocking it. Thomas went to it and pushed. Hinges protested but the door moved. He had forced it half open when the giant hit him on the back of the neck.

Thomas went to his knees, rolled aside as a bare foot came at his face. He grabbed it, using the man's momentum to unbalance him. The monk went over like a felled tree. His head cracked on the corner of a stone and he lay still. Thomas crawled across and felt his neck. A strong pulse continued to beat.

Thomas pulled himself up and returned to the door, put his shoulder to it and pushed. The cool air that came out to greet him stank of spoiled meat and he knew he had found the killing chamber. He also knew he should fetch Jorge, but if they had brought Adana here he needed to know her fate.

As he stepped inside he heard a voice, a young woman's voice, call out one word. "No!" But by then it was too late.

CHAPTER TWENTY-NINE

When awareness returned to Thomas it came slowly, tainted by the remnants of the poison that still flowed in his veins. He smelled the stink of corruption, heard someone nearby breathing fast and hard, felt an unexpected wash of heat across his back together with a faint breeze. When he opened his eyes the dark corners of the chamber bled away into spirals and he closed them again.

"Are you awake?" It was the same voice that had called out, quieter now so he heard the fear in it.

He nodded without opening his eyes, afraid of what he might see. Or simply afraid. Thomas had been in danger many times but wondered if this might not prove to be his last encounter with that dark enemy. Nearby the panting started again, each breath ragged with terror and he knew, despite his own raging fear, he had to be strong. Or at the least appear to be strong. When he opened his eyes again it took a moment for what he saw to register, the chamber appeared tilted until he discovered that was only his own head lolling to one side. Strong light cast itself across the floor and one wall, long shadows stretching out which slowly he interpreted as belonging to him and Adana. They were both tied. He felt coarse rope around his wrists and ankles and waist. He twisted, catching a glimpse of a tall window behind him before pain caused him to turn back. It explained the heat on his back and the cacophony of images.

"How long have you been here?" Thomas asked.

Adana's breathing increased its pace, and when she spoke her voice trembled so strongly she could form no words. Thomas heard her make an attempt to dampen her panic and try again.

"I woke before—before dawn."

"Did you see the man who attacked you?"

"He accosted me in the—in the market. Then again—" She broke off, gasping.

Thomas let it go. He knew what had happened, there was no need to make her relive it.

He shifted, testing his bindings, but they were firm. He managed to crane his head forward enough to see he had been stripped of all clothing, although someone had wrapped a stained loincloth around his waist. When he twisted sideways he saw it was more than they had done for Adana. She was tied to an identical cross, her young body revealed, showing marks at her elbows and thighs—the same marks Thomas had seen on the girl at the gate. He raised his eyes to meet Adana's and kept them there.

Her face was pale and her hands trembled beyond their bindings. She was petrified, barely rational beneath the weight of fear that lay upon her.

"Do you know where you are?"

She gave a shake of her head, biting at her bottom lip. "In the city somewhere?"

"We are in the monastery of Almodovar del Rio."

"The monk," said Adana, and Thomas was pleased to hear less trembling in her voice. "He attacked me and knocked me—knocked me out. When I woke I was tied, and then a man came in and—" The memory of what had happened triggered another wave of panic and she broke off.

"What man?"

Thomas saw her try to steel herself, her entire body shaking now even as her skin sweated.

"Another monk. He came in and drew on my—on my skin."

Her eyes skittered away as though by not looking at him he could not see her either.

"What did he look like?"

"He was tall, with—"

"He looked like me." Abbot Mandana stepped from the shadows. How long had he been standing there, watching them? "Where have you left your companion? My monks have searched everywhere and failed to find him."

"You tried to kill us."

Mandana smiled. "Not kill, only disable. I would not kill you when I need another subject for a special display. Where is he?"

Thomas made no reply, wanting Mandana uncertain over Jorge's whereabouts. Although he too wondered where he might be.

Mandana appeared unconcerned. He shrugged. "No matter. If he's fled his story won't be believed. Don't think someone's coming to save you. Either of you."

"He's gone to the city," Thomas said, "with a message for the queen. She will believe me."

Mandana smiled. "How did he escape? Our walls are high and the door is always locked."

"Jorge is resourceful. He will have found a way."

"Don't overestimate yourself, or him, Thomas Berrington. You might have wormed your way into the queen's affections, but she is never going to doubt my loyalty."

Thomas glanced at Adana but her gaze had turned inward and he knew she had escaped to some other place.

"Even you can't believe that—not after what you've done."

Mandana took a step closer. "And what is it I have done, exactly? Do you even know? How does a heathen such as you even begin to comprehend the glory of what I have created?"

"Madmen always justify their actions. We'll see what the queen says." Thomas spoke through the mask of his own fear. The more he saw of Mandana the less confident he was he would walk free of the situation.

"Isabel is like my daughter. I held her as a baby, I have been at her side as she grew into the powerful ruler she is. Do you honestly think she'll believe a stranger over me?"

Mandana moved to one side where a bench was set at right angles to their crosses. He went beyond it and tugged on a thick rope tied to a hook set into the wall. Thomas felt the cross he was tied to sway. It jerked as the rope came free of the hook. Mandana fed the rope through his hands, a series of pulleys linking it to the cross. Thomas twisted and saw the post hole was only closed on three sides. He wondered how many others had lain here. At least a dozen he knew of, but had there been others before then? Almost certainly based on the bones he had seen outside.

"She'll believe when presented with the evidence."

"Bones can be crushed. Bones can be hidden." Mandana grinned. "And bones can be broken." He laughed, tying off the rope now the cross lay flat. He returned to the bench where an array of tools and instruments were neatly arranged. He picked up iron tongs, studied them a moment before replaced them, moving them slightly so they sat in the same position as before.

"Murder is murder," Thomas said. "It's impossible to hide everything. I will make it my business to uncover your crimes."

"Not crimes, sir, nor murder, either. I prefer to think of what I do as sacrifice. Sacrifice in pursuit of a higher purpose. To raise my subjects to glory." Mandana glanced at Adana. She had sought refuge in unconsciousness, her body hanging slack from its bindings.

"There's no glory in what you do."

Mandana picked up a pot of liquid and a quill, walked closer until he was leaning across Thomas. He stared at his chest, his arms and legs, then leaned closer still. He used the feathers of the quill to trace the scars that criss-crossed Thomas's body. Some old, others more recent. Each touch was a promise of the agony to come. A vibration settled deep inside Thomas, and he fought to relax. He would not give this man the satisfaction of seeing his fear.

"Where did these come from? A surgeon should not carry such marks on his body."

"I wasn't always a surgeon."

"And I wasn't always an abbot, or even a man of God." Mandana withdrew the quill and dipped it into the liquid, allowing the excess to drain from the tip before running it across Thomas's chest. Mandana drew a line at the shoulder.

"Where do you keep the beasts?" Thomas said.

"Close. They do not share our intelligence so require little preparation. You and the girl, however, must know of what is to come if you are to make your contribution. And this sacrifice..." Mandana stopped for a moment while he marked Thomas's thigh. He stared at his work then shook his head, took a cloth and wiped the ink away, drew a second line around the knee. "This sacrifice is the most important. Do you know what week this is?"

"Of course."

"Even though you don't share our religion?"

"How do you know I don't? I've prayed with you and the queen, remember."

"I saw through that pretence. You couldn't live among the infidel if you believed in the one true God." Mandana glanced at Adana, frowning. "This time it will be perfect."

"Why two?"

"Good question. Yes, a very good question." Mandana marked Thomas's other leg, then took his cloth and wetted it in a bowl of clean water and wiped the mark from his shoulder that he had drawn there earlier. He traced the feather side of the quill along Thomas's right arm, seeking the perfect spot. "Adam and Eve rising into man and woman, separating us from the beasts. Or Mary Magdalene and our Lord Jesus Christ rising into glory through pain. As you will rise into glory."

"You're insane."

Mandana looked at Thomas, his eyes rational, his expression one of interest. "Aren't all visionaries accused of being such until the world embraces their vision?"

"Your religion preaches peace."

"For now." Mandana glanced at Adana, his eyes tracking over her body, the hunger in them disgusting Thomas.

"Let her go. Keep me and let Adana go."

"I can't do that," said Mandana, his eyes continuing to devour Adana's perfection, and it almost sounded as if the sorrow in his voice was genuine. "You see, for this act of glorification I need two subjects. One male. One female. And look—that is exactly what I have."

"Find someone else then. She is too young. She won't understand the meaning of this. The true meaning."

Mandana turned back to Thomas. "And you do? You presume to understand?"

"Then help me understand." Thomas wasn't sure what he was trying to do, but any delay in the abbot's plan might give Jorge time to fetch help. If that was what he was doing, and wasn't still sleeping away the day as he had been.

Mandana sighed. He turned to the table and laid his tools down, making minute adjustments to each until they lay where he wanted them. Then he picked up a blade. It was of a kind familiar to Thomas, who had used identical instruments to operate with.

"I don't think there is enough time to make you understand what great glory you are going to attain. Besides, do you believe she is here by accident? I have been watching you and your friend and know all about his family. The harmony of taking her was too sweet to resist." Mandana stared at Thomas, a glittering joy showing in his eyes. "It is only a shame it is not he who will be here to hear her screams." He laid the blade on Thomas's skin. Not cutting. Not yet.

CHAPTER THIRTY

Thomas felt the pressure of the blade against his skin and waited.

"Don't I deserve to know why you are going to kill me?"

"Oh, a better question." Mandana lifted the blade and tapped the blunt side against his palm. "Yes, a very good question." He turned the blade over and drew it across his own hand, a bead of blood welling to follow it. Mandana's face contorted into a grimace which turned to ecstasy. "Oh, I wish I was you. To experience the pain you are about to embrace."

"I'll gladly exchange places."

Mandana closed his fist. Blood dripping from it to splash against the flagstones.

"If only that was possible." He cocked his head to one side. "And I expect you have the skills to do the work. But the belief? I'm afraid the belief is missing. So it will have to be you who dies." He stepped close and this time the blade cut into Thomas's leg.

He expected it to travel deep, picturing what this man was trying to accomplish, recalling the figure he had so briefly studied after it had been cut down from the city gate. Somewhere an animal was being prepared even as Mandana worked. Thomas knew how he would accomplish the task. A deep cut above the knee to expose the patella, which would be worked loose, then releasing the tendons at the back and sides. Finally an axe or other sharp instrument to break the bone. He wondered if he would still be conscious when that time came. Somehow he thought he would, that Mandana would ensure he was so he could experience every moment of agony.

But instead of slicing through muscle the blade only kissed his skin, releasing a thin line of blood which trickled down his leg.

"I see you feel the pain even though you try not to. Only a little yet—a promise of what is to come." Mandana shivered. "I wish I had thought to take a medical man before. You understand what I am going to do, which will make the agony all the sweeter."

Thomas glanced at Adana. She had woken and was listening, eyes wide. He hoped her threshold for pain was low enough she would find solace in oblivion sooner than he.

"She's not worthy of sacrifice."

Mandana considered the statement, the blood stained blade loose in his hand. "You're right, of course. But what choice do I have? There must be a woman as well as a man. And the symmetry is too perfect. The daughter of your friend's brother. The fruit of his loins—something your friend can never emulate."

"Someone older would be better."

"Oh, if only I could. Someone who has experienced the world. Someone like your friend's new lover. The duquessa would be perfect, wouldn't she?"

"You could take her if you wanted. If you invite her to the monastery she will come." Thomas was willing to sacrifice Esperanza if it meant Adana going free.

"I don't think so. Not now. Especially if the eunuch has really escaped and raised the alarm." Mandana's dreamy expression gave way to instant rage and he used the blade on Thomas's stomach where no guiding marks had been laid. He would have continued, cutting wildly, had a hammering at the barred door not stayed his hand.

Thomas risked a glance downwards. The pain was horrendous, but there appeared to be only two shallow slashes across his belly.

When he raised his eyes Mandana was staring at his handiwork, the rage still on his face making him look even more like his namesake the wolf. He tapped the blade up and down in his hand, and Thomas could see him coming to a decision.

There was a second knocking at the door, louder, and a muffled voice.

Mandana turned and dropped the blade on the bench.

They were left alone. Outside Thomas heard voices come and go, some calling out, and he imagined the search for Jorge continued. He didn't think he had been found yet otherwise there would be more noise. He was starting to doze in spite of the pain in his belly when a loud rattle made him lift his head. Mandana was returning.

A figure appeared in the shade of the doorway, and Thomas saw that beyond their prison the day would soon be ending. The last day of his life. When the figure entered Thomas writhed in his bindings and shouted, "Get out! Run!"

Instead Jorge walked further inside.

"Help us, Uncle Jorge," cried Adana. For a moment she too fought her ties, but the pain it brought was obvious on her face and she soon stopped.

"I'll cut you free," said Jorge.

"There are instruments on the table."

Jorge turned and saw where Thomas was indicating. He went to the bench and picked up two blades, short knives with sharp edges that caught the fiery light of the setting sun that filtered through the high window.

"If they catch you they'll kill you," Thomas said. "Get out now while you can and fetch help."

"I won't leave you this way."

"Leaving is the logical course."

Jorge shook his head as he approached Adana. "Not everything is logical, Thomas."

"You're convinced in this folly?"

"I can't leave you."

"Then free me first."

Jorge glanced at him, his eyes averted from the naked form of

Adana beside him.

"I'll be more use if anyone returns," Thomas said.

It might make sense, but he saw Jorge was going to ignore him as he turned away and began to saw at the bindings around Adana's ankles. The rope was thick, coarse, and although the blade was sharp it was slow work. Three coils of rope held her feet. Jorge cut through the first and was part way through the second when Thomas heard another sound.

"Quick, hide, they're coming back."

Jorge dropped the knife to clatter on the floor and spun around, looking for somewhere to conceal himself, but the room was a square with bare stone walls.

"Climb," Thomas hissed. "Climb fast!"

Jorge turned, turned again. Voices came from beyond the doorway, arguing. Thomas saw a corner where the mortar between the stone blocks had worked loose. It was the only possibility.

"There," he whispered, hoping Jorge could hear him, relieved when he ran to the spot and reached up, working his fingers deep between the stone. The voices fell silent. There came a scuffling and then the door banged shut and the bolt was thrown.

Jorge stopped climbing.

"Keep going," Thomas said.

"They've locked you in again."

"They're still there, I can hear them. Hide in the rafters, and when they've gone make your escape. Whatever you might witness, you have to get away."

Thomas could see Jorge move a foot downward, but as he did so the bolt on the door was thrown once more and he started to climb again. He was only half way up when Mandana entered, but fortunately the abbot had eyes only for Thomas, Adana, and his new captive.

Thomas tried not to look as Jorge kept going, but it was almost impossible until he saw him pull himself up and sit astride a beam beneath the roof.

The abbot came into the room and stopped. Beside him stood Pero, immobilised by the idiot monk.

CHAPTER THIRTY-ONE

"Look—a friend has come to plead on your behalf." Mandana spoke close to Thomas's ear, the smell of spices rich on his breath. His hair hung loose to brush against Thomas's cheek, the sensation far too intimate. "Should I take his life in exchange for yours?"

"Let Adana go," Thomas said, even though he knew the offer was false. None of them would be allowed to leave the chamber alive.

Mandana shook his head, disappointed in a star pupil who had turned against him. Thomas stared beyond to where Jorge perched on the rafter, splintered in shards of orange light that streamed through gaps in the roof. His face shone with sweat from the heat trapped beneath the tiles.

"We have already had this conversation. I told you my reasons why I can't let her go. I need one man and one woman. Nothing else will work." He ran a fingernail across Thomas's chest. "So—do you want to exchange places with the priest?"

"He'll be missed."

"As will you. The great Thomas Berrington, brought all this way to treat poor, sickly Prince Juan. You would both be sorely missed. Until the parade, at least. And then the whole world will witness the ecstasy of your rebirth."

High above them Jorge moved and Thomas tried not to stare, afraid Mandana would wonder what he was looking at.

"I am not afraid of pain," said Pero, his words cut short as the giant clasped a hand over his mouth.

"No, let him speak." Mandana waved a hand as he pulled up a three-legged stool and sat. His hand traced Thomas's skin once more, following the dark lines drawn there. "You understand what I am creating, don't you, Pero. You're a man who understands the joy of pain."

"There is no joy in it," spat Pero, his face contorted with anger. "I suffer that I may appreciate the sacrifice made by our saviour the lord Jesus Christ."

"Indeed. Yes, indeed." Mandana stood and walked to the bench, leaned over and studied the instruments before selecting one. "Of course you understand. I knew you of all men would. Hold him tight, Sebastian, let us see if he speaks true or not."

Pero writhed within the giant's grip but escape was impossible. Mandana came close, the blade raised, but instead of cutting at flesh he sliced away the ties closing Pero's robe. The coarse wool fell away and Sebastian helped until Pero's chest was bared, his skin grey with dirt.

"Turn him," ordered Mandana. He leaned forward to touch the scars covering Pero's back. "I see you use the flail often, but have you ever felt true pain? The pain that brings glory? The pain our Lord felt?" He glanced at the giant. "Turn him back and hold him tight now."

Mandana's hand shot out, knife flicking, and a deep gash opened in Pero's chest. The priest screamed as Mandana worked the blade beneath his flesh, using his fingers to pull it clear, cutting deeper until ribs showed.

"Why did you come here?" said Mandana. "How did you know Thomas was here?"

"A note," gasped Pero. "He left me a note."

Mandana reached out with the blade but did not cut again. He looked into Pero's eyes.

"Who did you tell?"

"No-one. I came directly I saw the note, hoping I would be in time." He glanced at Thomas, who saw that Pero had known about Mandana. He wondered how long he had known. And why he had not spoken.

"I don't believe you," said Mandana, and his blade flashed. Pero put his head back and screamed.

"Enough!" Thomas shouted. "Let him go."

"You know I cannot do that. He has seen too much. Besides, when I have finished the gates of heaven will be thrown wide to welcome him, as they are to all believers who die in great agony." He worked the blade again, cutting to reveal more ribs, slicing the flesh that lay between them.

"No!" Thomas said, seeing what the abbot intended.

"Oh, but yes." For a moment he stopped cutting. Blood poured down Pero's chest to pool at his feet, but it wasn't enough to kill him, not yet. "Do you feel it, my friend?" Mandana leaned as close as a lover, his lips almost on Pero's cheek. "Do you feel the glory of God within you? Does the pain not bring Him close?"

He examined Pero's ravaged body, then reached in again to expose his beating heart. Thomas had seen the sight many times and was always awed when he did. Except this time the patient was alive and fully aware of what was about to happen.

Mandana pushed a finger into the gap he had created and touched the beating organ. Pero gasped and jerked.

"It is good you don't scream. Feel the pain, my friend, embrace it."

He touched Pero's heart again, pressing harder this time.

Thomas knew of places that would stop the heart in an instant, others that could bring it back to life. Did Mandana know these places, too? He must. His skill with the blade showed knowledge of anatomy, and Thomas wondered if he had not studied the art of surgery as well as soldiering.

Mandana turned away to the bench, his hand scattering instruments until he found the one he sought. A strong pair of shears.

"Kill him," Thomas said. "But not this."

"He has to feel every moment," said Mandana, his voice exultant, eyes filled with the fire of madness. Without hesitation he thrust the shears into Pero's chest. The sinews in his arms stood out as he cut through one rib, then a second. He stepped back, examining his handiwork.

Pero's head lolled towards his chest. Mandana grabbed his hair and lifted his head. He smiled as Pero's eyes fluttered open.

"Good. I thought you might be dead. But I see you were only resting a moment so as to better appreciate your passage into glory."

Pero made a sound in his throat that might have been words, but if so they meant something only to him.

Mandana cut again, once more, then reached in and worked two entire ribs free of Pero's chest. The man's beating heart lay fully exposed.

"God's wonder," said Mandana, his voice almost inaudible.

Is this how it will be for me? Thomas saw the enjoyment the abbot took in his handiwork, and knew it would. There was no escaping the pain that was to come. His only hope was Adana would be too weak to take it and her heart would stop of its own accord. A wish he knew might be granted when he glanced across to discover she had fainted clean away at the horror presented.

There was a soft crunching sound, another rib, and Mandana giggled as Pero emitted a strangled scream.

"Yes—the pain is your only guarantee of heaven." He cut again then leaned close, examining Pero's eyes. He nodded. "I think you can release him, Sebastian. He is a danger to no-one now."

The giant held on a moment longer, but when Mandana lifted his shaggy head he let his hold loose and stepped back. Pero's knees buckled. Before he could fall Mandana caught him, his white robe already stained with the priest's blood. He looked around, searching for something. Thomas couldn't see what it was until Mandana barked an order and Sebastian went into a shadowed corner, returned dragging a third crucifix behind him.

"Set it up. You know how."

The giant nodded, grinning as he laid the cross flat against a post hole as though it weighed nothing.

Mandana draped Pero's body on the cross and quickly tied it, not bothering to make the bindings tight. They would not need to restrict him long. Then Sebastian heaved on a rope and the cross creaked as it rose to vertical, dropping into its hole with a soft thud which caused Pero to raise his head and scream again into the roof space.

Thomas had thought him dead, but when he looked closer he saw the man's heart still beating inside the opened ribcage.

Die. Why can't you die and end this suffering?

Even as the thought came to him he knew Pero was too strong, too stubborn. He had seen it on their journey from Gharnatah. Then it had been an annoyance. Now it was an agony.

Mandana pulled the stool close and sat, hands resting on his knees, eyes locked on Pero.

"Kill him," Thomas said. "For the love of God kill him!"

"I believe I already have. Now it is only a matter of waiting."

"You're the Devil."

Mandana glanced aside, a brief flick of his eyes before they returned to Pero. "No, I'm the opposite of the Devil. I do this for the glory of God, not against Him. To show my love of His son and the suffering He accepted on behalf of us all."

Pero tried to breathe, but the agony of his wounds together with the pressure on his arms was too much.

Thomas wanted to look away but couldn't, and he knew a part of him was fascinated. He had never seen a man die so clearly, never witnessed the last struggling efforts a heart makes as it stutters and comes to a halt. He was as mesmerised as Mandana. He risked a brief glance upwards. Jorge was still suspended above, his face slick with sweat as he too watched the priest approach the great divide.

Pero tried to draw air into his lungs one more time, agony on his face, but it was impossible, his body too damaged, the pain too great. Thomas saw the thick muscled walls of his heart stutter and stop. A moment passed then it beat again three times before stilling, this time forever. Pero's body finally relaxed, hanging loose from its ties.

Mandana released a deep sigh and shook his head.

"Satisfied?"

He looked at Thomas. "Not especially, no. There should have been more pain." A frown touched his grey brow. "Tell me, how do I maintain the pain without them fleeing from it? You're a physician, you must know."

Thomas said nothing, refusing to react to the man's madness.

Mandana turned and stared up at Pero. He reached out and placed a blood-stained hand over one of the priest's feet, resting it there as though some essence of the man might still remain. If he hadn't moved he would never have known about Jorge. But he did reach out, and such are the vagaries of chance.

When the drop of sweat splashed on Mandana's wrist he frowned and looked up. The frown deepened, and then he saw Jorge crouched amongst the rafters.

"Sebastian."

"Run, Jorge!" Thomas yelled.

The giant scrabbled at the walls, but he had gone to a different place to where Jorge had ascended and could gain no purchase. Mandana stood and scanned the chamber, knowing Jorge must have climbed somewhere.

"There!" He pointed, and Sebastian charged across the room and leapt into the air, landing a good five feet up the wall, his thick fingers seeking purchase and finding it.

"The roof," Thomas shouted. "Go through the roof."

Mandana ran to the bench where his instruments were still arrayed and picked up a knife. He threw it into the rafter space but his aim was poor and it clattered back down, barely missing Adana, who thankfully remained in a faint.

Above them Jorge rose, gripped a beam for balance and punched at the roof tiles above. He opened a gap and thrust his hand through, pulling tiles free. Some fell to shatter on the stone floor and he flung others at the climbing monk. They broke over his head and shoulders to no effect.

Jorge worked faster to widen the hole until he could push his arms and shoulders through. Thomas watched as his feet lifted from the beam, kicking as he pulled himself onto the roof. At the same time Sebastian reached across and grabbed the same beam and in a single motion swung himself out and around to straddle it. He squirmed fast along the beam but Jorge was already gone.

Sebastian stood, not bothering with his balance, and thrust himself straight through the gap Jorge had made. A muffled cry filtered down as he caught sight of his prey. He pulled himself up, more tiles clattering down, and then he was gone.

Thomas could see the progress of the chase by the tiles that broke and fell beneath their feet, but he couldn't tell if Sebastian was gaining or not. Jorge was big enough, but the monk was half as big again, and in the end it was his weight that tipped the scales against him.

Tiles cracked and tumbled, then a whole section of roof fell loose and Sebastian followed it through. His hand shot out and grasped at a beam, but his momentum was too great and his grip tore free. He fell twenty feet, the sound of his landing greeted by a scream.

Mandana bellowed a wordless curse and punched Thomas on the thigh before turning to run from the chamber.

Thomas looked around, breathing hard, as if it had been he who had been chased. Pero's body slumped in its bindings, a pool of blood beneath his feet. The priest had surprised Thomas at the end. After discovering Mandana's guilt and seeing Pero enter the torture chamber his first thought was that he and Mandana were in this thing together. Pero's love of the flail would have made sense in light of Mandana's fantasies. But instead the priest had come to rescue them.

"Adana!" Thomas shouted, but the girl didn't move. He watched for a moment until he saw her chest rise and fall. He didn't blame her for seeking refuge in unconsciousness. If he had an opportunity he would end her life to spare her the suffering that was to come. For himself he believed he could bear it. He had borne great pain in the past and it always ended, easier to accept in memory than in the doing. Except this time the end of the pain would mark the end of his life.

Unless Jorge managed to flee—and someone believed him.

The giant Sebastian rolled over, grunting unintelligible curses. Thomas thought he must have broken a leg at least, but the man was indestructible. He pulled himself to his feet and staggered out after his master.

CHAPTER THIRTY-TWO

"I don't understand why we've been laid flat," said Adana.

They were her first words in a long while and Thomas had begun to wonder if she had escaped once more into oblivion. If she had he couldn't blame her, but she needed to be alert if they were to have any chance of escape. Mandana had returned with three new monks an hour after Jorge's escape and they had wound the crucifixes down until they now lay on their backs. The exquisite pain in Thomas's arms and legs had eased, but his body still ached from the cuts and blows it had received, and he wondered what had become of Jorge. He took the fact he hadn't been dragged into the chamber as a good sign.

"They're afraid we might die if they leave us hanging for too long," he said.

Adana made a sound part disgust, part fear. "Why should they care?"

Thomas tried to decide how honest he could be with Adana. "It's four days until Easter Sunday. Mandana will want us alive until then."

"Why?"

"It makes his work easier." He rolled his head and stared at her. "Can you test your bindings? I think Jorge might have managed to cut through one."

"What's the point? We're going to die anyway."

"Not if we escape."

"Escape?" Her chest heaved as she sobbed. "How can we escape? I can't even move!"

"Stop it!" Thomas allowed some of his own fear into his voice. "Try to work your feet loose." He pulled at his own bindings but his own feet were locked solid. There was a little play at his wrists but not enough to slide a hand through. The ropes were thick, tied in multiple loops around the wooden cross-piece. The coarse hemp cut painfully into his flesh when he pulled.

"Even if I get my feet free what good will it do? I can't walk strapped to this thing."

"I'll think of something."

"If this is the best you can think of you're not as clever as Uncle Jorge told me you were." But this time he saw her flex her legs. She had delicate ankles and pale toes. She moved her hips from side to side, lifting each leg in turn.

Thomas watched as the movement put pressure on the rope. He saw the rough hemp fibres pull apart. He had been right—Jorge had almost cut through the second rope and in their haste the monks hadn't noticed.

"It's looser," said Adana, a hint of hope in her voice.

"I can see. Try drawing your right foot up, it looks as though it might slide through."

Adana's thigh muscles trembled as she tensed, but her foot remained caught.

"Not so hard," Thomas said. "When you pull that much your foot tightens up. Try to ease it loose, not force it."

Adana's breath came faster as she did her best to obey. Her foot moved further, then caught.

"Try again," Thomas said. "Use a different angle."

"What angle!"

"I don't know. A different one." He was wondering how long they had before Mandana or one of his monks returned. He had expected someone before now. Hopefully Jorge's escape was causing them problems.

"It's coming!" Adana pulled too hard and her foot caught. She took a deep breath and forced herself to relax. This time her right foot slid through the rope and emerged, a red mark circling her ankle. She twisted and drew her left foot after it.

"Can you reach the floor?" Thomas said.

She dropped her heels, one each side of the wooden upright, hunched her back.

"My feet are on stone. But I can't drag this thing an inch."

"You don't need to. The blade Jorge dropped is next to your left foot."

Adana reached out, her eyes widening when her toes touched cold metal. She moved her foot and dragged the knife closer.

"What should I do with it?"

"Can you get both legs down on the same side of the cross?"

"I think so." She lifted her right leg and swung it over. She hung awkwardly, both feet on the same side as the central post, her flank stretched so tight every rib showed.

"See if you can grip the knife between your feet." Thomas had no idea to what purpose, but trusted something would come to him. He wasn't ready to give in yet, and any activity was better than the cloying sense of hopelessness that was the alternative.

Adana knew what to do better than him. She gripped the blade between her soles and raised her legs. She grunted as she lifted them higher, twisting until her legs lay flat against her breasts. She arched sideways with the flexibility possessed only by the young. Even so Thomas saw where her spine chafed against the wooden upright and knew she must be in pain.

"I think I can reach," Adana said, strain in her voice. Thomas was awed she could accomplish such a feat.

Adana laid the sharp edge of the blade against the rope binding her right hand. Tendons stood out in her neck from the strain of holding her position. Slowly she flexed. Each time she did the blade moved a little against the rope. Sweat gathered on her pale skin and ran down to drip onto the floor. At one point she almost lost her grip on the knife. If she had it would have been irretrievable—there was no way she could have reached it—but she grunted and managed to grip the knife more securely. The brief movement appeared to give her renewed energy and she sawed harder. The rope began to part.

Thomas glanced away, listening. Other than Adana's gasps he heard nothing. Mandana might return at any time, but he had no idea when, and if he worried about it they would never do anything. Perhaps they would be left undisturbed until morning.

Directly above them the hole in the roof showed a darkening sky. Would Jorge have reached Qurtuba yet? And if he had, would anyone believe his story? Mandana was close to the king and queen, a powerful man with wide influence. Jorge would have to convince them of the abbot's guilt before action was taken.

Adana gave a sudden gasp and Thomas jerked around at the sound of the knife falling onto the stone floor. Despair welled in him, but Adana sat up, turning, her right hand free. She had dropped the knife in a final effort, but the rope was already cut.

She stood and picked up the fallen knife, sawed at the knots trapping her left hand. Progress was swifter, and after only a few minutes she stepped down from the cross, rubbing at her wrists. She turned sideways on to Thomas, covering her breasts and sex with her hands.

"I'm a physician, Adana, I've seen naked women before. Get the knife and cut me free."

"Not me you haven't," said Adana, but she knelt and retrieved the blade. "Close your eyes and turn your head away."

Thomas sighed and did as he was told. He felt movement against his right hand as she began to saw at his ropes, pleased she had started there and not his feet. With one hand free he could, if need be, remove the rest of his restraints himself.

He smelled the fear in her sweat and knew his own body must stink, too. He wondered if they could use the same escape route as Jorge, whether Adana was capable of the climb. He wasn't sure he could manage himself, not with the pain Mandana had inflicted.

There was a sting against his arm as the knife cut through the rope and he jerked his hand free.

"My feet, Adana," he said. "I'll untie the other hand."

She moved to the base of the crucifix. She had barely started sawing with the blade when the door opened with a crash and Mandana strode in accompanied by four monks, one of them the giant Sebastian who no longer limped.

Adana spun around, her face contorted. She leapt at the abbot, knife raised above her head. Mandana grabbed her wrist, wrapped his arm around her waist and held her squirming body tight against his.

Thomas redoubled his effort to free himself even as he saw their position was hopeless.

"If I'd known you were going to be so helpful I would have placed the knife in your hand myself, my dear. We have come to untie you. Temporarily, of course. We're returning to Cordoba—to your final resting place."

Thomas wondered could he fight Mandana and his monks if he was free, determined to try even if his body did feel like it had been tumbled in a barrel full of rocks. He tensed, waiting for his other hand to be set loose, but before they untied him one of the monks picked up a hammer and swung it. Thomas saw it coming but could do nothing to avoid the blow.

CHAPTER THIRTY-THREE

Thomas jolted awake as his body jarred. He rolled his head to one side as nausea flooded through him, swallowed hard as his stomach clenched and saliva filled his mouth.

"He's awake," said one of the monks. "Shall I hit him again?"

"No—he can't escape, and I need him alive until morning."

"Thomas!" It was Adana's voice.

The urge to vomit faded and he craned his head, trying to take in his surroundings. He was strapped to a wooden pallet with one monk ahead and another behind. Adana was on an identical pallet below. They were descending through a narrow tunnel carved out of rock, the only illumination coming from occasional torches wedged into cracks in the walls. The monks stumbled awkwardly down the steps, each movement setting off a host of agonies in Thomas's body.

"Gag her." Mandana's voice came from ahead, but however hard Thomas strained he couldn't see him.

The jostling stopped and he heard Adana struggle.

Then Mandana came into view as he ascended the steps.

He leaned over Thomas. "I don't need to gag you as well, do I?"

Thomas shook his head, wishing he hadn't as a new wave of nausea washed through him.

"Where are you taking us?"

"No questions," said Mandana, "Unless you want Sebastian to hit you again?" He backed away and a moment later the jostling agony started up once more.

Thomas drifted through a miasma of pain, only brought back to full awareness as the descent came to an end. His pallet was carried into a rough circular courtyard barred on one side by a tall wooden gate. To either side sheer rock walls rose. More torches burned here, and the quarter moon Thomas had seen the night before cast a pale light. He shivered, but whether from cold or fear he couldn't tell. Their options were running out, closing down one by one, each missed chance reducing their odds of escape.

Mandana huddled to one side, talking with two of the monks. The giant Sebastian stood passively, awaiting instruction. Another remained near Thomas and Adana, who was twisting her head in an attempt to loosen her gag. Their pallets lay side by side, almost touching, and Thomas reached out a fingertip, just managing to touch hers. She stopped struggling and turned to look at him, fear and anger showing equally in her eyes.

"Relax," he whispered, hoping she could hear him. "We will need our strength later."

Adana's eyes widened in a question and Thomas nodded.

"If they make a mistake I'm going to try to escape. If I can't free you too, don't panic. I'll come back for you, I promise."

She gave a nod, her eyes lifting as Mandana came across to them.

He knelt beside Thomas and checked the ropes binding him. Across the courtyard one of the monks he had been talking with unbarred the gate and went through.

"Are you thirsty? Would you like water?"

After what the man had done to them Thomas couldn't believe what he was hearing, but nodded. Any opportunity to break routine. He expected the monks to lift the pallet so he could drink. Instead Mandana went to a small opening hacked into the cliff face and returned with a stone jug. He knelt again and tipped the jug, pouring a line of water directly onto Thomas's mouth and nose.

Thomas rocked his head in an attempt to avoid the water. This was nothing but more torture. His lungs burned, and when he was finally forced to take a breath he choked, coughing water back up.

Mandana stopped and moved across to Adana. He repeated the exercise, but this time the water fell on her gag and she writhed in her bindings, her back arching.

"Stop it!" Thomas barked.

Mandana turned. "You want me to empty the entire jug on you instead?"

Thomas glared at him.

"No, I thought not."

"Yes," Thomas said.

Mandana grinned, looking even more like his namesake, his yellow teeth long, feral.

"In that case…" He turned back and began to pour the water slowly, an expert at prolonging the agony.

Thomas was tempted to simply open his mouth and breathe the water in, to end the torment, but knew Mandana was too clever to allow that. Besides, small as the chances were, there might still come an opportunity for escape.

Mandana emptied the jug and rose. He walked back to the alcove, no doubt to refill it, but was interrupted as the gates were flung wide. The monk returned leading two mules drawing a cart. Mandana dropped the jug to shatter on the ground.

"Put this one on first. And check his ropes again. Then the girl."

The monks lifted Thomas's pallet and dropped it on the back of the cart. They pushed until he was hard up against the side then returned for Adana. Thomas tested his bindings and found them firm. But there was a long journey to Qurtuba yet.

As the monks knelt to lift Adana a figure appeared in the tunnel. The monks were turned away and didn't see as Jorge came to stand inside the doorway and take in the scene. *Damn the man,* Thomas thought, *why hadn't he run?* He knew Jorge wasn't capable of fighting these men.

Jorge stayed where he was, almost hidden in the darkness of the doorway. His head turned, seeking something.

The monks lifted Adana and carried her towards the cart. She was dropped on and pushed up until her pallet lay tight against Thomas's. Mandana drew Sebastian and the others to him. Thomas couldn't hear their words, but Mandana gestured into the tunnel. They weren't ready to leave yet. He watched as the man with the scarred face, the monk who had kidnapped Adana, disappeared into the tunnel. There was no sign of Jorge.

Thomas reached once more for Adana's hand, but instead of offering some measure of comfort his fingers sought and pulled at the rope binding her. She turned her head at his touch, her eyes going wide.

"I'm going to try and loosen your hand," he whispered. "If I can get it free reach across and do the same for me. Don't try to untie yourself until you've released me." He knew if he could get free they might still have a chance.

Adana nodded as he tugged at her bindings, a welling of emotion rising within him at her courage. The rope was badly tied, a rushed job, and her hand came free easily. He glanced at the dark entrance of the tunnel as Adana reached up and loosened her gag before starting to pull at his own ties. He wondered how long the monk would be away on his errand.

Mandana approached the cart and Adana fell still. Thomas turned his hand to cover where she had begun to loosen one knot.

"Perhaps I should untie you both when we get to Cordoba," he said, "and let you enjoy a final night of passion."

"She is fifteen," Thomas said.

"Age has nothing to do with it—she is a fallen woman. You know I only ever take fallen women. They infect this city—too many of them to count. There is never a shortage for my work." Mandana's hand reached out and stroked Adana's arm, rested briefly on her breast, and Thomas saw something flare in his eyes. Adana twisted from the touch and Mandana laughed, turning away. "Yes—I think I should release you both and see how long the lauded Thomas Berrington can resist temptation."

Thomas bit down on a reply. He wanted Mandana to move away. As soon as the abbot's back was turned he felt Adana's touch return. He had no idea how long the monk would take so lay tense as Adana's fingers worked. When he flexed his wrist he found the rope looser.

"Don't do that," Adana whispered, "it tightens the knots."

Thomas took a breath and forced himself to still.

A crashing sound came from within the tunnel. One of the monks laughed and went to the entrance, called inside for the man to be more careful.

Adana's touch continued its work.

"Try now," she said, her voice barely above the sigh of a breeze.

Thomas flexed his wrist. He was still tied to the pallet, but when he pulled, his hand came loose of the rope. He moved slowly, reached over and untied his other hand, then lifted his head and gazed down at his body marked with ink and scars.

"Keep watch while I free my legs," he said.

He waited a moment then sat up and leaned over, knowing if anyone turned towards them he would be caught. He worked as quickly as he could. He had almost freed one ankle when he heard Adana gasp.

The monk had returned carrying a heavy box. He dropped it to the ground, the sound of metal coming from within. He had gone back for Mandana's instruments of torture.

Sebastian knelt and picked the box up in one hand as if it weighed nothing. When he turned to the cart a bellow erupted from him. He dropped the box, scattering knives and pincers and cleavers across the ground as he started to run. Thomas worked frantically, but he knew he hadn't enough time to free his last leg. Despair flooded him.

It was then the returning monk drew a sword and swung at Mandana. The lunge was wild and whistled through the air half a foot in front of the abbot's chest.

Thomas cursed Jorge for not taking his training more seriously. The man could wield a blade now but totally lacked any killer instinct. At least Mandana's shout halted Sebastian, who skidded to a halt and turned back to protect his master. Thomas gave up all pretence at concealment and tore at his bindings.

He strained, pulling his foot through the loosened ropes,

tearing skin away. He knelt and watched Mandana and the three monks circling Jorge.

"Untie me!" Adana pleaded.

Thomas looked down at her, back towards Jorge, who was surprisingly holding his own. His blade work had improved since he and Thomas had taken lessons with Olaf, the Sultan's general, and it was obvious the monks thought him more skilled than he was. It was also obvious Sebastian had forgotten all about Thomas.

He slid from the back of the cart and padded across to where the giant monk had dropped the box.

"Finish him!" Mandana shouted, urging his men forward while remaining at a safe distance himself.

Thomas picked up a knife and returned to the cart. He sliced through Adana's ropes and lifted her down. Instead of turning and running through the open gate as Thomas expected, she darted to the scattered instruments and also picked up a knife.

"Help him," she pleaded. "Help Uncle Jorge."

Her voice was too loud and Thomas saw Jorge react to the sound of his name. His head turned at the distraction and he saw them crouching next to the cart. He waved a hand at them, his meaning obvious. Run.

The others had heard Adana, too. Thomas turned to them ready to fight, took a step and stopped.

"Sebastian—kill him. You two with me, now." Mandana drew a sword from his waist and walked purposefully towards the pair of them.

Thomas pushed Adana behind him but she resisted, her face set in a snarl, all her fear at the hands of Manadana coming out in a rush of wild anger.

Mandana's sword came down and Thomas ducked, deflecting the blow with his knife. He wasn't afraid—not yet. The abbot was a poor soldier, as generals often are, but the other two were more skilled.

Beyond the attackers Thomas saw Sebastian lunge at Jorge and cursed. Damn the man, why couldn't he just kill the monk? Instead he was trying to wound him. Sebastian simply ignored the gash to his arm and clasped his arms around Jorge, lifting his feet clear of the ground.

"Run, Thomas!" Jorge yelled. "Save her!"

Thomas feinted left as a monk came at him. He heard the blade of a sword hiss close to his ear and rolled aside. He dropped the knife and grabbed a cleaver in his right hand, a longer blade in his left. When he came to his feet the other monk was running at him. Thomas lowered his shoulder and lifted the man into the air, his knife slashing upward to meet resistance. He ignored the thrown man and feinted at the other. Mandana had fallen back, shifting his attention between Thomas and Jorge.

Sebastian began to walk into the mouth of the tunnel, Jorge gripped in his arms.

Thomas moved left, seeing the change in Mandana's expression, but he was too late. Mandana turned and ran after Sebastian and the heavy wooden door crashed shut. Seeing his master flee the remaining monk turned and tried to follow, but the door had been locked from inside.

Thomas approached him, stopping long enough to pick up the sword of the man he had tossed over his back, who now lay unconscious. He swung the sword lazily, circling, watching for an attack. Instead the monk threw his sword aside and sprinted for the gate. Thomas darted at him but couldn't move as fast barefoot on the stony ground.

All at once only he and Adana remained on their feet.

Thomas kicked the monk on the ground. When there was no response he rolled him over and stripped him of his robe. There were no clothes beneath other than a stained loincloth and Thomas decided he didn't need that bad enough to steal it. He tossed the robe to Adana who wrapped it around herself. It was far too big and dragged on the ground when she walked.

Thomas searched the cart. Beneath the seat that ran across the front he found a compartment with a blanket inside. He drew it out and pulled it around himself. Then he offered his hand down to Adana. She looked up at him, her face suddenly collapsing into tears she had held in check until that moment.

"What will happen to Uncle Jorge?" Her voice trembled between gasps.

Thomas lifted her bodily and set her on the seat. He urged the mules forward. The cart creaked as it passed through the gate and along a path which turned to lead down to the valley floor.

Thomas didn't bother with a reply. They both knew what was going to happen, although he did wonder where Mandana was going to find another female. Their only hope was to return to the city and try to find the place Mandana used for the final act of his mad entertainment.

CHAPTER THIRTY-FOUR

Thomas stood in a side-alley, jostled by crowds, half-deafened from the noise. Out on the main roadway soldiers marched past. Some blew trumpets while others beat drums, a cacophony of different rhythms and melodies filling the air. Even without their efforts the noise was overwhelming—a thousand voices all trying to be heard. Cheers rose in waves as pasos decorated with gold, their carvings ornate, moved through the streets carried on the shoulders of costaleros. The penitents moved past in groups dressed in nazareno robes, heads covered by long pointed capirote.

A woman jostled against Thomas and something pressed into his ribs. He jerked sideways, knocking into a man who pushed back. Thomas looked about, seeking refuge from the stink of those around him, but there was none.

He turned in the other direction and saw Daniel leaning against Adana. They had both told her to stay at home but she was insistent. Uncle Jorge had saved her life, she'd said. She couldn't abandon him.

They had spent the night searching for sign of him, resting briefly at dawn for Zanita to bandage Thomas's arm where he had been caught by a knife, and for Adana to bathe. She'd wanted to scrub off the blue markings where she would have been cut.

Daniel had wanted to inform the authorities but Thomas urged patience. Abbot Mandana was respected, a well connected member of the clergy, and Thomas knew how slowly and stubbornly the Hermandad operated. Going to Isabel and Fernando would take even longer. Thomas had roused Lawrence but the float that had been in the courtyard of the Church of San Bartolomu was gone. So they had come into the heart of the city where chaos reigned, because this was where the float was destined. A cold dread told Thomas that by the time the pasos arrived it would be too late for Jorge.

Adana leaned against the wall while her father's bulk protected her from the crowd.

"Can you remember what Mandana said?" Thomas leaned close to her. He needed sleep badly, they all did, but none would be taken until they found Jorge.

"You thought we were going to be changed on Sunday, but at the end, in the courtyard, he said he wanted us alive for today." Adana grimaced. "They call him the wolf. He looks like a wolf, but he's even more so inside. He's a cold-blooded hunter."

"What did he mean—changed?" asked Daniel.

Adana gazed at her father. She appeared to have grown ten years in maturity since being taken.

"Just like the others. We had been marked. He ... he wanted to keep us alive for today." She began to weep, bowing her head until hair covered her face. "He's dead, isn't he? Uncle Jorge's dead."

"No, he's not dead." Thomas's voice was louder than he intended, loud enough to convince himself, although the analytical part of his mind knew the truth. Jorge would have been transformed, and nobody could live through that.

A hand lay on his arm and Thomas shook it off.

"Where will they have taken him?" said Daniel. "We've already searched the church. You said you were sure it was where the victims were taken at the end."

"There are a hundred places he could be. We're better off looking for Mandana. He'll need to be part of the parade, and Jorge will be close by."

"What if he's running as we speak? He must know he'll be found out."

Thomas shook his head. They had already been through this. "He won't run. His arrogance won't let him. Power protects power, and Mandana's a powerful man. Powerful enough, he believes, to be above the law. He'll be here somewhere."

"With his pasos," said Adana, her voice barely audible.

"Yes, most likely. If he's in the city he'll have to be here."

Which is why they waited in a side street as other floats passed, the sack men holding them on their shoulders, staggering beneath the colossal weight of each. They had discussed splitting up and decided against it. If they found Mandana and there was any chance of freeing Jorge they would need to be together. Even if Jorge was already dead Thomas was ready to take vengeance. Daniel had provided him with a fresh sword. He wore it beneath the monk's robe he had taken from Adana when they returned, using it as some kind of disguise.

He climbed onto a ledge so he could gaze over the heads of the crowd. With the advantage of height he was able to see a new pasos approaching.

The penitents came first, some carrying crosses on their shoulders. This group's robes were dark blue, pointed scarlet capirote covering their faces and extending into points at least a foot above their heads. The crowd cheered, their voices mixing with drum and trumpet. Some scattered flower petals, others reeds. Thomas was almost dislodged from his perch as the crowd surged forwards.

The pasos came into sight. It was smaller than some, the wooden sides covered in gold leaf which had worn through in places. Atop the platform was a carved Christ carrying his own cross. Behind stood a Roman soldier, a short sword threatening. A statue of Mary Magdalene knelt beside the tortured figure.

It was only one more pasos, not the one they sought. If the one they sought even existed and wasn't a figment of Thomas's exhausted mind.

The noise rose to a crescendo, but once the pasos had moved

on the crowd relaxed, falling back. Food and water was passed around. In a few places some drank ale and wine, but most were too in awe of the religious ceremony to risk the wrath of their God.

Thomas dropped down and pushed his way through the throng to Daniel. The man looked almost as bad as Thomas felt, his face sweat-beaded and pale.

The noise of the crowd began to rise again. The three of them had been here since an hour after dawn and now it was mid-afternoon. The heat of the day lay oppressive across the city and Thomas knew the costaleros would be suffering beneath their burdens. He was sweating heavily beneath his monk's robe but couldn't remove it otherwise the sword strapped beneath would be visible. Daniel was also armed. Even Adana carried a small knife.

Thomas drew away, forcing himself through the crowd. People pushed back, some with angry words, but he ignored them all and when they caught sight of his face their objections faded to nothing. He pushed his way to the street, glanced behind and saw Daniel raise his head, his eyes tracking Thomas.

The next pasos was still hidden beyond a cross-street but the cheering of the crowd was ecstatic. White robed penitents led the way, some with crosses on their backs, others with them raised. Drums rattled and voices chanted prayers.

The front of the pasos appeared, moving slowly, swaying from side to side as the costaleros took tiny steps. It was another Christ and Magdalene and Roman soldier, but this time the cross was raised and a figure hung from it. Thomas pushed forward, trying to get closer because there was something different here.

It was the female figure who gave him confirmation. She knelt beside the cross, one arm extended, the rest of her body obscured beneath a silk robe that puddled the bed of the cart. Someone had nailed her hand to the wooden upright to prevent it falling free. As Thomas pushed closer still, forcing people aside, he saw her face was pale, bloodless, eyes open and staring. It was a face he recognised, one that told him how much Mandana knew about what went on in the palace. The figure was no carving—this was a real woman, Esperanza's life stolen away in order to make the tableau. In Mandana's twisted mind she was no more than another fallen woman.

When Thomas looked up he saw Jorge tied to the cross. Nails punctured his palms, trailing blood that dripped onto the wooden platform. Thomas reached his arm out, straining for the pasos, but the crowd was too dense. He turned his head, looking for help, saw Daniel barging his way through the crowd, figures scattering as he tossed them aside. When Daniel reached him he closed his hands around Thomas's waist and tossed him into the air. Thomas staggered as his foot caught the side of the pasos, reached out and tumbled onto the wooden boards. Which was when the figure of the Roman soldier swung his sword.

Thomas jerked aside, then his own blade was in his hand, clashing with the soldier's. Voices screamed, others cheered, thinking this was all part of the ceremony. As some people retreated Daniel pushed himself through and got a hand to the side of the pasos. One of the sack men tried to push him away but Daniel swung out and knocked the man to his knees. His sword came free even as he pulled himself up to join Thomas, who turned away, confident Daniel could hold the attacker at bay.

He drew a dagger and used the short blade on the rope tying Jorge's feet, ignoring the fight going on a yard away. If Daniel was defeated he would do something about it then.

The crowd was finally starting to work out something untoward was happening, but there was confusion. A gap opened as some of the costaleros deserted their positions and ran off. The pasos began to tilt.

Thomas pulled himself up the cross and hacked at the bindings on Jorge's left arm. They came free and he grasped Jorge's hand and jerked, pulling it free of the nail.

Jorge raised his head and screamed.

Thomas almost tumbled from the bed of the float. When he looked up Jorge was staring at him, blood coating his face from the crown of thorns wrapped around his brow. His left arm hung limp, dripping blood along his thigh.

"The other hand," gasped Jorge, and Thomas scrambled back up the cross. He slashed at the rope. This time Jorge pulled his own hand free, the nail sliding through his palm.

Thomas gripped Jorge as he fell, helped him down and laid him flat on the bed of the pasos. Daniel was still fighting with the Roman soldier. Thomas stared at Jorge a moment then turned and drew his own sword. With nowhere else to go the soldier leapt from the rear of the platform and ran off through the crowd, but not before Thomas recognised him as one of the monks from the previous night.

It was then the pasos tipped hard to one side and hit the ground, throwing them to the roadway. The body of Esperanza tumbled across the cobbles, her clothes falling open to reveal a calf's leg stitched against her hip. One arm remained human but the other was the foreleg of a wolf.

Oh, he grows brave, Thomas thought. *Brave or foolish.*

"Bonebreaker!" The word rippled through the crowd, which had formed a circle around them, a barrier to escape. Thomas got to his knees and tried to lift Jorge.

"Can you stand?"

"I don't think so. My feet..."

Daniel pushed his way through the crowd, grasped Jorge and lifted him without effort.

"Always the big brother," said Jorge without opening his eyes.

"Where is Mandana?" Thomas asked.

Jorge shook his head. Thomas reached out and squeezed his injured hand.

"I don't know, damn you," said Jorge, his voice barely audible. "Get me out of here."

Thomas looked around. The crowd was overcoming its shock. Already the sack men were returning, lifting the despoiled pesos to their shoulders. The remains of the parade was piling up behind and they had no option but to continue on, although what the remainder of the onlookers would think of an empty cross would prove interesting.

Daniel barged his way through, the crowd parting as if he

carried the plague. Thomas followed in his wake, but before they could reach the relative safety of the side street a clatter of hooves sounded and a voice commanded them to stop.

Daniel pushed on while Thomas turned to defend him. Fernando, King of Aragon and Castile, spurred his horse closer, pushing against the crowd.

"What blasphemy is this? Who dares disrupt the holy parade?" The king scowled as he took in the figures before him. Thomas knew exactly how they must look; him dressed as a monk, Jorge naked but for a loincloth, a crown of thorns around his head and blood trailing across his skin.

"No blasphemy is intended," Thomas said. "I need to speak with you in private, Your Grace."

"You would speak with me? Who are you to speak with the king?"

Thomas realised Fernando didn't recognise him in the monk's habit. He threw the hood back.

"I am—"

"Thomas!" The queen had arrived to join her husband. By convention they would follow at the end of the parade, accepting accolades from the crowd, dispensing small favours, coins and food. She slid from her saddle and rushed across, not to Thomas but to Jorge. Her hand came out, trembling, but did not touch him. "Dear God in heaven, what has become of him?"

"There is much you need to know, Your Grace. Things I cannot speak of here."

She took command, as she had so many times before. A pallet was brought from somewhere and Jorge laid on it. His eyes stared up at the sky, a deep, cloudless blue framed between buildings, and Thomas watched his friend let go and drift into darkness. Then the world spun around him, turning grey, and his knees gave way and he crashed to the ground.

CHAPTER THIRTY-FIVE

When Thomas woke he found himself in the bed he had hardly used, in the room assigned to Jorge and himself. His body ached and his skin burned where Mandana had cut him, but he knew none of his injuries were serious.

Thomas lifted the linen sheet and looked down at himself. There were a few new scars to join those he already possessed. No matter. He saw he was naked and washed, and wondered who had done that for him.

The answer came as the door opened and Sancha entered, carrying a bowl from which steam rose. Theresa followed with a tray. She set it down on a table and went out, returning with a second tray on which sat fruit and a bowl of something hot. Bread rested on a small side plate. She closed the door behind her as Sancha stripped the sheet from his body.

Thomas covered his groin but she only laughed.

"We have already seen all of you, Thomas Berrington." Her eyes twinkled. "And washed every inch of your body, as you have taught us. Now we are here to wash you again. It was you who said a body must be kept clean if it is to avoid infection."

"I can wash myself," he said, trying to pull the sheet up, but Sancha gripped it tight and he was still too weak to fight her. He sighed and laid against the bed. "All right, do as you will. Where is Jorge? Does he still live?"

"He is cared for close by. The queen had us dress his wounds but refuses any other doctor access. She says you must go to him when you wake."

Thomas dropped his legs over the side of the bed, uncaring for his nakedness. Sancha put her hand on his chest and pushed him back.

"You're not strong enough."

"I have to be strong enough," Thomas said, resisting the pressure. He stood and brushed past her, searching for clothes. "And the prince? Is he recovering?"

"He grows stronger every day. He asks after you. I think he trusts you now. Where have you been? And what have you been doing to yourself?"

"How long have I slept?"

"A whole day and more. It's Easter Sunday, close to dawn. The queen has been to visit. She sat with you for a time, but there are other matters she needs to attend to."

"Mandana," Thomas said.

"No," said Sancha. "Your heathen prince is taking up all the queen's time. The nobles argue endlessly over his fate. What is it you want to know about Abbot Mandana?"

"It was he who did this to me and Jorge. He kidnapped Esperanza and killed her." Thomas found his clothes. They had been washed and pressed. He pulled them on, ignoring the looks of Sancha and Theresa. "I need to see the king and queen, but first I need to see Jorge."

"She'll be here soon enough to visit you. Wait until then. Come back to bed, you need to rest and get strong."

He made his way towards the door, determined to find Jorge even if they refused to help. Agony flared through his feet and legs. He rested a moment, leaning against the back of a chair, then started up again. He was still a yard from the door when it opened and the short figure of Queen Isabel entered, waving her guards to remain outside.

She was looking at the bed and did not see him at first, turning in surprise. The look of shock and fear on her face led Thomas to believe she thought herself in danger, and he raised a hand to calm her as she recognised him.

"Cousin—you should be in your bed."

"We have to talk."

"You can talk from your bed. Here." She put her arm out. "Lean on me."

"I can manage, Your Grace."

"I have told you not to call me that."

"But you are a queen, and I am not even a citizen of Spain."

"You healed my son. His leg is straight and strong." She looked down at his bare feet where bruises showed. "He is perhaps even stronger than you. What is it you want to talk of? Your capture and torture? Do you know who did this to you?"

Thomas took a moment to catch his breath, annoyed at his weakness. Now the moment for accusation had come he felt a strange reluctance. He wanted time to think of how to tell the queen of Mandana's betrayal.

"I must go to Jorge, Your Grace."

She stared at him a moment before nodding. "Very well. Come to me afterwards. Come as soon as you can."

Thomas entered the room next to his. He stood in the doorway watching his friend. In repose Jorge's face had relaxed into a grace Thomas had feared he might never see again. It had been the hardest thing he had ever done to abandon him at the monastery, but had he not he knew most likely all three of them, he, Jorge and Adana, would now be dead.

He crossed the room, silent on bare feet, and drew a chair to the side of the bed. The scraping of wood on wood made Jorge mumble and open his eyes.

"You got away, then. Adana, too?"

Thomas nodded. "Don't you remember your rescue?"

Jorge shook his head, winced at a pain. "I remember nothing after he nailed me to the cross."

"Was it bad?"

Jorge stared at him for a while. "You know what it was like. You were both subject to his madness far longer than I was."

"And Esperanza?"

Jorge closed his eyes but tears forced their way past his lids. He spoke without opening them. "Her screams were terrible. I've never heard such a thing. I thought the sound of them would kill me before they did her."

"Mandana knew," Thomas said.

"The whole palace knew. He took her deliberately. A thousand women in this city he could have taken but he went for her. Even worse—" He broke off, but the memory too painful, forced himself to continue. "She walked in with him." His face convulsed with emotion. "He found her and told her I was injured. She came willingly, all the way into the room until it was too late. If I hadn't allowed myself to be seduced she would be alive now. I killed her, not Mandana. I did."

"You know that's not true."

"Has he been caught?"

"Nobody's looking for him yet. I go from here to the queen to try and persuade her of his guilt."

Jorge opened his eyes. "His guilt? Isn't it clear for all to see?"

"There are no witnesses," Thomas said. "It is our word against his. He could claim we have a vendetta against him. We are infidels, after all. Why would anyone believe us above one of their own?"

Jorge tried to sit up. "He can't be allowed to escape. Adana will testify."

"A girl? Who lives outside the city walls? No. But he won't escape. Even if the palace won't believe him guilty you and I know the truth. If nothing is done I will kill him myself."

Jorge stared at Thomas. "And I will help you."

Thomas shook his head. "I do it alone. I saw you at the

monastery, Jorge. You're no killer. Even with Adana in danger you couldn't bring yourself to strike the fatal blow."

"That was before he made me watch what he did to Esperanza. He had one of his men hold my eyes open so I was forced to witness every moment. The pain he put her through. I didn't think a body could take so much pain."

Thomas thought of Pero and the manner of his death. Yes—a body could take all manner of abuse and still fight to stay alive. He reached out and took Jorge's hand, held it while the man wept. When he could put the moment off no longer he released his grasp and drew down the sheet to examine his friend. Jorge lay with his eyes tight shut, and Thomas didn't know if he felt his examination or not.

Thomas found the queen with her son. Juan slept, his colour better than the last time Thomas had seen him. The room was warm, logs burning in the fireplace, filling the air with a sweet scent.

She turned as he crossed to her side. "How is your friend?"

"He will live. I need to tell you about what happened."

She released Juan's hand and stood, walked to stand in front of the fire.

"You were right. That man we executed wasn't the bonebreaker." She turned her head to look at him. "Do you know now who it is?"

Thomas nodded.

"Are you going to tell me?"

"I'm trying to decide whether you'll believe me."

"It is someone I know?"

"Someone close to you." He looked into her eyes, saw determination there. Yes, she was strong enough. *Am I,* he wondered? "The bonebreaker is Abbot Mandana, Your Grace."

She raised a hand as if to fend off a blow, took a step sideways, the tap of her feet sharp on the wooden floor.

"Who else accuses him?"

"Jorge, Your Grace. And a smith's daughter, Jorge's niece. You need to fetch Mandana in and confront him with the truth. Look into his eyes when he is accused."

She let her breath out in a long sigh. "I—" She shook her head. "Yes, I should. I will send a message for him to come." Her gaze met Thomas's. "But if he truly is the killer arresting him may prove difficult. He has many allies. And he is a respected member of the church. If there is one thing in this land I cannot go against it is the power of the church. I would not want to."

"If you can do nothing then I will have to kill him myself," Thomas said. He wanted her to know he was willing to do so.

"And be accused of murder in turn? No, I would not have you executed, and I doubt I could pardon you, not from that crime. Let me bring him before us and ask him to his face. You can be there if you wish but must say nothing. Your presence alone might be enough, but…"

"You know it won't be."

She firmed her stance and stared up at him. "I cannot accuse the man without clear proof. It is, as you say, the word of two strangers and a girl against one of the most powerful men in this land."

Thomas sighed and pushed the hair away from his face. "Then you know what I must do, Your Grace."

She stepped close and beat at his chest with her hands.

Thomas allowed her to continue then grasped her wrists. "He will be wary, Your Grace, and afraid of who knows. You have time to send someone to the monastery. There is one room there where they will find evidence. Likely there is more. And there are bones in the soil. I will take them and—"

"You will not!" She snatched her hands from his grip and turned away. "You cannot be seen to be involved or you will be in danger, too. Everyone you know will be in danger. I must talk with my husband, and the Hermandad, and…" She put her hands to her head. "To everyone I can. And I will have to be careful, too."

Thomas knew there was nothing more he could do. He understood the queen's reasons even if he disagreed with them. Perhaps letting Mandana think he had gotten away with murder would make him over-confident. Although he knew the abbot could not allow him to live. There would be some accusation, some falsehood spoken which would put both him and Jorge in peril.

CHAPTER THIRTY-SIX

It was late as Thomas made his way toward Prince Juan's room, knowing the queen would not be there. For the last ten days she had been at pains to avoid him and, once he accepted her reasons, he her. Her innate sense of justice made it difficult for her to be in his presence while Mandana continued to walk free, but there was nothing she could do to prevent it. The accusation against him was well known throughout the palace, but the church had closed ranks. Some refused to believe him guilty of anything, others believed him justified in his acts, helped by the fact all his victims except the last were prostitutes. At the start the queen had tried to explain the convoluted politics involved, but all Thomas asked was when would the man be punished. In the end she had stopped visiting Juan if she knew Thomas would be there. He in turn had learned when she was likely to be with the prince and adjusted his own routine accordingly.

As he turned a corner, head down, deep in thought, he didn't see the two men ahead of him until he almost walked into them. He drew up short, an apology on his lips. Then he saw who one of them was.

Abbot Mandana stood in pristine robes, an expression of amusement on his face.

"Ah—the sorcerer. I was only telling my friend of your exploits. I trust you are fully recovered from your injuries?"

A dozen responses flashed through Thomas's mind, none of them appropriate. It was two weeks since he had informed the queen of the events that occurred at the monastery, but here stood Mandana, still walking free. His influence was spread too wide and too deeply into the royal court and church for him to be openly accused.

"What, lost your tongue?" Mandana grinned. Thomas glanced at his companion but did not recognise him.

"I have nothing to say to you." Thomas went to push past but Mandana's hand came out and stopped him. Thomas grasped his wrist and twisted, pulling him close so he could whisper in his ear. A faint tang of burning clung to the abbot. "I am not your prisoner now, sir, and do not think me without claws of my own. You may think you've gotten away with your deeds, but you will answer to me one of these days." He released the abbot and pushed him away, walking fast to stop himself striking out. He heard the pair's voices behind him and Mandana's laugh.

Thomas had taken care not to be anywhere near the abbot since his return to the palace, and had warned Jorge to stay away from him, too. It had been a difficult conversation and continued to be so. Thomas understood why. He had suffered himself, but Jorge had lost the woman he claimed to love. His friend still asked every day when they were going to kill Mandana.

Thoughts of Jorge calmed Thomas's anger and after a moment he smiled. Yes, the time for revenge would come, and in the meantime it was good that Jorge spent most of his time with his new family. He had even tried turning his hand to a little smithing, which amused Daniel greatly.

Around him the palace slept fitfully, beyond its walls the city, too. An unusual heat even for Spain had plagued the city the past week, but today brought signs of relief. Dark clouds gathered to the north and an occasional rumble of thunder rolled across the land. Warm air and cool rain fought a battle, the victor as yet undecided.

Thomas found Sancha slumped half-asleep in a chair, but she rose as Thomas entered and came across to him. He scowled at the knowing look in her eyes, the soft curve of her lips. She had offered herself to him the night before and he had almost succumbed. The thought of her soft body pressed against his had grown increasingly seductive. Tonight he had come to the room with the intention of making good on her offer. His encounter with Mandana had only served to sharpen his arousal.

He was pleased the queen was not present. She came to Juan's room less frequently as the boy improved, and Thomas was sure part of the reason was to avoid him. Each time she came he asked for a progress report, and each time her reply was the same. Politics. Discussions are taking place. The church does not believe Mandana guilty of such crimes and they were questioning Thomas's tale. At least no more women had gone missing, and Thomas wondered if Mandana had stopped for good, or only for now.

Juan roused and sat up as he approached, and Thomas was glad for the distraction from his thoughts.

"How are you, Juan?" Thomas sat on the edge of the bed and laid his hand on the prince's throat, feeling temperature and pulse at the same time.

"Careful no-one hears you call me that," said the boy, "or you'll lose your head."

Thomas laughed. "Sancha has heard me, Theresa, too."

"I don't mean servants," said Juan, and Thomas felt his good humour fade. "And I am well, you know I am."

Thomas turned to Sancha. "Has he been standing a little?"

"Every other hour, for the quarter," she said.

"I don't like it—it makes my leg hurt."

"Standing will make it stronger. You will do as I say until you're well enough to have me beheaded."

Juan smiled shyly, restoring the mood between them. It wasn't the boy's fault, Thomas knew, merely the world in which he had grown up. "I have changed my mind on that. You can call me Juan if you want when we are alone, if I can call you Uncle."

"I am no relation."

"That does not matter. I have made my decision, Uncle."

Thomas shook his head. "It's time to sleep now."

Sancha had already prepared the draught. He took it from her and raised it to Juan's lips. The boy pursed his mouth and turned away.

"I don't want to be tossed into dreams anymore." His voice emerged strangled as he tried to keep his lips a tight line.

"Perhaps in a few days, even tomorrow. But this time tonight, for me, Nephew?"

Juan laughed and opened his mouth.

Thomas wiped the boy's lips and handed the empty beaker to Sancha. The draught he would normally give him was usually barely enough to make him drowsy. Thomas had been reducing the ingredients slowly to avoid any problems of withdrawal. Tonight he had deliberately made it a little stronger. He remained on the edge of the bed, talking until Juan's eyes grew heavy, then arranged his head on the pillows and stood, stretching.

"Are you sleeping here?" said Sancha. She had her back to him, washing the cup, tidying away the materials she had used to make the draught.

"I thought I might. It will save time if he wakes." Although he had not done so in several nights. "And you?"

"Will take the chair as usual." She finished what she was doing and glanced at him. "Help me pull the screen in front of your bed, Thomas. You will sleep better behind it."

"I may not hear Juan if he wakes." But he moved to one end of the tapestry screen and tugged on it. It was heavy, fashioned of dark wood, and the feet made a scraping noise across the floor tiles. Thomas glanced towards Juan, but the boy lay undisturbed.

Thomas felt a roil of emotion and lust and anger, everything mixed up inside, eroding what little will power he possessed. He was determined it would not be him who made the first move. But of course, when Sancha stepped closer, he knew he was unable to rebuff her.

She stopped inches from him, the scent of her body raw and arousing, the heat from her skin touching his.

"Was your concubine very beautiful?" She must have eaten an orange before he came in and its scent sweetened her breath.

"What do you know of my concubine?"

"All the palace knows of her."

"I will have words with Jorge about keeping matters private."

"It was not he but that poor priest. Pero returned knowing everything about you. Even before your arrival. Late last year word came of the clever Moorish doctor. Except when you arrived," Sancha laid a hand lightly against his chest and Thomas allowed it to remain there, "you were no Moor." She moved until she was closer. Far closer than polite society allowed, but Thomas knew what was going on here had little to do with polite society. "So," said Sancha, "was she? Beautiful?"

"Helena was, and is, exquisite. But..." He stopped. Why was he telling this woman anything?

"I am not beautiful," said Sancha.

"You do yourself an injustice."

"Do you think I am?"

Thomas smiled. "Don't go searching for compliments in case you are disappointed in what you hear."

"So you do not think me beautiful." All at once her breasts were pressed against his belly and she was looking up at him. Her hand had strayed lower and Thomas knew he should grasp her wrist to stop its search but did not. "No matter. I am skilled in other ways."

As is Helena, Thomas thought, but considered it was not the time or place to voice that sentiment. And why were they talking of Helena? It wasn't Helena that filled his mind with thoughts of betrayal. Jorge was right—he had to tell Lubna of his true feelings. Except Lubna too was far away, and when Sancha's hand found his cock and gripped him Thomas closed his eyes and groaned.

There came a sound at the door and she stopped, looking over her shoulder.

"Is it the queen, do you think?"

Sancha shook her head, her hand maintaining its grip, starting to move now. "She won't come if she knows you are here. And she knows you stay overnight. But if it sets your mind at rest I will lock the door."

"Will that not also raise suspicion?"

Sancha laughed. "God's teeth, Thomas Berrington, do you want me or not?" She laughed again, the sound coarse as her hand moved. "No—I already feel your answer."

"Lock it," he said. He was both disappointed and relieved when her hand stopped its ministrations and she moved away. He knew this was his last opportunity to put a halt to what was about to happen, cursing his weakness, his need to feel someone next to him that had brought so much trouble to his life. Even after Helena betrayed him he had allowed her back into his bed, unable to resist her beauty or her skill. As he now was unable to resist Sancha. There would be guilt, he knew, but that knowledge was not enough to prevent what was about to take place.

He watched the way her body moved as she crossed the room. She had just placed her hand on the heavy bolt when the door slammed open, catching her full in the face and knocking her cold. She fell to the floor and lay still as Abbot Mandana strode in, two armed men close behind, the giant Sebastian bringing up the rear.

Mandana stopped abruptly, glanced at the unconscious woman and gave his lupine smile.

"You should take care who you threaten, Thomas Berrington." He nodded to the men accompanying him. "Kill him. Sebastian, get the prince."

Thomas backed away from the approaching men, lust turning to instant rage. He lifted the bed to use as a shield as they slashed at him with their swords. He ran at them, forcing the men back, but knew unless he could find a weapon of his own he was dead. He snatched at a candle stand and flung it at the head of one. As the man ducked Thomas pivoted, swinging the end of the bed at the other, who raised an arm to block the blow. Except the bed was heavy and it caught him hard, knocking the sword from his grip.

Thomas pressed his advantage, throwing the bed at the first man who had recovered and was coming at him from the side. He rolled, grabbed the dropped sword and came to his feet. All his tiredness had disappeared in the moment. The only thing he saw were the two attackers.

The disarmed man reached to his waist and drew a dagger.

Thomas feinted, and as the man staggered he changed direction and aimed the tip of the captured sword at the other's chest. He expected to be parried, but these were more of Mandana's monks, ex-soldiers who had not fought for years. The sword entered the man's chest and caught on a rib. Thomas felt the moment's resistance and twisted, pushing hard. Blood gushed from the man's mouth and his knees went, dropping him to the ground.

The other came at him from the side and Thomas twisted, the dagger slicing through his shirt but missing flesh. He caught the man's collar and dragged him forward, punching him hard over the kidneys. The blow jarred his hand and for a moment pain lanced through the heat of battle, but Thomas had known pain before and ignored it.

He hit the man again on the back of the neck, kicked at his legs, brought him to his knees. Thomas stepped around the man and grasped his head. He lifted and twisted, felt vertebrae snap as the man went limp. Thomas tossed the body aside and turned to the bed.

But there was no sign of Mandana or the giant, nor of Prince Juan. The wolf had taken its prey and fled.

CHAPTER THIRTY-SEVEN

At least no-one doubted Thomas any longer, and Mandana had finally overstepped any boundary that could protect him. He was seen fleeing by palace guards and servants, Juan's limp body clutched under Sebastian's arm.

"He'll be slow with a captive," said Fernando, his hand on the queen's shoulder. Her face was pale as marble, lips compressed as she fought panic. "We'll catch him within the hour." He turned to Thomas. "You're coming, aren't you?"

Thomas nodded.

"As am I." The Duque of Carmona had entered the room, attracted by the cries of alarm that spread through the palace. "Mandana was my friend. I will not see him slain like an animal. He must be returned to stand trial."

Fernando threw an impatient look his way. "If you had not argued his innocence so strongly this would never have happened. Come if you must, as long as you can keep up." He turned back to Thomas. "Can you ride fast?"

"I can. We should be leaving. Now."

"We are. Wait for me in the courtyard."

Thomas started to turn but the queen's voice halted him.

"A moment, Cousin."

He turned back, waiting for her to speak, forcing stillness

against the rush of panic that filled him. Her eyes rose to his. "I should have taken you more seriously, and for that I apologise." She closed her eyes for a moment. When she opened them they were burning with a cold fire. "I should not have allowed politics to sway me from my belief, for I knew in my heart he was guilty."

"It is too late for regrets," said Fernando.

"Thomas must know my mind on this," said the queen, her voice firm. "You have served us with great loyalty, Cousin, despite being from a different land. Now is not the time, but when you return we will find some way to reward you."

A full moon cast enough light for them to see the roadway that snaked ahead above the river. Their horses' hooves thudded against the dry ground as they pushed them as fast as they dare in the dark. Thomas rode beside the king, three guards ahead, three more and Carmona behind. It was a small force but he believed they were enough. He knew Fernando's reputation in battle, trusted his own skills. The road ahead climbed, twisting into a stand of trees. To the north dark clouds had massed, their bellies lit by an occasional flash of lightning, the faint sound of thunder coming long after.

"We should have seen them by now," said Fernando, his voice broken by the jolt of riding. He had become one more man among others now. A man concerned for his son.

"They will know the roadway better than us," Thomas said. "And they had an hour's start by the time everyone was roused and we were ready to leave."

"At least we know where they're heading. What is the man thinking of? Does he believe kidnaping Juan will offer him a means of escape?"

If that is what he intends, Thomas thought. He considered the other reason Mandana might have for taking the boy, but dare not speak of it to the king.

They had still not glimpsed sign of their quarry by the time they rode up the steep track to the monastery. Thomas was trying not to think about what happened to him the last time he came this way, but the memory of that terror was still too fresh.

They arrived to find the gates were thrown wide, and when they rode inside there were no torches burning. Fernando dismounted and ran into the cloisters, Thomas close behind.

"They can't have gone already—there hasn't been enough time."

Thomas looked around. He entered a doorway, remembering the way to Mandana's rooms. A dozen lit candles showed papers lying torn and burned, ashes still glowing in the wide fireplace. He knelt and put his hand over them. Warm, but not hot.

"He did this before he came to the palace," he said. "He had no intention of returning here. He's taken a different direction."

Fernando kicked over a chair. "What does he think he's doing? There is nowhere in Spain safe for him, not after this."

"If he is heading for Spain."

"A ship? Does he plan to flee the country?"

Thomas stood and brushed ash from his hands. "There is somewhere else he could go—to al-Andalus."

Fernando stared at him. "He is a Christian. Why would he do such a thing? It would be even more dangerous for him than to stay in Spain."

"He's in possession of a valuable prize. He might be mad but he's not stupid—he's cunning like his namesake. You have the sultan of Gharnatah as your prisoner. Mandana knows you would give him up in return for Juan, and that he would be seen as the broker of the deal."

"Then we're wasting time here," said Fernando. "Come on, back to Cordoba and then onwards."

Thomas sat astride a horse next to Jorge as they rode out of the city across the old bridge. Ahead of them was Lawrence. On the way back to the city Thomas had talked for a long time with the king. Lawrence knew Mandana, he had argued, as well as any man—they had served together as soldiers, and he would know how he worked. Jorge—well, Jorge had refused to be left behind, despite the injuries that still pained him. And then there was Daniel. Somehow by the time they'd returned to the city word had spread even beyond the walls and Daniel was waiting beside his brother, swords at his belt. Thomas had finally persuaded Fernando to allow the pair to accompany them, but told Jorge to stay close to Daniel and Lawrence—and to stay away from Carmona.

Fernando rode at the head of the group, larger now than the group that had ridden through the night on a fruitless dash to the monastery. They were now a dozen and one strong. Large enough to be dangerous, small enough to move fast. Fernando had changed into the garb of the soldier he had once been, at ease in the saddle, his long hair tied behind his neck.

If they had taken a little time instead of rushing off they might have already caught their quarry by now. Mandana was seen leaving in the company of others, a group of at least twenty, possibly more. One of the riders had been small, and one observer reported him as being tied to his horse. The group was seen passing through the southern gate at midnight and crossing the roman bridge, but at that time nobody had any idea they were wanted men.

"If we find no sign of him by nightfall," said Fernando, "we will call on more men and widen the search." He had fallen back through their ranks to ride beside Thomas once they were on the far side of the bridge.

"He's gone south," Thomas said, convinced he was right.

"Likely so. But I have sent men out anyway—asked them to travel half a day's ride in all directions then return to the city. If they find a trail someone will ride after us with the news. We won't be able to travel as fast as one man can." Fernando stared down at his hands, shaking his head. "I can't believe he fooled us for so long. How could the man do that?"

"The deaths didn't start until last year," Thomas said. "Something happened to change him. Or he changed his method."

"What was it?"

"I don't know, and it doesn't matter. Perhaps we will find out when we catch him."

“When we catch him,” said Fernando, “he is a dead man. I won’t allow him to be taken prisoner. I’ll not give him a chance to spin some tale. Even though he has allies.” He glanced across at Carmona. “He dies out here.”

Thomas met Fernando’s stare. He would get no argument from him.

CHAPTER THIRTY-EIGHT

A pale line of light remained in the western sky, but Fernando decided to stop at an abandoned farmhouse before full dark. The threatened storm had finally arrived. Intermittent rain had troubled their journey all afternoon and now dark clouds moved between the hills, promising worse. Half the tiles were missing from the farmhouse roof, but one of the men managed to get wood burning in the filthy fireplace while another gutted rabbits. Fernando had brought his hound, Carmona another—both rangy creatures with shaggy coats whose narrow heads came almost to a man's chest. It was they who had chased down dinner, trotting back with slack animals clutched in their jaws. Bringing too many provisions would have slowed the group, and living off the land meant their meagre supplies would last longer.

Thomas sat with Jorge, their backs to the wall as the threatened cloudburst arrived, rain tumbling through the open sections of roof. Daniel crouched to one side, staring into space. Across the room Carmona, Esperanza's husband, stood beside Fernando. They could be discussing matters of state, something as trivial as tonight's meal, or his wife's infidelity.

"Does he blame you?" Thomas asked Jorge, cleaning the sole of his boot with a knife.

"For bedding his wife, or that Mandana chose her because of

me? I assume he's aware of both—everyone else in the palace seems to be."

"Keep your voice down," Thomas hissed. "How can you be so sure?"

"Because Esperanza was as open as the sky. No sooner did a thought occur to her than she had to express it. No sooner an urge than she had to act on it. I won't be the first she seduced. A husband must know how it is when married to such a woman."

Thomas gazed across the room towards Carmona, thinking the description of Esperanza could apply to Jorge equally as well. "He's quite a bit older than her."

"And it was likely a marriage of convenience, or politics."

"Did you ask her?"

"Strangely enough such topics didn't come up when we were together. And I would rather not be reminded of what I have lost. Nor what I was the cause of."

The rabbits had been spitted and sat above the fire, the smell of their roasting filling the air, the offal tossed to the dogs together with a squirrel they had run down. Thomas's stomach grumbled, and for the first time since returning to the palace he felt hunger clutch him. He could barely believe two weeks before he had been Mandana's prisoner. The agony inflicted on him then was no more than a fading memory. Even locked in the charnel house he had felt little fear. It was some lack in himself, he was sure, but not a trait he welcomed.

"What did you talk of, then?"

"We didn't. We had other matters to occupy us." Jorge looked away from Carmona and studied Thomas. "What about you? Have you taken either of those nurses yet?"

Thomas concentrated on the other boot even though it required no attention. "If we don't catch him before we reach the border with al-Andalus I'm not turning back."

"I know."

Thomas raised his eyes. "And you?"

Jorge laughed softly. "What do you think? How about Lawrence? Will he come with us? I like him—he's his own man."

"I'll raise the topic," Thomas said. "And you're right. I like him, too. What about Daniel?"

"He wants revenge for what Adana was put through."

"The king won't be able to follow."

"I know."

"Nor his men. They'll have to stay to protect him."

Jorge nodded, his gaze returning to the men across the room, but Thomas was sure his attention was all on Carmona, who had left the king's side and was now in conversation with Lawrence. The duque and Jorge had not acknowledged each other yet.

"So four of us," said Jorge. "Maybe only three. How many does Mandana have?"

"I killed the two he brought to Juan's room, but there'll be plenty of others. Not too many otherwise they will slow him down. Those who saw them cross the bridge said around a score, but I doubt he has many more."

"Do you really think he's travelling this way?"

"I know he is."

When Jorge stared at him Thomas smiled. "It's luck you enjoy such a feted life in the palace, my friend, for your skills in the field are sadly lacking."

"You've seen sign? Why didn't you say anything?"

"Because Fernando would have us chasing off through the dark after him."

"And that's such a bad idea? Mandana has taken his son. The man is a killer. I would have thought you more than anyone would want to see him caught."

"I do. But Mandana's not going to harm Juan. He's the only leverage he's got, which is why he took the risk of kidnapping him."

Jorge rubbed his knuckles across the top of his head. "I'm going to have to trust you. You know far more about such things. Tell me—what sign did you see?"

"The wood we passed through an hour ago—there were freshly broken twigs."

"Anything could have done that—the hounds chasing down those rabbits, a boar, anything."

"And this?" Thomas reached into his robe and withdrew a scrap of white cloth. He handed it to Jorge, making sure nobody else saw him do so. "That's from a monk's robe, just like Mandana's and those who accompany him."

"They won't be dressed as monks," said Jorge, passing it back.

"Mandana wore his robe when he came for Juan. It's his badge of office as much as the cross he wears. This is from that robe, I'm sure." Thomas tucked the scrap into an inner pocket. "Trust me on it."

"I do."

Thomas's gaze shifted as Lawrence strolled across to them, avoiding the rain falling through the open section of roof. He squatted between them, his face as benign as always.

"Did you see the wolves?"

"What wolves?"

Lawrence smiled. "And I took you for someone with keen eyes. As we came from those woods, after you found that piece of cloth, there was a pack of them. Big pack, too, ahead of us. I caught sight of them as they crossed the ridge. The dogs sensed them, too, which is why they stayed close after that." He dug at the packed earth with his knife, drawing shapes that might have meant something, but if so only to him. "It makes our hounds useless for tracking. Maybe the abbot truly is part wolf and they are his familiars."

Thomas thought through what Lawrence had said—the rational part, at least. The fact he knew about the cloth, but also his sighting. Thomas knew wolves. They were rarely dangerous unless they moved in a large pack or a man was injured, but he had been tracked by the animals in the past and was aware of how tenacious they could be once they had their sight set on prey.

"They wouldn't attack a large group of men," he said.

Lawrence lifted an eyebrow. "Are you so sure?"

"There must be a surfeit of prey in these hills. Why would they follow Mandana?"

"Because a wolf attracts its own kind," said Lawrence.

"I didn't take you for a superstitious man."

"Far from it. But with that man, who knows?"

Thomas shook his head, disappointed. He rose, his legs stiff from the ride, and crossed to where the rabbit was being cut into pieces. He would tell Fernando in the morning what he had found, to put his mind at rest they were travelling in the right direction.

CHAPTER THIRTY-NINE

The rain stopped a little after dawn but beneath the trees water continued to drip. The ground underfoot was soft, the horse's hooves sliding away, making riding difficult. Thomas reined his horse and swung from the saddle.

They had been on the road since before light showed in the sky, riding through the last of the rain that had fallen overnight. Occasionally as they travelled someone would discover a sign of Mandana's passing. Unless, as Carmona pointed out, it was somebody else entirely. Thomas ignored him, and so, it seemed, did everyone else.

The track began to climb. At times the hills drew close and they had to ride in single file. In such places Thomas sat up in his saddle, scanning the rocks and bushes. These were good places to set an ambush, but so far they had progressed unmolested.

The path descended into a valley where a white-foamed stream ran. They moved parallel to it through dense woodland, looking for a place to cross before climbing again. The trees stayed with them. Then the woodland opened out into a clearing. Around the edge dense foliage would have offered some shelter from the rain. A thin wisp of smoke rose from a fire.

Lawrence reached it first, Thomas close behind.

"Still embers in the heart," said Lawrence. "Four hours ahead at most, likely less."

"They don't seem in any great hurry," Thomas said as he squatted, reaching out to judge the residual heat for himself.

"Maybe they don't believe they are being followed."

"That last valley? A man perched at the top of the pass would be able to see back a good three hours. If it was me I'd have had someone there to check who was behind me."

"Mandana isn't you, nor me."

"He was a soldier. You served with him, didn't you?"

"He was a general—a poor general at that. It's not the same as being a fighting man."

Thomas liked Lawrence more and more, sensing in him some echo of himself. He liked his easy confidence and the flouting of rules he didn't agree with.

He surveyed the clearing. "There's not much shelter here. They'll be wet and cold." He thought of Prince Juan, stronger now, but strong enough for this?

"All the more reason to push on." Lawrence rose and offered a hand to Thomas, who took it. "You could have stayed behind, you know. Both of you. There will be fighting when we catch them. Your friend looks soft, but I think his brother will be all right."

Thomas ignored Lawrence's veiled accusation of weakness.

"The fire still doesn't prove it's them."

"Look around. Tell me what you see."

Thomas studied the ground, but he had already read the signs.

"Twenty-three men," he said. "The horses were tied over there." He pointed, then moved his hand, picking out other places. "Men slept there, there and there, in groups. The prince was there—the patch of dry ground is smaller, but there was a man close on either side of him. They covered him with an oiled sheet to keep him dry. It means they want him alive, at least for now."

"Which is good," said Lawrence, starting to walk away. "They have a purpose for him."

"Mandana kept both Jorge and me alive when he had no need."

Lawrence lifted himself into his saddle and waited while

Thomas did the same. "He had his own purpose. Your friend was meant to die on the cross like our Saviour." He spurred his horse into a canter. The others had gone ahead, knowing they would catch up.

"I don't understand why he marked me," Thomas said, wincing as his body protested. "If I was meant to die on the cross why mark me like Adana? And he stitched Esperanza, his Magdalena."

"I suppose you would have been too obvious. He couldn't have strapped one of his creations in full view. The woman's mutilation was hidden beneath her robes. And I think..."

Thomas heard the lack of emotion in Lawrence's voice, as if the killings didn't bother him.

"What is it you think?" he asked.

Lawrence glanced at him as the track began a twisting climb. "I think he was working towards that day, the day our Lord gave his life for all mankind. In his mind he saw it as a pivotal moment. That is why you were meant to live—until you could die on the cross."

"Do you think he believes his own logic, or is he just insane?"

"I've always found him highly sane," said Lawrence. "Single minded and focussed. These events surprise me as much as everybody else. The abbot has been part of the court for twenty years. If he was mad all that time he hid it well. I think this is more recent."

"Brought on by what?"

Lawrence slowed and turned in his saddle to face Thomas. "These are unstable times. The Inquisition has changed many things. When the king and queen set it up it was at Mandana's urging, but I believe none of them had any idea it would grow into the monster it has become." A tight smile compressed his lips. "I believe Mandana might have been dragged in too far—further even than Torquemada, who was already mad."

"And no-one suspected anything?"

"Important men of religion are allowed some leeway in their worship of God. And don't forget Mandana is one of those who makes the rules, who sets the boundaries."

Thomas urged his horse into a walk, waiting for Lawrence to

catch up before speaking. "They outnumber us. Doesn't that worry you?"

"They are three over a score—the fourth is the prince. We are eleven. Are those odds too great for you, Thomas Berrington?"

"We are thirteen," Thomas said.

"I wasn't counting your friend or his brother. But all right, twelve with the big man. Daniel, is that his name?"

"You know it is. Mandana will have chosen men who were soldiers."

"As was I. As is the king and the duque and his men. It's only the eunuch and his brother have never fought." Lawrence glanced across. "But I would wager on just the king, myself and you against their score."

Thomas allowed him to ride ahead, wondering if he had not revealed too much of himself during the long hours they had spent in conversation.

CHAPTER FORTY

It was Jorge who first saw the man on the bluff. He was fully a mile away and even when told where he was most of their party couldn't see him.

"Are we so close?" asked Fernando. As they had journeyed the trappings of state had fallen away and he had become one more man amongst others. It wouldn't last beyond their return, but Thomas welcomed getting to know the man who was going to end his way of life, comforted by the fact he bore no ill will to either himself or Jorge. Which was not something that could be said of Carmona, who made his hatred of Jorge plain.

"They'll have left him there to report," said Lawrence. "They could be another mile or more ahead." Despite his lowly status both Fernando and Carmona listened to him.

"Or there are others waiting," Thomas said.

"There was no-one before when you thought the same back there," said Carmona.

"It doesn't mean I'm wrong this time."

"What are the chances?" Fernando looked to Lawrence.

"It's where I'd set a trap. Look how the path narrows and the cliffs rise close on either side. A good archer or two hidden up there would cut us down in a moment."

"So we wait?"

Lawrence looked to Thomas, who shook his head.

"You go on, Your Grace," said Lawrence. "I'll climb the hill behind them. If they're there I'll take them out while they're watching you."

"No," Thomas said. "I can do it."

"I'm the better man for it," said Lawrence.

Thomas smiled without humour. "Stay with the king. I'll ride most of the way. Only the last few hundred yards will be on foot."

"We could send Jorge."

Thomas laughed, saw Jorge open his mouth to protest, but before he could Thomas kicked his horse into a canter. He rode fast without looking back, guiding the horse through scattered bushes along the side of the hill. When he glanced behind five minutes later it was to find no sign of his companions. He slowed, listening, but the noise of his own passage masked any sound the others might be making.

He let his horse pick its own way over jagged rocks which had been shattered by heat and frost. The entire landscape was blasted, stone tumbled on stone, only shallow-rooted birch and pine flourishing, and that not much. The sun had broken through and the ground steamed, tendrils of mist rising to be disturbed by his passage. The scent of loam and rock and water enveloped him.

He came to a small circle which was clear of stone, where grass managed to grow. Wild flowers were starting to bloom along one edge and bees circled, always able to find pollen however forbidding the territory. Thomas dismounted and left his horse to pull at the poor fare while he continued on.

He hadn't seen the watcher since he'd left their party but knew exactly where he would be, so was surprised to hear a noise when still a hundred paces shy of the position.

Thomas crouched, listening, and the noise came again. Someone coughed, the sound muffled.

He went on his belly and crawled around a moss-covered boulder.

A man sat forty feet away and ten below. He had a crossbow

but it lay beside him. He coughed again, holding the sleeve of his blouse across his mouth.

Thomas searched along the hillside, found another man, then one more. And still the watcher, if he remained where he thought him to be, was out of sight. He ducked behind a boulder and took stock. Four men, possibly more, waiting to ambush their party as they passed through the narrow gorge. Thomas checked his weapons, realised he had been stupid and left his bow on the horse. He considered returning for it, but knew the others would be almost at the pass. He had a sword and two daggers. It would have to be enough.

The man coughed again and someone whispered at him to shut up.

Thomas left his sword on the ground and crept around the boulder. He raised himself up and glanced to the right. The others were leaning forwards, intent on something out of sight. The man below had lifted his crossbow, a bolt already notched.

Thomas crept closer. Thirty feet. He moved on.

Twenty feet.

The man coughed again, his arm once more across his mouth, and Thomas moved fast, hoping the noise would mask any he might make.

Ten feet.

"They're coming!" A hissed message from along the hillside.

Thomas glanced right and smiled. He could see no-one, which meant they couldn't see him either. He came onto his knees, then his feet, crouching over.

The man reached for the crossbow he had put down while he stifled his cough. Before he could lift it Thomas sprinted. He clapped a hand over the man's mouth. At the same instant his blade sawed his throat open.

The man's struggle lasted only a second before he went limp. When Thomas turned him over to take his weapon he was gratified to see the man's cheeks marred by scratches. He should have known Jorge wouldn't have been able to kill the monk in the tunnel when he went back for Mandana's instruments. But now the man who had kidnapped Adana had paid for his sins.

Thomas lifted the crossbow and rose slowly until he saw the top of another head forty or so feet away. He lifted the bow, rose to full height, aimed and fired. This time the sound of the bolt hitting the man, and his cry, could not be muffled. Before anyone else saw him Thomas knelt and wound the crossbow back, inserting a fresh quarrel.

When he stood a bolt whistled past his ear. Instead of ducking, as most would, he rose tall and aimed. The man who had shot at him was frantically winding the mechanism on his own bow to send a second arrow. Thomas took his time, released, and saw his bolt embed itself in the man's chest.

There was one man left, but even as he moved across the hillside Thomas heard him scrambling away, saving his own skin. He didn't bother pursuing. He went across and took the other bow but left the third. It was too far and the ground too broken to risk. He returned to his horse and bullied it down as direct a route as he could then urged it to catch up with the others. He glanced at the sky. With luck they would catch Mandana before the sun set.

CHAPTER FORTY-ONE

"Did you take care of them all?" asked Lawrence as Thomas caught up with him. He had been waiting alone at the narrowest point of the track.

"One got away." Thomas rode on, knowing Lawrence would match him. Nothing else was said until they reached Jorge, who had drifted from the back of the group.

"I'll go tell the king," said Lawrence, and cantered ahead.

"Are you all right?" asked Jorge.

Thomas thought it should be he asking his friend, but all he did was nod and say, "I'm fine. We'll catch them today."

"Are there enough of us?"

"There are three less of them now."

Jorge cast him a look but Thomas was unable to decipher it clearly, unsure if it indicated approval or disgust.

"Have I changed so much?" he asked, staring ahead, afraid to look at the man he had come to call friend above all others.

"Of course you have," said Jorge. "It's understandable after what he did to you."

"He killed the woman you loved."

They had almost caught up with the others. Even as they spoke Thomas's gaze swept the ground that rose to either side. The head of the pass was visible now. He leaned out of his saddle and studied the ground. Their own passage showed clearly, but they had stuck to the middle of the path. Those they sought had not been so organised, leaving marks along the edges of the track.

Fernando had come to a halt ahead, Lawrence beside him. The two hounds ran on a hundred yards and stopped, waiting. From the right, obscured by rocks, came the sound of other animals, a brief yelp cut short. The wolves were still with them.

Ahead the path snaked down through rocks. Half way to the valley floor the trees thickened to obscure the roadway, but Mandana's group had not quite reached cover yet.

"We'll be on them in less than an hour," said Fernando. "We need to discuss tactics." He turned in his saddle as Thomas approached. "Lawrence tells me you killed three of them." He looked as though he couldn't decide whether to believe the news or not.

"Like Lawrence I have a past," Thomas said, unsure of why he felt the need to explain.

"So it seems." Fernando glanced around. The rest of their party waited at a distance, as if respecting the discussion taking place, and Thomas wondered if Fernando saw the three of them as the true leaders of the group. If so, how did Carmona feel about that?

"They'll be well into the trees by the time we reach them," said Lawrence. "They may even be starting up the far side."

"We'll do well to catch them before they reach the river," said Fernando, "but if we can we'll have the advantage of height."

"It won't matter under the trees," Thomas said. "It will be nothing but confusion and noise, the same as every other battle. I'll go for your son, Sire, and protect him."

"That's my job," said Fernando.

"You know it makes sense for me to do it. You'll draw too much attention."

"Can we take him alive?"

Thomas knew Fernando referred to Mandana. The discussion regarding his son was settled—he had merely felt the need to make a token protest.

"He won't take his own life, but I think he'll fight to the death rather than be captured. He won't allow himself to be taken back to Qurtuba to stand trial."

"It will never come to that," said Fernando. "He will disappear out here. And no word of what we do must pass beyond our number."

"Not from me," said Lawrence.

"Nor I," Thomas confirmed.

"Your friend and his brother?" It was obvious Fernando had no need to include his own men or Carmona.

"Jorge keeps more secrets than your city holds, Sire."

"Then we are secure." He lifted in his stirrups and shaded his eyes. "They are almost at the tree line. We should follow as fast as we can. We can talk tactics as we ride."

"They may set another ambush," Thomas said. "It will be more difficult to deal with under cover of the trees."

"I don't think they'll risk losing any more men," said Lawrence.

"It's going to be dark in a few hours," said Fernando. "That wolf pack bothers me. They're not usually as tenacious as this, and if they decide to attack once the battle starts it will be a problem we could do without."

"We'll reach Mandana well before sunset," said Lawrence. "The wolves are only doing what they always do. They sense the coming fight and are looking for easy prey, but they won't attack a man with a sword."

"I'm not so sure we'll catch them so easily," Thomas said. "They must know we're close. They'll speed up now."

"They are more than us," said Lawrence. "The bigger the party the slower it travels."

"They won't stop when it gets dark, not with us behind them," said Fernando. "We might have to ride through the night and it will be black as pitch beneath the trees."

"Then we catch them before then," Thomas said.

But when the others urged their horses down the slope he stayed where he was. Once he was alone he lifted up from his saddle and looked forward beyond the group, beyond Mandana, to where the land rose to high hills. To where the borders of al-

Andalus lay. He had a decision to make, but first there was a battle to fight.

He spurred his horse into a gallop, jerking on the reins to follow the receding group of riders. The beast would tire quickly but he wouldn't need to ride hard for long. They clattered down the roadway, metal horseshoes striking sparks from stone that had been laid by the Romans over a thousand years before.

CHAPTER FORTY-TWO

It was chaos, as battle always is. However well a man plans, events slap him in the face with the reality of chance.

There was a plan, of sorts, but the plan was to ride as hard as they could and plough into the enemy. And it looked as if it was going to work until an arrow took one of the king's soldiers in the throat. His horse panicked and ran into the woods. The man astride it clutched at his neck, but only until he cracked his face open on a branch. He was flung from the horse to land in an ugly heap, unmoving. They were down to twelve men already.

More arrows flew but the pursuers were moving fast now, and the archers—only three by the look, the others dead on the hillside—were trying too hard and their arrows flew wide. A crossbow was accurate and powerful but took too long to reload.

Thomas rode through it all, the shouting and clatter of hooves fading to nothing as his awareness concentrated to pinpoints of action.

He saw Lawrence leap from his horse, bow already in hand, notch an arrow and fire. The first shot fell short, but the second caught one of the archers in the shoulder.

To his right Jorge swung his sword as if he had done so all his life, parrying one thrust from a man on his feet, threatening a second who was struggling with a weapon which had caught in his belt.

Fernando bullied his way through a group of four men, a sword in each hand, controlling his horse with his knees. He was heading directly for the far side of the enemy group.

Mandana sat astride a white mount, Prince Juan draped across the horse's shoulders. He had a knife in one hand and his head turned, sucking information from the fight, judging whether to join in or flee.

Grey shapes ran through the woods, keeping their distance for now as they yelped in excitement. The wolf pack that had trailed them for the past day and a half was coming close for the kill. Intelligent creatures, this was the reason they had shadowed the two groups, knowing that when men fight there will be easy pickings.

A man ran at Thomas whirling a morning star over his head, the ugly weapon whistling each time it came close. Thomas leaned back, letting the heavy lump of studded iron swing harmlessly in front of his chest. Then he slid from the saddle and used his knife to cut the soldier's throat, made vulnerable as the momentum of the heavy weapon carried his body around.

Something hit him on the back and he turned. Another man stood there, his sword slicked with blood. Thomas snapped awareness to his own body, but it wasn't his blood. He stepped towards the man, sword in one hand, knife in the other.

Men screamed, some in agony, others with bloodlust.

Time slowed. A familiar cold fire filled Thomas. He strode again and the soldier's eyes lost their certainty.

"Run while you can," Thomas hissed, but he knew he would have to kill him, saw the man recognise the fact himself and started to turn. Thomas followed, but before he could strike Lawrence leapt past him and thrust his sword through the soldier's flank.

"Get the prince!" shouted Lawrence.

Thomas turned, placing his back to Lawrence. They began to move sideways, each protecting the other. Neither man attacked unless they were threatened, but moved steadily through the melee. By the time they had closed half the distance Mandana had seen them coming. He turned his horse and cantered away through the trees, the giant Sebastian running behind. Thomas parried and struck at an attacker, softening the blow so his sword point barely broke flesh. He pushed harder, the man falling backwards from the pain, then he was behind them.

"There," said Lawrence, pointing, and Thomas broke away and sprinted through the trees, feet slipping on moss-covered rock. He saw Lawrence run the other way.

Thomas glimpsed a wolf running at him. He swung his sword and the animal darted aside, loping up the slope to join its companions. Their whining barks filled the air, the animals snapping at each other in their excitement.

He scrambled higher before ducking down at the sound of hooves. He found himself on a rocky outcropping above a path forged by boar. It led to a small clearing where Mandana pulled his horse to a halt. He looked around as Sebastian lumbered out after him. His gaze passed directly over Thomas without taking in his presence.

Movement drew Thomas's gaze and he turned as Lawrence appeared on the far side of the clearing. He must have run around and come from the other side. Thomas started down the near vertical slope, then stopped.

Lawrence scrambled into the clearing and walked to Mandana's horse. He gripped the reins. Mandana leaned down and spoke, their heads almost touching.

Something heavy crashed through the undergrowth behind. Thomas spun around as a wolf leapt at him, its jaws a savage snarl. He threw his hands up and fell sideways, tumbling down the slope to land awkwardly.

Thomas rolled to his knees to find Lawrence a yard in front of him, sword extended. Thomas felt around for his own and came up empty.

"Kill him!" ordered Mandana.

Thomas stared up at the man he had grown to like. He thought of warm evenings spent in conversation among the scent of orange blossom. He believed even Laurita had begun to warm to his presence—or at least stopped resenting it.

Lawrence raised his sword, the tip circling in front of Thomas. His eyes found his own weapon now, lying three feet away, too far to reach. He laid his hand on the knife at his waist and saw Lawrence's eyes follow. Something moved across Lawrence's face, some reflection of a question, likely the same one Thomas was considering. Which of them was better? He knew there was only one way to find out.

Except Lawrence lowered his blade until the tip rested on the ground. "No. I've had enough—if you want him dead kill him yourself."

As Thomas started to rise chaos erupted.

Lawrence lifted his sword to sheath it as something thrummed past Thomas's ear. An arrow embedded itself in Lawrence's arm. Thomas turned, caught a glimpse of Daniel standing on the outcrop he had fallen from himself, then Sebastian was on him, one hand gripping his hair, lifting him into the air, the other swinging a hammer blow to his belly which rendered his body incapable of drawing breath.

Lawrence swayed on his feet, the arrow's shaft projecting from his arm. Blood had already soaked the arm of his robe. He staggered away to stand next to Mandana, grabbed at Juan's shoulder, but his grasp was weak. He managed to pull the boy from Mandana's saddle but hadn't the strength to drag him away. He staggered a yard or two, leaving the boy curled on the ground beneath Mandana's horse, before a grey shape sped into the clearing and leapt against him. A second joined in, then a third. Sebastian uttered a bellow and dropped Thomas. He moved fast, wading into the brawl. A wolf came squealing out. Sebastian got his hands around another's head and twisted it as Lawrence scrabbled across the ground, his knife finding the throat of a third. Mandana's horse whinnied in panic and skittered away from the carnage.

The wolf Sebastian held broke free, its jaws locking instantly around his arm and the giant monk roared. A fresh wolf ran into the clearing, larger than the others. It slowed, not leaping immediately. Thomas started towards Lawrence, who was dragging himself away. Some memory of friendship, even if it had been false, demanded he come to the man's rescue, but he stopped as two more wolves appeared. These were less measured and tore into Sebastian. One buried its jaws between his legs, head twisting as blood blossomed. The other went for his stomach, ripping, shredding clothing and flesh. Its face dug deeper, emerged with a mouthful of entrails.

Sebastian went to his knees. As he did the large wolf trotted up and casually bit his neck, blood spilling in a sheet across the ground.

Lawrence had dragged himself to the edge of the clearing. Thomas grabbed his sword and ran towards Prince Juan, who had risen to one good knee, head still bent. Thomas grabbed his arm and pulled him away. Something came at him and he raised an arm. Instead of the animal he expected, it was a wolf of a different kind. Mandana had returned, bullying the panicked horse back. His sword descended in a savage blow.

Thomas parried the strike, which was meant for Juan, not him. He struck out with his dagger but succeeded only in inflicting a flesh wound to Mandana's leg, but it was enough to make him withdraw.

Thomas heard a cry and something crashed into his shoulder. He spun to find a dying wolf scrabbling at an arrow embedded in its flank. When he looked beyond he saw Daniel still atop the outcrop, his bow drawn, eyes scanning the carnage below.

Sebastian had stopped screaming. Three wolves tugged at his body, spilling liver and lungs and blood across the ground, snapping at each other as they fought over the delicacies. Of Lawrence there was no sign. Mandana hesitated on the edge of the clearing, rage on his face, then some spark of reason surfaced and he turned his horse away and rode into the trees.

In a second Thomas felt his strength drain. The pain he had

been suppressing rolled through him with a wild vengeance and his legs gave way. He sat hard, head spinning.

The prince crawled to him and climbed onto his lap. Thomas wrapped an arm around the boy and held his sword out in an attempt to protect them both. But the wolves were occupied with Sebastian's remains, and Mandana and Lawrence were gone.

Thomas jerked his head around at a sound, but it was only Daniel coming into the clearing, bow still aimed at the snarling group of wolves.

"Are you all right?"

"I'll live," Thomas answered. "Can you lift him?"

"The prince? Of course."

Daniel grasped the boy and plucked him from Thomas's lap. Juan clung to Thomas's familiarity but Daniel was too strong. The boy struggled for a moment then stilled as Thomas got to his feet.

"You're safe, he's with us," he said to Juan. "He's Jorge's brother."

"The eunuch? Can eunuch's have brothers?"

Thomas would have laughed but was too weary. "Yes, they can have brothers. Not children, but as many brothers as they want."

He spun around at the sound of barking, but the wolf pack was moving away, running fast through the trees in the direction Mandana had fled, leaving Sebastian's savaged body on the ground. Thomas saw Daniel put his hand over Juan's eyes and turned his head away from the sight.

CHAPTER FORTY-THREE

"Take him to his father," Thomas said. "But only if the fighting is over." He laid a hand on Juan's cheek. "Trust this man, Prince. I have other matters to attend to."

"Are you going to kill Abbot Mandana?" asked Juan, and Thomas smiled, remembering this was no ordinary boy but one, even at his tender age, being groomed to rule a kingdom.

He gave no answer other than to kiss the boy on the brow. He turned away, picked up Lawrence's discarded sword in his left hand, and strode in the direction Mandana had fled.

He hadn't gone two hundred paces when he realised he had been too hasty. He should have returned to the others and mounted a horse. He slowed, uncertain, reluctant to go further only to have to turn back. He had started up again, deciding if he ran he might match the abbot, when a shout on his left sent him in that direction. His feet flew across stony ground beneath the trees as he listened for the voice again.

He came to a shallow clearing and skidded to a halt. Two figures stood in the centre, neither of them Mandana.

Jorge was circling backwards, breathing hard, fear plain on his face.

Esperanza's husband, the Duque of Carmona, paced him, sword raised, an expression of hatred distorting his features. From the far side of the clearing a stray member of the wolf pack came fast towards the pair. Jorge swung wildly as the wolf leapt but his blade landed flat. The wolf's momentum took it past and instead of returning it ran on, seeking its companions.

"Can't you even kill a wolf?" said Carmona. "What excuse for a man are you?" He spat on the ground and closed the distance between them. Thomas was torn. His instinct was to rush down and intervene, to put himself between his friend and Carmona. But he wanted to see how Jorge coped. Thomas knew Jorge could wield a sword, knew he could defend himself, but could he kill? For that was what this was coming to, the pair of them circling each other in the clearing. Only one of them was going to walk away from the confrontation.

A howl sounded in the distance. Both Thomas and Jorge turned in the direction it came from. The howl came again, accompanied by the yapping of the pack, and Carmona swung a lazy blow to clash against Jorge's lowered sword.

"Defend yourself, man!" He scowled. "God knows what my wife ever saw in a creature such as you." He swung his sword again, teasing. "Do you know how it dishonours me that the whole palace knew you were bedding her?"

"It wasn't me that did the chasing," said Jorge, and Thomas was gratified to see the taunting. An angry man was more likely to make mistakes. He shifted sideways so he was hidden among the undergrowth but still close enough to intervene if needed. "You know I wasn't the first." Jorge sneered. "I doubt I was even the hundredth. You think me not a whole man? What manner of husband allows his wife to act in such a way?"

Carmona's sword darted in from the side, but Jorge parried the blow and struck his own, driving him backwards.

"You weren't the same as the others," said Carmona when the attack slowed. "She had her playthings and I had mine, but you..." He shook his head as if failing to understand.

"I gave her what she wanted," said Jorge as he circled to the left. "I gave her what you never could."

Carmona tracked him. Thomas moved deeper into cover.

"What she wanted? She was my wife. Since when has what she wanted got to do with anything?" He shook his head. "I couldn't allow it to go on. Not with everyone laughing behind my back."

"She was coming away with me," said Jorge, surprising Thomas. He had known Jorge was besotted but this was the first he had heard of this.

"So she told me." Carmona moved fast, coming within striking range. "Why do you think I gave her to the abbot when he came asking? It solved both our problems rather elegantly."

Thomas cursed as Jorge bellowed and struck at Carmona—the anger transferred from one to the other in an instant. He broke cover and skidded down the slope into the clearing, but neither man saw him, both locked in a fight to the death. Thomas moved closer, waiting for a moment.

Jorge's sword craft had improved over the year he had been taking lessons, but Carmona was also skilled. There was little in it and Thomas knew he would need to intervene to save his friend. There was a gulf some men are incapable of crossing—that between skill and the coldness needed to kill.

He paced backwards, not wanting to distract Jorge, but his movement did the opposite. As Jorge's concentration faltered Carmona stepped in and his blade sliced through flesh. It was only a shallow wound but it would slow Jorge, and the injury was to his sword arm.

Carmona grinned, circling the tip of his sword, choosing a spot.

"This is for my wife."

And he attacked, coming hard and fast. His blade sliced through Jorge's robe and Thomas saw more blood. Then Carmona was stepping back clutching at his own side, blood pumping through his fingers.

Jorge stepped close to him, gripping his sword in both hands.

"No—*this* is for your wife." He swung the blade hard in a vicious blow that almost severed Carmona's head from his shoulders. Jorge went to his knees as Carmona toppled sideways, blood jetting across the forest floor, but only for a moment before his heart stilled.

Thomas walked towards Jorge, who knelt with his head down, great sobs jerking his body. He looked up at Thomas

"He killed her. Not the abbot—he was only the tool. Carmona killed Esperanza because of me!"

Thomas pushed until Jorge lay on his side, ripped his robe and examined the wound. It looked worse than it was. Carmona's blade had entered through the flank and gone straight through. It was nothing that would kill him as long as the wound was cleaned and dressed. And the right man to do that was already there. He used his knife to tear Jorge's robe, pushed him until he could wrap the linen around the wound, binding it tight, then he checked his arm and bound that too.

"Can you make it back to Fernando on your own?" he asked as he helped Jorge to his feet.

"Which way?"

Thomas pointed. Jorge looked confused and stunned. Thomas knew why. It wasn't his wounds, but the act of killing a man. It was something that could never be undone. Something that changed a man forever. Thomas knew exactly what Jorge was going through, for he had taken that step himself. Except, for him, he had been thirteen years old and had lived with the knowledge of what he had done all his life since.

He waited until Jorge started towards where the others would be. The sound of battle had stilled. Even the wolves had fallen silent as Thomas made his way back to the pursuit he had interrupted.

CHAPTER FORTY-FOUR

Thomas crouched on the edge of a gully. From far below came the sound of rushing water, but there was no sign of it. The ground at his feet was stained with blood, but whether it was canine or human was impossible to tell.

Four wolves lay dead, their jaws trapped in perpetual snarls.

Scraps of Mandana's white robe were scattered about, stained crimson, but there was no sign of his body, nor of Lawrence.

Thomas grabbed a birch trunk and leaned out over the gully. If Mandana had fallen some sign of him might be visible. Or had he jumped? A rational man might consider it a kinder death than the one the wolves offered, but Mandana was hardly rational. Both he and Lawrence might have allowed the wolves to take them, embracing the pain they claimed would ease their passage into heaven.

Thomas drew back and searched for evidence of what had become of them, but he saw nothing. The ground was too disturbed to extract any meaning from it. He returned to the gully for one final look. Nothing. But as he started to pull back something caught his attention. He had been searching too far down, trying to find evidence at the base of the cliff. Higher up, almost within reach, lay a gruesome object.

A hand was caught on a bush four feet down. It had to be

Mandana's—the rings of office still on his fingers. Thomas edged as far as he could and stretched out, but it was at least twice as far as his reach. He looked around for something to help. A stick wouldn't be of any use, more likely to dislodge the find rather than retrieve it, the same for his sword. Then it came to him. He untied his belt and looped the end, leaned over once more and lowered it. His first attempt missed. The second bumped against the hand, threatening to send it tumbling after its owner. The third time he adjusted his approach and eased the loop over the fingers until it lay up against the angle formed by the thumb. Then he lifted. For a moment the hand pivoted and almost slipped free. Thomas allowed it to rest on the bush once more and tried to tug the belt tighter. When he tried again the hand came half way up before it began to slip, and this time he jerked hard. The hand escaped from his belt and flew into the air. As it fell he snatched at it, his own fingers closing around those of Mandana's which were barely cold. He rolled away from the edge, clutching them to his chest.

"Thomas!"

Prince Juan sat astride a captured horse. There were several spare now, and this was a fine stallion, grey-flanked and skittish. Thomas took the reins and stroked the beast's neck until it calmed.

"How is your leg, Prince?"

"I think I could walk on it a little now. Do you want me to show you?"

Thomas laid a hand on the boy's good thigh. "Stay in the saddle. It will benefit from more healing yet." He turned as Fernando approached.

"Did you kill him?"

"No," Thomas said. "The wolves did that."

"You saw the body?"

Thomas shook his head. "It fell into a gully. But I found this." He drew the hand from beneath his robe and heard Juan make a sound. Fernando gazed at it without expression.

"Well—it certainly looks like Mandana's hand."

"The rings?" Thomas asked.

Fernando nodded. "Yes, those are his rings." He glanced from the grisly find to Thomas. "I would prefer to find the rest of him as well, to be sure."

"He's dead," Thomas said. "Even if the wolves didn't kill him the fall would."

Fernando beckoned a man over and Thomas held out the abbot's hand.

"Put it in a sack," said Fernando. "It will be our proof he is gone for good."

"What will you do about the monastery?" Thomas asked, walking beside Fernando as he returned to his horse. His men were dragging the dead to one side where a shallow pit had been dug. Thomas had seen no sign that Jorge had returned and an edge of worry nagged at him.

"Appoint a new abbot," said Fernando. "One who will clean the ranks of heretics and madness. One not addicted to the notion of pain."

Thomas said nothing. He knew it was foolish to point out there were more and more clerics addicted to the idea of pain.

He cupped his hands to assist Fernando into the saddle.

"Will Juan heal?" He was the king again now, looking down on Thomas, his face already changed from that of the man who had ridden beside them in pursuit of Mandana.

Thomas nodded. "He is more than half healed now, but he will need to stay off the leg another month."

"You'll be looking after him, won't you?" Fernando looked around at the remaining men dragging bodies to the pit. "We didn't lose too many, did we?" His attention moved outward. "Although I haven't seen Osman."

Thomas patted the flank of Fernando's horse. "He didn't make it, Your Grace. His body is over there, in a clearing."

Fernando turned in the saddle. "We should take him back with us. I'll send men." He frowned down at Thomas. "Do you know what happened?"

The truth, or a political lie? Thomas couldn't see what benefit the truth would bring now. "Looks like he chased one of them—no, more than one, several."

Fernando shook his head. "I told him he was too old for this, but he insisted on coming. I think he wanted vengeance. For his wife."

Yes—better the truth remain locked away. Thomas turned at the sound of feet kicking through leaves, but it wasn't Jorge, only Daniel returning.

Fernando glanced in his direction. "The brother of your friend —he fought well. I hear he's a smith."

"He is, Your Grace." The matter of Carmona appeared to be settled, with little concern at his loss.

"I'll see what I can do for him. The palace has a constant need for weapons."

Thomas smiled, remembering something Daniel had said to him when they'd first met. "He does not fashion swords for show, Your Grace."

"Good," said Fernando. "We have need for weapons of war, not fancy." He nodded. "I'll send someone to talk with him. He makes good swords, I take it?"

"The best."

"I thought he would. What about your other friend, Lawrence?"

Thomas thought of Laurita, wondering did she know of her lover's involvement, and what would become of her if knowledge of it became public.

"Dead, too. I think he chased Mandana. Looks like the wolves got them both. It would be good if you could find a post for his housekeeper."

"Of course," said Fernando. "He was a good and loyal soldier." He kicked his horse's flanks and started along the path that would lead him through the woods and on towards Qurtuba.

Thomas stood in the clearing as men began to depart. His own horse waited patiently, tied to a tree, snuffling beneath the leaves in search of something edible. He walked across and checked the saddlebags. Blanket, provisions, a bow, a spare sword. He stroked the horse's flank, seeking a little comfort. He had returned to himself again, and as he always did when he lost his humanity in battle he felt the rise of guilt. Except this time it didn't fill him as once it used to. Mandana had been evil. The man deserved to die. Lawrence, too, and Carmona.

Thomas tried to think what he had missed in Lawrence, what clue there had been to his guilt, and found nothing. Although he had turned against his master at the end, so perhaps the man harboured doubts and there had been no guilt to find. He had been charmed by the man, by his intelligence and his background which almost matched his own. Except, Thomas knew, he could never be seduced by the philosophy of pain as Lawrence had.

He looked around, wondering where Jorge had gone to, hoping he was safe. The clearing had more than half emptied, the last of the bodies being dragged to a pit by one man while another started to fill it, the operation perfunctory. Thomas knew animals would find the corpses soon, likely even before nightfall. Once they left this place the natural order would resume.

He glanced across the clearing a final time then swung onto his horse. He bullied it with his knees, fighting its momentary reluctance as he turned it away from the direction the others had gone and turned east towards al-Andalus.

Jorge called out to him before he'd gone a mile.

Thomas slowed and reined his horse to a halt, sat waiting while his friend caught him up. Ahead the land fell away in waves into the distance. Somewhere out there, across some pass, beyond a ridge, lay home.

"Is he dead?" asked Jorge, not needing to say who.

Thomas nodded, examining Jorge's face. It appeared unchanged, the same benign expression there as always. But beneath the surface there would be a change.

"The wolves took him. Lawrence, too."

"Lawrence?"

"He was with them. I should have seen it—living next to the church, the records he kept. He would have been able to pick out subjects for them. I think he most likely pointed them towards Adana, as some kind of—I don't know, punishment? Although what either of us did to deserve punishment I don't know."

"You're trying to impose some kind of logic on events," said Jorge. "And you know where madness is concerned that doesn't work." He looked away, out towards the distant hills, their tops painted red from the lowering sun at their backs. "You know you can't do this, don't you."

Thomas stared at him, his eyes tracking Jorge's face, his body. Blood marked his shirt at the waist, a smaller stain on his arm

"I can't stay here."

"The prince needs you. And the queen has become your friend. Her husband too, now. Are you going to abandon them?"

"I don't belong here. I belong in Gharnatah."

Jorge looked at him but said nothing.

Thomas's horse whinnied and stepped sideways, took three paces forwards. He pulled it up short with a tug of the reins. Thoughts raced through his mind, memory tumbling on memory, of the journey from his home in England to this land, of the things he had seen and the things he had done. Of the things he had lost and the things that still awaited him.

He lifted himself from the saddle, sat again and got comfortable. His right knee pressed into the horse's flank and, obedient, it turned.

"Damn you," Thomas said, and Jorge reached across to slap him on the back. They both urged their horses into a canter, hoping to catch the others before darkness fell.

HISTORICAL NOTE

Throughout Breaker of Bones the rulers of Spain are referred to as Isabel and Fernando. Historical sources indicate that these were the preferred names, rather than the Isabella and Ferdinand used today, so I have chosen to use this form of address as more likely to be in common usage at the time.

I am indebted to the book *Isabel: the first Renaissance Queen* by Nancy Rubin Stuart. Although this book is long, and has some idiosyncratic typography in places, the research and breadth of information provided was invaluable.

The Sultan Muhammed XII, Abu Abdallah (known as Boabdil to the Spanish) was indeed captured and brought to Cordoba around the time the book is set. According to records he was captured on April 21st 1483, but I have him captured slightly earlier to fit in with the falling of Easter Week (Easter Sunday fell on the 30th March 1483), which is obviously integral to the plot of Breaker of Bones. What is true is that after his capture Muhammed was retained as a prisoner for many months before any decision was made on his fate.

The development of anaesthesia is only acknowledged from 1830 onwards. However, there are records in which Theodoric of Lucca, Italian physician and bishop who died in 1298, is said to have used sponges soaked with opium and mandragora for surgical pain relief (History of Anaesthesia website). The same source cites that in 1540 Valerius Cordus first synthesised diethyl ether by distilling ethanol and sulphuric acid. Based on this I believe it is not beyond the bounds of possibility that Thomas could indeed have created his own form of ether 50 years earlier. There are records of recipes to ease pain to be be found in both Greek and Roman works, and the physicians of al-Andalus had access to a huge library of works, many since lost, from the east.

In April 1483 Prince Juan, the son of Isabel and Fernando, was 5 years old, approaching his sixth year. As far as I know he did not break his leg, but I have invented the incident of him falling while running downstairs to support Thomas's journey to Cordoba.

What I found fascinating was the relationship of Isabel to English royalty, which is alluded to very briefly in the book. Isabel was the great-great-granddaughter of John of Gaunt through his marriage to Constance of Castille and through their daughter Catherine. And of course, most people know of Catherine of Aragon, Isabel's daughter born two years after Breaker of Bones is set, who came to England to marry first Arthur, Prince of Wales, and later King Henry VIII.

I am not aware of any person known as Abbot Mandana—he is a pure creation of fiction—but there does exist to this day the Castile del Almodovar del Rio, which is set on cliffs above the Guadalquivir a few miles east of Cordoba. The castle was originally of Moorish construction and is currently in private hands but open to the public.

In the next book Thomas returns to Gharnatah, but this is not the end of his involvement with Isabel and Fernando, nor of their children.

If you enjoyed this book then you can find out more about the tales of Thomas and Jorge on my website:

www.david-penny.com

You can also sign up to the mailing list there and be the first to hear of new releases and updates, as well as exclusive offers.

If you *really* liked this book why not let others know by leaving a review on Amazon or Goodreads.

ABOUT THE AUTHOR

David Penny is the author of the Thomas Berrington Historical Mysteries set in Moorish Spain at the end of the 15th Century. He is currently working on the next book in the series.

Find out more about David Penny
www.davidpennywriting.com

Printed in Great Britain
by Amazon

26142438R00179